I0523332

HARD JOB

Reightman & Bailey Book Two

Jeffery Craig

This is a work of fiction. All of the characters, organizations, and events portrayed in this novel are either the product of the author's imagination, or are used fictitiously. Any resemblance to individuals living or dead is entirely coincidental and the product of the author's imagination.

Cover design by LaLima Design
Cover images ©Artophoto|Dreamstime & ©Giuseppe Parisi|Dreamstime
Author Photo by Clayton P. King

HARD JOB: Copyright © 2016 by Jeffery Craig Schwalk. All rights reserved. No part of this book may be reproduced or transmitted in any form or by any means, electron or mechanical, including photo-copying, recording, or digital reproduction or by any information, storage or retrieval system or process without the direct written per-mission from the author. For further information, please contact the author at Jeffery Craig, 2903 River Dr., Columbia, SC 29201

This edition printed and distributed by IngramSpark and Lightning Source, Inc., La Vergne TN USA 37086

ISBN – 978-0997486612

BOOKS BY JEFFERY CRAIG

Done Rubbed Out: Reightman & Bailey Book One

Hard Job: Reightman & Bailey Book Two

Skin Puppet: Reightman & Bailey Book Three*

Little Deaths: Reightman & Bailey Book Four*

*Forthcoming

To those who read the early version, and to CPK,
always.

A New Day

JOHN BROWN DIDN'T sleep much after he made it home from the botched hit on Toby Bailey. He cleaned his gun and sat down in his favorite chair and just thought things over. "It all got too complicated, too fast," he told himself. He'd known it was risky, and he'd hated taking unnecessary risks. He didn't like it when there were too many pieces in play, and right now there were more than he thought wise. Last night unfolded very differently than he'd planned, and a simple drive-by murder had gone to hell because of it. He wished they'd just called it off and waited for another opportunity. John Brown wondered if he'd even hit the man he was supposed to take out. He got his answer when the phone in front of him buzzed.

U KILLED A COP

He stared down at the phone as he digested the words. He wasn't sure what to say. It was unfortunate, but the screw up wasn't his fault. If his employer had listened to him, none of this would have happened. He was inclined to just ignore the message, but knew there'd be a high price to pay down the line if he did. He thought it over some more, and decided he could at least respond.

SORRY, he eventually typed, adding a sad, frowny face after the word. When he didn't receive a response, he typed a question:

THE MARK?

He waited.

ALIVE

Now John Brown was worried he wasn't going to collect his pay, and that wouldn't do at all. He'd done his best, and he deserved his money. He wasn't about to let himself get screwed again by the person who'd hired him.

WHAT NOW? He typed, after thinking though the possible impact to their already hostile relationship.

The response didn't take long.

WAIT

John Brown could do that. He turned over the phone and got up from his chair. He had plenty of other things to do today, and there was no point in worrying about what might happen next. He didn't like worry. It made things complicated.

He locked up his gun and headed for the shower. A shower was always a good way to start the day. A shower always made him feel better. He emerged from the steam a few minutes later, fresh and clean, and took a look in the mirror. He liked what he saw.

His hair was a medium brown, neither too straight or too curly. His hazel eyes picked up the colors around him, but never caused comment. His body was good, but not overbuilt or worthy of immediate notice – at least with his clothes on. He wasn't model handsome, but that suited him just fine. Being too good looking wasn't an asset in his line of work.

He changed expressions a few times and then grinned. He could be whoever he needed to be, and that was perfect. His grin turned into a smile as he studied his reflection for a second more. John Brown was ready for a new day.

CHAPTER ONE

TUESDAY MORNING, MELBA sat on the edge of her bed staring at the alarm clock on the nightstand. She tried to summon up the inner strength to move, but found that no matter how hard she tried, she just couldn't. She'd been sitting and staring at the clock for forty-seven minutes.

When she finally dragged herself through the door of the apartment the night before – hurt and distraught over Sam's death – she forced herself to walk painfully to the kitchen where she pulled a bag of frozen peas out of the freezer. Needing something to dull her aches, she poured herself a glass of wine. After the first taste, she found she didn't want it. She poured the liquid down the sink then carefully lowered herself to the floor of her small kitchen. She dug around in one of the cabinets until she located a dusty, old bottle of scotch – a holiday present from a few years ago. She pulled herself up, using the edge of the counter for support. She filled the wine glass with several fingers worth of dark, smoky liquor and drank it down, choking once as it burned a trail down her throat. Then she filled the glass again.

Melba stuck the bag of cold peas under one arm, lifted the bottle with one hand and the wine glass in the other, and hobbled to her bathroom. There, she undressed, dropping her clothing on the floor and leaving the pieces where they fell. She eased herself onto the side of the tub and propped her injured leg up on the toilet, and applied the peas to the swollen knee. She slowly finished her second drink while the cold penetrated the puffy flesh. After twenty minutes, she tossed the peas into the bathroom sink and cautiously stood up, testing her knee.

She filled the tub and managed to maneuver her body into the water. There she sat, washing herself over and over as tears slid down her cheeks and eventually dropped, one by one, into the hot soapy water. She stayed in the tub until the water cooled, then pulled herself upright and placed her good leg on the bathmat then lifted out her other leg using the back of the toilet for balance. She reached for a towel and wrapped it around her wet body and sat down.

She poured another inch or so of scotch into the glass and lifted it to drink. Before it touched her lips, she lowered it and set it down on the bathroom counter. She heaved herself up from her seat, and stood by the sink looking into the mirror. "Not much of a surprise, Reightman," she said dully to the reflection in the glass, "but you look like absolute hell." She considered her tear-ravaged face and her rat's nest head of hair. She picked a hairbrush and gave the graying strands a few half-hearted swipes before deciding she really didn't care how it looked. She dropped the brush to the counter and picked up the wine glass and poured the scotch down the sink. She'd never cared for scotch.

Melba dried herself off and pulled her faded blue bathrobe from its hook on the wall and eased it over her body. After knotting the belt, she picked up the bottle of scotch and the wine glass and looked down at the now-thawed bag of peas, trying to figure out how she could manage all three items. After giving the problem more consideration than it warranted, she wedged the wine glass in one pocket and the floppy plastic bag of vegetables into the other. With the scotch in one free hand she half hopped, half limped, back into the kitchen.

She filled a sandwich bag with ice from the freezer and looked at the peas. "What the hell?" she asked, then pulled a plastic cereal bowl out of the cabinet. She ripped open the bag and poured the peas into the bowl, which she then carried, hobbling, to the sagging couch. Propping her leg up onto the coffee table, she balanced the bag of ice on her swollen knee and ate the peas with her fingers, one at a time from the bowl on her lap.

She sat on the couch for a couple of hours, staring at the empty cereal bowl and occasionally looking up at the dark screen as if there was something on that caught her interest, although the television was turned off. She felt like crying, but didn't have any tears left. She took the now-melted bag off of her knee and placed it in the cereal bowl, which she left on one of the old couch cushions. She tested her knee, eventually deciding that the swelling had gone down a bit. She stood up and went into her bedroom and eased herself down on top of the covers.

She stared up at the ceiling in the dark room for the rest of the night, thinking about everything that had happened. She recalled the night she'd answered the dispatch call and had walked into the Time Out Spa for the first time to discover Geri Guzman arranged on a massage table, his naked body marred by multiple cuts and slashes across his chest and around his neck. She remembered Toby Bailey as he'd been then; his innocent pale blue eyes, floppy hair and deceptively slight frame causing him to look younger than his actual years. They'd all been bewildered by how the murderer had made their way in and out of the room without leaving a trace. She was still perplexed, because that puzzle had never been solved. She reflected on the next day, when she'd met Madame Zhou, Toby's seemingly ancient, incapable attorney, who'd surprised them all with her brilliant mind and inscrutable demeanor. She replayed the discovery of Lieberman's involvement in a case which had since spiraled out of control, and the discovery of his death by apparent suicide. She'd never believed the former City Coroner had taken his own life, but had yet to disprove it. Finally, she reviewed the last several hours, from the moment she and Sam had rushed to meet Toby and review the new evidence he'd found in the lockbox Geri Guzman had rented and filled with a set of ledgers and photographs implicating some of the most prominent social and government leaders in the entire city. Try as she might, she couldn't erase the image of bright lights rushing down the street, blinding her for moment as the gunman fired at Toby, but instead killed Sam Jackson, her partner of many years.

Over and over again, the image replayed in her mind, until she sat up and turned on the bedside lamp, and swung her feet off the bed. There she stayed; staring at the alarm clock on the nightstand, counting down the minutes until it would sound its wake-up call, signaling it was time to begin the day.

An hour later, and only through grim determination, she managed to wrap her knee to give it extra support, then dressed herself and hobbled to the kitchen. She poured a cup of extra strong coffee. Her phone buzzed in her purse and she reached across the counter to retrieve it.

"Hello," she croaked, her voice rough and gravelly from screaming and fighting to get to Sam the night before.

"Detective Reightman, I am sorry to be calling you this early, but there is something we need to discuss." Melba recognized Zhou Li's voice, although the old woman sounded uncharacteristically gentle this morning.

"Yes?" Reightman's voice was a bit clearer this time. Zhou Li continued to speak and Reightman listened carefully to her words, answering the few questions she was asked. "Alright," she responded when the woman paused. "I'll see you both at headquarters a few minutes before eleven." Zhou uttered a few more words, and then ended the call.

Reightman stuck the phone back into her purse, smiling a grim, wintery smile. She finished her coffee slowly, waiting for the caffeine to hit her tired, shocked system. She rinsed the cup and gathered her things. Thirty minutes later she walked through the glass side doors of Police Headquarters.

Toby also had difficulty sleeping that night.

After Officer Mitchell took him back to the lockbox so he could stow the ledger and the photographs, he climbed the stairs to his apartment and called Madame Zhou. He filled her in on what had happened and relayed the information she needed to be prepared for tomorrow. Then he watched from his bedroom window until the last police vehicle left the front of his business, the Time Out Spa. Two uniformed officers remained stationed outside the entrance and he knew there was probably another one inside the building.

He took a shower, once again washing blood off of his body. This time, the blood belonged to the man who'd saved his life. Detective Jackson had thrown him out of the way when he'd realized the truck speeding toward them was intent on doing them harm. Toby had lost his balance and had fallen to the sidewalk as shots rang out from the vehicle. His own arm had been grazed by a passing bullet, and Sam Jackson had been killed in his place. And it was all because of the things Geri Guzman had done.

When the hot water turned to cold, Toby leaned against the shower wall and thought about Geri. He remembered him as he'd been when they'd first met, young and beautiful and full of life. He thought about how Geri had changed into a cold, calculating individual, entrapping and blackmailing those who could provide money and services or smooth the rough patches a business owner was bound to run into. In some part of his mind, Geri had believed what he was doing would ensure that Toby never had to worry about those things. Toby wondered if there wasn't something more behind his actions. Geri had never really had a family, or a place where he belonged until he met Toby and was taken in as part of the family. As a result, he'd never felt like he had much to offer, and always believed himself obligated for the help Toby and Grams provided when he and Toby went to school.

Geri was killed because of his actions, and others had died as well. Dr. Lieberman, the City Coroner, had been one of Geri's clients, and had supposedly killed himself. He'd confessed to Geri's murder, and driven by some form of sick obsession, had removed the foreskin from Geri's body while it was in the morgue. Perhaps he had killed Geri, but the ledgers and photographs raised a lot of doubt in Toby's mind. The collective evidence found in the lockbox had convinced Detective Reightman and Detective Jackson that there was good reason to reopen the murder case. It was that evidence that led to the death of Sam Jackson tonight, and would have claimed Toby's life if things had gone differently.

Toby remembered the night he'd found Geri murdered and laid out on a massage table in one of the treatment rooms at the spa. His green eyes had stared toward Toby as he stood in the doorway, shocked and horrified by what he saw. There had been blood that night as well; pools of blood on the floor and dripping down Geri's chest to the massage table and then onto the floor. Toby could still remember the sound of blood hitting the polished wood. He'd been arrested that night. Detective Reightman believed he'd stabbed Geri with a hunting knife engraved on the hilt with his name. Thankfully,

Madame Zhou had proven the knife wasn't his and that he'd been eating dinner when the murder happened. She and Toby had cooperated ever since, trying to help the police find the real killer.

Geri was dead and buried now, but Toby knew it wasn't over. He just hoped Detective Reightman could marshal the support she needed to follow this through to the end. But most of all, he hoped she'd be able to recover from the blow of Detective Jackson's death. He'd been her partner, but most of all, he'd been her friend. She'd been wild with grief and anger tonight and had lost control of herself. Toby winced when he remembered how he'd slapped her, trying to bring her back to her senses. She had needed his help and Toby intended to keep on giving her all the help he could. She didn't know it yet, but Toby was her friend, too.

Shivering from cold, Toby turned off the water and stepped out of the shower, quickly wrapping himself in his robe and drying his hair. He crawled into bed and remembered Geri's green eyes and white smile. He wondered if he'd ever fall in love again. Still turning the question over in his mind, he finally fell asleep.

When Reightman arrived at work she stowed her purse, refusing to look at Jackson's desk. Before doing anything else, she made the walk to Chief Kelly's office, her progress slow as she tried not to favor her knee too much.

Nancy stood up from behind the desk and walked around and gave her a warm, comforting hug. "I'm so sorry, Melba," she said quietly before pulling away. Bad news always traveled fast around here.

Reightman ducked her chin in acknowledgment and then glanced at the Chief's closed door. "Is he here?"

"No, he hasn't made it in yet, Melba. I expect him in a few minutes though. I don't know if he'll have time…"

"You'd better start clearing his calendar, Nancy, for the morning at least –if not the entire day."

Nancy heard the steely undercurrent in Reightman's voice and moved back behind her desk, opening Kelly's calendar on the computer. "Do you want me to call you when he gets in, Melba?"

"No. I'll wait for him." Reightman moved to the wall across from Nancy's desk and leaned back, relieving some of the pressure from her knee.

"Okay, but it may be a while before gets in."

"I'll wait."

Ten minutes later Kelly strode in, headed for his office. He was talking on his phone in a low, hushed voice. When he noticed Reightman leaning against the wall, his eyes widened and then narrowed in irritation. "I'll have to call you back," he said to whoever was on the other end of the call and stowed the phone in his pocket. "Detective Reightman," he greeted her, his voice clipped and harsh. She thought she saw something flicker deep within his eyes before he looked away from her stare.

"Chief Kelly," she greeted him in return, while standing quietly and waiting for what he'd do next.

Kelly glared at Nancy – who looked away nervously – and then walked to his door. He opened it and entered the office, firmly closing the door behind him. Once again, Reightman leaned against the wall.

"Melba," Nancy whispered urgently. "I don't think this is a good time."

"I'll wait." Reightman replied.

A few minutes later, Nancy's desk phone buzzed. The admin picked it up quickly after shooting a quick, anxious glance her way. "Yes, sir, she is." She listened for a minute and then placed the phone back into its receiver. Nancy looked up at Reightman with a worried frown and gave a little shake of her head before standing up and leaving the desk.

She'd just cleared the area when the door to the office opened, and Kelly growled, "Reightman, in here – now!"

Reightman pushed herself up from her place against the wall and entered the office, positioning herself in front of the desk with her arms held behind her.

Kelly's stormy eyes glared at her as she stood there calmly. "I don't have time for you this morning," he informed her, with angry, dismissive emotion coloring each word.

"I understand you're busy, but in this instance, you'd better make the time, sir." Reightman was surprised to hear how cool and detached her words sounded. It was as if someone else was standing in front of his desk, observing their exchange.

"Who the hell do you think you are to stand there and tell me I'd better make time?"

Reightman looked into his flushed, angry face and felt her own anger rise up to the surface. She forced herself to keep her voice level. "I'm the Detective who saw her partner shot down in cold blood last night," she said simply. "I'm the Detective who held Sam Jackson in her arms as he died. I'm the Detective who has a few things to say to you."

"Why the hell were you there, Reightman?" he screamed the question at her from across the desk separating them. "What did you think you were doing by dragging Jackson into more shit at that god-damned spa? When you called last night, I knew you were up to something, so I ignored it. I knew you were probably digging around in things better left alone and I was right. I don't have time for any more of your crap!"

"My crap, sir?" She watched him, curious about what he'd say

"Yes, Reightman, your crap! Insisting that you needed to keep investigating, when the case was already solved. Making up stupid, convoluted theories so you'd have something meaningful to do with your time. You must have felt pretty damned special chasing after clues to solve the biggest murder in years. That crap, Reightman." When she didn't say a word in self-defense or justification, he narrowed his eyes and cruelly added, "Sam Jackson is dead because of you and your fucking crap."

She didn't even wince at his words. She just let them wash over her, insubstantial in light of everything else. "We were there last night to review new evidence related to the Guzman murder case – which you'd have known if you'd answered your phone when I called, or bothered to call me back, sir."

"The Guzman case is closed! Get that into your thick head!" he yelled. When she once again failed to respond, he added in a hard, cutting voice, "Because you couldn't accept the fact that it's closed, you got Jackson killed last night. Because you couldn't leave well enough alone, a good man was shot to death."

This time, Reightman closed her eyes at his words. She'd said those same things to herself over the last nine hours – over and over again. She hadn't made peace with them yet, but she'd willed herself to painfully accept the part she'd played. When she opened her eyes, she saw Kelly took a small step back, startled by what he saw on her face.

"Jackson was a good man," she agreed, ice coating her every word. "He was also a good detective. He knew what the evidence we saw last night meant, and thought the case needed to be opened again. He knew it shouldn't have been closed in the first place – not without more work." Reightman watched the Chief's face closely as she readied her shot. "You know what he told me, sir? He said the man he once thought he knew – a man he respected – would never prematurely announce a murder had been solved, and would never have bought into an easy suicide verdict for Lieberman. That man would've looked for answers until every loose end was tied up, and not even the smallest possibility of doubt remained. That man he thought he once knew – was you." She saw her words register and then with her voice filled with sorrow and regret, added, "I accept the fact I contributed to his death. There's no way around that." Before the cold, satisfied smile could fully form on his face, she added with more force, "But so did you, sir, the minute you agreed to make the damned premature announcement – the minute you caved under pressure and took the easy road. And the minute you didn't call me back."

The look on Kelly's face frightened her with its intensity, but she pushed herself to continue. "Or was it something more, Kelly? Was it more than caving in from the pressure? Were you paid off to make this all just go away, sir?"

His eyes widened in outrage at her accusation and for a moment, he simply stared at her in disbelief. "How dare you?" he finally hissed across the desk, spittle falling from his lips.

"I dare, because it's time for the truth," she snarled back. "It's time to get to the truth about how Geraldo Guzman died. It's time to dig until we find the truth about Lieberman's death, and the truth about why two men – one of them a former officer on your force – tried to gun down Toby Bailey last night and instead…instead killed Detective Sam Jackson."

Kelly recoiled from her response, but quickly recovered and looked down at her from his superior height. He smiled cruelly, and nodded in satisfaction at the thought that crossed his mind. "This little show you're giving right now will end your career, Reightman. I can promise you that!"

"Maybe it will, sir." Reightman accepted his statement at face value and had in fact, already thought through that possibility. However, she wasn't going to back down now. She met his flinty eyes and gave him a smile of her own. "But this case may end yours. God help you if you were involved in this – in any way. If there's any mercy for you at all, it may be determined you were simply negligent and afraid to lift up the wrong rocks because you were frightened by the worms you might find underneath."

Kelly's eyes shifted away and after a tense moment, he sat down in his chair. He looked up at her from under his brows and leaned back, hands clasped together in front of his chest. "Where is all of this so-called evidence, Reightman?" he asked in a cool, silky voice

"The evidence we reviewed last night is still in Mr. Bailey's possession. He'll be arriving here this morning to turn it over, in the presence of his attorney." Once she'd gauged his reaction to that piece of news, Reightman leaned into the desk until she was face to face with him. "Madame Zhou's bringing along a few other guests to join the party, just to make sure it's all above board – and to make sure there is no possibility anything will be *misplaced*." In some remote and detached corner of her mind, Reightman enjoyed watching his face pale at her words. Her cold smile widened. "A shit storm like this city has never seen is about to be unleashed, and it looks like you might just find yourself right in the middle of it."

She pushed up from the desk and looked down at the man sitting behind it. He refused to meet her eyes. Nodding to herself at what she saw, she continued. "Madame Zhou recommends that you bring a few folks of your own. I believe she suggested Tom Anderson, Dr. Evans and perhaps someone from the Mayor's office. It'll even things out. She already has the City Attorney's confirmation, and I believe she mentioned that some nice woman from the DA's office will also be in attendance." As she walked to the door she added over her shoulder, "The big pow-wow is scheduled for eleven this morning, sir. In the large conference room. It'd be best if you were on time."

"Reightman?" Kelly's still angry – but less hateful – voice came from the desk. "I wasn't paid off."

"I hope that's the truth and I hope all of your misplaced anger and threats are because you know you were wrong. I hope the way you're acting has something to do with your own contribution to Sam's death. Maybe it is – maybe it isn't," she said from the door, allowing her doubt of his innocence to color every word. "Regardless, you better decide how you're going to play this. Either you do what's right and support me while I try and find the truth, or you continue down the path I fear you're already on. That path will have a very bad ending, sir. If I can promise you anything, I promise you that."

"You're a bitch, Reightman," Kelly said from his chair

She paused for a moment, with her hand on the doorknob. "*That is the truth, sir.*" Reightman left the office before he had a chance to respond.

When Reightman returned to her desk she found Jones and Mitchell waiting for her. Neither chose to sit in Sam's chair and had instead dragged two chairs close to hers. Both of the men looked tired and downcast, but she thought Mitchell in particular, looked more haggard than his years warranted. "*He was also there last night, and kept me under control during the worst of it,*" she reminded herself as she hobbled toward them.

They stood when they saw her approach, and she took her own seat without greeting them.

Detective Jones glanced at Mitchell and then spoke. "I'm sorry about Detective Jackson. I just heard this morning he'd been killed. If I'd known, Detective Reightman, I would've been here sooner."

"Thanks, Jones," she answered quietly, turning toward the two men so that she wouldn't have to stare at Sam's desk.

After an awkward silence, Mitchell told her what she'd want to know. "They found Helliman."

The news caused her to look up sharply. "When? Where is he?" she asked as she stood from her seat

"He was found last night, ma'am. He was in his truck about two miles from where…" The young cop broke off for a moment and until he'd swallowed his own grief. "He was found about two miles from Capital Street, shot once in the head."

The statement hung in the air until Reightman nodded once. "Good." She took her seat, but kept her eyes on his face. "He didn't deserve to die quickly," she resumed with harsh condemnation, "but at least the bastard is dead."

Neither man responded. Mitchell's face was pale and drawn, and Jones stood by his side, his own face chiseled out of stone.

"Any word on the shooter?" Reightman eventually asked.

"No," Jones answered. "There are a couple of teams out trying to gather word from contacts on the street, but without a description – and with Helliman unable to tell us anything – it doesn't look good."

"Are they working the vehicle? The shooter had to have left behind some evidence."

"Tom Anderson has a team working on it, but I think it'll be a day or so before he'll know anything. If he doesn't find anything concrete, it might be a dead end. If that's the case, it'll be almost impossible to find the shooter."

Reightman considered his words and discarded their message as insignificant. "I'll find him. Sooner or later, I will find the man who tried to kill Toby Bailey and did kill Sam." There was no doubt in her voice, and both men looked away from her expression.

"Are you positive they were aiming for Bailey?" Jones asked.

"Yes, and they would've been successful if Sam hadn't....if Jackson hadn't pushed him away and placed himself in the line of fire." All three of them were quiet, giving the man a silent moment of respect. "The shooter did hit Toby," Reightman continued, after she was sure she could trust herself to speak calmly, "but it was only a flesh wound."

"What do we do now, ma'am?" Mitchell asked.

"I'll have an answer for you later today." She studied his face as he looked down at her and made a decision. "In fact, Mitchell, I want you to attend a little meeting I'm going to later this morning. It starts at eleven o'clock and will be in the big conference room off the side hall. Can you meet me there a little before?"

"Yes, I don't think that'll be a problem. They haven't told me where I'll be assigned next."

"Should I plan on attending as well?"

She thought it over before shaking her head. "No. I don't think so, Jones." She saw the disappointment on his face and shrugged. "I may need you later though, depending on how the meeting goes. I'll either ask for your help with something, or ask you to help carry my things out to my car."

"Is this meeting going to be bad, ma'am?"

She was surprised Mitchell didn't sound worried or nervous – just curious. It was almost as if he wanted time to prepare himself for whatever might be coming. "I won't lie to you and tell you it won't be, Mitchell. I can only promise that I'll try and keep any of the firepower from turning on you – if I can. Regardless, I think you need to be there, especially after last night."

"I'm not worried about myself, Detective Reightman. I'm worried about you."

She was startled by the protective quality in his voice. "Thanks, Mitchell. I appreciate your concern, but I'm a big girl and can take care of myself." She smiled up at him and at Jones, even though the smile didn't reach her eyes. "I appreciate your offer to attend as well, Jones. But like I said, I think it's probably better to keep you out of it right now. If the worst happens, someone needs to be able to pick up the pieces." Both men nodded their understanding. "I think that's all for now – I've got a few things I need to do."

"Where should I meet you?" Mitchell asked her before he left

"Good question. Let me think for a sec." She thought over the jockeying that would be going on right now if her fears were well-founded, and made the safe decision. "I think it'd be best for you to just meet me right outside the conference room doors, Mitchell. If we meet here, someone might get some warning I'm trying to loop you in, and that wouldn't benefit you down the road."

"I'll be there, ma'am," Mitchell assured her and then turned and made his way through the maze of desks to where ever he was headed

"Let me know when you need that help," Jones reminded her. "Regardless of which type it turns out to be. My money's on the first option."

"I wish I was as sure of that as you are. Now get out of here. I have a couple of things to do to prepare." She watched him walk away and then turned to her computer. She had to search for a while to find the electronic files she needed, but she finally located them. She typed an email and attached the files and sent it off to its destination. Then she stood and crossed around to Jackson's desk

She went through his files slowly and methodically and pulled all the information she could find related to the Guzman case. She added a few of his filled notebooks to the stack after looking through them to determine if the dates were in the range she needed. A lump rose up in her throat as she scanned over his familiar handwriting. She forced it down and carried the stack of stuff around to her desk and started sorting it into piles – the things she knew were either true or false, and the things she wasn't sure about yet. *"I wonder what happened to the notebook he had with him last night."* She picked up the phone and dialed Tom Anderson. He didn't answer, so she left him a voicemail asking about the notebook. Then she called down to the morgue.

Dr. Bridges answered and Reightman explained what she was looking for. After she finished, Bridges assured her they'd look for it, but said she hadn't seen anything like it when she'd processed Sam's clothing. "I'm sorry, Reightman," Bridges added before hanging up. Melba knew her words had nothing to do with the missing notebook.

At 10:30 AM her phone rang. She spoke to the caller and concluded by saying, "I'll be sure and bring some. Thank you for thinking of it." After she hung up the phone, she pulled out a tea bag and headed to the breakroom. It seemed that every few feet someone stopped her and expressed their regret over Jackson's death. She forced herself into automatic pilot and made the appropriate responses. She wouldn't allow herself to think about it too much until this was all over. Otherwise, she wasn't sure she'd have it in her to do what needed to be done.

She carried her mug back to her desk and waited for the tea to finish brewing. As she inhaled the scent which she found calming – even today – she went over her plan for the meeting to come, building layers of mental and emotional defenses and focusing on her desired outcome.

Her conversation with Zhou Li earlier in the morning played through her head and she smiled a cold, nasty smile, thinking about what this city was in for if the powers that be didn't play their cards right. If circumstances were only a little different – if Jackson was here with her for this one – she was almost certain she'd be looking forward to the next few hours.

She finished off the tea and picked up her purse and went to the ladies room. As she was washing her hands, she caught sight of herself in the washbasin mirror. She looked tired and worn-down, and her face was swollen by the tears and grief of the last ten hours. *"Not much I can do about that,"* she conceded. When she forced herself to meet her own eyes in the mirror, she was pleased to see determination in them or – maybe – even the desire for revenge. *"Whatever it is, it'll have to do, Reightman."* She pulled some lipstick out of her purse and applied a little, blotting the excess of on a paper towel. She took another look in the mirror. *"That helps a little,"* she decided. She replaced the lip color and dug out her wallet, opening it to retrieve a few bills. She cursed under her breath and stuffed the wallet back in her purse. She shouldered the heavy bag and started out the door to make her slow, halting way to the conference room. By the time she made it, she could feel her knee starting to swell again.

Mitchell was waiting as promised, right outside the double doors. When he noticed her approach, he started toward her and she motioned him to the side, about ten feet away from the room's entrance.

"Here's what's about to happen." She laid out what she knew of the plan.

When she finished, he looked back at the double doors. "They're not going to be happy, ma'am."

She didn't detect fear or worry on his face, just the simple acceptance of the facts. "No, they're not. But if they don't do things my way, they're going to be less happy, Mitchell." She sighed, feeling a tiny amount of regret. "I don't like what I'm about to do, but I can't let it all get swept under a rug somewhere. And that's what would happen." When the young cop started to object, she shook her head sadly. "I wish I believed differently. I used to, but I've seen it happen time and time again over the years. A case gets stale and cold and there just isn't any urgency anymore. It becomes easy to ignore that file stuck on the corner of a desk somewhere – and ignoring the file is encouraged, in little, insidious ways. Sometimes, it's even blatantly encouraged. If I felt I could trust the people around me, I wouldn't have to do this. But I don't trust them. I don't trust anyone now, except Toby Bailey, Zhou Li, Jones, and you.

"You don't trust the Coroner or Anderson?"

The young man was incredulous when she shook her head. "I want to trust Tom, and Doctor Evans, but I can't."

"How about the… I mean, what about Chief Kelly?"

"No. I don't trust Chief Kelly," she answered regretfully. He was wide-eyed at her admission, so she tried to explain. "There's something bad going on here in the city and…and I think it's permeated every department I can think of – or is trying to get a foothold wherever it can. I think it may already have a foothold here." She studied his face carefully, before telling him what she knew to be true. "Somehow, someone found out we were meeting Toby Bailey last night and didn't want what he found to see the light of day."

His eyes widened and then his face went very still as he processed the meaning behind her words. "I think I understand what you're telling me," Mitchell finally answered, once again accepting the situation for what it was. "What do you want me to do in there?" he jerked his head toward the doors.

"Tell your part in the events of last night, if needed. Otherwise, just watch and listen. Pay attention to what's said and done, and watch everyone's face and body. I won't be able to focus on that as much as I should. I'll be busy with other things."

"That doesn't sound like much for me to do. I'm willing to help more, if you need me to."

"What you'll be doing may end up being very important, Mitchell." They started to walk toward the doors, but she stopped him. "One more thing – do you have any money on you?"

"I think I have a little," he said, pulling out his wallet. "How much do you need?"

"You got a five?"

"Sure." He pulled out the bill and offered it to her

"Thanks, Mitchell," she said, taking it from his hand. "I'm good for it."

"What do you need the money for, ma'am?

She thought about telling him, but decided he could wait and see. She suspected that Mitchell had hidden depths and it'd be more fun that way. "Watch and learn, Mitchell. This day should be very educational for you."

CHAPTER TWO

WHEN THEY ENTERED the conference room, Reightman noticed most of the planned attendees had already arrived. This room was like every other city-owned conference room with its dull grey walls and utilitarian furniture. The ubiquitous orange chairs were arranged around a large table with a worn and scarred top. There was no attempt at comfort or style. It was simply a space for large numbers of people to meet when there were things to discuss. Often, those discussions were unpleasant and today would prove to be no exception.

Toby Bailey and Zhou Li sat on the far side of the table, side by side. The aged Chinese attorney had a stack of legal documents stacked neatly in front of her, as well as a familiar, leather covered memo pad. Toby's satchel was slung across his body, clearly demonstrating that nothing in his possession was up for grabs. His face was pale, and his hair threatened to fall forward and hide his pale blue eyes. They both offered small, sad smiles, acknowledging her entrance.

To Toby's right was Dr. Evans, and to her right was Tom Anderson. Although each noted her arrival, neither offered any form of greeting, although they followed her progress with their eyes. Reightman was sure they were wondering what this was all about. She hoped they were prepared for an interesting morning.

Seated across the table from them were Jessica Lautner, the senior Assistant District Attorney and Jerome Hollingfield, the City Attorney. Lautner and Hollingfield sat with their heads together and were engaged in a hushed conversation. Reightman couldn't make out their words, but from their body language it was clear their exchange was not amicable. The representative from the Mayor's office had not yet arrived, nor had Chief Kelly.

After scouting the lay of the land, Reightman selected a seat at one end of the table. She slid the purse off of her shoulder and looped it over the chair back, and put her yellow legal pad on the table. Mitchell followed her lead and took his place on her left. That left the chairs at the opposite end of the table for Chief Kelly and the – as yet unknown – representative from the Mayor's office.

Moments later, Kelly entered through the double doors, followed by a thin, middle-aged man carrying an old-fashioned briefcase. Reightman recognized Adam Wilkenson, the Mayor's Chief of Staff, and realized the city was pulling out the big guns today. Wilkenson was a powerful force in the city and had the air of rarified elegance sometimes found in scions of older local families. He gave a short, abbreviated greeting to the City Attorney, but didn't bother to greet the representative from the DA's staff. Obviously, he considered her to be beneath his notice. He followed Kelly to the end of the table opposite Reightman, and took his chair, as did Chief Kelly. Neither looked toward Zhou Li or Toby Bailey. While Wilkenson was occupied with opening his briefcase and removing the items he anticipated needing, the Chief leaned back in his chair and glared at her across the long table. He pursed his lips at the sight of Mitchell and eyed him speculatively.

After everyone was seated and situated to their satisfaction, Chief Kelly exchanged a brief glace with Wilkenson then growled down the table. "Well, Detective Reightman, we're all assembled for your little party. I suggest you get this circus started."

Without replying, Reightman stood from her chair and walked directly to Zhou Li, who rose from her chair as Reightman approached. Without saying a word, Reightman handed her the five dollar bill she'd caged off of Mitchell. Zhou took the money into her left hand and held out her right. Reightman shook the offered hand and bowed slightly. Madame Zhou returned the small bow and seated herself back in her chair, placing the money into her vintage purse as she settled into her place. Reightman moved back to her place and took her own chair.

All the individuals present watched the interchange between the two women. As Reightman took her seat, she noticed Kelly frowning slightly at Zhou. Hollingfield, the City Attorney, sat back in his chair with a speculative look. Jessica Lautner leaned slightly forward in her chair and folded her hands on the notepad in front of her, with a tiny, amused smile on her face. Dr. Evans and Tom Anderson both looked from Kelly to Reightman, sensing the tension in the room, but not understanding the reason behind it. Mitchell looked confused, trying to determine what Reightman had just done with the five dollars he'd given her.

Impatient with the delay, the Chief addressed her sharply, "If you're finished with whatever little game you're playing with Mr. Bailey's attorney, I'd suggest you get started."

Reightman ignored Kelly, and looked placidly down the table toward him. He tried to figure out what her expression meant, but eventually gave up. His face reddened and he started to comment again, but Wilkenson – the Mayor's Chief of Staff – leaned in and spoke a few words into his ear.

Kelly's flushed deepened, and he glanced back toward Wilkenson. When the man gave him a single nod, he glowered at her and then attacked. "Reightman, I said, get this meeting started! You're wasting the valuable time of everyone seated at this table with your ridiculous games and posturing. I've absolutely reached the end of my patience with you, you stupid woman. Either get things started or be prepared for an official reprimand in your file."

She met his gaze across the length of the table. "I'm sorry, sir. I wasn't aware your previous comment was directed at me. You must have misunderstood. This isn't my meeting."

"Dammit, Reightman!" Kelly shouted. "Get this started or we are all going back to the jobs we should be doing instead of sitting here twirling on our thumbs."

Reightman had seen the Chief angry before, but she'd never seen him come so close to losing his control in a gathering like this. "Sir, as I've already made clear, this is not my meeting."

For a moment, she thought he was going to be able to hold on to his uncertain temper, but after another whispered comment from Wilkenson, she could see him begin to boil. She could see a blood vessel throbbing in his forehand and braced herself for the expected explosion. He didn't disappoint.

"That does it!" He said in a loud, thundering voice as he shot up from his chair. He sneered at her, and then continued with a cutting voice laced with derision. "I should have known better than to have placed a stupid broad in a position with any level of responsibility! Women simply cannot accept authority and are absolutely incapable of doing this sort of job. They don't have the balls for it! They're fine as secretaries and meter maids but not much else. As a matter of fact…"

"Chief Kelly! Hollingfield cut him off, realizing Kelly had just stepped into dangerous territory. "I don't think this is the appropriate venue for this, and your comments are out of line."

Kelly started to retort, but sputtered to a stop as he realized what he'd just said in provoked anger. He sat back down in his chair, avoiding the shocked stares coming from all of those present.

Madame Zhou smiled in satisfaction as she began writing notes on her tablet. The tiny old woman looked up the assembled group, peering at each of them from behind her thick-lensed glasses. "My apologies to all of you who have taken time out of their day to attend this briefing and discussion. I must also apologize to Detective Reightman especially, for suffering this unprecedented outburst in my stead. You see, this meeting is not hers. It is mine. Or rather, it has been called by me on behalf of one of my clients, Mr. Toby Bailey."

"Perhaps you would care to explain then, ma'am, what exactly this meeting is all about." Jerome Hollingfield suggested.

"Madame," Zhou replied from across the table. Reightman struggled to suppress an involuntary smile as the elderly woman corrected the City Attorney. "I prefer to be called Madame Zhou."

There was a moment of silence, and then a small patronizing smile formed on Hollingfield's face. "Well, if you insist. I suppose I can indulge you and play along."

Zhou's voice whipped across the table. "I am afraid I do insist! And Mr. Hollingfield, I would suggest you wipe the patronizing smile off of your face and learn proper manners. I have been a highly respected, practicing attorney, accredited in most of the States in this country, for longer than you have been alive."

Before Hollingfield could respond, Jessica Lautner leaned over and hurriedly whispered something in his ear, obviously taking great pleasure in informing him just who was sitting across the table. After Lautner finished, Hollingfield looked across the table, somewhat abashed. "My sincere apologies, Madame Zhou."

Zhou barely spared him a look before she resumed her explanation. "We have called everyone here today to present to you new evidence discovered by Mr. Bailey. This evidence has a direct bearing on the murder of Mr. Geraldo Guzman."

"The Guzman murder has been closed, I believe," Wilkenson – representing the Mayor – replied with feigned surprise.

"Inappropriately so, I assure you." Reightman couldn't quite decipher Zhou's expression as she addressed the man, but it looked like extreme distaste.

"I believe all proper procedures were followed, and the results of the investigation have been signed off by Chief Kelly," Wilkenson said with an almost imperceptible glance toward the Chief. "I don't think there's really any need to waste our time further."

"Both my client and myself, as well as Detectives Reightman and Jackson – a good man who was killed in the line of duty while examining and making provisions to safeguard this new evidence – feel further investigation is warranted in light of what has occurred over the last few days."

"And what exactly is this evidence, *Ma'am?*" Wilkenson asked, purposely insulting the diminutive attorney with both the form of address he used, and the emphasis he placed on the word.

This time, Madame Zhou ignored the form of address and simply went on with her explanation. "The evidence consists of a number of quite surprising photographs of several of this city's leading citizens engaging in a variety of sexual acts with the murdered man." Her comment had everyone sitting upright in their chairs, beginning to listen with interest. "In addition," Zhou continued, "we have evidence which demonstrates many of these same individuals were being blackmailed by Mr. Guzman, and paid large sums of money to prevent the photographs from being made public." Zhou surveyed the people around the table, making sure of their attention. "This evidence – when taken into consideration with open questions raised during the investigation which were ignored or brushed aside by the others — offers motives for murder and calls into question the validity of both the Guzman case's closure and the suicide ruling made by the acting Coroner regarding the death of Dr. Benjamin Lieberman."

"I beg your pardon, Madame," Patricia Evans said from her place at the table, "But are you questioning my ruling?"

Zhou gave an apologetic nod to Evans before she replied. "With the greatest respect for your abilities, Doctor, I'm afraid I must."

Evans didn't comment, although her brow creased slightly.

"Let's take a look at this evidence then," Wilkenson suggested in a patronizing tone of voice. "I, for one, can't wait to see what collection of crap you've assembled."

Reightman winced, but was sure Zhou could handle him.

"Mr. Bailey has agreed to share this evidence with everyone here today. This group was assembled at my request to protect his interest, and to ensure each piece of material was presented and witnessed by all present. This is to prevent any accidental misplacement or inadvertent destruction of the material." When Wilkenson motioned to her impatiently, she added, with some relish, "However, Mr. Wilkenson, you will not be viewing the material."

Everyone nervously looked around the table in reaction to her declaration. At first, Wilkenson couldn't believe what he'd just heard, but he quickly recovered his wits and changed tactics, aggressively defending his prerogatives. "I *will* view the evidence with everyone else in this room *Madame*, and I don't think you can stop me. You do understand I'm here representing the Mayor in this ridiculous matter?" The pompous edge to his voice was familiar to everyone seated at the table.

"I do understand your role here today, perhaps better than many others. I am also well aware of who you are. Indeed, you are quite recognizable."

"Then surely even you can understand why I must be allowed to view the materials. In fact, I insist on viewing this evidence before the others, and in private, so I may access its validity. I will then consult with the Mayor and make a determination of whether *anyone* should be asked to waste any more time on this nonsense."

Chief Kelly nodded his head in agreement. "I think your suggestion sounds like a sensible approach — the first sensible thing I've heard this morning. Don't you agree, Hollingfield?" When the City

Attorney shrugged, signaling he really didn't care one way or the other, Wilkenson smiled condescendingly. "You see Madame Zhou – we're all in agreement. You will provide me with the materials. After my review, I'll make a recommendation on how – and if – we'll proceed."

"No, Mr. Wilkenson. I will not consent to that." Zhou replied serenely. "Indeed, your directive regarding how we should proceed firms my resolve and strengthens my understanding of why you must *not* see the evidence, under any circumstances, and most certainly not in private."

Zhou's calm but firm rejoinder confused Wilkenson for a moment, but once again he regained his aplomb and responded mockingly, "I think *you* are *absolutely* crazy, Madame whoever-the-hell-you-think-you-are! I've made a perfectly reasonable suggestion, which you refuse to even consider." Wilkenson's tone changed as he presented his ultimatum. "Unless you can give me one good reason why my suggestion shouldn't be accepted and acted upon, I will insist all city employees withdraw from this nonsensical meeting and get on to more important things. Is everyone here in agreement?"

Reightman noted those who agreed with Wilkenson, and those who were holdouts. The city officials were in clear agreement, although Dr. Evans hesitated before following the lead of the others. Jessica Lautner and Tom Anderson were silent and each wore a different, but equally considering expression on their faces. Zhou Li carefully noted each individual response on her legal pad.

When she didn't offer comment, Wilkenson smiled; gracious in his victory. "So, Miz Zhou, are you ready to share whatever possible objection you have, now that we're all in agreement?"

Zhou Li considered him for a moment and then bared her small white teeth in what might – from a safe distance – be considered a smile. "Certainly, Mr. Wilkenson. In fact, I will do better than to provide you one reason. I will provide several. Firstly: You, Mr. Wilkenson, are the senior member of the Mayor's staff, and as such you wield a very high level of influence over most, if not all, of the city departments which fall directly within the Mayor's purview. That has been adroitly demonstrated just now." She tilted her head slightly in a birdlike gesture. "Would you agree with my assessment?"

Wilkenson shrugged with false modestly before he answered. "I make no bones about it. I *am* the senior official on the Mayor's staff. As such, I set the tone for how most city departments react to any given situation."

Zhou nodded her acceptance of his evident power. "From your comments, I feel we can all agree you are indeed able to influence opinion and bring the departments into line when needed. This brings me to my second reason. Shall I tell you what my second reason is, sir?"

Wilkenson chuckled loudly, his amusement and pity for the old, foolish woman plain to hear. Kelly shared a pleased expression with him. *"He's absolutely delighted that Zhou is being made to look foolish,"* Reightman realized as she watched the byplay at the opposite end of the table.

"Very well then. Thank you for indulging an old woman, Mr. Wilkenson. I will remember your kindness as I share the rest of my reasoning with the group." Zhou paused until she had the attention of everyone seated at the table. Reightman suppressed a shiver when she realized Zhou looked like a small, dangerous predator preparing itself for a strike. "My second reason for denying you access to any of the material is this: you are one of the individuals shown engaging in sexual acts with Mr. Geraldo Guzman."

The individuals around the table reacted in different ways: Kelly looked unsure of what had just happened, but recognized the floor had just dropped out from under his side of the table; Hollingfield was both shocked and disgusted; Lautner sat back in her chair with her arms crossed thoughtfully, not looking at anyone else in the room; Patricia Evans gave a short bark of surprised laughter, which she attempted to disguise by clearing her throat; and finally, Tom Anderson looked directly at Reightman with one eyebrow raised in query.

Zhou continued her relentless summation, not bothered in the least by the reactions around her. "Thirdly, your name appears in the ledger book detailing the sums of money paid to Mr. Guzman, complete with the totals and the dates of payment. Your account is *quite* impressive, and perhaps should be investigated by the staff accountants on the city payroll. I am sure they will have questions about where some of the funds originated. Shall I continue explaining how, because of these reasons, you have a possible motive for desiring the death of Mr. Guzman and, should the case be reopened, must be considered a suspect?"

Wilkenson's face was as white as a sheet and he sat absolutely motionless at the end of the table next to Kelly. When he failed to respond to her question, Zhou finished up her slaughter. "Mr. Wilkenson, you have the contacts, the influence and enough outright power to stymie *any* investigation, much less one by which you stand to lose as much as this one promises in terms of cost. You have in fact, admitted it – rather boastfully – and tried to do just that here in this room today."

Wilkenson sat back in his seat, dazed and in shock. He shot the old lady an incredulous look. "You've ruined me ..."

"No, Mr. Wilkenson. You ruined yourself. "Zhou's voice held no pity for the humiliated man who had treated her so dismissively a few minutes earlier. "As soon as I described the evidence in our possession, you should have excused yourself from the discussion and then explained yourself to the Mayor. Instead, you chose to try to intimidate me into allowing you to view the materials and to take control of them. My concerns about the safety of the evidence have been fully justified."

Wilkenson continued to stare at Zhou Li, with horrified and shameful understanding of what had been exposed to those present. He slowly gathered his things from the table and placed them in his briefcase – avoiding eye contact with anyone at the table. Then he quickly left the room.

"Oh, man..." Mitchell commented with the slightest of breaths from his place at Reightman's side.

Once those seated around the table had absorbed what had just happened, Madame Zhou spoke again. "Mr. Hollingfield, I assume you are able to represent the Mayor, as well as the City's interests, now that Mr. Wilkenson has left us. Is my assumption correct?"

Hollingfield took a quick look around the table and then answered, "Yes, I am."

"Excellent," Zhou responded. "I suggest we proceed, if everyone is in agreement." Once they'd all signaled their assent, the old attorney continued. "The nature of the evidence we have in our position must be handled very carefully if it is to be used properly and effectively, and in an ethical manner. I must insist what we discuss remain extremely confidential. I have grave concerns about how the material will be safeguarded, and about how the investigation will unfold when the case is reopened – and it will be reopened."

Hollingfield spoke from his seat opposite Zhou. "Madame Zhou, with all due respect, I'm not certain the city will agree to reopen this case. It will require further discussion."

"Perhaps additional discussion will be required," Zhou agreed. "However, if needed, I will make certain public opinion demands the case be reopened."

"Do I understand you to say you would make this information – information you yourself have described as highly confidential and sensitive – available to the public?" Lautner, the senior assistant DA asked carefully.

Zhou exchanged a look with Toby and then nodded. "Yes, although that would be our choice of last resort. However, we are committed to finding the truth behind these deaths and are prepared to go to extreme measures to do so."

Immediately understanding the repercussions, Hollingfield asked "What would we need to agree to in order for the information to remain in official hands?"

Zhou consulted her notes a moment before answering. "First, the case must be opened. Secondly, all matters pertaining to the investigation must be under the authority of the department's senior Homicide Detective, Detective Melba Reightman."

"Absolutely not!" Kelly objected. "Reightman's too close to this case and I don't have confidence in her ability to handle something this important. In fact, I've questioned her judgment many times before, and have been meaning to take disciplinary action and demote her from her senior position for some time." He waited for Reightman's reaction, and when he saw she wasn't going to say anything in her own defense, he dismissed her. "If this case is reopened, it will be under my direct supervision and handled by a different team entirely."

Hollingfield considered the Police Chief's words. "If that's the case, Chief Kelley, we'd have to make other arrangements."

"It is the case. I don't trust Reightman to keep any information to herself. She's shared more information with Mr. Bailey and his attorney than was ever advisable."

"Do you mean Detective Reightman didn't maintain proper confidentiality of information?" Hollingfield asked.

"Yes, that's exactly what I mean."

"That in and of itself would be a dereliction of duty, and reason for disciplinary action. It could certainly explain why there are some unanswered questions about this situation." Hollingfield looked in Reightman's direction, making his disapproval clear.

"Yes, you are correct," Kelly agreed. "As I've already mentioned, I've had concerns about her performance for some time."

"Exactly how long have you had these concerns, Chief Kelly?" Zhou politely inquired.

"For well over a year, and perhaps for as long as two years."

"Oh dear, this does complicate matters." Zhou's voice sounded surprised and worried. "You must find her very difficult indeed, Chief Kelly."

"That calls into question the need to reopen the investigation," Hollingfield added with concern. "I'm afraid any further action on this case will have to wait until the matter of Detective Reightman's ongoing performance is handled to the Police Department's – and the City's satisfaction."

Zhou Li considered everything that had been said, and then asked hesitantly, "Assuming your concerns are validated, Mr. Hollingfield, how long do you think it…I mean, how long would it be before you'd be able to agree on behalf of the city to proceed with reopening the case and resuming the investigative activities?"

Hollingfield tightened his lips and looked toward Chief Kelly. "Well," he mused, "I think we should be able to tie things up in a relatively rapid fashion, say – two or three months?" He waited for Kelly's confirmation

"That sounds about right. These things do take time and we want to make certain Detective Reightman is treated equitably. For a matter this serious, she may even feel the need for some sort of representation if things should move to the point of a formal hearing and possible demotion – or dismissal." He looked down the table to see what impact his words had on Reightman and was surprised when she simply gave him a tight-lipped smile.

"Oh…this is even more complicated than I feared," Zhou said sadly, fluttering about in her seat. "Can you explain one thing to me, Chief Kelly?" she directed a hopefully expression toward the end of the table. "You see, I'm finding myself confused."

Distracted by Reightman's response, it took him a minute to turn back to answer the question. "I'll try to help in any way I can."

Zhou Li smile sweetly in his direction. "Thank you, that is very kind." Reightman watched as Zhou's expression changed, and if the circumstances had been different, would have felt sympathy for what Kelly was about to experience. "Perhaps you can start by explaining what exactly you're getting out of all this?"

"I don't understand what you are asking." Reightman could see Kelly's irritation starting to rise again.

"Then I will try to simplify for you," Zhou Li told him, with none of her former sweetness. "What benefit are you receiving for your efforts in trying to discredit Detective Reightman?"

"I'm not trying to discredit her! I've simply shared my long standing concerns regarding her judgment and her performance of her job duties."

"I find myself very disappointed in you, Chief Kelly." Zhou pulled a few pages from the stack on the table and held them in one hand. "Here, I have copies of Detective Reightman's performance reviews for the past five years. In addition to those, I also have several letters which have been placed in her file – many from you, Chief Kelly – over the same period of time. The most recent letter from you commending her for outstanding performance was dated less than five weeks ago."

"Where did you get those?"

"Why, I received them from Detective Reightman, of course."

"Those are confidential documents and are not to be shared casually with anyone outside of the Detective's direct chain of command, and certain city officials." Hollingfield told her sternly. "Detective Reightman knows better than to share them with anyone not falling within those boundaries. She's in violation of city policy by that action alone."

"I believe there are a few exceptions to that policy, Mr. Hollingfield. One such exemption allows for an individual to share any of his or her own documents, or documents relating to him or herself, with an attorney engaged for the purposing of representing them." Zhou looked at the City Attorney with an expression of inquiry. "Is my understanding correct, sir?"

"Yes, but I fail to see—"

"Exactly! You fail to see much of anything this morning, Mr. Hollingfield. Detective Melba Reightman has engaged me to represent her. We finalized our binding agreement this morning. You witnessed it in fact."

"We all witnessed it," Jessica Lautner acknowledged from her seat at Hollingfield's side. "Detective Reightman handed payment to Madame Zhou and they shook hands, signifying agreement and making it binding and legal. Detective Reightman is perfectly within her rights to share these documents – and a great many more – with her attorney."

"May I see those documents?" Hollingfield asked after he thought over the possible ramifications.

"Certainly," Zhou agreed pleasantly, as she stood and handed him the papers. "But I will want them returned."

Hollingfield quickly read though the presented documents and looked up at Kelly when he'd finished. "Kelly, perhaps you'd care to explain yourself? These indicate that you held Detective Reightman in the highest possible regard – and in fact, you indicated she's ready for promotion when the first opportunity arises."

"But I—"

"Gentlemen," Zhou interrupted "I must caution you to say nothing more. You see, I intend to represent Detective Reightman in the suit we will be filing against the city as soon as I obtain her agreement to proceed. Anything you say now will certainly prejudice your case and ethically, I am obligated to warn you."

Hollingfield head snapped around at her comment. "What suit?"

"The lawsuit which will claim she has been discriminated against, harassed, and disparaged due to her sex."

"That's ridiculous!" Hollingfield exclaimed. "You'll never have such a claim substantiated."

"Won't I? All of us in this room heard her direct superior – the senior official of the city department in which she is employed – make a series of remarks this morning." Zhou quickly consulted her notes. "He said, and I quote, "I should have known better than to place a stupid broad in a position with any level of responsibility – women simply cannot accept authority and are absolutely incapable of doing this sort of job. They don't have the balls for it! They're fine as secretaries and meter maids but not much else." Those comments, along with his transparent and unsuccessful attempt to discredit Detective Reightman, will provide a strong basis for our suit – especially in light of the new non-discrimination policy which has been adopted by the city. Fortunately, I have a room full of credible witnesses to both Chief Kelly's attempt to discredit her, and also to the inflammatory comments made by him."

"We would counter sue, showing that Detective Reightman failed to follow procedure and broke official policy by sharing information about an ongoing murder investigation with you and your client."

"I would advise you to not waste the time or the taxpayer's money, Mr. Hollingfield. The sharing of information was approved by the Mayor's office and cleared by your own staff. Chief Kelly shared the good news with me himself. I am sure there is documentation somewhere. We do all seem to be fond of paper trails. A subpoena for information should garner what I need to have your suit dismissed as being completely without merit."

Hollingfield knew she had him. Kelly looked down silently at the table.

"I am afraid I have more unpleasant news for you, Mr. Hollingfield," Zhou said apologetically as she handed him an additional set of documents. "I am sharing these with you, in advance of them being officially served, as a professional courtesy." She waited until he had taken the documents into his own hand before adding pleasantly, "I filed this suit this morning, against the city for the mistreatment of and damage done to Mr. Geraldo Guzman's body while it was in the custody of the city morgue, under the care of Dr. Benjamin Lieberman."

"You're claiming damages of eighty million dollars," Hollingfield whispered in horrified disbelief after reviewing the new set of documents

"Yes, I realize we will probably not receive that much, but I suspect the final total will be quite acceptable. Jurors have proven to look unfavorably on the desecration of the dead. I would also have included damages for the loss of Mr. Guzman's private property, but the items were located by Detective Reightman and Mr. Anderson and eventually returned." Before the dismayed City Attorney could comment, Zhou presented another set of documents to him. "I'm afraid I am not quite done. The documents I've just handed you will also be served through official channels. They outline my intent to sue this department for the improper arrest of my client, and to ask for damages for the harm done to his character. Unfortunately, there were a number of reporters present as Mr. Bailey was cuffed and taken to jail and that caused him great emotional distress. In fact, the financial harm done to him and to his business by the public comments made by city officials has not been factored in the damages I'm seeking, so I'm afraid I will have to amend my filing. I do hate having to rework documents."

Zhou Li turned to the assistant DA. "I also have one small matter for your office, Ms. Lautner. I will be asking for an official grand jury investigation to be opened regarding possible corruption and the use of undue influence by city officials to prejudice this department in both its disposition of the Guzman murder and in the suicide ruling in the death of Dr. Lieberman."

Jessica Lautner glanced across the table at Dr. Evans, and then cleared her throat before cautiously asking, "May I ask what information you will present to support your request, Madame Zhou?"

"It is actually a chain of events. I believe they will be found curious. In short, I will share the discussions we have all had this morning, the content of which will be supported by most – if not all – of the people sitting here. In addition, I will point to the vilification this department was subjected to by a member of the City Council and the complete turnaround in relations demonstrated immediately following the public announcement of the Guzman case closure and Dr. Lieberman's death, which was characterized as suicide. Furthermore, the kind words spoken by the same Councilman at a recent rally at the City Park will be presented to bolster up my request."

As she was talking to Lautner, Zhou had another thought spring to mind. "Oh Mr. Hollingfield, I really must caution you that the expression of hateful, discriminatory and derogatory comments made by a member of the city council against a class of citizen protected under the new non-discrimination and defamation policy is putting you on shaky ground. Especially since those same comments were made on city owned property. It would be a pity if someone – or a group, perhaps – came forward and filed a suit against you for that as well. We wouldn't want that, would we?"

After Hollingfield mumbled something which Reightman couldn't quite make out, Lautner replied to Zhou's previous comment, "Madame Zhou, with all respect – and I use that word sincerely – I don't honesty believe you have enough concrete evidence to warrant such an investigation. Unless you have something else to tie everything together, I'm afraid your attempt to muster an official investigation would fail."

"Oh dear," Zhou replied in a mournful voice. "I hate to prematurely share anything, but I suppose I must. Ms. Lautner, I feel confident action will be taken because, you see, Councilman Sutton Dameron is also included in our photographic line-up, with each transaction documented and cross referenced. Mr. Guzman kept such excellent and complete records, although I can't say I approve of how he was using his bookkeeping skills."

Lautner jerked with surprised shock as the enormity of what had been revealed rippled through the rest of the room. Kelly set at the far end of the table and Reightman could see in his face the bitter realization of how thoroughly he'd been drawn into the web of duplicity and how members of the city's brass had betrayed his trust. *"His pride, his temper, and his capitulation to members of the city's hierarchy, has led him here,"* Reightman observed to herself as she looked down the table. *"And those things, combined with my own actions, ultimately resulted in Sam's death."*

As she struggled with her depressing thoughts, she felt Hollingfield's eyes on her. She glanced up and saw his considering look before he turned back to Madame Zhou. "What do you want?"

"It is very simple, Mr. Hollingfield. We want the case reopened – although I *do not* want it announced as such. All of this needs to be played very close to our collective chests, so to speak. Additionally, we want the responsibility for the investigation placed into Detective Reightman's hands, and we expect the full cooperation of the city –

every department – to be given to her, with no interference. We want the provisioning of any needed resource without argument or delay. Also," Zhou looked at her client, "I want protection for Mr. Bailey."

Toby started to object but Zhou was adamant in her demand. "No, Toby, don't argue. Everyone seems to have overlooked the fact it was you who was the target last night. You *will* be protected until this has reached its conclusion." She turned back to Hollingfield. "And now, the final thing: we want Detective Jackson to be honored for his selfless part in saving Mr. Bailey's life. It won't mean much to his family now, but perhaps it will one day."

Hollingfield was silent for a couple of minutes as he thought over Zhou's list. He turned to Jessica Lautner who gave him a short nod. He looked to Evans and Tom Anderson, who readily indicated their agreement. He looked down the table to Kelly, who agreed in a quiet, shamed voice. Finally, he turned to Reightman. "Assuming I can get agreement from the Mayor, do you agree with Madame Zhou's demands, Detective?"

Reightman hesitated. She agreed with most of them, but she didn't know if she'd be able to meet the old woman's expectations. She couldn't bear it if she failed Toby and she knew she'd have difficultly surviving if she failed herself. Mitchell nudged her foot under the table, jostling her injured knee. She looked Chief Kelly in the eye and he gave her a grim smile, followed by an almost imperceptible nod. She looked down the table at Toby where he waited expectantly for her answer, his pale blue eyes unblinking. "Yes," she answered.

Hollingfield rose from his seat. "I must step out to brief the Mayor and gain her agreement. Shall we take a recess?"

"That is a fine idea, Mr. Hollingfield. I could use a break myself. This has been a tiring morning for me. I'm not as young as I once was, and I find it difficult to keep up."

Reightman couldn't stop herself from grinning openly at the lady's comment. *"If you weren't keeping up this morning, I don't think anyone would survive it when you were."*

She walked around the table to where Chief Kelly sat. She'd never trust him again after what he'd tried to do to her this morning, and might never get past his behavior of the past few days. But…"Sir," she said, in offering. "Would it be possible for Nancy to order us some lunch before we get started again?"

"I'll see to it," he answered gruffly. He stood from the chair and looked down at her. "Reightman…"

She met his eyes and knew he was embarrassed by the day's events. She also knew that although he'd been made to cooperate, he wasn't her ally and might never be one again. "Save it, Chief, I have more important things to worry about."

"Yes," he agreed. "You do. Get your ducks in a row, Reightman, and pray for luck. You're going to need it."

"Yes, sir," she said quietly to his back as he left the room. She wasn't sure if his comment had been made in encouragement, or in threat. She hobbled back to her end of the table. The ache in her knee reminded her she needed to stay in the chair as much as possible.

Mitchell encompassed everything he'd witnessed with a single word, "Wow."

"Not very descriptive, but I think it about sums it up," she kidded him gently. Then more seriously, she added, "I'm going to need your help, Mitchell."

The young cop pursed his lips, looking older than his years for a brief second. "Yes, you are." He looked down at his shoes. "I know I'm not Jackson, ma'am. But I'll do whatever I can to help and you can be damn sure I'll have your back."

"Mitchell?" She waited until he looked up into her face. "You're right, you're not Jackson, but….nobody will ever be him. You'll do just fine."

He headed to the vending machine to get them each a soda, and she leaned back in the chair and closed her eyes. "*Get the bastards,*" she heard Jackson say in her mind. And she replied, "*I will, Sam….I will.*"

Things moved along quickly that afternoon. Hollingfield returned and informed the group that the Mayor had given her approval for Zhou Li's *requests*. Their agreement was documented by Hollingfield himself and Zhou patted him approvingly on the hand as she took the signed document from him. "I knew you showed promise, Mr. Hollingfield." The somewhat nonplussed City Attorney also informed them that Wilkenson had resigned directly after leaving the meeting.

Dr. Evans was excused for the remainder of the day, as her attendance that morning had been for the purpose of providing any additional details pursuant to her findings. She was still smarting from Zhou's questioning of her ruling, but after having witnessed the exchanges of the morning, she decided not to make an issue of it.

Once everyone else was settled back in their chairs, Zhou turned to Toby. "Alright, Mr. Bailey – I think it is time. Start by telling us how this evidence came into your possession."

Toby walked them through the events from the moment he had been given Geri's letter to the arrival of Jackson and Reightman at the spa. After he finished, he opened the satchel and pulled out the brown envelope, the ledger and the small white envelope containing the key and the diamond earring.

Reightman slid the white envelope to Tom. "These need to be tested for prints, and for DNA. There may be something on the earring. I don't know about the key."

Tom signified his agreement and then Toby handed the other items to Reightman.

"I think we should view the photos first." When no one objected, Reightman unfastened the brads and pulled out the large stack of photos. She laid them on the top of the table and sorted them into small stacks, organized by the individuals represented in the images. All told, there were fourteen sets of pictures – thirteen of which featured easily recognizable faces. As the attendees grouped near the stacks, there were occasional exclamations of surprise, which were quickly stifled as the potential impact to the community was realized.

While the photos were examined and their subjects named and described, Toby found himself understanding how and why his business license had been so easily approved, how there had been no issues raised by the zoning commission, and how anything needed from a city department had been obtained effortlessly and at very reasonable cost. "*I never questioned any of it,*" Toby realized. "*I thought Geri had just done some research and found the best deal, the most efficient path, or the right argument.*"

"Who do we think this is?" Tom asked, tapping on one of the images

"I don't know," Reightman answered as she picked up the photos of a man, maybe in his mid-to-late thirties. The body was well-toned, although not possessed of Guzman's musculature. "The only identifying feature is the tattoo."

Tom examined the picture, and then jokingly asked, "Anyone in here have a tattoo?" His effort to provide a little levity was met with blank looks. "What?" he asked. "I think it's a perfectly reasonable question given all the revelations presented today."

"Ummm...I have one," Mitchell admitted, not understanding Tom was joking. "It just...not there." He trailed off, his innocent face blushing bright pink.

"I want to see! Why don't you show me?" Lautner teased him mercilessly. 'Or do I have to guess where it is first?"

"Uh...uh...well...."

"Mitchell, she's just yanking your chain," Tom came to his rescue and reassured him with a smile.

Zhou Li rapped gently on the table top, bringing them back to the matter at hand. "If you will take a look through the ledger, I think you will find all of the photographs have been referenced with their respective financial transactions."

Tom took up the book and looked through the contents, occasionally checking a date and time stamp of an image with an entry. "We might be able to tie these to the financial records of each of our celebrities. However, we will need probable cause to get the records."

"I might be able to help with that," Lautner offered. "However, we should be prepared to run into a few roadblocks."

"I'll have one of the financial gurus on the forensics team take a crack at streamlining the information." Tom noticed the concerned expressions directed at him from both Reightman and Zhou Li. "The young lady I have in mind to help is completely trustworthy," he assured them. "She'd better be – she's my wife's cousin, and her momma would have her hide if she ever got herself involved in something like this."

Reightman glanced at Zhou Li, and when the old lady shrugged to let her know that the decision was in her hands, Reightman agreed. "Alright, Tom, but tell her to keep the information close. She might have the best intentions, but I want to make sure we keep anything having to do with this buttoned up tightly."

Tom agreed and handed the book off to Hollingfield, who only flipped through a few pages before giving it to Lautner.

Reightman considered her next move. "I think we need to talk about who will be assigned to help with this." She turned to Kelly. "Sir, do you have any suggestions?"

"I can recommend a couple of folks to handle any legwork you need, but I'm hesitant to make any recommendation for the investigative team, given my own damned gullible involvement. Do you have anyone in mind?"

Reightman considered a few choices. "Yes Chief, I'd like to keep Mitchell involved, although I'm not sure how to best use him. But there'll be plenty to do and I'm sure we can keep him busy. I'd also like Detective Jones assigned to me, since he is the most senior detective we have that I trust completely. If I could have a couple of others – maybe Detectives Monroe and Caldwell – I think that would be sufficient. I don't want to add too many folks into the mix. In fact, I plan to parse out the tasks and information carefully so no one has access to the full ball of wax – except those of us in this room."

"I'll get them all pulled off their current assignments, and have them report into you. It'll be in morning before I can make it happen."

Reightman started to push the issue, but thought through the current departmental constraints. "Understood. I realize we're short-handed, but I'll need them first thing in the morning." She raked her fingers through her hair, and realized she was about out of stream. "I think the only other thing we need to do tonight is to arrange for Mr. Bailey's protection. I think we can use a couple of teams of patrol officers. It'll mean pulling from the regular patrols, but I don't see much choice."

"I'll get with the duty officer and get a few teams assigned in rotation." Chief Kelly offered. "I assume you want them to start as soon as we leave here?"

"Yes. I think a presence on Capital Street will deter anyone looking to finish last night's job, although I'd like someone to shadow Mr. Bailey for the next few days – full time. Any thoughts?"

Kelly folded his arms across his chest and thought the roster of officers he'd trust. He finally shook his head. "I don't know. It's a pretty tricky role to fill. The person has to be trust worthy, but also needs the right mindset to accept Mr. Bailey's life choices – no disrespect or judgment intended, Mr. Bailey"

"I'm not easily offended, sir, and I appreciate your consideration. The truth is, I'm probably the most boring queer they'll ever meet."

The Chief looked away, clearly uncomfortable with Toby's comment.

After a moment of awkward silence, Mitchell spoke up. "I'll do it."

"Are you sure, Mitchell?" Reightman asked, both surprised and pleased he'd stepped up to the plate. "It'll mean really long hours, and will cut into your private time. There won't be much relief."

"Yeah, I'm sure. I can handle it for a few days. If it gets to be too much, I'll let you know and we can try and figure out something else."

After running through the list of other possible candidates in her head, Reightman was convinced there weren't any other choices. This would be an opportunity for Mitchell to prove himself, and might just clench a permanent promotion for him. "Ok then, Mitchell. If you're sure."

"I'm sure, ma'am."

"Can anyone think of anything else we need to cover this evening?" When no one raised their hand, Reightman decided to shut things down. "Why don't we call it a day? It's been a long and difficult one, and I didn't sleep at all last night after…after…." The sorrow inside rose up again, making it difficult for her to continue.

All the attendees understood what she was trying to say, and one by one, they silently filed out of the room until only Zhou Li, Toby, and Mitchell remained.

"Detective? I have something for you." Toby opened his satchel and pulled out a small object which had been carefully wrapped in paper. "It's Detective Jackson notebook – the one he had with him last night. I found it after you left."

Reightman took it from his hand, trying not to choke up again. "Thank you, Toby."

"I don't know if it has anything important in it, but I knew you'd want it anyway."

"Yes, I do. It's important to me, regardless of what's inside." She placed the wrapped notebook on her yellow legal pad and then turned back to him. "Did you find it after you slapped me?"

"Yes." He looked away from her, embarrassed by what he'd done.

"You did the right thing, Toby," she assured him. "No telling what I would've done without you and Mitchell there to keep me under control." She included both Mitchell and Toby as she said, "Thank you."

"Detective Reightman," Zhou Li interrupted gently, so as to not shatter the moment. "I rode with Toby this morning. I was wondering if Officer Mitchell could escort him outside, so he can bring his car around and pick me up near the entrance. Toby, if you could also take this stack of materials it would be a big help. I really am very tired."

"Sure, that's not a problem, Madame Zhou," Mitchell agreed. Reightman was pleased to see he'd adopted Zhou Li's preferred form of address. Good thing he was a quick study. She didn't think she could handle another lesson in manners from the old lady today.

"Thank you, Officer," Zhou said appreciatively. She waited until the two young men had gathered up the files and documents and left the room. She then turned to Reightman. "Detective Reightman, I have been unable to express my heartfelt condolences to you until now, and for that, I apologize. Detective Jackson was a wonderful man."

Reightman could feel tears threatening and blinked her eyes to try to prevent them from falling. She was too late. "Yes, he was, Madame Zhou."

"Focus on the wonderful things you remember about him, as well as the things which exasperated you at times. It will be painful, but it helps with the healing. I know from my own experiences." Zhou watched the Detective thoughtfully until Reightman had herself in control once more. "Detective, if there is anything I can do in the days ahead, please let me know. I am happy to help anyway I can."

Reightman nodded as she wiped away her tears with the back of her hand. "There…there is one thing you can help me with, Madame Zhou."

"What is that, Detective?"

"Well...could you help me buy....I mean...I need a dress, for Sam's funeral. Can you help me find one?"

Zhou was silent as she remembered the Detective's reaction when Moon had suggested she buy herself a dress. That day she'd told Moon that either she or Detective Jackson would have to be dead and buried before she'd be caught in a dress. It had proved to be a prophetic statement and was almost too much to bear thinking about now. "It would be my honor, Detective," she replied, her own voice tight with emotion. "I will alert Moon and will give you a call in a day or two to arrange a time to assist. We will both be delighted to help."

"Thank you."

"Certainly, that is what friends are for," Zhou replied as she gathered her few remaining things

"We're...we're friends?" Melba asked slowly, surprised by Zhou Li's use of the word.

Zhou tilted her head and peered through her glasses. "I can tell you must be very tired, dear. Otherwise you would already know the answer to that question." She reached out and gently patted Reightman's arm. "Since I am very tired myself, I will answer – just this once. Yes, Detective Melba Reightman, we are friends." Zhou gave her a very wise smile and started toward the door.

Melba watched her go, and knew just how lucky she'd been today. If Zhou Li hadn't been by her side, things may have turned out very differently. She picked up her heavy purse and gathered her things. Her knee was hurting, and she was looking forward to getting off her feet. *"What a day, Reightman,"* she thought as she hobbled to the exit. Grateful it was over; she turned off the lights, and gently closed the door.

CHAPTER THREE

After Toby and Mitchell dropped Madame Zhou off in front of Green Dragon and carried in the files she'd brought with her, Toby thought about what he needed to do next before going up to his apartment.

"Officer Mitchell, do you mind if we swing by the supermarket? I need to pick up a few things. I didn't think about having someone else around and I think the fridge and pantry are pretty bare."

"That's not a problem, Mr. Bailey. I can pick up a few things too. You shouldn't have to worry about feeding me while I'm around – I eat a lot!"

Toby gave a small grin at the Mitchell's admission. "Oh, I think I can probably manage to feed us both. I make a great tuna casserole. It shouldn't take too long to get what we need and then we can come back here. I live right upstairs in that building." He pointed out his apartment and realized there might be a problem. "The only thing is, I live on the third floor and there isn't an elevator."

"That's fine, Mr. Bailey," Mitchell assured him. "I don't mind taking the stairs. Hey, do you mind if we stop by my place so I can pick up some things?"

"No. I figured we'd need to do that sometime this evening. In fact, why don't we stop there first? You'll need to tell me how to get there."

Mitchell gave Toby the directions and ten minutes later Toby pulled up in front of a small duplex.

"This looks pretty nice, Officer Mitchell. I didn't even realize this neighborhood was here. Have you lived here long?"

"Thanks. I've been here about three years. Mr. Bailey."

Toby decided all this formality was ridiculous. After all, this guy was going to be living with him for the foreseeable future and was certain to see him at his worst. "Officer Mitchell, since you're going to be all up in my business over the next several days, I think you can stop with the 'Mr. Bailey' routine. Call me, Toby, please."

Mitchell hesitated, and then gave a reluctant shake of his head. "I think Detective Reightman would have my head if I did that, sir."

"What she doesn't know won't hurt her – and do not, for any reason, keep calling me 'sir'! It makes me feel old and feeble and I bet we're close to the same age. In fact, you might even be a couple of years older."

Mitchell decided Toby might have a point, but fair was fair. "Okay. But if I call you Toby, then you have to call me Anthony or, if you'd prefer, Mitchell. As long as were alone, that is. I really don't want Detective Reightman on my ass."

"It's a deal. Do you prefer Anthony, or Mitchell?" Toby asked as the young cop unlocked the front door.

"Mitchell is fine. I never really cared for the name Anthony, and I *hate* the nickname Tony." Mitchell made a sour face. "My middle name is even worse." He opened the door and ushered Toby inside.

Toby took a quick look around, and was surprised to see the place looked comfortable and well put together. A leather sectional was accented with several bright throw pillows and there were a few nicely framed prints on the walls. It was not at all what he'd expected a cop's home to look like. "This place is great, Mitchell! And just so you know, I don't think Anthony's a bad name at all. I kind of like it, but somehow, Mitchell suits you better. What's your horrible middle name?"

Mitchell looked over his shoulder as they crossed through the small living room. "If I tell you, you have to swear not to tell anyone else."

"Come on, Mitchell, it can't be that bad."

Mitchell didn't answer, but turned back to him, waiting. Realizing what he was waiting for, Toby earnestly agreed. "Okay, I swear never to tell a soul. Cross my heart and hope to die."

Mitchell turned back around and mumbled on his way into the bedroom, "It's Horatio."

"Oh, man! I'm sorry. You're right – that's an awful name.

"Remember, you promised never to tell a soul!" Mitchell hollered back.

Toby poked around the living room, checking out the sound system and the books on the shelves. He could hear Mitchell rummaging around in back of the house, but decided he'd better stay in the living room. A few minutes later, Mitchell came out of the bedroom carrying a small duffle bag and a few hanging clothes. Toby stepped forward to take the bag, and then they were out the door and Mitchell was locking up.

The next stop was the grocery store, and Toby filled up a shopping basket. Mitchell tossed a few things in the basket, some of which made Toby cringe.

"Moon pies? How can you stand to eat those things?"

"I like 'em! I got used to eating them in the dorm so I guess now they're comfort food."

Soon, they'd finished checking out and were back at the apartment. Toby made his famous tuna casserole, which Mitchell eyed suspiciously. "This is tuna casserole?"

"Yeah. Why? Don't you like it?"

"Well, it sure isn't what I expected." Mitchell took a few more bites, and decided it wasn't terrible, just very filling. "Good thing I'm going to be going up and down those stairs though. This stuff really sticks to the ribs."

They ate dinner and sat out on the terrace for a while, talking about inconsequential things. Mitchell had a kind of bouncy energy, but in spite of that, was actually very good company. He reminded Toby of some kind of friendly dog – maybe a golden retriever – with his sandy golden hair, big brown eyes, and solid build.

After a couple of hours, Toby found himself yawning. "I'm beat," he eventually said, standing and stretching. "You have to be pretty tired too."

"Yeah, I am. Today was really intense, and I was worried about how things were going there for a while. Man! That Madame Zhou is something else! I wouldn't want her gunning for me. She shredded those guys today."

"Yeah, she *is* pretty intense sometimes, but she's really very nice. I've gotten to know her over the last couple of weeks. I knew her a little before, and she's done some legal work for me, but we never talked much. Over the last few weeks I've learned more about her and I really like her. She sure doesn't put up with any bull." He stretched again and headed inside. When he got to the French doors he stopped and looked back at Mitchell. "Are you coming in, or are you going to stay out here for a while?"

"I'm coming in. I'm your bodyguard, and where you go, I go too. At least, that's how I think it works. I've never been a bodyguard before."

"I've never been body-guarded before, so I guess we're even. Just stay out of the bathroom when I'm in there!"

Toby brushed his teeth and changed into a pair of sleeping shorts. He'd just crawled under the sheets with the pillows propped behind his back when there was a knock on the bedroom door. "Toby?" Mitchell asked from just outside.

Toby got out of bed and opened the door. "Yeah?"

Mitchell brushed past him and stepped into the room, inspecting it thoroughly. He even checked the windows to make sure that they were securely locked and that there was no access from outside. He turned toward the big bed and nodded. "That'll do," he informed Toby.

Mitchell took off his shoulder holster and removed the gun, checking the safety. He placed it on the nightstand closest to the door and took off his shirt, which he folded and draped over the back of the chair placed near the bed. He sat down and started taking off his shoes and then his socks.

When he stood and unbuckled his belt, Toby snapped out of his daze. "Whoa there! What're you doing?"

"Getting ready for bed," Mitchell told him, very matter-of-factly. He stepped out of his pants and started folding them.

"What do you mean?" Toby asked, trying his best not to notice Mitchell's well-built frame and the faint dusting of golden hair which covered his powerful legs and chest. "There's a perfectly good bed in the guest room. I know it's just a full size, but it should be comfortable."

"Not gonna' happen," Mitchell informed him as he tossed his folded pants on the chair. He turned back to Toby, who realized the cop was now wearing only a snug-fitting pair of light blue boxer trunks – which left very little to the imagination. "If someone managed to get into the apartment without me knowing it, they could conceivably make it into this room. If you needed help, I wouldn't be able to make it here in less than a minute or two and a lot can happen in that time. Besides, I told you – where you go – I go."

Toby took a deep breath, and forced himself to maintain eye contact, even though he was tempted to let his eyes roam to more interesting places. "Mitchell, I appreciate the thought and everything, but couldn't we just stack cans in the hallway or something? That way, if someone got in, they'd make a lot of noise getting back here and give us plenty of warning."

Mitchell considered the suggestion, but shook his head. "I don't think you have enough cans to make a difference. But that was good thinking and it gives me another idea." He shut the door and then pulled the chair over to it, and tilted it back slightly so the back leaned just under the door knob. Mitchell tested his arrangement by trying to open the door a few times, and then stepped away satisfied. "That won't hold for long if someone really wants in, but it'll give me some extra time. It is never a bad thing to have extra time in a situation like this. Remember that." Mitchell walked back to the bed and started pulling back the covers. "You going to use all those pillows?" he asked as he eyed the stack on the opposite side of the king sized bed.

Toby struggled to keep his mind on other things while the nearly naked man moved a few pillows, causing the muscles of his torso to flex and shift. He forced his eyes back up to the cops face. "Mitchell, aren't you worried about sleeping in here? I mean, you know I'm ...gay."

Mitchell stopped what he was doing and looked up. He gave Toby's body – clad only in a mid-thigh pair of sleep shorts – a slow, deliberate once over, letting his eyes linger for a few seconds. "You're good looking and all and you have a very nice body. I really like the happy trail, but frankly, you're not my type." Mitchell went back to pulling back the covers and then reached for a pillow. In mid-reach he caught Toby eyeing him and gave him a bad-boy grin. "I like 'em ten years older than you, twenty pounds heavier, nice and furry, and I prefer my men to have a beard. If there's a little silver in the beard and in the hair, that's even better."

Toby was speechless. He tried to get something to come out of his mouth but couldn't. After a couple of tries he finally managed to stutter, "You're….you're….?"

"Yep, I'm a card carrying, cock loving homosexual," Mitchell informed him agreeably as he climbed into the bed. He checked his reach toward the gun and moved it a little closer. "And before you ask, no, I'm not seeing anyone, but I do have my eye on a nice silver daddy. He thinks I'm too young for him, but I'm working on changing his mind. As far as the mechanics go, I'm versatile. Sometimes I pitch and sometimes I catch – depending on the guy I'm with. Beyond that, I haven't experimented much, but I do keep an open mind." He reached over and turned off the light on his side. "I think that should cover things – being this is our first night sleeping together and all. I think it's best to keep some mystery in our relationship. If you have any more questions, I'll probably answer them tomorrow – if I don't have to shoot anyone tonight. So, climb into bed and get some sleep." Mitchell lay down on the bed and pulled the sheet up to his chest

Toby closed his mouth, which had fallen wide open during Mitchell's pretty exhaustive commentary. He walked over to his side of the bed and got in, wondering how he was every going to get to sleep now. He turned off the light and rolled over on his side with his back facing Mitchell. In the darkness, he heard the man a few feet away shift slightly in the bed

"Hey, Toby? You have an awfully nice ass, too – in addition to the happy trail. Good night."

"Good night," Toby responded, shell-shocked by the compliment. He tried to find a more comfortable position, trying not to disturb the man next to him. He listened to Mitchell breathe in and out, and soon his eyes grew heavy and he dropped gently down into slumber.

Sometime during the night, he woke, startled and afraid. Before he was even fully aware, Mitchell pulled him close to his body and whispered softly, "Go back to sleep, Toby. It was just a nightmare."

"Sorry," Toby mumbled, before he fell back to sleep.

Mitchell smiled in the darkness and pulled him closer, before his own eyes dropped shut again.

John Brown walked across the roofs of the Capital Street businesses, careful not to make a noise. He had climbed up one of the buildings in the back, using the remnants of an old attached service ladder that had never been removed. *"That's not very safe,"* he observed. *"All kinds of criminals could use that ladder to get up here, and you can walk across the roof to any of these businesses."*

He stood on the roof of Passed Around, well back from the edge. He watched the patrol cops parked below. Occasionally one would exit the car and walk up and down the block, leaving their partner behind. They concentrated mainly on the building across the street, paying special attention to the stairwell providing access to the apartment above the vacant shop space.

John Brown looked across the street to the apartment he thought belonged to the young man he'd been hired to kill the night before. About an hour ago, John Brown had seen a light go off in the building on the third floor. *"Probably his bedroom,"* he decided. Unfortunately, there wasn't a good way to get into the apartment as long as the patrols were outside. Maybe he'd have a chance if they got sloppy or lazy, or if he could create a diversion to redirect their attention. *"That's a possibility,"* he decided. *"If I get the word to take care of the kid after all, I'll have to give that idea some more thought."*

He crossed the roof quietly, making his way back the way he came. John Brown climbed down the old ladder. Once he was back on the ground, he gave it a frown. *"Someone needs to take care of that. It'd be a shame for something bad to happen one night because of that ladder."*

The next three days flew by. Reightman's team was out on the street checking for any whisper of news, hoping for tiniest hint which might lead them to the shooter. So far, nothing worthwhile had been discovered. Jones hit on a promising lead and had spent the last couple of days running it down – but it had turned out to be a false trail.

Tom's team finished their work on Helliman's truck, but ran into an unexpected problem. "There are about a hundred different finger prints on that damned truck, Detective," he told her, frustration evident in his voice. "About half of them belong to members of the force."

"Isn't that odd, Tom?"

"No, not really. It would be if Helliman hadn't been a cop, but I always saw a whole passel of guys hanging around that pick-up when it was parked in the lot. I'm sure pretty much everybody in this precinct has had their grubby fingers all over it."

"So, nothing unusual has turned up," Reightman disappointedly cut to the chase.

"There is one thing, but I'm sure it's to be expected. The whole passenger side was wiped down with some kind of cleaning solution. Whoever did it cleaned things up pretty good. There were only a couple of prints found around the top of the door frame and on the edge of the windshield, but they could have been there forever. When we ran them, they all turned out to belong to members of the force." Tom flipped over a couple of pages in his notes, reviewing what had been found. "We found a few dyed black cotton fibers. The thread strands are twisted, so whatever it came off of was stretchy. The significant thing is they were only found on the passenger side. We're trying to run down a few samples so we can test for similarities. I'll let you know if we make progress."

"Has your financial wiz made any giant leaps forward?" Reightman asked hopefully

"Some – but I wouldn't call her progress anything close to a giant leap. She's created a small database linking all the transactions with the photos for easy referencing and review, which should prove helpful as we go along. She's working on what few financial records we've been able to get our hands on, but that's proving to be hard going since we have limited means of accessing them – legally. We might have more luck if we pulled in the Feds, although that would open a can of worms we're not prepared to handle. They have more resources they can pull from to get the sorts of information we need, but we'd probably have to give up control of the investigation if something caught their interest."

Reightman wasn't thrilled with that idea, but knew the Feds could access information off limits to the regular police. "We may have to do it, Tom. If we don't make some progress soon, we'll have to get help from somewhere."

"You're right," he agreed grudgingly. "Just hold off for as long as you can. Something will pop." He fiddled with some things on his desk for a minute, while trying to frame his thoughts. "I went back over all of the stuff we collected from the Lieberman scene. Given what I know now, your crazy theory about a hustling hitman might not be so far-fetched. If I consider the people we know were involved with Guzman, there's plenty of resource to make something like that happen. I've also reviewed the Coroner's notes again, and found something interesting. The amount of booze in his stomach doesn't fit with the alcohol levels in his blood. It's nothing too obvious, but it feels off to me. You might want to touch base with her again, and see if she has any ideas."

"I don't think Dr. Evans is too happy with me right now."

"Patricia Evans isn't one to hold a grudge, Reightman. I spoke with her yesterday when I went to get a copy of her notes. She's not entirely comfortable with what's happened around here, and she's appalled at the things Lieberman did to Guzman's body. I know you were upset about her ruling, but give her a break. I think she's just trying to keep things going down there and to catch up on work left over from years of bad management."

Reightman knew he had a point, and decided a chat with the Coroner might be worthwhile. "Speaking of Doctor Evans, did she mention any unusual findings from Helliman's autopsy?"

"No, nothing out of the ordinary." He hesitated a moment, before getting to the next thing he had to tell her. "Ballistic testing did confirm the bullet which killed Helliman came from the same gun that killed Jackson."

Reightman's chest tightened a bit, but she focused of what Tom had said. She realized that any mention of Jackson still hurt, and probably would for a while. "So, we know the same person fired the gun which killed both of them."

"No, not exactly. Technically, we know the same *gun* was used to kill both of them," he said gently, realizing she was trying to get past Jackson's death and do her job. "I think we can work on the assumption the same person pulled the trigger in both instances, but we should remember that assumption might have to change.

Reightman left him feeling that at least work was getting done, even if there weren't many answers yet. *"If we do the work, we will find the answers,"* she assured herself, and moved to the next items on her list.

Thursday afternoon a call came in from the switchboard and was routed to Jackson's desk. Detective Jones was spending a lot of time there these days and he answered the call. She forced down a surge of resentment when he picked up the receiver, but she fought it down, knowing it was unreasonable to feel that way just because the some-one who answered Sam's phone wasn't Sam. She did, however, stop what she was doing to listen to Jones' side of the conversation.

"I'm sorry, but Detective Jackson isn't available," Jones told the caller, glancing apologetically toward Reightman. "I'm Detective Jones, and I'm helping out for the time being." Reightman felt tension build inside her when she heard Jones refer to Sam, but it eased when she heard the next words.

"She did?....You're sure it's the same person, Mr. Gold-bleum?....Yeah, I got it....I'll try and drop by later this after-noon....Yes, sir, thank you for calling." He hung up the phone and wrote a couple of notes down on a scratch pad before looking up into her expectant face.

"Sorry – I had to write down a thought before I lost it," Jones apologized. "As you probably heard, that was Mr. Goldbleum from the pawn shop where the knife that killed Guzman was found. He said the same person who bought the knife came in today, except this time, they were selling, not buying."

"She," Reightman said.

Jones looked puzzled until he understood what she meant. "Yes – sorry. He said the woman who bought the knife was selling today. *She* brought in some expensive jewelry. It was too rich for his blood and sent her on her way. About an hour after she left, he remembered he was supposed to call us."

"Is there video footage of the woman?"

"He's not sure. I'll head down there later this afternoon and see what I can find out. If there isn't video, I'll try and coax a workable description out of him. If it sounds legit, we can get one of the staff artists to work up a drawing of some sort."

"I guess it's the best we can do." Reightman found herself running the photos Toby had provided – via Geri Guzman – through her mind. "Maybe she'll be a match to one of them," she mused, not realizing she'd spoken out loud.

"What?" Jones asked

"Nothing," she said. "Just thinking out loud."

"I hear that's common with you old folks," Jones joked as he stood up from the chair. "I'm going to go get a cup of coffee from a *real* coffee shop on my way downtown. Would the offer to buy you a cup entice you to come with me to visit Goldbleum?"

"We old folks have to watch our caffeine intake, Jones. So, as appealing as your offer is, I can't. I have another errand to run in another hour or so anyway."

"Okay. I guess I'll just have to pay full price then, since you won't be with me to get the senior's discount."

"Jones?" she said

"Yeah?" he answered

She almost said 'shut up', but changed her words at the last minute when she realized those were part of the shtick she'd shared with Jackson. "See you later," she said instead.

After Jones left, she sat back in her chair and looked over the small partition separating the two desks. "*It's time,*" she decided. "*Jones shouldn't have to keep working around Sam's things.*" She went down to the copy center and grabbed a couple of cardboard paper boxes. She carried two boxes back to the desk and spent the next forty-five minutes packing up all of Sam's belonging. She made herself pack methodically, and focused on the packing itself, instead of who the items had belonged to. Upon opening one drawer, she found a stack of the small notebooks Jackson had always used. She pulled them out and put them in her own desk. She might never use them, but she'd have them as a memento of sorts.

When she finished packing up everything, she went to the breakroom and pulled out a bottle of cleaning solution. Bringing it back to the desk, she cleaned every surface and wiped down the computer and the phone. She threw the paper towels in the trash and stacked the boxes, and then picked up the phone and dialed Nancy.

"Hey, Melba," Nancy answered.

"Hey," Reightman responded. "Can you have someone come by and pick up the boxes by Jackson's desk? I've packed up everything, and it might be nice to get them to Alice."

Nancy was quiet for a second or two. "Sure, I'll send someone over in a few minutes. Will you be there?"

"No, I'll be away for the rest of the afternoon."

"Okay, no problem." Reightman could hear Nancy smack her gum before she continued. "If they're all stacked up, I'm sure they'll know which ones to take."

"They're pretty much the only packed boxes around here. One more thing – can you order Detective Jones a nameplate for the desk? If he's going to be hanging out around here, people might as well know where to deliver his mail. "

"Yeah. If I get it ordered today, it'll probably be here soon. The supplier's pretty fast."

After Nancy hung up, Reightman sat in her chair, looking at the boxes for a good long while. She finally stood up and pulled her purse out of her drawer. Just as she was shouldering the bag, a young man came around the corner wheeling a dolly

"Are these the boxes to be picked up, ma'am?"

She looked at the name tag on his shirt. "Yes, Jimmy, these are them." He started to load the boxes, but she stopped him. "I know this is going to sound weird, but….could you wait until I'm gone before you load them up and take them away?"

"You leaving soon?"

"I'm leaving right now."

"Then waiting's no problem at all, ma'am."

She quickly walked away so she wouldn't have to see the boxes leave. *"Come on, Melba, it's time to go buy a dress."*

CHAPTER FOUR

CHRISTINA DAMERON PULLED into the parking space a few yards down from Le Bistro Rouge, a trendy lunch spot few miles from the downtown business district. She checked her watch, hoping that she wasn't too late. Marilyn Shaw absolutely hated to be kept waiting. She hurried through the brass trimmed double doors and scanned the interior until she spotted Marilyn seated at a small table near the back. She threaded her way through the space, occasionally exchanging brief smiles of recognition with the other lunch patrons.

"Marilyn, I'm sorry if I'm late," Christina apologized as she took a seat across from Marilyn at the cozy table for two.

"You're not late. I just got here a few minutes ago, myself. Traffic coming in from the lake was terrible."

The waiter handed them each a menu. "Good afternoon, ladies. My name is Jules and I'll be serving you today. Can I bring you something to drink before you order?" He placed a glass of ice water down in front of each of them.

"I'll have glass of the house white," Marilyn looked up at him and smiled invitingly, noting his continental good looks and the tight shirt stretched across his chest.

"I'll have the same," Christina decided, after weighing the chance of being seen by an ultra-conservative constituent while drinking during lunch, and the almost immediate benefits of having a drink. Alcohol won. Jules smiled and informed them he'd be back soon.

"Do you know what you are getting?" Christina asked as she looked over the menu.

"I know what I'd like for an appetizer," Marilyn purred. "I could just about make a whole meal out of Jules."

"I don't think he's listed under either the appetizer or the entrée section of our menu." Christina placed her menu down on the table, having decided on the watercress and endive salad served with roasted beets and goat cheese. Remembering the Shaw's liked their quips to be appreciated, she added with a touch of playfulness, "I must admit though, I did see something which resembled Jules listed under dessert."

Marilyn laughed coyly while skimming one perfectly manicured nail down the menu. "Yes, the French pastry horn served with crème sounds delicious."

Jules returned a brief moment later with their wine. "Are you ready to order?"

After each of the women communicated their choices and sampled their wine, Marilyn folded her hands on the table. "How have things been going, Christina?"

Christina inwardly groaned at Marilyn's opening gambit, but managed a small smile. "To tell you the truth, things haven't been going as well as I'd hoped. Ever since Sutton's disastrous rally in the park over the Labor Day weekend, everything has seemed a bit off kilter. I've been working diligently to get the campaign back on track and I think I'm making some progress, but there's just so much I can do."

"Ephraim did mention Sutton's speech wasn't as well received as we all hoped. He said something about there being a lot of undesirables who kept pulling Sutton off track and caused quite a ruckus."

"Yes, they certainly contributed to the situation, but I'm not sure it was the only factor."

"What else could it have possibly been?" Marilyn asked.

"Well, sometimes I feel Sutton's messages don't appeal to a broad enough demographic. He seems to focus too heavily on..." Christina trailed off as she tried to find the right words.

"Deviant sinners, who threaten our morally and righteously earned lifestyles?" Marilyn suggested with one slighted arched eyebrow.

"Maybe. I just wish he'd ease up on the message a bit, and work to make himself more likeable to a broader range of people." Marilyn responded with a somewhat stony look, so Christina quickly added,

"Of course, I totally support the conservative line on which we have built our platform, and thoroughly approve of the work we're doing to clean up our society and to promote wholesome, Biblical based values."

Marilyn studied her intently and then lifted her wine glass and took a swallow. "Of course you do, Christina. No one has ever doubted your dedication, or the level of support you've given your husband." She ran a finger around the rim of the glass. "What do you think his chances are? With the election, I mean."

"They're fairly good." Christina answered, trying to inject some confidence into her voice. "We have a very loyal base and thankfully, a single serious contender hasn't emerged. The two liberal candidates are splitting the voters, which gives us an advantage."

"That's encouraging," Marilyn said approvingly. "How is the fundraising going?"

Christina was spared the immediate need to answer by the appearance of their waiter. As Jules placed her food down and then turned to do the same for Marilyn, Christina tried to figure out how best to answer the question. The problem was, contributions had dropped off significantly over the past week, especially after Sutton's Labor Day rally, and they were feeling the strain. There'd been a lot of unplanned expense and they were almost broke. She hoped Marilyn had no idea how deeply the Dameron family had reached into the campaign pot to tide themselves over during the past month.

"Doesn't that look wonderful?" Marilyn complimented as Jules leaned in to refill her water glass. Christina couldn't tell if the other woman was referring to her food, or her waiter.

"I hope you ladies enjoy your lunch," Jules said as he backed away from the table.

Marilyn followed him with her eyes, and then sampled her serving of chilled soup and looked across the table. "I think we were talking about the current state of the fundraising efforts?"

"Thanks for reminding me. To answer the question, I'd say our fundraising is going about as well as can be expected," Christina speared a beet from her salad, thinking the color matched both Marilyn's lipstick and the large cabochon rubies in her ears. "Money's tight for everyone, and we're appreciative of every dollar we receive. Expenses are high though, and I expect they'll climb even higher as we get closer to November. I'm just worried I won't be able to stretch the pool as far as I'll need to." Christina considered the woman across the table as Marilyn lifted a spoonful of the lime green soup to her red mouth. "I don't suppose….?" she ventured.

Marilyn finished her spoonful and blotted her mouth with a napkin. "I'm afraid not, Christina. Ephraim has already donated quite generously to Sutton's campaign, and I'm afraid my own circumstance are somewhat strained at present. I've had a number of unexpected things come up." She filled her spoon again before adding. "Perhaps I can manage a little something in a few weeks after I've covered everything for which I'm already obligated."

"Of course, Marilyn," Christina replied quickly. "I know how much monetary support you've both already given us, and both Sutton and I are extremely grateful. I didn't mean to impose further."

Marilyn lifted one of the crostini which had been served to accompany the soup, and bit into it with strong white teeth. Small crumps fell from her mouth onto the table cloth. "You didn't impose Christina, and I'm aware of how grateful you are. I'd help if I could, but it's not possible at present." Marilyn wiped her mouth again and picked up her wine glass. "I'm sure you'll manage to handle everything without my help. You're like me. You always find a way to get things done and you don't let anything stand in your way."

"Thank you for your confidence in me, Marilyn," Christina replied and then redirected the conversation to other things.

"Did you ladies leave room for one of our special desserts," Jules asked after he cleared their luncheon plates. "I think you might enjoy the French pastry horn, with cream."

Marilyn considered his suggestion with sultry eyes, but ultimately declined. "It sounds delightful, Jules, but I'm trying to watch my intake. Once I have the first taste, I can't seem to stop myself from devouring every last bite."

Christina declined as well, and soon Jules returned with their tab. As he placed the small leatherette folder on the table, Marilyn looked at her pointedly. After a moment spent trying to interpret the other woman's expression, she caught on. "It's my turn to treat, I think." She picked up the check and reviewed it. "*How can one lunch for two cost so damned much?*" she asked herself as she pulled out her wallet and removed a credit card, hoping the charge would go through.

"Are you headed off to take care of campaign business?" Marilyn asked she touched up her lipstick.

"No, not right away. I have a rather pressing errand I need to run. What about you? What do you have planned for the afternoon?"

"I have an important stop to make as well, and then I'll head back out to the lake to make sure Emeline has dinner under control." Marilyn sighed heavily. "I know it sounds clichéd, but it really is difficult to get good help. It seems they always make the most stupid mistakes, and they cost an absolute fortune. Even something that's supposed to be a simple job costs an arm and a leg."

"Are you expecting a large group tonight?" Christina asked as she slipped on a pair of sunglasses.

"No, just a little mother and son get together. Ephraim has a dinner meeting this evening, so I thought I'd take the opportunity to catch up with my boy, and talk over a few things he might be able to help me with. It's a sin how little we see each other."

"Does he live far from here?"

"No, he lives here in the city. Now that I think of it, you probably met him at the fundraiser we hosted a few months ago. We don't see each other as much as we should." Marilyn shrugged as she got up from the table. "But, I guess that's to be expected. He's all grown up now, with his own interests and obligations."

After saying their goodbyes, Christina watched as Marilyn stepped into her luxury sedan and found herself wondering how much the car had cost Reverend Shaw's congregation. Obviously, she and Marilyn had very different definitions of a strained circumstance.

As she walked back to her own car, she reflected on past times when she'd never had to worry about a damned thing.

As the youngest child and only daughter of the senior branch of the Martelli clan, the world had been hers for the taking. Spoiled and petted by her adoring papa and three brothers, Christina Martelli had only to point her finger at something and it was hers. As she'd grown older and had become more actively involved in her family activities, they had pinned their hopes on her – certain that she would be the one to bring them back to the heights of their former glory as a premier flying act in the competitive world of circus performers.

Christina had learned all there was to know about the family business and showed incredible promise. She wanted more, but didn't know what she was looking for. Whatever it was, it wouldn't be found in Sarasota, Florida. Of that, she was sure.

After a series of loud and angry arguments, her father had finally thrown his hands up in disgust and agreed that she could attend college out of state, as long as she promised to keep herself in shape and return to the family fold after she obtained her degree. She'd assured him that she would and had packed her bags and headed off to discover the world.

In her junior year, she met Sutton Dameron and her world had changed. He was totally different from the men she'd grown up with and she was enthralled by his collegiate good looks, pale skin and the auburn hair that he wore a little longer than others on campus. Although his looks were a decided contrast to her family's swarthy skin and dark hair, it was his outlook on life that spoke to her most strongly.

Sutton wanted to change the world. His own family was noted for supporting various liberal causes and he argued passionately with their circle of friends about the need for affordable healthcare and programs to benefit the poor. He was a champion for the disadvantaged in those early days and she aligned her thinking with his own until she convinced herself that his causes had always been hers.

They dated seriously for a number of months until March of that year, when Sutton asked her to marry him. After joyfully accepting, she phoned home and broke the news to her family. The discussion had not gone well.

"What do you mean, you're getting married?" her mother asked.

Christina explained how she'd met Sutton and enthusiastically pointed out all of his excellent qualities. Her mother listened patiently until Christina reached the end of her situation, and then cut to the chase.

"Your father is not going to be happy about this, Christina. After all, you did promise you'd come back her after college and help rebuild the act."

"But mama, that's not what I want anymore. I know that papa's going to be disappointed, but that's not the kind of life I see for myself."

"What's wrong with our life?" Antonia Martelli asked with a sharp edge to her voice.

"Nothing's wrong with it, mama! It's just that I can't see myself as a circus performer."

"And what do you see yourself as, young lady? A stay at home mother?"

"No! But would that be so awful if it was what I wanted?"

Antonia sighed into the phone. "No. If that was what you really wanted it wouldn't be so bad, Christina. But I had such hopes for you. We all did. I wonder if this isn't just a passing fancy."

When Christina assured her that it wasn't, her mother sighed again.

"So be it, Christina. But you'll have to be the one to break the news to your father. I think it would be best for you to bring this man home this weekend and let us all have a look at him. If he passes muster with the family it will make things easier in the long run."

"You'll help me with papa?"

"I'll make you no promises until I've met this Sutton Dameron character. If he's everything you say, you won't need my help.

Christina hung up the phone feeling a little better, but knew the hard part was still ahead of her.

That weekend, she and Dameron drove down to Florida to visit her family. She carefully coached him on what to say and how to act and hoped for the best. It didn't take long for her to realize her family wasn't at all impressed with the man she'd chosen to spend the rest of her life with.

"He's weak!" he father shouted after dinner. Sutton had been taken out to see the sights by her two brothers, leaving her alone with her father and mother.

"He's not weak! I know he looks small compared to this family but he's not weak."

Her father shook his head in disgust and had turned away from her.

"Your papa doesn't mean weak in that way, Christina." Her mother spoke from her place on the sofa. "He means that his character is not strong."

"How can he tell that?" Christina retorted. "You only met him four hours ago!"

"Sometimes it doesn't take long to tell," her mother had responded gently. "He is not the kind of man we want for you. This one is not for you, Christina. You need someone who will be a true partner and won't change his position every time the wind blows."

Christina was confused by her mother's words. "What do you mean mama?"

"What I mean is this man refused to hold his own with any of the family when they challenged his position. Instead, he adjusted his words and demeanor to make a more favorable impression."

"But, he just wanted you all to like him."

"I know. But how can we even begin to like him if we have no idea of who he really is?"

They'd discussed and argued for another hour before her father finally put a stop to it all.

"Enough!" he told her forcefully. "I have listened to everything you have to say and it makes no difference to what I feel. You may not marry this man and throw away your future."

"I will marry him, papa."

"Not if you want the support of this family," he informed her matter-of-factly. "Not if you want to continue on with your education. Not if you want to be welcome here."

Christina was shocked by his pronouncement. "You'd force me out of the family over this?"

He was silent for a moment as he considered his next words. "Christina, I would do more than that to keep you from making what I know will be a terrible mistake."

She turned to her mother with an incredulous look in her eyes. "Mama?"

Antonia looked toward her husband and then back to her daughter. "I'm sorry, but in this I agree with your father. This man is not for you. It would hurt me terribly to lose my daughter, but that would eventually happen anyway if you marry this man. Choose carefully, Christina."

Christina could tell by her mother's tone and the set of her father's jaw that there was nothing to be gained by further discussion – at least for tonight. Thankfully, they hadn't demanded that she stop seeing Dameron. She decided she just needed more time for them to get to know her future husband and was certain she would eventually change their minds. After all, they'd never denied her anything before.

For the remainder of the weekend, Christina acted like the conversation had never occurred. Her family was cordial and pleasant. Not realizing that this was not normal Martelli behavior, Sutton never knew anything was wrong, and never suspected that their polite social engagement disguised their absolute loathing. People loved and accepted by the Martelli's knew they were in favor by their inclusion in the constant barrage of loud, boisterous arguments and the inevitable feuds that sprang up at a moment's notice. They were never treated the way they treated him. On the drive back, he even remarked that he thought he'd made a good impression. Unwilling to disappoint him, she'd simply agreed and set about making her plan.

For the next year she was a dutiful daughter and joined in on every family occasion. She took every opportunity to include Sutton, although she knew her parents disapproved. She even decided to spend the summer back in Florida helping out with the flying school. In her spare time she agreed to help fundraise for a local charity, hoping to make useful contacts for the future. She needed to learn the ropes in order to support Sutton's ambitions when the time came. Before leaving for school to start her senior year, she once again broached the topic of her marriage and was once again disappointed.

"I've already said all I have to say on the topic," her father informed her, as he checked the rigging in the practice arena of the school. "My opinion hasn't changed. If anything, I'm more certain than ever that he's not the man for you."

Christina was forced to accept the reality of the situation and after some serious soul searching and weighing the consequences, she made her own decision. She was as stubborn as her parents – it was a Martelli trait. That Christmas, against her family's objections, Christina became Mrs. Sutton Dameron. Her family resigned themselves to the loss of their daughter and her father even paid for the wedding so as not to lose face within the community.

However, the moment they were pronounced man and wife, her father cut off her funds as promised and she found she was not welcomed back home for any reason. Sutton was bewildered, but didn't say much. Christina had kept her family's real feelings from him for this long, and would continue on with the deception. Sometimes, Sutton just wasn't very bright, and she suspected he really didn't care anyway. As long as she was there to shield him from disagreeable things, Sutton was perfectly content.

It didn't take long for Christina to realize just how difficult it was to make ends meet without the generous check her father had provided. She took on a series of part-time jobs and somehow managed to make ends meet although circumstances were very strained. All those things she had taken for granted when her papa was footing the bill were now out of reach. She learned to take care of her own grooming needs and shopped sales and online bargain sites for her clothing. She cultivated a no-nonsense, streamlined style that eventually became her signature. It helped that her lithe, toned body – honed from the combination of a lifetime of exercise and her mother's good genes – was the perfect showcase for no-frills clothing.

The Dameron's first child was born a year later. Christina hoped that would soften her parent's resolve and to some extent, it did. She and the baby were allowed back home for the occasional visit –as long as Sutton didn't accompany them. Eighteen months later, a second child was born, but there was no change in her family's attitudes.

Things were a little better on the home front. Sutton secured a job with a local life insurance firm specializing in mutual funds and a steady income stream significantly eased some of the financial strain. A year later he decided to run for city council and to her surprise, won on a liberal platform. She ignored his frequent late evenings and occasional overnight business trips, rationalizing to herself that he was simply working to make contacts. She even adjusted her thinking again, aligning with the more conservative attitude Sutton had gradually adopted. He'd rationalized that there was more money to be had from conservative donors than from the inconsistent liberals. After a few passionate arguments, Christina laid her principles on the altar of greed and ambition and got with the program. She would be the perfect, supporting wife, and make certain that there was no crack in the façade she carefully constructed. Then one day while sorting his clothes for the dry cleaners, she stumbled upon something that changed her life.

She'd been in a hurry as she quickly checked the pockets of his dress slacks for anything that might ruin the clothing and had simply placed the small handful of items on the edge of the dresser. She turned to place the trousers on the rest of the pile, when her mind caught up with what she had found. *"Why are there condoms in his pockets?"* she wondered. When she finally discovered the answer, she decided her mother and father had been right after all. Sutton was weak.

But she'd married him and had hitched her star to his. For good or bad, Christina was determined to make things work no matter how hurt she was. She wouldn't allow anything to spoil the future she envisioned for herself. She and Sutton were destined for great things and she wasn't about to let anything get in her way. After a few months passed, she wondered why she'd even thought it was a big deal. It wasn't like he was seeing other women.

As she started her car and drove back home, Christina Dameron firmed her resolve. If anything or anyone tried to take away what she'd worked so hard for, they'd be sorry. For a moment her fingers toyed with the large solitaire pendant Sutton had given her a few years ago. Regretfully, it would have to go. It really didn't matter to her. It was just another sacrifice she was willing to make on the path to glory. And besides, the matching earrings were already lost.

Melba stood in front of the cheap full-length mirror tacked to the back of her bedroom door and looked at her reflection critically. It'd been at least a year since she'd worn a dress of any kind, and this dress was totally different from anything which had ever taken up space in her closet

The dress in question was made of black linen, and seemed to drink in all of the light in her bedroom. It sounded awful, but somehow, it wasn't. *"Maybe it's the thin black silk trim or maybe it's the cut,"* she considered. Whatever it was, the black dress was as far from awful as she could imagine, even though the occasion which warranted her purchase was a terrible one. As she balanced herself against the door to put on her sensible, low heeled black shoes, she thought about Moon's comments from the day before, when she'd modeled her final selection for Zhou Li and the shopkeeper.

"This dress captures perfectly the doleful and sorrow-filled state in which we approach the ritual of mourning, and yet, with the right accessories, it would be a perfectly elegant tribute to a sophisticated celebration of culture, possibility and the absoluteness of refined good taste."

Melba didn't know about all of that, but she did know she looked better than she'd looked in as long as she could remember.

Moon had urged her to purchase a hat to complete her ensemble, but Melba had demurred, knowing she was already pushing things as far as the reaction from her co-workers was concerned. She might live down a dress, since it was being worn as an expression of respect for the man who'd been her friend and partner for the past several years, but she'd never, ever recover from showing up anywhere – even Sam's funeral – in a hat.

"*At least the weather's not too hot today*," she consoled herself. An early season cold front had dropped down from the north, bringing evening rain showers and a breath of cooler air. It was almost bearable, even with the high humidity. Melba gave one last brush to her hair, checked her lipstick and picked up the smallish purse Moon had convinced her to buy.

"While possessing a weathered, functional usefulness – which is in fact a style acceptable for a busy career woman going about her normal daily business," Moon had declaimed, "for a funeral, your everyday purse simply will…not…do."

Melba transferred a few items into the small black bag, telling herself she could probably survive a few hours without her trusty sidekick of a purse. "*At least this one's lighter*." She picked up the sleeker accessory and loaded it with a handkerchief. She gave herself one more look in the mirror, straightening her shoulders as she did. "*Here we go, Reightman. Keep yourself together and get through it. If you do that, you'll have done great.*"

Sam Jackson's funeral was the city at its finest. From the honor guard of uniformed police officers on gleaming motorcycles which escorted his body to the church where generations of his family had worshiped, to the four members of the mounted equestrian officers who had stood vigil beside the hearse and accompanied the cortege as it made its slow progress to the city's oldest cemetery, the force turned out in its finest to honor one of their own.

The simple service in the church was more of a remembrance than a goodbye, and the pews filled with family, friends, co-workers and city dignitaries spoke to the love, affection and respect in which Sam had been held. On the steps of the church, the Mayor had presented the city's highest honor to Alice Jackson. The quiet, graceful lady who had been Sam's wife carried herself with calm, mournful dignity. Melba could see the telltale signs of grief etched on Alice Jackson's face, but she could also see the strength of will and the deep faith every spouse of a serving police officer found to sustain themselves as their loved ones went into danger to protect the city and its citizens.

Melba managed through the service better than she'd feared, but the burial itself was more difficult. It was there she realized her partner was gone for good. A chapter of her life closed as Sam Jackson's mortal remains were lowered into the earth. Alice Jackson stood by the grave until the coffin finished its descent, and then took a covered, box-shaped structure from her eldest son. When its draping cloth was removed, Melba realized it was a small wicker cage. Alice gently removed a single dove. After closing her eyes in silent prayer, Alice flung her hands toward the sky and watched as the dove winged its way upward with an eerie rustle of fluttering wings.

Melba followed the dove's progress with tear streaming eyes until she could no longer make out its form. "Goodbye, Sam," she whispered. "Put in a good word for me when you get there."

She drove herself home and took off her black dress and hung it carefully in her small closet, then removed her shoes and got dressed again in one of her usual outfits. She transferred the items from her black purse into her large, heavy bag. She added her badge and her weapon and went back to work to solve Geraldo Guzman's murder, and in the process, find the man who had gunned down Detective Sam Jackson

Detective Jones arrived back at headquarters thirty minutes after Reightman had seated herself at her desk with a mug of fragrant tea. He stood by the side of desk for a minute, taking in the clear surface that had held Jackson's odds and ends only the day before.

"I figured you'd appreciate not having to work around that stuff," Reightman said as soon as she realized he didn't know how to react.

"If you're going to be hanging here around bothering me every day, I guess you'd better have a desk you can call your own."

"I have my own desk, or at least one I can share," he said gruffly, trying to hide the fact he knew how hard clearing away Jackson's things had been for her. He knew, without a doubt, that it had been Reightman who'd boxed up the items. She would've never allowed anyone else to remove even a single pencil or pen until she herself decided it was time.

She shrugged at his comment and took a sip of tea. "Well, if you don't want to use it, someone else will. Eventually, I'll be assigned a new partner."

Jones sat down in the chair and ran his hands over the desk's clean, uncluttered surface. "Any idea who it'll be?"

"No, but I'm pretty sure Chief Kelly will take my recommendation into account before he makes the decision," she said. "I kind of thought I'd ask if you might know anyone who'd be interested in moving from another unit over to homicide – even if it does mean they'd have to put up with me."

She could see a spark of interest in his hazel eyes.

"Well, the last part's a really hard sale," he said, keeping his face free of expression. "I might know one guy, though. He's a pain in the ass himself, so it might be a good fit."

"I think I might know who you're talking about," Reightman said, mirroring his expression, "and he *is* a real pain in the ass. I hear he's a pretty good detective though, so I could probably put up with his crap – not much mind you – but I might be able to handle just a tiny bit." She looked over at him, sitting behind the desk which used to be Jackson's. "Seriously, would you be interested?"

"Well, I don't know. It's a big decision and I'd have to think about it. After all, the Homicide Unit is a big step up from working burglaries and white collar crimes." Jones paused for effect, and a split second later said, "I've thought about it, and my answer is yes, Reightman." When she gave him a tiny fractional smile to reward his class clown theatrics, he asked her seriously, "Would you really make a recommendation to Kelly?"

"Yes, but don't get your hopes up too high," she warned. "He might have someone else in mind. I'll raise it with him the first of next week though, now that I know you wouldn't consider it cruel and unusual punishment to be stuck with me."

"I know it wouldn't be a done deal until the Chief agreed and the paperwork went through, but I appreciate the vote of confidence." He gave her a look of gratitude and then looked back down at the desk. "You know what? I think I'll just head over to the supply closet and grab a few things I need if I'm expected to get any work done. I'll move the rest of my stuff over in the next few days – if you think it'd be alright."

Reightman shrugged. "You might as well have your own stuff over here where you can get to it. The worst thing that can happen is you'd have to move everything back."

"Good point. Can I bring you anything?"

"Nope, I think I'm all set for supplies."

Jones walked away and Reightman took another sip of her tea. Kelly would probably accept her recommendation and she thought Jones was a good choice. She'd liked his cocky attitude and he'd been a big help over the last several days – filling in wherever needed. She just hoped she wasn't just missing Jackson and making her recommendation too soon, but time would tell.

Jones returned a few minutes later with his arms laden down with enough office supplies to outfit the entire floor. He laughed at her expression. "They were having a two for one sale over in the supply closet and I thought I'd load up while the prices were good. Gotta' love a sale!"

He proceeded to organize things to his satisfaction and she looked over her list of outstanding items. "Hey, Jones, what did Goldbleum have to say? Was there any video?"

Jones rolled his eyes and let out an exasperated breath. "I have to tell you that Mr. Goldbleum is a real piece of work. First of all, there's no video. He has his system set to record over the existing tape every hour. He says it's cheaper and he's not made out of gold. Personally, I think the old man probably has the first nickel he ever made – from back in 1901."

"That's a disappointment. Was he able to provide any sort of description?"

"Yes, if you can call it that. Let me read it to you." Jones pulled a folded piece of paper from his front pocket. "He said the woman was average height, not heavy, and had hair of average length. When I asked him what color her hair was, he said he didn't remember and he never remembered things like that – unless it was some kind of weird color, like that those crazy kids are wearing now days. When I asked him about her eye color, he said he had no idea, just – wait for it – average." He looked up and saw her grimace at the useless description. "He was more helpful when I asked about the items she was trying to sell, but still wasn't able to be real specific. He said she had a load of pretty impressive jewelry – all kinds of stones and some nice pearls. He was particularly interested in one pendant she had with her. He said it was a really big rock, a diamond, from what I gather. He made her an offer, but she said she couldn't let it go for that. He gave her the names of a couple of other places to try, although he figures she'll be disappointed with their offers as well."

"Did he share the names of the places he recommended?"

"Yes, I have them and will swing by each of them later today. I'll also check out all the other pawn shops in town just on the off chance someone may have taken a couple of items off her hands. We might get lucky. We just might get lucky and stumble on to something."

"It's probably worth a shot. I just wish he'd been able to give you a better description of the woman – and the jewels." Reightman didn't bother to hide the disappointment she felt.

"Me too. I thought we were on to something. Instead, I get to spend several hours driving all over town asking pawnshop owners if an average woman came in trying to sell some nice pearls and a 'big rock.' Still, I think it's worth a shot."

Reightman sighed and pulled the purse from her drawer. "I need to drive down to Capital Street and check on Toby Bailey and Mitchell. It's been a few days since I've had more than a brief update, and I want to see how things are working out with our impromptu bodyguard program."

"Mitchell's been assigned to keep Bailey safe?" Jones asked. Reightman recognized a surprised note in his voice and wondered what it signified

"Actually, Mitchell volunteered and he seemed like the best – if not only – choice. He's been on the job since Tuesday evening." She was curious about the expression on his face. "You seem surprised and…something else. I can't read your expressions yet, so you might as well just tell me what you're thinking."

"Well, I think Mitchell is a fine cop, and deserves a chance to prove himself. I was glad to see the Chief decided to keep him on plain clothes detail. I've gotten to know him pretty well over the last couple of weeks and like what I've seen. But…oh never mind, it's probably nothing."

"Come on, Jones – out with it."

"Mitchell would be an ideal choice for this sort of duty in most cases. But….oh, what the hell….Mitchell's a homosexual."

"Mitchell's gay?" When Jones nodded affirmatively, Reightman thought over her reaction to the new information. "I'm a little surprised, I guess. I've never given much thought to what his preference in that area may or may not be. Truthfully, it doesn't matter to me how he lives his personal life as long as he does his job."

"I feel exactly the same way, Reightman. In this instance, however, Mr. Bailey is also gay. With them thrown together like this, I worry things might become a little too personal – if you catch my drift. Potentially dangerous situations can lead to all kinds of things which wouldn't happen otherwise."

"Sounds like you speak from experience, Jones."

"Not really." Reightman wondered if his response was a little too quick for it to be the whole truth. After a minute, he added, "I just wouldn't want to see the two of them get hurt, or to have some kind of physical attraction compromise Mitchell's role."

Reightman considered what he said and gave a weary sigh. "Thanks for telling me about this, Jones. I don't think Mitchell would step over the line, but I will have a cautioning word with him." She turned to leave and then stopped. "Jones, as a favor – keep Mitchell's orientation to yourself. A lot of people around here aren't as open minded as you and me and I'd really hate to see anyone give him a hard time about this."

"I wouldn't have even said anything to *you* if it wasn't something I thought you needed to be aware of. I've no desire to see anyone dish out a bunch of ignorant, prejudiced crap to the kid."

"Thanks, Jones, I appreciate it. I guess I should have asked, but do you want to come along?"

"Thanks for the offer. Any other time I would – even though I've been warned about your driving, I think it'd be best for me to try to track down the mystery woman with the boat load of jewels for sale."

"I'll have you know I 'm a perfectly good driver! Whoever told you otherwise is just trying to give me a bad rep."

He laughed at her mock glare. "See you later, Detective Reightman."

"See you later, Detective Jones." She left him sitting at the cleaned and restocked desk which was now his, and would stay his, if she had anything to say about it

Reightman thought she'd find Toby and Mitchell at the spa since Toby was working to get everything ready for the reopening tomorrow. She checked in with the uniformed detail before walking through the door to Time Out. As she'd anticipated, Toby was finishing up the paint in the backroom and Mitchell was stationed in the hallway near the door, leaning up against the wall. He straightened when he saw her headed his way.

"Good afternoon, ma'am," he greeted her with a smile on his face. "I thought maybe you'd forgotten all about us."

"Not a chance of that, Mitchell, although to be honest, I thought for sure I'd have made it down here to check on you before now. The last few days have been harder than I'd expected. I appreciate the reports you've been sending though, and you seem to have things pretty well under control."

"Thank you, Detective." Mitchell cleared his throat and added, "I was sorry I had to miss Detective Jackson's service, but after talking it over with Mr. Bailey, we decided it was best to stay in the area. I know he was disappointed, but we agreed the closer we stayed to home base, the less chance there was something might go wrong."

"I appreciate that, Mitchell, and I think you and Mr. Bailey made the right choice. I know you thought highly of Detective Jackson, but believe me, he would've not only understood your decision, but he also would have approved."

Reightman continued down the hall and entered the back treatment room, noticing Toby had changed the color scheme to deeper greens and rich gold tones. "*He probably wants a change, so he's less reminded of the events which had happened in this room,*" Reightman thought, knowing it was going to be hard for him regardless. "I see you're pretty close to finishing, Toby."

"Yeah, I'm almost done in here and I think we'll be as ready as we can be for tomorrow. I know for sure that the staff will be glad to get back to work full time."

"Are you ready, Toby? I mean, personally ready?"

He stood up and wadded the used painter's tape he'd removed from the molding into a small ball. "To tell you the truth, I'm not sure. We do need to get this place up and running again – the bills aren't going to magically pay themselves." He looked around the room, checking out his handiwork and then shrugged. "But frankly, I'm not real excited about the business right now." He took a deep breath before continuing. "I hope I get my excitement back. I've tried to schedule things over the next week or so in such a way I won't be using this room very much and that'll help." He threw the tape into a nearby wastebasket and added, "I know you understand….about things being hard."

"Yes, I do understand, and you're right – it's hard. You'll get through it though, even if it's only one day at a time. Eventually, every single one of those days adds up and you realize you're going to make it after all."

"That's almost exactly what Grams told me last night. If the two smartest women I know – three, if you count Madame Zhou, who had similar advice – tell me it gets better with time, then it must be true."

"I'm honored to be in such august company. Those other two ladies have been through far more than I have." She walked around the room, looking at the changes. "This room looks good, Toby." She turned back to him. "How are the bookings for the reopening looking?"

He made a small moue of distaste. "Not nearly as well as they should be. It'll be a while before things get back to the level they were before all this happened. I'll keep plugging away though, and as long as nothing else goes wrong, we'll survive until it rebounds."

"I have every confidence things will work out. You'll make it work.

"I hope you're right," he said and then changed the subject. "Any news you can share with me, Detective – about the investigation?"

"We're working on a few leads, but these things take time – especially if we're trying to be as careful as possible, and covering everything twice to make sure we don't miss anything." When she saw his disappointed face, she decided to just tell him the truth. "Toby, we aren't making the progress I thought we would. Truthfully, we're running into one dead end after another and I'm about out of ideas. I wish I had better news – as much as you're wishing the same, I bet. But we've both been through too much together since Geri was found for me to not be up-front with you about our progress."

He'd been watching her face intently as she spoke, and was satisfied by what he saw in her expression. "I appreciate you told me the truth, Detective Reightman. I *am* disappointed there hasn't been some kind of big break, but I trust everyone working on this is doing their best." In effort to break the solemn mood, he added, "If I didn't think you were, I'd unleash Madame Zhou."

"All I ask is that you give me warning before you do, so I can get out of town!" Reightman laughed. "Seriously, she's amazing. I don't think Tuesday would've gone nearly as well if she wasn't such a tiger."

"I think you mean dragon," he corrected with a grin. "Tuesday did wear her out, though. I haven't seen her since then, although I've talked to her on the phone a couple of times."

"I saw her yesterday and although she did seem tired, I think she'll be fine. After all, she has enough mysterious herbs and potions over at that shop of hers to jump start anyone, no matter how tired they're feeling." She took one more look around the room at his handiwork. "I like the new colors – good choice. But now it's time for me to let you get back to work. I need to have a word or two with Officer Mitchell before I go, but I won't keep him too long."

"Thanks for stopping by, Detective Melba." He grinned at the look she gave him. "You can pretend, but I know you like it when I call you that."

"I still haven't decided," she retorted, although he was right. "Good luck with tomorrow, Toby – keep your chin up. And if you have any ideas that might help us make progress, let me know and I'll seriously consider them." She walked out into the hallway and over to the young officer on duty. "Hey, Mitchell, you think you can spare me a second or two?"

He walked down the hall toward the room where Toby was working. "If you think it'll be okay to leave him alone, Detective Reightman."

"We're just going down the hall a few steps, or maybe," she opened the door to the other treatment room, "we can step in here." Once they were in the room – with the door slightly open on Mitchell's insistence – Reightman studied his face. "How are things going?"

"I think things are going fine, ma'am. I haven't seen anything suspicious during the last couple of days. I would've said something to you if I had."

"I know you would have, and I'm glad to know there hasn't been anything you thought warranted reporting." She thought about how she should approach the real topic she wanted to discuss with him. "How are things between you and Mr. Bailey?"

Mitchell was confused by her question. "I think everything's fine. We seem to be getting along and he hasn't been any trouble at all. He isn't thrilled about having someone assigned to him twenty-four hours a day, but I think we're making it work." A small worried frown creased his forehead. "Why do you ask, Detective? Did he say something?"

"No, and if there was a problem I know him well enough to be absolutely certain he'd have said something." Reightman noted the relief which appeared on Mitchell's face and forced herself to come to the point. "I hate to ask this, but I need to, Mitchell. There isn't anything of a personal nature going on between the two of you is there?"

It took a minute for him to understand what she was asking. "Someone told you about me, didn't they?" Reightman couldn't decide if he sounded worried, or angry.

"Someone did mention your orientation to me." Before he could interrupt, she continued, "And I don't give a damn who you're attracted to or what rings your bell, as long as it doesn't affect your ability to perform you duties. Mr. Bailey is a personable and attractive young man and–"

"Yes, he is, Detective Reightman," Mitchell cut in before she could finish. "I like him, but I don't think I *like* him. After the last three days it would be like…hitting on my best friend."

Reightman gave an internal sigh of relief. Mitchell's earnestness appeared to be totally genuine. "Thanks for reassuring me, Mitchell. I really didn't think there was anything inappropriate going on. If you were attracted to him, and weren't assigned to keep him safe, I'd be all for you two seeing each other or – whatever." Her next words were more difficult for her, as she'd never been in the position she was in now – that of giving a young officer the benefit of her, and Sam's, limited wisdom. "Let me just share something for you to think about, Mitchell. What you do with it is your decision, but you might find it helpful, somewhere down the line."

"Any advice that you're willing to share is appreciated, ma'am,' Mitchell said, although his voice and expression were now somewhat guarded.

"I'll try to make it short and sweet. In a nutshell, sometimes it's hard to avoid forming attachments with people involved in the cases we investigate."

"Like you and Mr. Bailey, you mean?"

"*Touché, Mitchell.*" Reightman thought. "Yes, in a way. Much like you, for some reason I associate Mr. Bailey with a best friend, or a brother I never had." When Mitchell nodded, she continued, "It's important to try and remain as objective as possible – especially when the situation is a dangerous one. That means we sometimes have to step back from the person involved, even if our instincts tell us to do otherwise. It's fine to like Mr. Bailey, but if possible – and it might not be – try to hold off on forming any kind of attachment, even one of friendship. It'll help keep you focused and might prevent you from hurting too badly if something terrible happens."

"Nothing's going to happen to Toby Bailey if I can help it, Detective."

"I hope you're right, Mitchell. I felt exactly the same about Detective Jackson, but ultimately I wasn't able to stop the person who killed him."

Mitchell put her hard confession into the context of his feelings for Toby. "You knew and worked with Detective Jackson for a long time, ma'am. This situation is different, but only because I haven't known Toby – I mean, Mr. Bailey – for as long as you knew Detective Jackson." He paused to see what her reaction to his words was, and when he saw that she wasn't going to object, he continued. "I understand what you're telling me and I think it's probably good advice. I'll do my best to step back some, but, Detective?" He looked

earnestly into her face. "I think it might already be too late to be objective."

Reightman had caught his use of Bailey's first name, but given her
own feelings for Toby she didn't mention it. She couldn't even find a
reason to try and make him step back from what was obviously,
friendship. She hadn't, even when she knew better. "In that case,
Mitchell, do your damnedest to make sure nothing bad happens. It
hurts like hell when it does."

"Detective? I appreciate you taking time to talk to me about this,
and…for accepting me for who I am. It means a lot, and I'll never
forget it."

Once, Sam had told her that he'd always remembered the kind
advice given to him by a more senior officer and had tried to explain
how much it had always meant. She thought of all the times he had
been so generous with sharing the benefit of his experience with others, and suddenly knew what kind of personal satisfaction he'd received from mentoring others. She forced down the lump in her
throat and gave Mitchell a mock glare. "Don't start getting all mushy
with me. I'm not used to it and it makes me cranky and weepy and
you don't want to see either." She smiled up at him as she opened the
door. "It's time for me to let you get back to your job. Stay safe, and
keep your eyes open. I have a feeling things are going to start to unfold pretty soon. I just hope we're ready for what's headed our way."

As Reightman walked past the reception desk, she stopped and
looked up at the photo of a young Toby Bailey. His mother had perfectly captured the moment which had given the spa its name. The
young boy, seated in the hard backed wooden chair pouted down at
her, with his arms crossed defiantly across his chair. He was in time
out, until he 'found a better mood to get in', Toby had explained to
her the first time she'd seen the picture. She'd known it was him the
moment she saw it, but today, the resemblance to the man she'd left
in the back treatment room seemed to be less obvious. Maybe it was
because the small boy staring down from the wall hadn't yet experience the heartbreak and trauma with which his older self was becoming all too familiar. She thought of what might still be ahead, and
couldn't suppress the small shiver that tingled down her spine. *"Lord
— and Sam, if you're listening — please send us what we need to make it*

through this mess safely. Any help or good ideas you can send down to us would be much appreciated.”

She stepped out onto the sidewalk and looked over to the patrol car across the street, situated between Zhou Li’s shop and the stairs which led to Toby’s apartment. The officers on duty were good men and would keep watch on her neighborhood. She looked down the street at each of the quirky businesses occupying this section of Capital Street. Six months ago, she wouldn’t have given the shops – or their owners – a second thought, but now she found herself caring a great deal about this small stretch of downtown.

“When,” she asked herself as she drove away, *“did these people become my friends? And when did I start thinking about this place as my neighborhood.”* She never did come to an answer, even though she was still thinking about it later that evening while the scent of jasmine tea filled her lonely apartment.

CHAPTER FIVE

SATURDAY WAS PRETTY much a mixed bag for Toby. He was happy the spa was up and running and the remaining staff were thrilled to slide back into their work routines. He'd lost a couple of employees over the past couple of weeks because they weren't able to go without regular work. The rest of the staff managed to hang in with him though, and made ends meet by stepping in to handle a fair number of outcalls from area hotels. One or two had picked up fill-in shifts waiting tables or tending bar around town. As he reviewed the appointment book with SarahJune before opening, he realized – even with a reduced staff – Time Out would be able to handle the work-load. There were far fewer appointments scheduled for the upcoming two weeks than he'd anticipated.

"It'll get better, Toby," SarahJune reassured him. "We should have known this time of year would be slow. Folks are trying to get back into their routines after summer vacations and have just fin-ished getting their kids back in school. I bet things will start picking up in a few days."

Toby flipped through a couple of pages in the appointment book, noting the missing names of some of the spa's regular clients, and then closed the book and handed it back to her. "I hope you're right," he said. "Maybe we should put together some promo packs and flyers. I can carry them around to some of the area businesses like I did when we first opened." He watched the water from the wall fountain flow down the ridged rock backdrop while he thought about anything else that might help. "I guess we could offer a discount coupon. That worked pretty well when we were trying to get started."

"Yeah, it did." SarahJune agreed. "I'll go grab some of the flyers and business cards and start putting together some packets. You want to add those little samples of body lotion?"

"Sure, we might as well. I think everything you'll need is in the lower right-hand cabinet in the back treatment room."

As SarahJune went to fetch the supplies, Toby walked over to where Mitchell was standing in the front of the reception area looking out the big glass windows. "You're quiet this morning."

"Really?" Mitchell seemed surprised by Toby's observation. "I've just been thinking about some stuff. You'd better enjoy it while you can. If I remember, the other day you asked me if I ever shut up."

Toby laughed at Mitchell's reminder. "Well, you do seem to find plenty to say most of the time, when you're not being all official and cop-like." When Mitchell grinned at his characterization, Toby added, "You know, you can't lurk out here staring out the window all day. You'll scare away what few customers we have left."

"I guess I could find a magazine to read or something. I guess I hadn't realized how much I'd stand out in here."

"Yeah, me either. I'm going to need to take some marketing brochures around to a few places in town later this morning, so we'll be out of here for a couple of hours. After that, I have a lot of stuff to catch up on in the office and you can hang out with me back there." Toby stopped him before Mitchell could suggest an alternative. "And, no, you can't stand outside the hall between the office and the spa treatment rooms. I think most of our customers would think it was creepy, unless you want to put on a fluffy white robe and pretend you're waiting on an appointment."

"I don't think that would be a good idea. Detective Reightman would come unglued if she saw me like that." After a moment, Mitchell shyly added, "Beside, I've never had a massage before."

"Never?"

"No, but I've always wondered what it would be like."

"I'll tell you what, once this is all over, I'll make sure you get the best massage the Time Out Spa can provide."

"Really?"

"Sure, it's the least I can do. After all, you've put up with me for the last three or four days, and who knows how long we still have to go before this is wrapped up." Toby gave the cop an evil grin. "I'll book you with Brigette, for one of her special deep tissue torture sessions." Toby assumed a very stern expression and mimicked the sturdy German masseuse. "You vill lay dere very still. Dis vill not hurt – much. Ja?"

Mitchell's eyes widened in unfeigned fear. He'd met the bossy, militant Brigette just this morning when she arrived to make sure *tings vere in der proper order.* She'd taken control of the whole place within five minutes and Mitchell was kind of scared of her no-nonsense, take-charge-but-take-no-prisoners demeanor and didn't want it directed his way. "Ummm…I'm not sure that'd be very relaxing."

"Actually, Brigette is one of the best therapists I have ever known," Toby told him. "She has about twenty-five years of experience and I was lucky she was looking for a part-time position when her son left for college." He smiled at Mitchell's still wide-eyed face and added, "I'd tell her to go easy on you since you're a massage virgin."

"Thanks – I think," Mitchell was not at all enthused. "I think I'll go find a magazine or something to read before we leave." He started to head back to the break room and looked back over his shoulder, "Don't even think about unlocking the front door until I get back."

"Aye, aye, captain," Toby saluted, and then stretched and turned to the desk where SarahJune was opening the boxes containing the extra spa literature and the free samples. "Need some help? The sooner we get these put together, the sooner I can start trying to drum up some business."

Melba spent her Saturday morning doing some grocery shopping and catching up on her laundry. An hour or so later, she was sitting on the couch with an improbably plotted detective novel, prepared to spend the afternoon immersed in the adventures of Master Detective Justinian Copperfield as he tried to solve the case of the missing Burmese Champion show cat. She'd progressed through the first few chapters of nefarious doings when her phone rang. Melba dog-eared her page and answered.

"Detective Reightman, I'm sorry to interrupt your Saturday, but I did have a couple of things I wanted to talk to you about - if you have a moment?"

"Hello, Madame Zhou," Melba replied, recognizing the lady's voice. "I'm not in the middle of anything important, so you haven't interrupted a thing."

"I'm glad," Zhou replied. "The first thing on my mind is to inquire about how you are doing. I wasn't able to get to you yesterday at Detective Jackson's service due to the huge turnout, and so I thought I would check on you today."

Melba did a quick internal check of her current mental and emotional state. She was still depressed, of course, but she did feel more normal than she had in a while. "I'm doing as well as can be expected. It's going to take me a while to come to terms with what has happened, but I'll be alright." She remembered her conversation with Toby the day before. "How are *you* doing? Tony mentioned you were still feeling tired."

"I was worn out from that tedious meeting on Tuesday. I will never understand why people have to be bludgeoned into getting with the program. It would save so much time if they would just realize I was going to get my way regardless of their antics. However, I am feeling much better today."

"I'm glad to hear it. Toby and I were a little worried."

"I am perfectly fine, Detective, but I appreciate your concern. Now, the second item I wanted to check with you about is regarding the tea I made for you – not the jasmine, the other tea. How is it working for you?"

"It's working very well, Madame Zhou. In fact, it's almost miraculous."

"I am delighted to hear it. That blend always worked well for the members of my family. I will start working on another batch."

"Thank you. Please let me know when it's ready and I'll stop by. And please include a bill this time."

"I will, Detective. Now that you are hooked, I can make back my initial investment," Zhou's girlish laugh echoed over the phone, and Melba found herself wondering just how much investment the old lady was going to try to recoup. She decided it didn't matter – the tea was worth its weight in gold.

"The third thing I wanted to know is whether you have plans for this coming Tuesday evening? The "Ming Palace Chinese Flying Wonders" are going to be performing, and a friend has given me two tickets. I would be delighted if you were able to join me."

Melba thought through her non-existent social calendar and accepted. "I'd love to join you, Madame Zhou. The only caveat is if something should occur regarding the investigation, I could find myself in a situation where I'd be unable to attend."

"That is a given, Detective. However, we will *plan* on you being able to attend the performance with me. As a matter-of-fact, I was wondering if you would mind driving us that evening. I'm finding driving once dark is becoming troublesome for me."

Melba readily agreed. Anything which kept the octogenarian off the streets after nightfall was worth it in her mind.

"Thank you, Detective. I believe that very satisfactorily completes all the items I called to discuss. I am sure you would like to return to your own activities, and I have a flat full of fall mums to put into the pots on my terrace."

"It sounds like you have a busy afternoon ahead, Madame Zhou. Thank you again. I'm looking forward to our outing on Tuesday." After hanging up, Melba picked up her book and thumbed through the pages until she found her place. She was soon once again caught up in the mysterious caper of the missing cat.

John Brown had spent every available minute during the last couple of days checking up on various people of interest. He attended the funeral of Detective Sam Jackson and noted the impressive turnout. At the cemetery, he watched the Detective's widow release the white dove, and had to wipe a single tiny tear from the corner of his eye. *"That was a beautiful moment,"* he thought, recalling the bird's winged passage up into the sky.

He'd also spent a good deal of his time keeping an eye on Toby, and the police detail shadowing him. Early Sunday morning he watched the two men rush down the stairwell onto the sidewalk to commence their morning jog. The young cop running at Toby Bailey's side was dressed in a pair of modest training shorts, athletic shoes, a departmental t-shirt and had his weapon holstered over his shoulder. In contrast, Toby wore only a pair of running shoes and a brief pair of nylon shorts. The sun glinted off his ash blond hair and played off of his lean, toned body. *"He's got a nice pair of legs on him and a really fine ass,"* John Brown noticed as the men stretched for a minute and then took off down the street.

Forty minutes later he saw them return, wet with sweat. The young cop was breathing heavily, trying to catch his breath. Toby was not breathing as hard, since he was a well-seasoned runner, but his skin was slicked with a glistening sheen of moisture and the thin shorts clung damply to what little skin they covered. The young man bent over to adjust a lace on his shoe, and John Brown found himself mesmerized for a moment by the flexing, tight muscles of Toby's backside. *"Damn, that's nice!"* he exclaimed under his breath, before wondering what caused him to even notice. Once the shoelace was properly tied, he saw the golden young man straighten, and the cop at his side reached over and clapped him on the shoulder. They laughed together as the cop flung the water which had attached itself to his fingers and palm off onto the pavement. Toby Bailey pushed the cop playfully in the chest, and John Brown could tell he was making some laughing rejoinder to a remark the cop had made.

John Brown watched the two men head back up the stairs, and realized what strong feeling was welling up inside him. He was jealous – pure and simple. He was jealous of the young cop who had obviously formed a bond with the man John Brown had been hired to kill. He pushed the feeling down. He didn't think he was gay, and besides, he didn't have any experience with that particular emotion. His relationships had always been on a for-hire basis, and jealousy didn't factor into those situations.

Later that night, he climbed up the old attached ladder leading to the rooftops of the shops on Capital Street. *"That's going to cause trouble,"* he observed again when he reached the roof and looked down at the ladder. He walked across the flat expanse of asphalt covering the roofs until he was directly across from the apartment he knew belonged to Toby Bailey. In the dark night, John Brown watched until the bedroom light was turned off.

"Good night, Toby," John Brown whispered to the apartment window opposite him. "I'll check on you again tomorrow."

Monday brought the start of a new week, but didn't, unfortunately, bring any new leads in the ongoing investigations. By the end of the day Tuesday, Reightman was more than ready for the diversion Zhou Li's outing promised. After making a quick stop home to change into something more appropriate for a night out, she pulled up in front of Green Dragon, where Zhou was waiting by the front door. To her surprise, Toby and Mitchell were also waiting expectantly.

When she pulled into a nearby parking place, the three made their way to her car.

"I hope you don't mind, but I was able to get a couple of tickets for tonight and I thought we could all ride together."

"That's not a problem at all, Toby – the more the merrier," Reightman agreed as Mitchell held the passenger side door open while Toby helped Zhou Li get settled into the front seat.

Soon they were all in, buckled up, and headed to the city's performing arts arena. Once they made it to the lobby, Toby and Mitchell started to split off from their small group. "Our seats are further back than yours," he explained. "I was lucky to even get two seats together, so I'm not about to complain."

After agreeing where they should meet after the performance, Melba carefully escorted Madame Zhou to the seats she'd secured for them. Melba was surprised to see herself seated dead center in the orchestra section, about eight rows back from the large curtained stage. She noticed several of the city's elite seated around her, although thankfully, none she'd seen in naked, photographic glory.

"These seats are wonderful," She commented to her companion as she helped Zhou arrange the heavily embroidered silken shawl the elderly woman wore draped over her thin shoulders.

"Yes, they are very acceptable," Zhou Li responded with imperial dignity, certain the privilege of such excellent seating was only her due. Amused for a moment at the thought of Zhou Li sitting in the nose-bleed seats in the top tier of the theatre, Melba settled back into her seat and leafed through her program.

"I wonder if they'll have animal acts."

"I don't think so," Madame Zhou replied, "although the last time I saw this group perform they did have one act which included tigers. It was quiet impressive. However, the Ming Palace troupe is more renowned for their feats of acrobatic dexterity and flying maneuvers." She leafed through her own program and bared her tiny teeth in delight. "I am so looking forward to this, Detective! I will be anxious to hear your thoughts after tonight's performance has concluded."

"I'm looking forward to it as well, Madame Zhou," Melba replied. As the orchestra started to play and the lights began to dim, she leaned over to the lady. "I think they're ready to begin."

Once the lights were down, the orchestra increased its volume. The woodwinds and brass were joined by the rumbling sound of several large drums, which increased in tempo until suddenly, all sound stopped. The lonely sound of a single flute played a couple of mournful measures, and then the lights came back up and the curtain was raised.

Melba watched in wonder as she took in the single figure of a striking young woman posed on the stage. The performer was wearing an elaborate jeweled and embroidered robe of deep crimson and gold, and on top of her head was a towering headdress with beads and pearls hanging from the many small winged points. The headdress reminded Melba of pictures she'd seen of the palaces in the Forbidden City. The woman on stage held herself perfectly still in front of an elaborate backdrop of deep cobalt blue featuring large, highly stylized white and gold birds. As the orchestra began to play the next measure, one by one the birds began to unfold and open their wings to the beat of the music. After a moment, Melba realized the birds were members of the performing troupe. A single bird launched into the air followed by the rest. The stage soon filled with carefully choreographed movement as the performers balanced and tumbled from each other's shoulders and hands. The beautifully robed woman joined their number, moving gracefully among the flock of dancers and tumblers until she was lifted high in the air by two troupe members. Her robes unfurled and Melba realized they represented brilliant red wings.

More tumblers and dancers joined the white birds, this time simply costumed, but carrying sticks or wands with long streamers attached, in all of the colors of fire. None of the swirling streamers were as brilliant as the woman's crimson robe, but were shades of vibrant orange and yellow with a few deep bluish-purple tendrils dancing among them.

From the side of the stage came a horde of tumblers carrying large swaths of billowing grey and black fabric. The fire-colored streamers whirled around the woman, now held aloft by only a single pair of hands. The woman spread her wings gloriously in time to the music as the streamers of colored fabric danced more wildly about her. Suddenly, the orchestra sounded a high, terrible piercing note, and the woman stretched out her throat as if she were in terrible pain. She dropped from her height, and the swaths of dark fabric billowed outward and down, to cover her body.

The music was still for a moment, until slowly the flute began to play again. Melba could see the fabric on the floor begin to move gently. She could barely make out the horizontal bar being lowered from the fly space above the stage. A single red-clad arm parted the fabric and reached upward and grasped the bar. Slowly, the woman was lifted from the mound of dark fabric, revealing the same woman – sans fantastic robe and headdress – wearing only a skin-tight garment of crimson. Higher and higher the bar was raised above the stage, carrying the figure upward, and then it started to swing. Other bars were lowered from the ceiling, and from each bar hung a figure dressed in the same cobalt blue as the backdrop. Each of the suspended figures dropped wide fabric panels of the same blue, which turned almost transparent under the lights. The crimson woman flew from figure to figure caught by out-stretched hands, or held for a moment wrapped in the fabric. The crowd watched breathlessly as the woman tumbled and flipped and turned in the air, seeming at times to drop, only to be caught and flung through the air again. The figures in blue began to fly through the air as well, and moved from the bars to fabric, until it was impossible to tell where one stopped and another started. Just when it appeared the frenzied action couldn't continue another moment, two large, dyed lengths of silk unwound from somewhere high above the stage. They hung about three feet apart. Painted on each of them was a huge stylized wing.

The movement of the acrobats built to a climax while the music increased in tempo and volume. Suddenly, the woman was flung from the back of the stage and flew toward the audience. Melba's breath caught as the woman reached out and grabbed the panels, one in each hand. She stretched out her arms, supporting herself with the fabric as she hung motionless between them in the form of a cross.

The stage was now empty of performers, except for the woman. She was lowered slowly to the floor and the white bird figures erupted from the sides of the stage and circled her, their fantastic wings screening her from view. One by one, the birds spun off from their dance, and resumed their original positions on the backdrop. The woman was revealed, once again crowned with her headdress and wearing the red and gold robe. The white birds stilled on the backdrop, and the central performer resumed the pose which had started the show. The lights lowered to the sound of a single, mournful flute.

Thunderous applause burst out from the audience, peppered with shouts and whistles of appreciation. Melba turned to Madame Zhou. "That was the most fantastic thing I've ever seen," she whispered.

"It was only the first act of the evening, Detective," Zhou Li answered. "It will only get better from here."

Trying to imagine what could possibly be better, Melba settled back in her seat. Zhou Li was right. It only got better.

In the car back to Capital Street, everyone talked about their favorite parts of the performance.

"I liked the times when the performers used the big pieces of silky fabric to move about above the stage," Mitchell commented excitedly. "I was amazed the fabric could support the weight, given how delicate it looked. It just seemed to float down, before catching the acrobats and flyers in the folds."

"I've always enjoyed watching that as well, Officer Mitchell," Madame Zhou agreed. "I think the technique is referred to as aerial silk. It became popular after being used by the circus headquartered in Montreal – the one which now has several shows running in Las Vegas."

"I've seen them on TV – there was a special about them on last spring. It would be fantastic to try it! I hear you can learn at some of the circus schools," Toby said from the backseat.

Melba listened to their conversation as she navigated the car. After a while, everyone fell quiet. Toby asked, "Any news, Detective Reightman?"

Melba knew exactly what he was asking. She turned onto the exit which would take them downtown. "No, not yet, I'm afraid. I'm working hard to keep myself from getting too frustrated. I just don't know what to do next."

No one spoke for a moment. "Perhaps it is time to cast out a net of some sort and see what kind of fish can be caught," Zhou Li said in a tone Melba couldn't quite decipher.

"What do you mean, Madame Zhou?" Toby asked.

"I'm not sure. The thought just popped into my head. I'm sure one of us will think of an answer, though. These things always work out."

Melba pulled in to the space in front of the Zhou's building on and got out of the car to wait politely while the two men helped Zhou Li from the car and escorted her up the curb to the sidewalk. "Detective, I never heard you comment on which part of the performance you enjoyed best." Zhou's head tilted to one side as she waited for Melba's answer.

Melba tried to recall each fantastic act. "I enjoyed them all, but I think I liked the first act the best – the one with the woman in the crimson robes."

Zhou Li nodded her approval. "Ah yes. I believe that was the story of the firebird, Detective Reightman – or the phoenix, to those of us from Asian cultures."

"I liked it the best, too," Toby agreed. "It spoke to me somehow, but I wasn't sure what it was supposed to mean. It was kind of sad, but at the same time, not sad at all."

"You are correct in your impression, Toby," Madame Zhou assured him. "As to what it meant….well, the story is about living and loving and dying and then rising triumphantly from the ashes and flames to do it all again." She started for the door to Green Dragon and then turned back to them where they stood on the sidewalk. "It is about life, really, and overcoming adversity to come back stronger than before, prepared to tackle the next challenge." She smiled sweetly from the door. "I can understand why you both liked it." Melba saw the old woman gently caress the little finger which was missing its first joint. "I like it also," Zhou said as she unlocked her door. "It has always been a favorite of mine."

On her way back home, Melba kept turning the conversation over in her mind. Something was setting off an alarm, but she couldn't figure out what it was, or what warning it was trying to give.

Toby and Mitchell got ready for bed, but Toby found himself full of restless energy. He pulled on his sleeping shorts and walked into the living room. As he started to open the French doors, Mitchell came out from the bathroom. "Where do you think you're going, Toby?"

"Just out here – it's perfectly safe. No one could ever get up here."

Mitchell frowned and shook his head. "You know better. You're not going out there alone."

Toby sighed heavily. This constant vigilance was getting to him. "I just want to step out here for a few minutes. I'm restless and won't be able to sleep until I settle down some."

"Okay. That sounds reasonable, but I'll go with you," Mitchell compromised. "I promise I'll even be perfectly quiet."

Toby opened the door and the two men stepped out onto the terrace. Toby looked up at the stars. "Aren't they wonderful?"

"Yeah, it's a pretty nice view. Don't you feel self-conscious though? I mean we're out here almost naked and anyone could see us."

"Mitchell, don't be ridiculous. No one can see us up here. I lay out here all of the time *completely* nude. The privacy is part of the reason I choose this apartment."

"It seems exposed to me – or maybe I'm just not feeling comfortable right now. I'm not used to walking around outside in my underwear."

Toby looked over to his friend, standing a few feet away. Mitchell was wearing a pair of mid-thigh black briefs that clung to his body and didn't leave much to the imagination. "I think it's nice to be out here nude," Toby said. "You should try it sometime."

Mitchell shook his head. "I don't know about that. I guess I'm just shy."

Toby gave his friend a mischievous grin and reached for the drawstring of his shorts.

"Toby, what are you doing? Stop playing around."

"There," Toby said as he reached down to pick up the shorts from where they'd fallen to his feet and placed them on the small table. "Now it's your turn."

"Toby...I...uh..."

"Come on, Mitchell. Drop those drawers," Toby instructed sternly. Mitchell didn't make a move and stood silently with his eyes adverted, until Toby realized what the problem was. "Mitchell, I'm not trying to put the move on you. Besides, you've already told me you aren't interested in me. So, this isn't a big deal at all." As he waited for Mitchell's response, he added, "I double dog dare you."

Mitchell finally turned his head back to face Toby. Keeping eye contact the entire time, he reached down and pulled down the briefs, stepping out of them one leg at a time. When he held them in his hand, he walked to Toby and held them out to him. "Satisfied?" he asked.

"Yep!" Toby grinned in delight and placed the briefs on the table next to his shorts. Then he turned to look out over the city. "Just relax, Mitchell – you're already undressed, so go with the flow and enjoy the feeling. Come over here and look at the lights. They're really beautiful."

Mitchell walked to stand beside him and looked out over the city. The two stood a few feet from each other and looked out into the night.

"What are you thinking about, Toby?" Mitchell asked as he started to relax.

"Just about some of the things Madame Zhou said when we got back."

A very gentle breeze blew across the balcony and played softly across their skin, causing Mitchell to sigh softly at the sensation. "This is kind of nice," he reluctantly admitted.

"Told ya so." After a few more minutes, Toby yawned. "I think I can sleep now. You ready to go in?"

Mitchell found himself disappointed it was time to end this new experience, but it was getting late. "Yeah, we probably should get some sleep."

The two men turned to walk back inside, and Toby moved to the table to pick up their discarded undergarments. From the open door,

Mitchell laughed. "You might as well just leave those there. I usually sleep naked anyway."

A beautiful imaged flashed through Toby's mind as he remembered being pulled close to Mitchell after waking up frightened a couple of nights before. "Okay," he said finally, walking through the door behind his friend.

"Hey, Mitchell?"

"Yeah?"

"I like your tattoo. It's just the right size and in the perfect spot to accentuate your very best ass-set."

Mitchell didn't react or say a word as he walked back toward the hall to the bedroom, but Toby could see the backs of his ears turning a bright red. Toby laughed.

From across the street, John Brown watched as the two men stepped out onto the terrace. He wouldn't have been able to see much of anything if he hadn't been perched on the highest part of the roof, up on top of a small shed housing the H/VAC equipment for the building below.

His breath caught in his throat as he realized they were almost naked, and when he saw Toby drop his shorts, and then the young cop do the same, he had to close his eyes and let the breeze wash across his face for a while before he could look again.

He saw the men joke with each other as the stood stand side by side on the terrace looking at the city lights. There was nothing sexual in anything they did, or in their interaction with each other. They were just two young men, naked in the night air, innocent and at peace for the moment. John Brown felt something surge inside himself, but he couldn't put into words what it was.

After a few minutes, he saw them go back into the apartment, leaving the discarded, irrelevant garments on the table on the terrace. Through the dimly lit apartment window, he watched as Toby closed the door.

John Brown slowly climbed down from his perch. When he reached the flat rooftop he looked out into the city. He slowly removed his own clothes, until he stood naked in the night – just as they had done.

The same breeze which had brushed their skin now brushed his, and he shivered – not from cold, but from longing. *"I'm glad I didn't kill him."* He stood on the rooftop a long time, wondering how he had come to be there, naked and alone on a late summer night.

That night while Toby slept, he dreamed.

He stood in the center of the empty stage, completely nude. He could see Mitchell, also nude, waiting in the wings to one side, and on the other side he could make out the transparent hazy form of someone he thought was Geri. He looked from one to the other and then turned around and looked behind him. Perched on the backdrop were Detective Reightman and Zhou Li, watching and waiting to see what he would do. Next to Melba Reightman was a dim figure he could recognize as Sam Jackson.

Toby turned around and saw a man he recognized as Doctor Lieberman staring up at him from the audience. A few seats away sat Helliman, sneering.

He turned back to the three on the backdrop. "I don't know what I'm supposed to do?" he said.

"See what you catch," Madame Zhou said and suddenly he was borne up into the air by two white birds. They lifted him high above the stage until he could barely see the floor and then swooped back down. On the stage floor he could see a group of people, naked in the lights. They were trapped in yards and yards of black and gray fabric, billowing around them like some sort of angry sea, and he recognized some of them from the photos he had found in the lockbox.

Another bird, this time a glowing red, flew near and dropped a net to him. He grasped it in his hands and looked at the knotted strings. "I don't know what to do," he told the red bird. The bird opened its beak and he heard a voice he thought belonged to Grams say, "It's time to go fishing, Toby Bailey."

The white birds took him closer to the floor of the stage and after looking back toward the figures on the backdrop, he unfolded the net and cast it down on to the people below. As he started to reach for the end of the net to pull it up, he saw one of the figures reach up toward him, with a hand flung out it denial. He couldn't make out the face, but he could read the tattoo on the back of one shoulder. "Alias."

He reached for the net again, and hauled it up, using all his strength and will. He pulled and pulled, and as the figure caught in the net started to lift from the grey fabric, Toby turned back to the figures behind him. "I think I caught something!" he shouted.

The three on the backdrop nodded and smiled at him proudly. He felt his arms weakening and he looped the net through the white birds' sharp beaks. "Help me?" Toby pleaded.

The birds swayed in the air, unbalanced by the weight of the net and the figure it held. They released Toby's arms and he began to fall, looking up at the birds as they struggled to hold on to their burden. He twisted as he fell, and saw Mitchell standing beneath him with outstretched arms.

"It's okay, Toby," Mitchell cried up at him, as he braced his legs. "It's okay – I've got you."

Toby fell faster and faster toward the floor. "Help me!" he heard himself scream.

Mitchell smiled confidently up at him. "Toby, I've got…"

…you," Mitchell told him as he jerked awake.

As he felt himself being pulled gently up against the friend who lay beside him, Toby gasped for breath, "I… was falling."

Mitchell pulled him closer and said, "It's okay, Toby. I've got you – safe and sound. Now, go back to sleep."

Toby closed his eyes again, and slept.

The next morning as he was pouring them both a cup of coffee, Toby said, "Mitchell, I think I know what I need to do."

Mitchell took the offered cup. "What's that?"

Toby told him and Mitchell stared into his face and into the pale blue eyes without saying a word. Then he tightened his jaw and put down the cup. "We'd better call Detective Reightman," he said. "She's not going to like this."

"I know," Toby said. "But she'll agree. We're running out of options – everything else has failed."

"She might agree, Toby, but she's still not going to like it."

Toby lifted his cup to his lips but quickly set it down. A tiny drop of coffee sloshed over the rim – jostled by his trembling hand. "I'm scared," he whispered.

"Me, too, Toby."

They stood in the kitchen looking into each other's eyes. When Mitchell nodded toward him, Toby reached over and picked up his phone from the counter. He dialed the number and waited.

"Detective Reightman," he said when she answered the phone. "I have an idea. I know what we need to do."

On the other end of the line, Reightman listened as he told her his plan. She ended the call and sunk back into the cushions of her couch. She thought over Toby Bailey's proposal, turning over the possibilities in her mind while the coffee in her cup slowly cooled.

CHAPTER SIX

WEDNESDAY AFTERNOON INCLUDED an argument or two, some shouting and a lot of worry. Melba slumped exhausted into one of the chairs in Toby's apartment where she, Zhou and Mitchell had gone over every detail. As Toby sat pensively on the sofa and Mitchell stood looking out the door, it was Zhou Li in the kitchen who broke the deadlock.

"I don't really care for this plan, Toby. I think it is very dangerous and puts you at a great deal of risk." As Toby started to object to yet one more rationalization of why he shouldn't proceed, Zhou held up one tiny hand. "Let me finish, please. I am old and I am getting to the end of my limited patience." When he sunk back into the sofa with one bare foot curled up underneath him, and she confirmed no one else was going to attempt to interrupt her, she continued. "While we have all given many reasons why you should *not* attempt to carry out your plan, I do not think any of us – other than you yourself – have discussed why you *should*." She walked over to the chair which set catty-cornered to the couch and placed her hands on the back of the padded backrest.

"Here is what I believe," Zhou continued when she had everyone's undivided attention – except that of the man still standing by the French doors. "I believe this offers an excellent possibility for you to lure the person, or persons, involved with Geri Guzman out into the open. I believe with proper preparation, Detective Reightman and Officer Mitchell can arrange to keep you safe. The fact is, you're not safe now, as demonstrated by the need to have someone with you all day, every day, until the murderer is caught. By moving forward with your suggested approach, you will be taking a reactive situation and making it into a proactive one. I believe the police have reached the point of not knowing what to do next, and the worst thing possible for all of us would be for this investigation to be allowed to grow cold from lack of progress. Isn't that correct, Detective?" the diminutive woman asked.

"Yes," Reightman answered from her chair, sounding tired and defeated.

"I thought so. Detective Reightman, please keep your spirits up!" Zhou Li turned back to the man seated on the sofa. "The final thing I believe about your plan Toby is this: I believe you need to do it, for yourself and not for anyone else. I don't think you will be able to put this behind you until the person who killed Geri is found, and prosecuted to the full extent of the law."

Zhou moved to the front of the chair and sat down carefully, folding her small hands in her lap. "Toby, you have handled yourself well – remarkably so – in my opinion. But answer this: have you grieved for the loss of your friend? I mean really grieved?"

When he finally shook his head, Zhou had her answer. "Then that, Toby, is why we should do this. To let you get on with your life, after you have grieved Geri's loss of life."

One by one the people around the room agreed, with Mitchell being the last holdout. "Toby, are you sure about this?"

"Yes, Mitchell, I am."

The young cop joined the rest of the group. "Then I guess we better start refining the plan, Toby." He looked into Reightman's eyes and remembered the advice she'd given him. He nodded, with acceptance and acknowledgment that she'd been right about the price of forming this bond and shared the realization that neither of them would've changed their relationship with Toby, even if they could. "I couldn't bear it if something bad were to happen, so we better make damned sure it doesn't."

Reightman reached out and took Mitchell's hand in her own. She gave it a gentle squeeze, knowing they were in perfect agreement. "Let's get started then." She rose from the chair and the others followed suit, following her to the small dining table.

Toby's plan was elegant in its simplicity, although it presented problems of both a personal and professional nature.

Toby would place an ad, similar to the kinds Geri had used to attract his...benefactors. The ad would be posted on two electronic bulletin boards which were scanned and read by a large cross section of the population. In order to weed out as many responders a possible, he'd request a photo of some sort – body only and as near to nude as they were willing to provide. Then, the team would compare the photos received to those retrieved from the lockbox Geri had rented. Once reasonable verification was made, Toby would agree to meet with them to provide the agreed upon service.

This was where Toby had difficulty. He wasn't sure how he'd manage to provide any services, so to speak, to anyone who was a potential suspect in Geri's murder, but he'd just have to find some way to get through the sessions. He didn't even try to justify it morally, or ethically. His focus was now on bringing the killer to justice. He'd have to play the rest out as best he could.

The clincher to the plan – and the event which would hopefully draw out the killer – occurred after the initial session was over. Once the client was verified as one of the individuals in the collection of photographs, he'd hand them a copy of one of their photographs from the lockbox collection. Then he'd indicate he intended to carry on with the same arrangements Geri had made with them to ensure the photos remained private.

Again, Toby ran into an ethical dilemma. He abhorred what Geri had done, and now he was perpetuating the same actions. He worried about the effect on those innocent of anything more than looking for companionship on a for-hire basis. He had no problem with people doing whatever they needed to do to meet their own specific needs, as long as no one was physically or emotionally hurt. But this was different. He pushed those concerns aside as well, deciding he'd make some form of restitution, somehow and someway, for any additional pain he caused as he enacted the plan to flush out the killer.

Once Toby presented the photos and made his position clear, he'd provide his contact details and hopefully, one or more of the responders would panic and attempt to meet Toby at a secluded location – maybe even the spa. There, Toby reasoned, they'd once again attempt to end the life of the person who'd threatened them.

The difficulty with the plan lay in determining how to gather evidence of the responder's wrongdoing and intent to harm, and – more importantly – how to keep Toby safe.

"The first thing needed for the initial meeting is a safe location," Reightman said pragmatically, now she'd resigned herself to the idea the crazy plan was going to be put into motion, "where Toby can meet with the suspects. Once we have a location identified, we can wire it for recording and provide a reasonable level of protection in case something goes wrong during the first meeting."

"Why can't we use the spa?" Toby asked, having now put his personal reservations aside.

"I think it could be too much traffic in and out and might raise suspicions. After the first round of meetings is over, and we decide how to move forward, I think the spa would work fine. Theoretically, we'll have the field of suspects narrowed down by then."

"How about a hotel room then?"

After thinking it over, Reightman shot it down. "No. I think it'd be difficult to arrange security and to get it wired. Someone would be bound to talk, and the public nature of a hotel would make it less attractive to our targets – given how recognizable many of them are, and how carefully they'll want to protect their privacy."

"And under no circumstances are you to agree to meet any of them at their homes, or someplace they suggest." Zhou sternly directed. "There would be no way to prepare those locations properly to collect what is needed or to keep you safe." No one argued with her position, or even wanted to. They all knew better, and she was right.

"How about a rental apartment?" Toby suggested again.

Everyone thought it through. There was the potential exposure concern to work through, but all other criteria would be met. They agreed it was a good contender.

Mitchell hadn't contributed much to the conversation up to that point. He listened intently from his place at the door to each part of the discussion but stayed uncharacteristically silent. Finally he spoke up. "My place." When the others looked to him for explanation, he continued. "It's centrally located, we can control the security, wire it for sound, and I know the ways into and out of both the neighborhood and the duplex."

"Mitchell, why would you agree to let us use your place for this? Wouldn't it be weird?" Toby asked before Reightman could essentially do the same.

Mitchell looked at his friend for a moment before he spoke. "I'm all in on this, Toby. When I say I'm all in on something, you can believe I mean it." He went to the kitchen for a glass of water while they mulled over his offer.

"It *is* perfect," Reightman said carefully, worried that Mitchell would retract the offer – and worried he wouldn't. "Are you sure, Mitchell?"

Mitchell took a big gulp of ice water before he answered. "Yes, ma'am, I am."

Reightman canvassed the opinions of the rest of the group before agreeing. "I appreciate this, Mitchell."

"No problem, Detective. Like I said before, I'm all in."

"So am I," she confirmed. "It looks like we've settled on our location and the basic approach. Now we need to decide who to let in on this surprise party we're planning?"

"Who do you suggest, Detective? Zhou asked as she went back into the kitchen. "Toby do you have any tea – I thought I would put the kettle on."

"Yes, Madame Zhou – let me get it for you. If you'd fix me a cup as well I'd appreciate it. I never get tea to turn out as good as you do."

As he went to help Zhou Li, Reightman thought over her question. "I'll need to get the Chief's approval, even though technically I have the authority to proceed on my own. This is too risky not to bounce it off of him."

"Aren't you afraid he will vacillate and delay on approving the decision, Detective? I must say, I've not been pleased with the kind of man Chief Kelly has turned into."

Reightman was not pleased by the Chief's recent behavior either, but decided not to comment. "I want to cover our asses on this, Madame Zhou. Regardless of what anyone of us thinks of Chief Kelly these days, he was a good detective in his day. He may be able to help us find and plug any holes in the plan."

"As you say, Detective, you have the authority to decide these things," Zhou agreed, without agreeing at all. "Who else do you feel should be brought in on our operation?"

"The city attorney and someone from the DA's office. Jessica Lautner would be my choice."

"I agree Ms. Lautner should be included, and Hollingfield has some promise if he would take the chip of his shoulder and remove the rigid object from his posterior."

Toby laughed out loud at Zhou's turn of phrase. "I don't think you considered your audience when you made that last comment, Madame Zhou." Reightman had never seen anyone tease the old lady before, and was curious to see how she'd react.

"Just because the thought of something rigid up the posterior sounds appealing to some members of our group, it doesn't follow that Mr. Hollingfield would," Zhou replied tartly, although Reightman thought she could detect a hint of amusement in her elderly voice.

Her comment sent Toby over the edge, and as he laughed delightedly, Reightman noticed Mitchell was struggling to hide his own grin. "Let the hilarity ensue," she said, quickly redirecting the conversation before it got totally out of control. "I think I should also assign a detail to be in the area, close to Mitchell's place. And after the first meetings, I think I have to insist any second meetings take place at the spa after regular business hours."

Zhou occupied herself with pouring the hot water over the hand-assembled bags of tea, and Reightman could smell the familiar fragrance of jasmine wafting from the kitchen. "Did you make enough for one more cup?" she asked hopefully.

"Yes, Detective – I anticipated you might enjoy one."

"Thank you, Madame Zhou." Reightman went over her mental list. "Assuming all systems are go, I think we need to talk about the wording for the ad, Toby."

"Yeah – I guess we better." Toby handed Reightman her still brewing mug of tea, and went into one of the back rooms. A moment later he returned with a pad of paper. He laid it on the table and went back into the kitchen and dug around in one of the drawers - hoping to locate a pen or pencil. He finally found what he was looking for, and trudged back to the table. He sat down the chair and looked down at the paper.

After a minute had passed in which he'd not written a single word, Reightman asked, "What's wrong Toby?"

Toby looked up from the paper and gave them all a shaky smile. "As soon as I write this down, it'll be real." He looked and sounded as if he was just now realizing exactly what he was going to have to do in order to carry through with his plan.

"You don't have to do this, Toby," Zhou said gently as she took her seat, cupping her warm mug with both hands. "Nothing has been set into motion yet, and we would all understand if you couldn't go through with this. Many of us would be relieved."

Toby closed his eyes and took a deep, steadying breath. He shook his head to banish his doubts and began to write. When he finished, he laid down his pen and pushed the pad into the center of the table.

One by one, they all took turns reading his words:

> "Looking for relief from stress and worry? I offer FULL service body work for discriminating individuals who know what they're looking for. Reasonable rates. Please provide body picture – or face picture if comfortable. No replies without photo. In calls only."

Reightman cleared her throat. "I think it looks pretty good." Zhou agreed, but Mitchell frowned as he looked over what Toby had written. "I think it could use a little more work." He reached over and took up the pen to create his own version. When he finished, he pushed the pad of paper into the middle of the table for their review.

Reightman felt her cheeks flush slightly as she read the words on the page:

> "Hot hung and full of cum young masseur offering personal relief to di$$ciminating professionals. I'll relieve ALL your stress and work your body from head to toe while taking care of everything in between. Some think I'm expen$$ive – but trust me – you'll never forget our $e$$ion together. Show me what you've got – full body pic required before scheduling. Complete discretion and centrally located private location. Respond now - just a few full$service appointments available. You'll love what we do together."

Zhou Li read the proposed ad, and then took off her glasses and cleaned the lenses with the tail of her shirt. She placed them back on her tiny face, and indicated the paper in the middle of the table. "I think we have a winner." She took a delicate sip of her tea. "Officer Mitchell, you are a man of hidden talents."

"We'll need a picture of me to post along with the ad," Toby said as he re-read the words on the paper. "I'll need to show them the goods." Everyone tried not to look his way as they realized how far he was willing to put himself out there. "I can probably take a selfie to use," he added.

Mitchell gave him a cheeky grin. "I don't think you need to worry about that. After all, I'm a pretty good photographer."

Reightman pretended she hadn't heard the implied offer. "Is it a go then?" she asked as she stood from the table. When all had agreed it was, she cautioned, "Don't post this until I've briefed the rest of the people who need to know. I will try to give the green light by noon tomorrow." Toby agreed with her directive, and she turned to Mitchell. "I'll be in touch tomorrow to arrange the wiring of your place. I think I'll bring Tom Anderson in the loop – he likes special projects like this."

"Sounds good, ma'am."

"Detective Reightman, do you mind walking me down to my apartment? I hate to ask, but since it is long past dark, I am somewhat worried about navigating the stairs."

"I'd be happy to, Madame Zhou. I was planning to take my time going down anyway so I don't stress the knee."

Soon the two women said their farewells, and Toby was cleaning up the mugs and glasses. Mitchell went about turning off the lights and lamps in the front rooms and checking that the front door was locked. Toby heard him open the French doors and step out onto the terrace. *"He's probably checking the perimeter – again."* He dried his hands on a towel and folded it over the edge of the sink, and turned off the kitchen light. He rounded the corner of the counter and walked to the door to check what Mitchell was doing. He stopped in the doorway.

Mitchell was standing in the silvery moonlight, as they'd stood together on the terrace the night before. He was looking out over the city.

"Mitchell, what are you doing out here?"

"Thinking. I thought I might try it while I wasn't wearing any clothes. After all you introduced me to the concept last night. I think I like it." Mitchell grinned over his shoulder and then turn back to look out over the city. He rolled his shoulders, causing the muscles in his back to flex.

"Mitchell, it's late and I think…"

Mitchell looked back at the man standing in the darkened doorway. "Toby, come on. Just take off your clothes and join me. We have to take the photo you need in a few minutes, so you're going to have to get undressed anyway."

Toby didn't move from the door and finally, Mitchell said, "Just humor me. I have some things to say, and for some reason. I think this is the best way for me to say them."

"Mitchell, you've really taken to this new tradition," Toby joked, hoping to relieve some of the gravity in Mitchell's voice. He stripped down, letting the clothes fall as he removed them. He walked out onto the terrace to stand next to Mitchell. They stood side by side, without saying a word, just looking out over the lights gently illuminating the downtown district.

After they had been there for a while, Mitchell reached over and pulled Toby to his side, with his arm draped over Toby's shoulders and began to speak. "I have very strong feelings for you, Toby. I don't know for sure how I'd categorize how I feel, but maybe 'love' will do for now." Mitchell turned his head to view Toby's profile. He studied it for a minute, memorizing the features. Then he tilted back his head, looking up at the moon shining overhead. "You know I'm worried about this plan – we all are. But I know you need to see it through." Mitchell paused as he collected his thoughts. "I'm concerned about what this will do to you. Not the physical danger – I'll make sure you're safe and so will Detective Reightman." Mitchell laughed as he looked at the moon. "It feels *really* weird to say her name while I'm naked."

"Yeah, I guess it kind of does."

"Toby, don't let this hurt or damage you – who you are inside, I mean. Come out of this whole. Protect yourself and build whatever walls and defenses you need to do that. Whatever happens, I want you to know I think you're doing the right thing, and I'll be by your side every step of the way."

"Thanks," Toby responded after he had swallowed the lump in his throat. "That means a lot to me."

"Toby, will you let me do something?"

"What, Mitchell?"

Mitchell took a while to answer, continuing to gaze up at the moon. "Will you…let me kiss you?"

Toby felt his heart skip a beat. "What about your silver daddy?"

"He's not here," Mitchell said simply. When Toby gently punched his arm, Mitchell gave an apologetic laugh. "That probably didn't sound the way I meant it."

Mitchell turned until he was almost facing the man next to him. "What I meant to say is you're special to me, Toby. This is probably the last time we can be together like this for a while – if ever. Tomorrow, I'm going to have to step back, and be a cop." He indicated them, standing closely without a single item of clothing. "I won't be able to think like a cop if I'm thinking too much like your friend – especially a friend who feels totally natural and comfortable when we're together like we are now. Before last night, I'd never stood naked outside before in my life, much less with another person, and now, here I am again." Mitchell looked back up to the sky and let out his breath. "The *cop* can help protect you, Toby. I don't know if the *friend* can do that nearly as well."

"So…you want to kiss me as a…friend?" Toby asked uncertainly.

Mitchell considered the question as he looked into Toby's eyes. "I don't know what I want, exactly. I just know I want to kiss you – tonight – here – while there's nothing at all between us. Not my job, not the things that we're afraid might happen, and not what happens after this is done. Just here and now, for this minute we're together – I want to kiss you …and have you kiss me in return."

Toby reached out and gently traced the line of Mitchell's brow, trailing his hand gently down the cheekbones and jawline. "*I wonder what he'll taste like?*" he wondered as his fingers brushed Mitchell's lips. "Yes." He pulled Mitchell in towards him.

Mitchell placed one hand on his shoulder, and another gently on his waist, as he leaned in. Their mouths met briefly, and Toby pulled away. Mitchell studied his face and then pulled Toby close again, bringing their lips together tightly. This time, their kiss lasted longer as they explored each other, teasing with lips and tongues. Toby felt his body react, and could feel Mitchell swell against his thigh. They continued to kiss until Mitchell reluctantly pulled away. He took a deep breath and leaned his forehead against Toby's.

"What does this mean, Toby? I don't think I understand what this reaction I'm having to you means."

Toby stepped back until he could see all of him. His blue eyes moved from Mitchell's face and down to his strong chest and flat stomach, until it reached the proud, generous flesh reaching up from the nest of curly brown hair. He looked up into Mitchell's face again, catching his eyes with his own. "It means you've just given me something wonderful and special to remember, and it felt fantastic to both of us. Thank you, Mitchell." They held eye contact for a minute more, searching and wondering.

Toby knew he needed to break the mood before it overwhelmed him, and took them both down a path they'd regret. It would be wonderful for a while, but that path, Toby realized in the moonlight, might never be right for either of them. He knew they'd be friends forever, but maybe never lovers – certainly not here and now on this night when there was so much stretching out before them. Toby understood what they'd just shared was beautiful, but also tempting. It needed to end before turning into something neither of them was ready for, or able to handle. He reached down and gave his cock a playful little tap, setting it gently swinging. "It means *this* happy guy thinks you're a damned fine kisser, but knows he won't be getting more than that." He gave a devilish grin as he reached out and gave Mitchell's cock a little tug and squeeze. "And it means your silver daddy is a damned fool if he lets *this* get away from him."

Mitchell realized what Toby was doing, and even knew he was right to do so. He allowed himself a moment of regret for what might have been, and then returned Toby's grin with one equally as devilish. "I think you are *more* than camera ready, Mr. Bailey." He cupped Toby's cock in his hand as if checking its heft. "I always knew I'd make a good fluffer – now I have proof!" Toby danced back from Mitchell's hand, laughing at the comment.

"We'd better head inside and get those pictures taken while everything's at its best advantage and the produce looks ripe and succulent."

"Yeah — I'll take your pic and then you can take a couple of me." Mitchell looked down at himself and grinned. "This might just tempt my silver-haired gentleman into sampling my wares."

Later, after much laughter and a lot of horseplay, they agreed on which photo to post. Toby had captured one especially playfully erotic shot of Mitchell at his very best. They picked up their discarded clothes and put them away. Toby pulled on his sleeping shorts and Mitchell pulled on his briefs before crawling into bed. After reading a while, Toby lay down on his side to watch Mitchell as he slept.

"Thanks for the kiss, Mitchell," he said quietly to the sleeping man. Toby adjusted his pillow and very gently touched his fingers to the man's lips. *"You tasted like clean, warm rain on a September night,"* he thought as he closed his eyes. *"Someone is going to be a very lucky man one day."*

CHAPTER SEVEN

BY NOON ON Thursday, Reightman had let all the people on her list know what they were planning.

Her meeting with Chief Kelly was tense, to say the least. They were both struggling with the situation between them, and with Reightman's new, temporary authority. Reightman was still resentful of how he'd tried to damage her credibility, although she still didn't understand his motivations. She wasn't sure he understood them either, and she was certain he'd never offer more than the very brief and grudging apology he'd made the day after the events in the big conference room. Regardless of all that, he listened to her explain the plan and agreed it was worth a shot.

"Don't let things go south on you if you can help it, Detective," he said when she wrapped up. "There's a lot of room for error here, especially if you flush someone out from under their cover." He leaned back in his creaking chair. "If there's more than one person involved in this, it could get real bad."

"Do you think there is more than one person involved?"

Kelly tightened his lips and chewed on the inside of his cheek, while he thought it over. "Maybe," he reluctantly answered. "The thing that bothers me is that if the murders are somehow connected, as you suggest – and I'm still not sure they are connected – then it's damned odd the killings were handled so differently."

"You mean the first murder was done with a knife, the second made to look like a suicide and the final..."she broke off at the thought of that final murder.

"And the third and final was a drive-by hit," the Chief finished for her, his eyes hard and flinty. He leaned forward in his chair. "These three different killings which – if they were done by the same son-of-a- bitch – tell us something about the person who did them."

"They don't fit a normal profile," she said as she realized where he was headed. "And whoever did them was very creative."

"You're abso-fuckin'-lutely correct, Detective," he said sarcastically, as if she were a child who couldn't manage to tie her own shoes. "But there's one more thing about these murders you need to consider." Kelly waited for her to make the connection. "Think, Reightman!" he barked at her. "What the hell else have you learned from the scenes where the bodies were found?"

"The killer knew what we would be looking for, and took great pains to cover his tracks," she answered slowly.

"And how might he – or she – have known how to do that?"

"They've killed before or… they've had some training. The same kind of training we've had."

"Or both," Kelly said as he leaned back again. "They may be trained *and* they may have killed before. Not one or the other." He sighed and folded his hands on his stomach. "I hate to think it might be a cop, but we all know how many tentacles this seems to have – if you are right about your theories."

"Do you think I'm right, Chief?"

"Hell if I know, Reightman." He growled. "You have a *possible* motive for some powerful folks to want Guzman dead. You have a weapon for the Guzman murder but haven't tied it to anyone yet. Lieberman's death is…" Kelly spread his hands and then dropped them back into his lap, "something else, altogether. Maybe Lieberman *did* kill himself because of guilt and remorse over killing Guzman. He had to be half crazy – the way he cut off a piece of the man's dick." The Chief scratched his head as he thought about it. "It may be someone did kill Lieberman and make it look like a suicide because Lieberman knew too much or was involved somehow." He looked ruefully her way and added, "I hate to admit it, but after turning it over in my mind a few times, I can't see how that fat fuck could've killed Guzman and gotten away without leaving something behind."

"And Sam?" Reightman asked the Chief.

"Yes, and Sam. One of four things happened there, Reightman. The first scenario is Jackson was hit as he was trying to shield Bailey. The second scenario is Jackson knew something the killer didn't want him to keep on knowing and Jackson was the actual target all along. The third – Jackson was in someone's way. In the way of what, I don't know. And the fourth is that Jackson was somehow involved himself and was inconvenient to keep around."

"Sam Jackson would have never been involved in any of this, and you know it!"

"No, Reightman, I don't. I *believe* he'd never be involved. But, I don't *know* it." After a minute, he leaned back again. "About our conversation concerning Detective Jones and his assignment – I'll accept your recommendation, provisionally, and somewhat against my own inclination."

Reightman bristled at his tone. "Don't you trust my judgment, Chief?" she asked pointedly.

"Here are my provisions," Kelly continued, ignoring her question and the attitude behind it. "He proves himself capable of doing the job to my satisfaction. This is a step up for him and he needs to learn the ropes." Reightman nodded her agreement. "The second provision is after a six-month period, you still think he's the right choice to be your partner. There may be a million reasons why you may decide he is, or isn't. But give it six months, and then decide. I was inclined to say no because I think it is too soon after Jackson's death for you to make this decision."

"I understand, sir."

He stood from the chair and said, "Then I think we are through here, Reightman. I appreciate the briefing."

"Yes, sir. You've given me some food for thought."

He stopped her as she reached to open the door. "Would you send Nancy in on your way out?"

"Hey, Nancy, the Chief wants to see you," she told the admin as she exited Kelly's office.

"He better have finished up the paperwork I'm waiting on," Nancy said with a touch of menace. She rose from her desk and picked up another full file folder. "What he doesn't know, is I've got more for him."

"He's going to love that," Reightman turned to leave, but realized she had a question. "Nancy, did you get the nameplate ordered for Detective Jones?"

"Sorry, Melba – I forgot to update you. It's backordered. It should be in Tuesday or Wednesday. If you *really* need it earlier I could try to order one from somewhere else, but the city has a contract with this supplier and I'd have to get approval for an exception."

"No, there's no need to do that. There really isn't any hurry."

"Okay, Melba. I promise to call when it gets here." Nancy scurried in through the Chief's door and closed it behind her.

When Reightman arrived back at her desk, Jones was unwrapping a pulled pork sandwich.

"Looks good," she said as she took a seat and pulled out her phone. She started to dial Toby, but set the phone back down. "I just got through talking with the Chief," she said, watching him slather coleslaw unto his sandwich. "How can you eat that on your sandwich, Jones? Only barbarians do that."

He shrugged as he put the bun back on top. "Have you ever tried it?" He took a big, manly bite and closed his eyes in appreciation. "Umm, umm good," he hummed around the sandwich.

"No, I haven't tried it," Reightman admitted. "And after seeing you in action, I don't think I'll ever want to. It's just…disgusting…"

"No one who's seen me in action has *ever* used the word disgusting to describe my performance." He leered at her suggestively from across the desk and took another bite.

"At least use your napkin! You have some kind of white juice caught on the corner of your mouth. It's gross!"

"Sometimes things get messy when you're doing them right." He poked out his tongue and licked the white coleslaw ooze from his lips.

She threw a pencil at him and he ducked. "Hey – that's not fair!" Jones protested with a laugh as he scooted his chair back into a safer range. "You can't attack me when I don't have a way to defend myself."

"One of these days you'll learn that I don't play fair – I play to win."

He laughed again and took another bite, this time wiping his mouth primly. "So, how was your meeting with the Chief," he fished.

"It was fine," she said, deciding to make him work for an answer. "I just gave him an update on all of the work the team's been doing."

"Anything else?" he asked innocently, as he took another bite.

"Yes…a few things. We talked about his golf game and about the new flower beds he put in for his aunt," Reightman fabricated. "I think next weekend he's going to help her put in some mums and other fall flowering plants." She smiled brightly. "Oh yes, there was one more, small item…."

"And what was that?" he asked with a perfect air of non-concern.

"He wanted to talk about the recommendation…" she smiled again, "…I gave him – about a carpet cleaning service I used. He thought his Berber rug was looking a little dingy." She pursed her lips and the nodded. "I think that was about it. Why do you ask?"

"Reightman, I'm going to flick coleslaw all over you in just about ten seconds. You know perfectly well what I'm trying to find out. Did he go for it? Will I be assigned as your partner?"

"Oh! I totally forgot to bring it up with him!"

Jones opened his sandwich and scooped up a big glob of slaw with his finger. He bent the finger back like a catapult and waited. "One…Two…Three…" he counted.

"Jones – don't you dare fling that slaw at me!"

"Five…Six…Seven…Eight…"

"Alright! Alright, already!" His finger slowly returned to its original position, although Jones didn't remove the slaw. "I did raise the idea and he agreed, but he wants the assignment to be provisional for about six months while you learn the ropes over here in Homicide."

Jones licked the slaw off his finger. "That's fair. I do have a lot to learn about procedure, and how we engage and assign other resources, and… a lot of stuff I don't have a clue about yet. Was there anything else that concerned him?"

Reightman didn't respond immediately, trying to think how to best frame the Chief's other provision. "Yes, there was. He wants me to be sure I really want you as my permanent partner. He thinks I might be rushing into things because of Jackson's death."

Jones folded up the white paper his pork and coleslaw lunch had been wrapped in and then stuffed it into the white carryout bag. "I think that sounds pretty fair, too. That'll give us time to figure out if we can work as well together as I hope we will." He started to toss the bag in the trash and Reightman stopped him.

"Don't do it! I don't want to be smelling old pork and slaw juice for the next two days. They only dump the trash around here twice a week, and the next day for that is Sunday. Take it to the breakroom and put it in the trash there – far away from my desk."

"Yes, ma'am! I hear and obey," he saluted her sharply. "I could use some of the sludge they call coffee anyway.

As soon as he walked away, Reightman picked up her phone and dialed Toby. After she told him they were all clear and to post the ad, they agreed that Tom Anderson would contact Mitchell directly about getting his place ready. She had just finished the call when she noticed Jones coming up from behind her.

"What's cookin'?" Jones plopped down in his chair and looked across the desk.

"Oh, nothing much. I was just checking in with Toby Bailey and giving him a short update."

"Hmmm…" Jones eyed her closely while playing with the toothpick hanging out of his mouth. She looked away and scrolled down her contact list.

"What?" she asked as she put the phone back down into her purse.

"Why do I get the impression you're not telling me everything about your call with Bailey?"

"Probably, because I'm not." He took the chewed toothpick out of his mouth and dropped it in the trash. "Look, Jones," she waited until he looked up at her. "There're a whole lot of balls in the air right now and I'm trying to keep them separate so they don't hit each other. There are very few – and I mean very few– people who have all the pieces. I'm going to keep it that way as long as possible."

"But, I'm your partner. How am I supposed to help if I don't know what's going on?"

"That's a more than fair question. I guess you can help by…just keeping you own balls spinning."

Jones grinned at her last comment. "That's almost too good of a line to resist – but I will." He opened his desk drawer and pulled out his keys.

"Where are you off to?" Reightman asked as he stood up and pushed his chair under the desk.

"I'm just going to spin my balls." He chuckled at the glare she shot him. "I've got a few things to follow-up on at a couple of the pawn shops and I thought I'd start before it gets too late. Is there something else you need for me to do? The pawn shops can wait."

"No, go on and follow-up on that. Maybe you'll get lucky."

"Now, I just can't resist that one – after all, it is Friday and what man doesn't want to get lucky to start the weekend?"

She groaned. "You're a menace, Detective Jones. Go on – get out of here."

He walked around the desk and then leaned over toward her. "Reightman, would you have told me what was going on with Bailey if I was Sam Jackson?"

She flinched at his words and looked up at him, hurt plain in her eyes.

"I'm sorry," he said as he saw her expression. "I shouldn't have said that."

"No, you shouldn't have," she agreed, rubbing her temples. "I get your point though."

Jones nodded. "I'll see you later. Call me if you need something."

After he'd gone, Reightman looked over at his desk. "*If you were Sam Jackson, I wouldn't have to tell you. You'd already know.*" Almost immediately, she felt guilty. "*That's not fair, Reightman. Jones can't help it he's new and hasn't learned to read your mind yet – and you are keeping him out of the loop.*" She wrestled with that, and then had another, more insightful thought. "*Most of all, your new, provisional partner can't help the fact he's not Sam.*"

Toby and Mitchell met Tom Anderson at Mitchell's place early that afternoon. Tom walked through the front of the house and then turned to Toby. "Where will you be doing whatever you're going to be doing?"

"I thought I'd set up in the guest bedroom. There's not much stuff in there and we can move most of it out if we need to."

Tom followed the two men to the back of the house and gave it a thorough inspection. "This is a pretty good choice – only one window and there's a big climbing rose covering almost half of it. Anyone who tries to come in through there would get pretty scraped up in the process." He looked over the assorted pieces of furniture in the room and then made a suggestion. "If I were you, I'd leave most of this stuff right where it is. It will look more authentic if you do – like you use it for other things when you're not pulling in tricks."

"I'm not pulling in tricks."

Tom Anderson looked at him sternly. "Look, Reightman has filled me in on what you're planning to do. Whether you want to admit it or not, you *are* pulling in tricks. The sooner you reconcile yourself to that, the better off you're going to be."

Toby's stomach gave a lurch as he realized Tom Anderson had a point. "I guess you're right, sir."

"Yes, I am, and stop with the 'sir' crap. It makes me feel like an old geezer, or like I should be wearing black leather motorcycle chaps and a pair of aviator glasses – and absolutely nothing else." Tom thought about those possibilities with a reflective smile on his face. "I wonder if my wife would like that." He shook himself out of his momentary fantasy and got back on track. "Call me either Tom, or Anderson – everyone else does."

"Okay, Anderson. You should call me Toby."

"See, that's so much better," Tom approved. "Now the other reason I'd leave the stuff positioned like it is now, is because it will help hide any wires. I'm going to use mostly wireless technology, but I want one wired mic for backup." He pulled out the small hutch desk and looked behind it. "Are you going to use a table or just the bed?"

Toby looked toward the full sized bed and tried not to think about why he might be using the bed. "I'm going to use a table. I brought a portable model, and it's out in the living room. I thought I'd set it up after you're done."

"Alright, I have an idea about that, too." He looked at his watch and frowned. "We need to get this show on the road. Why don't you two move the dresser and this desk out from the wall and I'll go get my stuff out of the van. Mitchell, do you mind if I drill into the walls? I'll try to keep it small."

"Sure, Anderson. But keep it to as few places as possible. I'll need to patch them when this is done. Otherwise, I'll never get my deposit back when I decide to move out of here."

Toby and Mitchell moved the furniture as requested, and soon Tom busy at work. "Where are you and Reightman going to be while Toby makes like a 'working' boy?"

"Detective Reightman thought she'd set up in the garage. I'm going to be in the next room over. Since the only bathroom is in the hall, there shouldn't be a reason for anyone to go in there and I'll be closer to Toby if there's trouble."

"That's good thinking, but you're going to have to get up in the attic and help feed the wire over to the garage. I don't do attics."

A couple of hours later, they were finished and the furniture was back into position. "Okay, let me test this out. I'm going to the room next door. You two talk normally, although try to vary the pitch and the volume level a few times." He gave Toby an amused grin. "Since I'm not going to be in on the action, go ahead and make some hot, moaning sounds. That way, I'll get a preview and won't feel left out." Toby blushed bright pink as Tom left the room.

"Okay, fellas – action!" Tom called from the next room.

Toby and Mitchell talked, modulating their voices through different volumes and ranges, stopping when Tom wasn't satisfied with the reception. He made a couple of adjustments to the equipment. "The wireless isn't picking up as well in the garage as well as it should. There must be some metal or something in the walls causing the interference," he explained. "Okay, let's try it again." A couple of more tries and they were done. "Toby, go get that massage table and I'll show you what I have up my sleeve for that baby."

Toby carried in the table and set it up. Tom dug around in his bag and pulled out a small electrical device. He adjusted the settings and applied some Velcro to the back and applied the coordinating portion of Velcro to the underside of the table, on the right side near the top. "This little beauty is a panic device – like they use in high-end stores. You push this button and it'll send a signal to Mitchell and Reightman to let them know something bad's going down. It won't make any sound in here, so no one will know you pushed it." He handed the device to Toby. "The big rectangular button in the middle is what you push. Usually, people wear these on their belts or on their waistband, but I guess under the circumstance, you won't have a belt or waistband to attach that critter too. So, stick it to the Velcro under the table and let's test it out. Try to get used to pushing the button from several different positions. Who knows where your arm might be?" He grinned and wiggled his eyebrows before walking out of the room.

Toby tested the panic button several times, trying to get used to reaching for it unobtrusively from several places around the table. Anderson came back into the room and verified it had worked. He looked around the room one more time and, as a second thought, pulled another panic button out of the bag and attached it to the mattress right under the headboard. "Just in case your party of two moves," he explained. Once again they tested it, and Tom declared he was satisfied. "I think I've done all I can here," he said as he packed the tools back into his bag. "As per Detective Reightman's instructions, I'll want to do the spa tomorrow, if possible. What time do you close on Saturdays?"

"The last appointment is at three o'clock, so you could start as early as four-thirty. Everyone should be long gone by then."

"Let's plan on me meeting you around five then. I'm going to bring Laurie so she can get some on the job experience."

"Thanks for your help, Anderson." Toby held out his hand to shake.

Tom took it and gave it a firm squeeze. "Be careful. If you have the slightest feeling your safety is compromised, press one of those buttons, okay?"

"Yes, I will."

After leaving Mitchell's place, they headed back to Toby's apartment for dinner. Mitchell firmly overruled any more tuna casserole or spaghetti dinners, so they ordered a couple of pizzas. After finishing off the food, Toby got out his laptop and sat it on the coffee table. He opened it and logged into the email account he had set up for just this purpose and waited for the mail server to download.

"Oh shit!"

Mitchell came out of the kitchen where he'd been putting away the leftovers. "Don't worry about it, Toby. Just because you haven't gotten a response yet doesn't mean anything. You just posted the ad early this afternoon."

"That's not the problem, Mitchell. The problem is, I have twenty-two responses. "

"Already?" Mitchell asked, astonished.

"Yeah – oh wait. Another one just came through. I now have twenty-three."

Mitchell came over to the sofa and looked at the emails waiting for a response. "Do you have the copies of the photos Detective Reightman gave you?"

"Yeah, I do." Toby went to the back room and come back carrying a folder. He placed it on the coffee table and took a seat back on the sofa in front of the computer.

Mitchell took a seat beside him and picked up the folder. "When you open the photos, I'll look through these to see if there's a match." Mitchell's voice was suddenly serious and professional. "Don't reply to any of them before we've been through them all. If there's a match, we need to call Detective Reightman before proceeding."

Toby leaned in toward the laptop and opened the first email from nastyboy42. "I can already tell he's not a match. There weren't any Asians in the group." He read the message and looked at the user name. "He certainly is a nasty boy! He says he's forty-two, but that was at least ten years ago. I think we can move on."

Toby worked through the emails as Mitchell checked the submitted photos against those in the file folder. Before they made it half way through, a small chiming sound singled another response had been received. Toby rolled his eyes as Mitchell checked for match and then they studied the final results.

"Out of twenty-four response we have two matches: Mr. Carlton Brookmeyer, whose father owns that big bank, and Officer Fred Lamont. Let's call Detective Reightman. I can already tell you she's not going to be happy about Lamont."

She wasn't. Toby couldn't remember any of the words she used as having come out of her mouth before, at least not in his hearing.

"I need to tell Chief Kelly about this, Toby, so don't respond to him yet. We'll probably need to get the City Attorney involved as well. I think you can go ahead and arrange something with Brookmeyer though."

As Reightman was speaking, another chime sounded.

"Hang on, Detective Reightman. I just got another one."

He clicked on the username righteousstud9 and opened the email.

"Is it a match?" she asked impatiently.

Mitchell handed him a photo from the file with the name of the individual written on it. "Yes," Toby answered.

"Who is it?" Reightman waited.

"Sutton Dameron."

"Are you positive, Toby?"

"Yes, and so is Mitchell."

Reightman was silent for a moment. "Toby, I need to let Hollingfield know about him, too. Don't respond to him either. I'm going to track down the Chief and the City Attorney and I'll try to call you back in an hour – make it an hour and a half."

After she ended the call, Toby handed the photo back to Mitchell and pulled up the email from Brookmeyer. He took a deep breath and placed his hands on the keys of the laptop.

"You can still step away from this, Toby. We'd all support you."

"Thanks, Mitchell, but I can't." Toby began to type. After a couple of exchanges, his first appointment was booked. "Well, that's done. We're scheduled for eight o'clock tomorrow night."

Mitchell got up from the sofa and went into the kitchen. Toby heard him open a beer. He didn't come back out for a long time.

Reightman called him back about an hour and twenty minutes later. By that time, he had received another four emails, but only one match. The match was Katherine McLarity, the Judge McLarity's granddaughter.

"Is *everyone* in this town looking to get laid tonight?" Reightman asked with sarcastically. While she ranted and raved, another email came through, also from Katherine McLarity. Toby opened the email and burst into laughter.

"What in the hell are you laughing about?" Her exasperated tone set him off again.

"I'm sorry about that, but I just got a second email from Ms. McLarity."

"What's so damn funny about that?"

"Well, she wrote to say she's sorry, and hopes she didn't inconvenience me, but she's changed her mind. She's decided she's going off men, for now, and is going to stick to women for a while. She's met a nice lady at her office, with whom she's going to try and form an attachment."

The phone was dead silent, but eventually Reightman started to chuckle and snort and then broke into peals of laughter. "You're right, that is funny! Her grandfather would have an absolute cow. I think he'd prefer knowing she was hiring men to service her needs, rather than switching to women."

"One thing I can say for Katherine McLarity – she sure has good manners and writes a nice note. I wonder if I'd have received a hand written thank you note after…you know."

"It wouldn't have surprised me if you had, Toby," Reightman replied, after getting a fresh set of giggles and snorts under control. "Listen, I finally tracked down both Kelly and Hollingfield. They said to proceed with both contacts. The Chief said to be extremely cautious with Lamont and not to set him off in any way. Kelly said that was really important. Did you contact Mr. Brookmeyer?"

"Yes. I'm supposed to meet him at eight o'clock tomorrow night."

There was a pause before Reightman spoke again. "We'll be ready, Toby, I promise." She gave him a moment to let her assurance sink in, before adding in a brisk, businesslike tone, "Reach out to both Lamont and Dameron. Try to arrange things so you meet one more tomorrow, and one on Sunday."

"Alright. I'll let you know when I have everything arranged. Do you want me to call you if we get another match tonight?"

"Why don't we check around eleven? Anything that comes in after that can wait until tomorrow. Does that sound okay?"

Toby agreed and sent responses to Lamont and to Dameron. By the time he talked with Reightman at eleven, he'd arranged to meet Lamont at eleven o'clock Saturday night and Dameron at seven o'clock Sunday evening. When their check-in was finished, Toby turned off his phone and closed the laptop.

"Are you okay, Toby? Mitchell asked about twenty minutes later.

"I guess I'll have to be." Toby rose from the sofa and stretched. "I could use a hug though."

When Mitchell didn't reply, Toby looked in his direction, perplexed at the lack of response "Mitchell?"

"I'm sorry, Toby, but, I told you I was stepping back."

"Yes, you did." Toby nodded in understanding. His friend was now just the cop. "I think I'll go shower."

Toby stood under the hot, almost scalding water, thinking about the three men he was going to try to entrap over the next two days. *"Did one of you who killed Geri? Or am I still waiting to hear from the person responsible?"* He leaned back into the spray, letting the water spill over his face and down his chest. When the water began to cool, he turned off the shower and pulled down a towel. He dried himself, and combed his hair. When he looked in the mirror, he didn't understand what he saw in his reflection, and wasn't sure he wanted to understand.

On Saturday, Toby tried to keep busy and did everything he could think of to keep his mind occupied. Much sooner than he'd hoped, the day was over. After everyone had left, Tom Anderson arrived, accompanied by Laurie. Toby showed them around the spa, and they conferred over where they might place the electronics. After some very grim but purposeful consideration, Toby decided the best place for him to meet with the potential murderer was in the room where Geri had been killed. There would be a fine sense of justice served if they were able to catch the murderer in the same room he'd committed the first, horrific act.

Right at seven o'clock, Mitchell indicated it was time for them to leave. Tom and Laurie weren't done with their work so Toby made arrangements to meet them back at the spa early Sunday afternoon. Mitchell escorted them out while Toby threw a few things he needed into a duffle bag. Toby turned off the lights and locked the front door, and then he and Mitchell walked to the car. Toby looked out the passenger side window as Mitchell drove, neither in the mood for conversation.

"I was worried you'd been delayed downtown," Reightman greeted them from her place at the small breakfast bar. She was nursing a cup of coffee and had a portable carafe sitting on the counter near her.

"No, nothing delayed us. I wanted to give Anderson and Laurie as much time as possible before having to leave. As it turns out, they have to come back tomorrow anyway." Toby took a few bottles of water from his duffle bag and placed them into the refrigerator, keeping one for himself. "You want a bottle of water, Mitchell?"

"No, but hand me one of the diet colas. I think I'm going to need the caffeine."

The three of them stayed in the kitchen another few minutes, although the conversation was stilted and each was occupied with their own thoughts. Reightman checked her watch and stood from the barstool. "I think it's time to get situated, Mitchell. I want to make sure all of the equipment is working, and it might be good to give Toby a few minutes alone before Brookmeyer arrives."

Mitchell agreed, and he and Reightman left the kitchen. Toby finished his water and grabbed a couple more from the fridge before picking up the duffle bag and going back to the room where he'd set up. He took off his shoes and socks and changed into a pair of athletic shorts and a sleeveless t-shirt, leaving his feet bare. He took a small dopp kit out of the duffle and went into the bathroom and brushed his teeth. Then he splashed water on his face. Toby went back into the guest bedroom and took a couple of towels from his bag and put them on the dresser. He arranged the bottles of oil and lotion next to them and them adjusted the table position so that everything was in arms reach. He threw a sheet on the table, smoothing out the creases. He didn't bother adding a top sheet, realizing tonight's sessions probably wouldn't call for the usual professional draping.

He removed the copy of the photo he would need for the first session and folded it in half, placing it on the small desk, held down by the stapler. Finally, he checked the position of the panic button underneath the table and the one hidden at the head of the bed. When he was finished with everything he could think to do, he sat on the edge of the table and waited.

After what seemed like a long time, he checked the time. "Nine minutes after eight." He quickly scanned his phone for missed messages, and just as he was done, the front doorbell rang. Toby froze, immobile for a moment, until the doorbell rang again. He forced himself to walk out of the bedroom and into the hall.

Mitchell stood in the doorway to the other bedroom. "I'll be right here," he assured him, before stepping back and gently shutting the door.

Toby walked to the front door, and after taking a deep breath, he opened it.

"Hi," the man on the doorstep said shyly. "I hope this is the right place. Are you, Bailey?"

It took Toby a second to remember he'd used his last name in the ad. "Yeah, I am." He gave the man a small smile. "And if you're Carlton, you're in the right place. Come on in." Toby stepped back and held the door as the man stepped into the living room.

Carlton Brookmeyer stood slightly over six feet tall, appeared to be in his mid to late thirties and had a thin, willowy built. Toby noticed his skin was bright red, as if he'd been out in the sun a lot. He held his hands tightly at his side, and Toby noticed he seemed apprehensive. "Is something wrong, Carlton?"

The man darted his gaze back to Toby. "No, nothing's wrong. I'm just a little nervous, I guess."

"I'll have to see how I can help you relax then. That's why you're here, right?" Toby gave the man what he hoped was a sexy smile. Apparently it worked, because Carlton relaxed.

"Yes," Carlton said, attempting a sexy smile of his own, while giving Toby a slow appraisal. Carlton's smile grew slightly larger, liking what he saw.

"Follow me then, Carlton. I'm set up in the guest bedroom." Toby turned to lead the way, looking back over his shoulder to make sure that Carlton was following. "Coming?"

Carlton gave what Toby thought was supposed to be a lascivious smirk. "Not yet, but I hope to be soon."

Toby felt his smile freeze, but quickly arranged his features into a more normal expression. "Let's head on back, and we can get started."

Once in the room, Carlton seemed surprised at the set-up. "You're going to use a real table? The guy I was with…I mean, that I went to before, just used the bed."

Toby turned toward the dresser and busied himself rearranging the towels so Carlton wouldn't see the expression on his face. "*He means Geri.*" Toby turned and made himself smile. "I thought we'd start on the table, Carlton. I can explore your body more fully when you are stretched out under me. Is that okay?"

Toby saw the man's Adam's apple move as Carlton swallowed and looked at the table, eager to begin. "That sounds fun." He looked back up at Toby, unsure of about what was supposed to happen next. "I almost forgot," he said reaching into his front pocket. "You're probably waiting on this." He pulled out a roll of bills and handed it to Toby. "It's all there, just like we agreed. You can count it if you want."

Toby took the small roll of bills from him. "I trust you, Carlton – there's no need to count it. Now, why don't you get undressed? Do you want me to use oil, or lotion?"

"Lotion, I guess…." Toby could hear him removing his clothing so he grabbed a bottle of lotion from the dresser, picked up a towel and turned back to Carlton who now stood completely naked a few feet from the table. His frame was loosely muscled, with a little extra softness around his waist and hips. There was a smattering of dark hair on his thin chest which continued down to his groin. His entire body was red, just like his face. Toby tried to think of something to say to put the man at ease. "You look like you have been getting some sun."

"I go to the tanning salon several times a week. I don't tan easily, but I like a little color on my skin. I think it makes me look better."

Toby didn't comment, thinking that Carlton would look much better if he'd refrain from tanning beds entirely. "This lotion should feel good on your skin." Toby walked to the table, continuing his perusal and noting the somewhat large identifying birthmark which appeared prominently in the photos.

Carlton noticed where he was looking. "I know, it's ugly, isn't it? I've been thinking of having it removed."

"It's not ugly at all." Toby assured him. "It makes you unique." Carlton Junior was already standing at attention. "*He's willowy all over,*" Toby thought distractedly, before sternly reminding himself what was at stake. He quickly looked away from the eager appendage, and focused on the man's red face. "You're all tense and …stiff, so why don't you get up on the table and we'll get started. Face down to start." Carlton positioned himself on top and then rolled over awkwardly and stretched himself out on its length.

Toby walked toward the table with the bottle of lotion in his hand. "Is the room warm enough, Carlton?"

"Yes, its fine. I bet it'll get hot in here before too long!"

Toby was at a loss for a witty rejoinder, so made few adjustments to the man's position and then poured a little of the lotion into the palm of his hand. He placed the bottle between Carlton's slightly spread legs, and rubbed his palms together to warm the liquid. He leaned slightly forward and placed his hands on Carlton's lower back, right above the buttocks. The man jerked slightly and Toby firmed his hands. "Just relax. Carlton." He worked his way up the spine until he was in the middle of the shoulders.

"Bailey?" the man on the table asked. "Aren't you going to take off your clothes?"

Toby forced his hands to keep moving, trying to get past the re-vulsion running through his body. "Yeah, I just wanted to get you good and slick first." He stepped away and closed his eyes briefly, overwhelmed by the situation. He took a few steading breaths and quickly removed his t-shirt and rolled it up before tossing it on the bed. Then he unbuttoned his shorts. At the sound of the zipper being pulled down, Carlton lifted his head and turned to watch while Toby pulled them down and stepped out of them. "You can leave the jock-strap on. It's sexy."

"Thanks." Toby walked back to the table and added more lotion to his hands. He massaged the man's shoulders and back and then each of the arms. He worked his way down the sides and then spent a considerable about of time on Carlton's glutes and thighs. As he worked his way up the man's inner thigh, Carlton started to tremble and spread his legs slightly wider. As he began to moan softly, Toby suddenly realized what was happening. *"Oh shit! I hope I can make this short and sweet."* Toby increased his pressure slightly and nudged the man's legs apart. He climbed up on the table and positioned himself between the man's legs and continued rubbing the now lifted but-tocks, parting the cheeks as he did. He moved his hands back to the thighs and stroked the inner flesh, moving his finger upward until he brushed the ball sack. The volume of Carlton's moans increased while he rubbed himself against the sheet. Toby blocked everything out of his mind until the man arched his back, and with a few frantic thrusts, came. Loudly. *"Well, Mitchell and Reightman certainly heard that,"* he thought in dismay.

Toby quickly removed himself from the table and Carlton turned over, evidence of his relief apparent. "I'm sorry I finished so fast, Bailey, but your hands felt really good and I kept imaging you behind me in that jockstrap. I couldn't help myself."

"That's okay. The main thing is you enjoyed it, Carlton. Now let me clean you up, and I'll finish with a real massage. For some reason, I don't think you've ever had one before." Twenty-five minutes later, Toby finished. "How was that?" he asked.

"It was nice," Carlton decided. "I liked it – just not as much as the first part. Next time, I think I'd like you to work the front first, without the jockstrap."

"*I hope there isn't a next time!*" Toby hoped fervently as he pulled a towel from the stack on the dresser. "Yeah, that'd be great." Toby handed Carlton the fresh towel. "We're done, so you can wipe yourself off and get dressed now."

Toby reached down and picked his discarded shorts from the floor and pulled them on. Then he put on his t-shirt and walked to the desk. "*Now, we can net the fish.*" He pulled the photocopy out from beneath the stapler and walked to the man who was sitting on the edge of the bed, pulling on his socks. "I have something for you." Toby handed Carlton the folded paper.

Carlton unfolded it and looked at the picture. "That's me," He said, puzzled. "Where'd you get this?"

"A friend left it for me, Carlton. Someone I think you knew, intimately." Carlton continued to look at him with a confused and unknowing face, so Toby clarified, "The other masseur you used to get together with for some fun."

Carlton's face cleared as he realized who Toby was talking about. "Oh! You mean, Jerry." He looked back down at the photo. "Yeah, I recognize him now that you mention it. You can't really see much of his face but I'd recognize his dick anywhere. What am I supposed to do with this?"

"I thought we could come to the same arrangement you had with him."

Carlton frowned in concentration, trying to remember what deal he'd made with Geri. "You want free checking and automatic overdraft protection on a business account? That's no problem – just come on down to the bank and I'll set it up. I do that for a lot of people."

"I think your arrangement with him included a lot more than that. You know – to keep this all private."

Carlton's forehead creased again. "I'm not sure what you mean. I booked with Jerry a lot, sometimes several times a week, and he'd let me pay in advance for several sessions at a time. Sometimes that amounted to a lot of cash." Carlton shrugged and slipped on his shoes. "You want to make the same arrangement? I don't have that much cash with me, but I can bring it next time."

"Aren't you worried I might show this photo, and the others he left me, to someone?" Now Toby was the one confused.

Carlton stood from the bed and tucked in his shirt. "No, not really. My family knows I'm gay, and there are worse – much worse – photos of me already out on the internet. There are a couple of really hot videos, too." He laid the used towel back on the table. "Hey, Bailey, I hope you weren't thinking you could blackmail me or anything. That would be dumb, because there's nothing to blackmail me with – certainly not *that* photo. Besides, I think it's illegal to blackmail someone." Toby shook his head, Carlton smiled approvingly. "Good. Now come on down to the bank any afternoon this week and I'll get you set up with an account. I'll email to set up some more appointments, too. Why don't I pay you for about six in advance?"

"Sure," Toby agreed, wondering exactly what had happened. "That'd be great, Carlton." He held open the door to let the man out of the room and Carlton spotted the bottles of water.

"Can I take one of these? I'm really thirsty."

"Sure." Toby felt slightly dazed as he offered him one of the bottles. "It's important to hydrate after a massage." He escorted Carlton Brookmeyer to the front door, and decided to give him some advice. "Carlton, I think it would be better to lay off the tanning beds. They're really bad for you, and you could end up with some really awful skin damage. Plus, I think you'll actually look better without your skin being so red."

"You may be right, Bailey. Thanks for the advice, and the hot session!" With a satisfied, contented smile, he walked out the door and Toby and watched him drive away.

Mitchell was already in the back room when he got there, and Detective Reightman joined him a few seconds later. Toby placed the used towels in the middle of the table and started rolling the sheet over them.

"Well, that was anticlimactic," Reightman said.

"Not for Brookmeyer!"

Reightman shot Mitchell an annoyed glance, feeling her face flush at his words. "Well, speaking of that – which I would just as soon we not–"she said irritably as she handed Toby the white plastic garbage bag she'd brought into the room with her, "bag those up in this. If we need a DNA sample, I guess we've got one." After Toby had tied the bag shut, she took a black marker and wrote Brookmeyer's full name, and the date and time, on the bag. "Based on the last part of your conversation, I think we can move Mr. Brookmeyer to the bottom of our suspect list, but I'd rather keep this until we're sure. I'll get it to Tom tomorrow and he can take the samples he needs."

"Have him burn it all when he's done," Toby said, disillusioned and frustrated by his experience. "I don't think I'll want those towels anymore."

Reightman nodded, understanding his disappointment, and carried the bag out of the room.

"Are you all right?" Mitchell asked, handing him a bottle of hand sanitizer.

"I think so. It was no worse than I'd expected. In fact, it was better. I didn't have to do as much to…" he let the words trail off as he finished with the hand cleaner and handed the bottle back to Mitchell.

Mitchell put the bottle back down on the dresser. "Brookmeyer did…uh…finish kind of quickly." When Toby didn't reply Mitchell added seriously, "Toby, they probably won't all be that easy."

"I know. I just hope this isn't all for nothing." Toby checked the phone for the current time. "I have about an hour and a half before the next one shows up. Do you mind if I use your shower?"

"No, help yourself. I think you'll be able to find anything you need in there. You want me to find some food or something?"

Toby picked up his t-shirt from the bed and started to the door. "No, I'm not really hungry. I'll get some more water when I'm done showering."

Mitchell heard the bathroom door close and then the sound of water being turned on.

"How is he?" Reightman asked as he entered the kitchen.

"I'm not sure. He said it wasn't as bad as he expected, but I can tell he's really bothered by the whole thing. He's taking a shower now." Mitchell started pulling out bread and a bag of chips. He rummaged around in the refrigerator for a while. "You want a sandwich?" he asked, over his shoulder. "I think I have some lunchmeat and a few slices of cheese that are still good."

"Sure, might as well." A few minutes later he placed a small plate with the assembled sandwich in front of her. "Are you going to make one for Toby?"

"He said he wasn't hungry."

"Make him one anyway. He needs to eat something or he is going to be a nervous wreck."

"More of one than I am already, you mean?" Toby asked as he walked into the kitchen drying his hair with a towel.

"Yes, that's exactly what I meant. You need to eat."

Toby didn't argue with her and soon had his own sandwich. Mitchell and Reightman watched him eat as he worked his way slowly through his meal. "You were right," he acknowledged when he finished. "I do feel a little better."

"I told you so." Reightman watched as he took his plate to the sink and then grabbed a bottle of water from the fridge. "Toby, the next one may be challenging. Lamont is a mean son of a bitch from all accounts, and the Chief said to be really careful." She waited until she knew she had his full attention, and continued, "I know it may be difficult, but do what he says and remember where the panic buttons are in the room. Keep their location in mind the whole time you're with him."

"You think he'll try and hurt me?"

"I don't know what to expect. Toby, but I want you to be cautious. Mitchell and I'll be listening, and if you press the button, we'll be there as quickly as we can."

Toby screwed the cap back down on his water and grabbed a couple of additional bottles. "I think I'll go get the room ready."

After he had gone, Mitchell put his own plate in the sink. "Do you really think things could get bad, Detective?"

"For Kelly to warn me about another cop is a huge red flag. I want us all to be ready for the worst, Mitchell." She took her own plate to the sink and rinsed her hands. "I wish Toby was better able to defend himself."

"If he was cornered I think he'd put up a pretty good fight. He's in great shape and he's a lot stronger than he looks."

"Yes, but he hasn't been trained to defend himself and Lamont, on the other hand, has years of experience." She dried her hands and folded her arms across her chest. "I wish he was trained with a firearm as well."

"You do think this *could* get really out of control." Mitchell felt a tingle of fear inch up his spine.

"What I think is if things don't get bad tonight, they might some other night."

Mitchell didn't like what he was hearing. "I can't do anything about it now. But tomorrow, I'll take him out to the range and start teaching him what he needs to know."

"I should have thought of that myself. If he seems to be getting the hang of it, stop at one of the sporting goods stores and have him pick out a weapon. This is the only time I can think of when I'm glad there's not a waiting period in this state. Under the circumstances, it's better to be safe and have one, than not have one if he needs it."

"I don't know if he'll agree to buy a gun, Detective Reightman."

"Oh, he'll agree, or will by the time I'm through with him." He shivered at what he heard in her voice. "I'm heading out to the garage to get myself situated. You better do the same. Thanks for the sandwich, Mitchell."

He walked back to the bedroom and looked through the door to the guest room. Toby was sitting on the table with his legs hanging off the side. "I heard you in the kitchen. I heard you and Detective Reightman talking and you don't have to worry about me causing a big scene about getting a gun or learning to shoot. I've never wanted one, but I do need to learn to defend myself. Just teach me the very best you can." Before Mitchell could respond to Toby's comment, the doorbell rang. With one worried looked at Toby, Mitchell hurried into the next bedroom.

CHAPTER EIGHT

OFFICER FRED LAMONT, long-term member of the City Police's vice squad, stood just about five foot ten inches tall. He was powerfully built, although there was a thin layer of fat covering his body. As Toby ushered him through the door, he noticed Lamont's leering mouth and the hard dark eyes undressing him where he stood. "Aren't you just the sweetest thing," Lamont drawled. "I bet you're even sweeter without all those clothes. Where are we headed, Bailey? I've been looking forward to this all day, and I'm ready to get started."

"I have everything set up in the back Mr...?"

"Just call me Sir," Lamont suggested with a hint of command. "I'd like that. It won't take you long to get into the habit – I promise." His face hardened when Toby didn't immediately respond as instructed.

Reightman's warning lashed through his mind and Toby felt a thin layer of sweat break out beneath his shirt. "Yes, Sir." Toby could feel the hair on the back of his neck rise at a cruel satisfied expression settled in to place on Lamont's face. "If you'll just follow me to the back, I have everything ready." Toby could feel the other man's eyes on his back as he led the way to the room at the back of the house.

When they entered the room, Lamont reached into the breast pocket of his rumpled jacked and pulled out a long narrow wallet. As he opened it and removed two large denomination bills, Toby caught a brief glimpse of the shoulder holster under his blazer. "I believe this is what you're waiting for, Bailey."

Toby reached out to take the money, but Lamont caught his wrist, holding it in a tight grip. "Aren't you going to say thank you?"

Toby swallowed, tasting apprehension in the back of his throat. "Thank you, Sir." Lamont slowly released his wrist and Toby had to work to keep himself from rubbing the skin. "Why don't you go ahead and get undressed, Sir," Toby suggested, placing the bills on the dresser on top of the money Carlton had given him. He took a deep breath, steeling himself for what he feared would be a very unpleasant experience.

"No. You undress first, while I watch," Lamont instructed. "Make it good. I want to get all of my money's worth." As Toby started to remove his shirt, Lamont stopped him with another demand. "Move that damned table out of the way first. We aren't going to need it for what I have in mind." Toby moved it slightly out of the way. "No. Put it up tight against that desk."

Toby moved the table as directed, realizing that the panic button was now effectively blocked. He turned back to the man who was closely examining the furnishings in the room as if he were looking for something. Lamont removed his jacket and threw it on the table, and rolled up his sleeves. Tony shivered again at the sight of the strong arms covered in coarse black hair.

Lamont turned back to him and narrowed his eyes. "Go stand in the center of the room and strip off those clothes. I want to get a good look at what I'm buying…Toby."

Toby stopped in his tracks, shocked at the mention of his name.

Lamont's smile of satisfaction was terrifying. "Yes, I know who you are. I did my homework. You're almost a celebrity in some circles, although not as well-known as your friend, Guzman. I figured you were going to try to run the same scam on me Guzman did, and I have to tell you, boy – it's not going to work out at all like you'd hoped." While Toby stood frozen in the middle of the room, Lamont walked to the dresser and picked up the cash on top. He held the bills up so make sure Toby saw what he held before he rolled them up tightly and shoved them down into his pants pocket. "I think it's time I got some of my money back – money that piece of trash whore Guzman squeezed out of me over the last few months, right up until he was killed. I was glad to see someone had the guts to give Guzman what he deserved."

Toby tensed when Lamont reached up and unfastened the flap of leather that held his weapon in place. Lamont followed his eyes and laughed low in the back of his throat. "I told you to strip!" Lamont reminded him harshly. "You'd better get started if you know what's good for you. You're going to need to listen better, or I'm going to have to teach you to mind. You won't like that at all, but I will."

Toby began to undress, and Lamont watched him covetously as he removed each piece of clothing. "Just toss them on the table, boy – real easy."

Toby did as Lamont instructed and tried to control his trembling. *"Please let the recording equipment be working,"* he prayed silently, hoping Reightman and Mitchell were ready to intervene if this got any worse.

"Now, you're going to stand there real quiet while I inspect the goods and tell you how our little arrangement is going to work." Lamont touched his gun to emphasize he meant business and then walked over to where Toby stood. He reached out and grabbed Toby's chin, jerking it so Toby was forced to look him full in the face. "You're pretty nice looking, but I'm not sure about those damned, pale eyes." Lamont released his chin and rubbed his rough hands across Toby's chest. When he reached the nipples, he pinched tightly and twisted them. "Here's what's going to happen, Toby. You can keep up this little racket – I insist you do – but you're going to give me fifty percent of everything you make from your whoring. You're also going to provide me with copies of any and all incriminating photos you manage to take, and I'm warning you, you'd better take some or I'll slam your ass in jail with the other whores after I beat you to a pulp. You understand me?" He twisted the nipples harder, until Toby cried out in pain.

"Yes! I understand," he answered, blinking in pain and powerless despair. When he saw Lamont's eyes fill with hope he'd get to teach him a lesson after all, Toby quickly add, "Sir."

Lamont removed his hands and walked slowly around Toby, looking him over like he was a horse or dog for sale. When Lamont was directly behind him, he nudged Toby's legs apart with his foot. Toby felt the cop place his hands on his ass and rub it appreciatively, before giving it a hard, stinging slap. Then, Lamont parted his cheeks and ran a finger down the cleft until it was resting against the opening.

Toby felt his finger circle, and then tap him forcefully. "You do have a nice, sweet ass, Toby," Lamont breathed into his ear. "You know what the other part of our little arrangement is? You're going to provide me your special services anytime I want them. Understand?"

"Yes, Sir."

"I knew we'd reach an understanding." Lamont circled back around in front of him. He reached out and fondled Toby's cock and then took his balls into one hand, squeezing them slightly. "You've got yourself some nice equipment down here, Toby. I'd hate for it to get injured over the course of our association." Lamont gave a tighter squeeze to emphasize his point, before releasing him. "But, I think what I like best about you, Mr. Bailey, is your lips." Lamont smiled and Toby didn't like the look in his eyes. Lamont stepped away, unfastening his belt and opening the fly of his pants. "As a matter of fact, the very first thing you're going to do for me is to get down on your knees and show me some appreciation with that pretty mouth. You're going suck until I'm dry. Understand?"

Toby couldn't bring himself to answer. Suddenly, Lamont pulled back and hit him in the gut, hard, with his closed fist. Toby cried out and bent double, trying to catch his breath. Before he could recover, Lamont grabbed him by the hair and flung him across the room until he hit the bed, sprawling against the headboard. Lamont was on top of him in a flash, pressing down on his chest and jamming one knee sharply between Toby's thighs. Toby cried out in fear as Lamont pulled his gun and held it to Toby's side.

"I told you not to make me have to tell you twice. Looks like you're one of those faggots who have to learn things the hard way. I'll ask you again – just once more – do you understand what you're going to do with that mouth of yours?"

"Yes, Sir," he whimpered, trying to shift his position on the bed. When Lamont jammed his knee in closer, Toby whispered, "I need to be able to move so I can…can do what you want me to do, Sir. I promise I won't give you any more trouble."

Lamont grinned in triumph, and eased his knee back. Toby struggled to prop himself up on the bed, slipping his hand behind the back of the mattress, trying to locate the panic button. "I need a little more room, Sir," he croaked out, hoping Lamont would ease back just a hair more. Lamont let up on the pressure, and as he did, Toby's fingers found the button.

A split second later, Mitchell was through the door with his weapon drawn. "Put down the gun and step away!" The cop's voice rang out in the room.

Reightman hurried into the room right behind him. "Don't do anything foolish, Lamont," she instructed him in a deadly voice.

Two patrol cops entered the room with weapons held at ready. Lamont slowly laid his gun down and raised his arms. "Isn't this a surprise," he said, standing from the bed. "What do we have here?"

Reightman walked forward as one of the cops picked up the discarded weapon. The other circled behind and jerked Lamont's hands behind his back and fastened cuffs to his wrists. "What we have, Lamont, is assault, assault with a deadly weapon, attempted rape, and extortion. I'm sure the DA and I will think of a few more charges to add before we're done." She nodded at the officers holding Lamont tightly. "Read him his rights and take him down to the station. I know that Chief Kelly will be delighted to see him. I'll be along as soon as I'm able." She holstered her gun, and stepped out of the way of the officers holding Lamont's arms. He shot her a glare of absolute hate, but didn't utter a word as he was led from the room.

Mitchell was helping a shaken Toby up from the bed. Reightman walked over and picked up his clothes from the table and handed them to him. "I'm sorry I had to let it go on so long, Toby," she apologized remorsefully, meaning every word. "I had to make sure we had everything we needed to put him away for a long time."

Toby turned away from her, vulnerable and exposed until he tugged on his shorts and pulled the t-shirt over his head. He turned back around and stared at her with his blue eyes. His pupils were so large from recent shock and fear they blended into the dark rings around the irises. "I'm ready to go home now," he told her with an unsteady voice. "I'm tired and I'm terrified and…I want to go home." He picked up his bag and his shoes and then looked at the table. "There's no reason to stay here any longer." He smoothed one edge of the sheet on top. "I'm already set up for tomorrow."

Mitchell fell in behind him as Toby walked out the door.

Melba Reightman slowly followed, turning off the light and gently closing the door as she left.

On Sunday, Toby slept so late that Mitchell thought he was going to have to wake him in order to meet Tom and Laurie at the spa. Just as he was about to knock on the bedroom door, Toby opened it and stumbled to the bathroom. Through the closed door, Mitchell heard the toilet flush and the faucet running. After a few minutes, Toby opened the door and went back into the bedroom. He stepped out of his sleep shorts and began digging around in a dresser drawer, looking for something to wear.

Wanting desperately to walk over and hug his friend, Mitchell held himself back, knowing better than to cross the divide he'd built between them. He couldn't, not if he had to let Toby continue on with this plan. So, he just watched silently while Toby dressed. "Aren't you going to shower?" he asked, hating the impersonal sound of his voice.

"I'll do it this afternoon." Toby replied, sounding apathetic and disinterested. "I don't want to keep them waiting." He shoved his feet into a pair of canvas sneakers. "Let's go," he said.

Toby said very little while Tom and Laurie went about their job, only speaking to answer a question or two. At one point Tom turned to Mitchell with slightly raised brows, inquiring what was wrong. When Mitchell only shook his head in response, Tom turned away and went back to his work.

They locked up and Mitchell followed Toby across the street and back up the stairs to the apartment. The minute they walked in the door, Toby slipped of his shoes and then began pulling his clothing off. He held the divested garments in his hands as he walked back to the bedroom and tossed them on the bed. Then he went into the bathroom and grabbed a large towel, a bottle of suntan oil and a pair of sunglasses. "I think I'll get some sun," he said as he brushed past Mitchell.

Mitchell followed him into the living room. "Toby, I don't know what to do, or what to say to help."

Toby stopped with one hand gripping the handle of the French door. "There isn't anything to say and I don't feel like talking anyway. I'm barely holding it together as it is, and I can't afford to lose it. Not yet." He dropped his hand from the doorknob and turned back. "I thought I understood what could happen, but I didn't until last night, when that man ran his hands over me like I was something cheap and dirty. And the worse part was, I couldn't do anything about it. Now, I know exactly how dangerous this is, for me and everyone else. I thought I understood why you had to step back from our…from the way we were, but I realized last night that I didn't really have a clue. I do now, and…I think you're right. I need the cop now. Later, Mitchell, I'm going to desperately need my friend." He turned around and opened the door, going out into the bright sunshine.

Mitchell watched him walk through the door, and pulled a chair out from the table to watch Toby through the door. Toby slowly stretched and began applying oil to his body. Mitchell had to look away when he saw Toby gingerly touch his bottom rib, tender and bruised where Lamont had hit him the night before. Toby lay down on the lounger and Mitchell stood up and took off his holster. He put on his sunglasses, and pulled off his own shirt. Carrying his shoulder holster and gun in one hand, he stepped out onto the terrace.

The young man raised his head up slightly. "I don't want to talk, Mitchell."

"That's fine with me." Mitchell adjusted the back of the lounger and took a seat. "But, where you go – I go. I said I'd be beside you every step of the way, and that's where I am – beside you."

They stayed in the sun for an hour, When Toby turned over and oiled the front of his body, Mitchell watched through his sunglasses, following the movement of Toby's hands as they covered every inch. When Toby lay back down on his back, Mitchell briefly closed his eyes.

Finally Toby said, "I think I've had enough for today. I'm going to shower." He stood up from the lounger and gathered up his things. Mitchell stood and followed as he went through the doors. "Do you mind fixing us something to eat while I shower?"

"No, not at all." Mitchell closed and secured the French doors and stood quietly until he heard the shower start. Then he went into the kitchen to see what he could pull together for dinner.

After they'd eaten, Toby picked up their plates and headed to the kitchen. "You better shower too. We don't have a lot of time until we have to be over at your place. I'll clean up in here."

"Thanks," Mitchell said as he rose from his chair and headed to the bathroom.

As he adjusted the showerhead spray, Mitchell placed his hands on the shower wall, and bowed his head and prayed.

John Brown had been perplexed for the last couple of days, and he didn't like it. He knew something was going on, but he didn't know what it was, exactly. He watched from across the street as Toby Bailey let the man and woman out of the door to the spa, and then a minute or two later, came back out with the other man – the cop he'd watched getting naked on the terrace – and walked across the street.

John Brown hunkered down in his vehicle, and a few hours later he saw them come down the stairs and get into the cop's car. He rolled up his window and started his engine.

As the driver pulled away from the curb, John Brown followed them, always remaining a couple of car lengths behind. When the car turned into a small subdivision, John Brown drove on past and then made a U-turn at the next intersection. He drove back and turned into the same subdivision, driving slowly down the streets until he spotted the car pulled up in front of a small duplex. He found a place to park on the side of the street, close enough to watch the house. He waived at a passing patrol car as it passed, and rolled down his window and turned off the engine. A short time later, he saw another car pull into the driveway and park behind the car he'd followed. He sat up straighter in his seat as he recognized the man walking up to the front door. "Someone's being a naughty boy tonight." He settled back down to wait.

At seven o'clock that night, Toby opened the door of Mitchell's house and faced Councilman Sutton Dameron. "Hello," he said as he opened the door. "I'm Bailey, and I've been expecting you."

Dameron gave him a smile in return. "Hi, I'm Chris. It's nice to meet you."

"Come on back, Chris," Toby said as he shut the front door and led the way to the back. "But you don't have to use that name – I know who you are. You're very recognizable these days and have made quite a name for yourself. I've wanted to meet you for some time now."

Dameron tensed, but then slowly relaxed when he saw the engaging, open smile Toby threw over his shoulder. "I guess it was pretty foolish to use a fake name." Dameron followed Toby into the back bedroom. "I guess you can call me Sutton."

"I'd like that, Sutton," Toby said as he closed the door. "Why don't you get out of your clothes so we can start getting to know one another?"

"Sounds good to me." Sutton handed Toby a few bills. "Here, this is for you."

Toby took the bills and laid them on the dresser while Sutton quickly removed his clothes and folded them neatly. Toby picked up a towel and a bottle of oil as Dameron put the tidy stack of clothing on the dresser.

"I hope you don't mind if I use oil," Toby said, holding the bottle out for approval. "I got a lot of sun today and my skin's really dry. In fact, I was wondering if you would mind rubbing some onto my back…and anywhere else you think needs it."

"I'd love to do that for you, Bailey. There's nothing like a little one-on-one personal contact to get to know someone." Dameron took the bottle from him. "You'll need to get undressed first, though. I can't wait to see what's hiding underneath those shorts."

Toby quickly pulled his shirt over his head to hide his expression, and then slowly unfastened his shorts. He folded both neatly, having noticed that Sutton appeared to like things neat and tidy. He turned his back slightly and then pulled down his briefs, letting them fall to his feet. He stepped out of them, and then bent down and picked them up. He stretched, taking time to displaying his best assets for the Councilman's appreciation. He placed the briefs on top of the other clothes and turned around to discover Dameron was stroking himself as he watched. Toby could see the beginnings of his arousal. *"Average all the way."* he observed. *"Or maybe slightly smaller than average. Fairly good body – even though he's short."*

"You did get some sun today," Dameron observed, as he picked up the bottle of oil. "Why don't you lay down on the table and I'll start rubbing some of this in. I'll make sure to get every crook and cranny."

Hiding his revulsion at the thought of Dameron touching him, Toby climbed onto the table and lay face down. He curled his hands around the edge and searched with one finger until he felt the edge of the panic device. He felt Dameron climb on top and position himself between his legs. Soon, the Councilman laid his oily palms on Toby's back and began to rub the oil into his skin. "How does that feel, Bailey?"

Toby gave a little moan, hoping it didn't sound too contrived. "It feels great." He sensuously shifted his hips a few times for emphasis. "You have great hands."

After that vote of approval, Dameron applied himself with more industry, working his way over every inch of Toby's back and shoulders. When he had reached the lower part of the back, Dameron said "It looks like you got sun on *every* part of your body. I'll just continue on down." When Toby didn't respond, the Councilman took silence as permission and worked the oil into Toby's cheeks and thighs, lingering much longer than necessary. "I think you should turn over now. It's time give the front of your body some attention."

Toby rolled onto his back with his hands slightly above his head, well within reach of the button. He gave the man what he hoped was a sexy, lazy grin and closed his eyes as Dameron dribbled oil onto his chest. "You're really good at this. Have you done this before?"

"A few times. There was another masseur who taught me a few things."

"Oh," Toby forced himself to ask calmly. "Was he a local guy?"

Dameron didn't answer for a moment. "Yes, he was," he finally replied in a guarded voice.

Toby didn't want him spooked. "Well you certainly learned how to use your hands." He arched his back until his ribs pressed firmly against Dameron's palms. He winced as the man's hands ran across his bruise.

"Wow! It looks like you have a pretty good bruise started. How did you get that?"

"Ummm…I fell against something yesterday. It's not too bad, just a little sore. You could move your hands…a little lower, though."

Dameron removed his hands, and Toby watched through half-lidded eyes as the Councilman rubbed oil onto his own erect member. The man moaned then placed his hands on Toby's abdomen and began to work downward. After a few minutes of undivided attention to parts of interest, Dameron sighed disappointedly. "Don't you like that? I don't seem to be getting much reaction from you down here."

"It feels great, Sutton," Toby assured him. "Maybe I'm just a little nervous. I've never done anything like this with someone famous."

"I'm not all that famous," Sutton Dameron said with false modesty. "I think I know what'll do the trick. Sit up for me and move your legs off the table."

Toby sat up and forced himself to put his legs over the edge of the table. "Like this?"

"Yes, but spread your legs wider and lean back and relax. You're going to really enjoy this."

Toby put his arms behind him and gripped the edge of the table, feeling for the panic button. He adjusted his arms and hands until his fingers found what he was searching for. Relieved, he leaned back, supporting himself with his arms. He watched as Dameron gave himself another few slow strokes and then dropped to his knees. Toby closed his eyes and tried not to think about what was happening as the man fondled him and placed his mouth over his limp flesh. After a few minutes of the Councilman's oral attentions, Toby felt himself stir, despite his best efforts. He sat up and placed his hand on Dameron head, making contact with the bare patch of skin Dameron tried so hard to hide. "I think you're getting results, Sutton, but stop for a minute. I have something in mind for you."

The man kneeling before him continued to work his mouth as he pumped himself furiously.

"Please stop, Sutton," Toby pleaded. "I really do have something special planned, just for you. You won't believe what I'm going to do to you next." When Dameron reluctantly pulled his mouth away with a wet drooling smack and looked up with eager eyes, Toby sighed in relief at his liberation. "You're going to have to see it to believe it. Here," Toby got down from the table. "Trade places with me."

Dameron stood up and sat on the edge of the table. Toby wiped off the excess oil and saliva off while Dameron continued to work himself, and went to the desk, where he picked up the photograph he'd left there earlier. He walked over to the Councilman and handed him the paper.

Dameron eased off his activity and took it from Toby's hand. As he unfolded the paper with one hand, his other hand abruptly stopped its busy work between his legs. "What…?" he asked as he removed himself from the table.

"It's a little souvenir from one of your previous encounters," Toby told him coldly as he pulled on his shorts. "A friend left it for me. I think you knew him. His name was Geri Guzman."

"You little faggot cocksucker!" Dameron shouted at him.

"Call me what you want, but I wasn't the one on my knees just now, Councilman." Dameron narrowed his eyes at him, and Toby could see his anger and suspicion. "I think the little arrangement you had with Geri will suit me just fine. It'd be a shame if that picture- and the others I have – were made public. I'm sure the voters – and your financial supporters – would find them very disappointing, not to mention the reaction they'd get from the press."

Toby saw something frightening flash in Dameron's eyes a split second before the man's fist headed toward him. Toby caught his wrist with one hand and squeezed tightly – just as Lamont did to him the night before. "I wouldn't try that again. If you do, I'd to have to make those photos public before we come to an arrangement."

"What do you want?"

Toby slowly released his wrist. "Exactly the same as Geri." Toby forced himself not to step back from the look on the enraged man's face.

"I'll give you exactly what I gave him," Sutton Dameron agreed coldly, thrusting the paper back at Toby.

"You can keep that copy, Councilman. I have more." Toby walked to the dresser and picked up the man's stack of neatly folded clothes. "It's time for you to get dressed. We're done here, but I expect to hear from you soon."

"It will take me a day or two to make arrangements." Dameron hurriedly pulled on his clothing. "I don't have that kind of cash."

"You have until Wednesday. If we haven't worked things out by then, well…" Toby indicated the paper Dameron held tightly in one hand, "I'm afraid I'll have to let everyone in on your dirty little secret." After Toby escorted the angry Councilman to the front door and watched him drive away, he headed back to the bedroom.

Mitchell and Reightman joined him shortly. "I think we just netted our fish."

"I think so." Toby pulled on his t-shirt and put on his shoes. "I just hope we can haul him into the boat." He picked up the oily towel and wiped down the bottle. "I thought that he was going to be worse than Lamont. He's very angry and looked like he wanted to kill me."

"Angry men make mistakes," Mitchell said.

"And they can be very dangerous. We're going to have to be very careful."

"We will be, Detective Reightman. You can count on it." Mitchell took the towel from Toby's hands and placed it in the trash bag he held.

"I am counting on it," Reightman said as she watched the two men walk out the door.

John Brown waited in his car until he saw everyone leave. *"Isn't this interesting?"* He watched the woman walk to her own car a few houses down and waited until she drove away. Then started his own vehicle and drove out of the subdivision.

Christina Dameron heard the front door open and shut as her husband returned home for the night. "How did your campaign meeting go, Sutton?"

He stalked past her into the study, almost slamming the door to the room. Wondering what was wrong, Christina got up from the couch and moved closer to the closed door. A few minute later she heard Sutton's angry voice.

"What do you mean, you won't help?" she heard Sutton shout into the phone. A second or two passed before she heard him say, in a quieter, more respectful voice, "No sir, I won't." When she heard his terse, "Goodbye," she hurried back to the sofa and picked up the magazine she had left on the cushion. She looked up from its glossy pages as her husband came into the room and went directly to the wet bar. He poured himself a drink and downed it, before pouring another.

"Is something the matter?" she asked.

Sutton took another drink and then pulled something from his pocket and carried it to where she sat on the couch. He threw it onto the cushion next to her and took a seat opposite hers on the matching loveseat.

Christina picked up the paper, and unfolded it. After her brain processed what the paper represented, she refolded it and placed it on the coffee table. "Again, Sutton?" Her husband didn't answer. "How could you be so stupid?" she shouted, and then looked at the photo again. "You just can't seem to stop thinking with your dick."

He shrugged and finished his drink and then got up and poured another. "We have until Wednesday night," he told her over the rim of his glass.

"Same as before?"

"Yes," he answered shortly. "Exactly the same."

"Sawyer?" she asked, guessing who he had called.

"The Reverend said we're on our own. He doesn't want anything to do with this."

"I don't know why you thought he'd help – he didn't last time." Dameron ignored her bitter comment. She watched him with glittering eyes from her place across the coffee table. "I guess we'll just have to handle it ourselves."

Dameron didn't say a word as she threw her magazine on the table and left the room. He drank until the decanter on the bar was empty, and then opened another bottle.

Things had been going so well until he'd been unable to resist temptation and found himself back in the same mess he'd just gotten out of. He really couldn't help it that he sometimes got the urge for something a little different. After all, variety was the spice of life.

He lifted the glass to his mouth and took a deep swallow of the amber liquid. He rolled his head on his shoulders and thought about his life.

Sutton came from a very liberal family. His father and mother had both gained a certain level of notoriety in liberal circles for the work on behalf of the environment and the needy. He'd been raised to understand that it was important to speak up for causes that were in danger because of humanity's never ending greed. He'd made a good start early on as a liberal spokesperson and had basked in the approval of family and friends. He appeared set for a brilliant future, until he'd realized the one uncomfortable truth about liberal politics – a cause could only be sustained as long as the money kept flowing. Once the gravy train came to a halt, other decisions had to be made.

In this conservative state, it didn't take long for funding to run out. Outside of a couple of larger cities, the political landscape was dominated by the old-line families and organizations who were primarily concerned with keeping the status quo firmly in place, and ruthlessly used every trick in the book to make sure that they maintained their position of leadership. Sutton had learned that truth the hard way as he'd suffered a few instances of humiliation and defeat, and the funds had totally dried up. About halfway through his first term, he decided to shift his focus and throw his lot in with those that were destined to win. Sutton liked winning and there was a lot more money to be had from people like the old bastard Sawyer than from the tree huggers and bleeding hearts.

No reasonable person could possibly blame him for switching teams. He laughed bitterly to himself as he thought about the irony in that last thought. He guessed he'd switched teams alright – and in more ways than one.

So what if he liked a little male companionship once in a while? It wasn't like he was going to leave his wife and children for a nice piece of ass or a big dick. As long as no one knew about his extracurricular activities, no one was going to get hurt.

He guessed he'd always been somewhat attracted to a good looking man. He could remember having urges as far back as high school when he'd found himself noticing the athletes in the locker room. He'd admired their easy camaraderie as they'd joked and kidded with each other and horsed around in the shower. There'd been many a late night when he'd brought himself off imagining his hands on their hard, toned bodies and theirs on his.

He'd never acted on his impulses until recently, but not because he thought there was anything wrong with it. Outside of the political concerns there was nothing to lose. He knew his family would have been accepting. In fact, they would have been more than accepting and would have flaunted the fact that they had a bisexual son for the extra credibility it gave them. And he was bisexual – he was sure of that. As much as he liked being with a man, he also enjoyed sexual relations with a woman. The fact he had two children attested to that, didn't it? He just enjoyed a change now and then.

Christina had known about his outside activities for years, and had never said a word. Her only request was that he be discreet and stay out of trouble. He figured she'd never said a word to anyone – especially her stuck-up family. They thought he wasn't good enough for their daughter anyway, and nothing he'd achieved over the last few years had changed their view. They'd be sorry when he was sitting in the Governor's Mansion or maybe even the White House. He savored that fantasy for a few minutes and then frowned. He took another slug of his drink and forced himself to think about the current situation.

How dare that faggot try to blackmail him? What right did he have to take advantage of Sutton's position? If only that damned Geri Guzman hadn't left the incriminating pictures behind for someone else to use!

He supposed the pictures in and of themselves weren't too bad. He picked up the crumpled paper from where Christina had left it, and smoothed out the creases. He thought he looked damn good in the shot, and some part of him was thrilled that he'd been able to hook up with such a fine piece of ass. Guzman could have graced the pages of any health and fitness magazine and would have sold a million copies by being on the cover.

Lieberman had introduced him to Guzman and that was about the only redeeming thing about that fat fuck of a City Coroner. If the good Doctor hadn't been such a weakling, none of this would have happened. He'd panicked and had lost Guzman's phone. Dameron turned his mind away from the events that had followed and focused on the picture he held.

The first time Sutton had watched Guzman undress he'd been speechless. All that smooth tanned skin had been a turn-on and when he'd seen what a treasure he had between his thighs, his mouth had literally watered. Guzman had taught Sutton a lot of things he'd never even imagined. He felt himself get excited at the memory of the first time he'd taken him in his mouth, and reached down to touch himself through his pants.

His ran through each of their encounters in his mind and finally unzipped his fly and pulled out his cock. When he got to the memory of that last night, he felt his excitement grow as he remembered how their relationship had ended. Guzman had been completely helpless and Sutton had enjoyed the feeling of vengeful power that had given him. He could feel his orgasm near as he imagined having Toby Bailey in the same position. Those pale blue eyes would be frozen in fear as he realized what was ultimately in store for him. He imaged everything that would happen when he had the young man in his power and with a shuddering cry, he came. After he regained his senses, he tucked himself back into his briefs and zipped his fly, not worrying about the damp mess he'd made.

As long as he took care of the problem before his supporters found out, everything would be fine. He lifted his glass again and drank deeply, then smiled in satisfaction. Anyone that got in his way would find out exactly what happened when he was crossed and Toby was next on his list. That would teach him to mess with Sutton Dameron.

He put down his glass and headed up the stairs on the way to his bedroom. He stopped a few steps from the top, wondering if he should check to make sure he hadn't stained the upholstery on the sofa. He decided it didn't really matter. If everything worked out as planned, he'd be able to afford new fabric. Hell – if everything worked out he'd buy Christina a whole house full of new furniture. He laughed at the thought of having the Sawyers over one night and arranging for the Reverend to sit right on the site of his emission. It would serve the bastard right.

CHAPTER NINE

DETECTIVE REIGHTMAN SPENT most of Monday morning talking with Hollingfield and Lautner, and then briefed Chief Kelly.

"Hey, Melba, I've got something for you," Nancy greeted her as she came out of Kelly's office. She handed Melba a small thin box.

"What's this?"

"The name plate you ordered," Nancy answered cheerfully. "I called the supplier on Friday and really chewed them out. I guess they didn't want me calling again, so they rushed it over to me today."

"That's great, Nancy! The timing couldn't have been better."

On the way back to her desk, Reightman's phone rang. She pulled it out from her jacket pocket, and hurried to answer it when she recognized who was calling. "Hello, Toby. What's up?"

"Dameron called me a few minutes ago, and Mitchell said I should call you right away," he said from the other end. "He apologized for the way he acted – said he was just taken by surprise – and asked if we could meet again. He said he was anxious for us to get together so we could put all of this behind us. He asked that as a show of good faith I should provide him a little consideration and finish giving him what he didn't get on Sunday."

Reightman stopped walking and leaned up against the wall. "What did you tell him, Toby?"

After a moment he replied, "I told him that I understood, and I'd be happy to help him celebrate the conclusion of our arrangement.

We've arranged to meet at the spa – Wednesday night, at eight-thirty."

"Okay. I'll call you tomorrow to arrange a time to get together so we can go over everything." She thought about the increasingly dangerous situation and whose lives were at stake. "Keep Mitchell close, Toby. Don't venture out of his sight until this is over."

"He barely lets me go to the bathroom by myself as it is."

"Good. That's his job. I'll talk to you tomorrow." She ended the call and walked slowly back to her desk.

"Hey, Jones," she said as she took a seat.

"Hello. Boss. I wondered if I was going to see you today."

"I've been tied up in meetings." She looked at the item she held in her hands and added, "I got you a little something." She reached across the desk, handing him the box."

"What's this?" he asked as he took it from her.

"Open it and see."

Jones opened the box and sat back in his chair, surprised and touched. "You got me a nameplate for the desk." He read the plaque on the front and polished one of the brass letters with a napkin.

"It's the least I could do for my new partner. Consider it a welcome present."

"Thank you," he said, his eyes shining. He placed the nameplate carefully on the desk and positioned it where she could see it.

"Vincent W. Jones," she read. "It looks good."

He came around to the side to view his gift. "I think so too. Thank you again. It makes me feel like I belong somewhere now."

"You do, Detective. And to prove it, I have one more thing for you – or rather – one thing I need some help with."

"Shoot."

"I need your help with the case we are working. You're going to become more involved now, so I think it's time to tell you everything that's going on."

Reightman filled him in with all the details and went over the plan for Wednesday night. When she finished, he looked across the desk and gave a low whistle. "You're aiming for the big dogs, Reightman." He shook his head at the enormity of what she'd just shared with him. "Thanks for telling me about all of this and you don't have to ask. I'll help any way I can. Do you need me to go with you tomorrow to meet with Bailey?"

She thought of all the things she was worried about, and decided that there were more important things for him to handle. "No, I want you to hang out at the pawnshops. The last time the murderer picked up a weapon, he purchased it from Goldbleum's shop and he may be shopping for a new one. Take a couple of officers and keep an eye out in case he follows the same pattern."

"That's a good thought – I'll take care of it. What time do you need me at Time Out on Wednesday?'

"Between seven and seven-thirty. That should give us plenty of time to do a final walk through and get you into position."

"Sounds good. Hey, I've been meaning to ask you something, but I keep forgetting." He pulled a sheet of paper out from his in box and handed it to her. "Do you think I really have to go to this?"

She looked over the information and grinned. "Yep – you do. The city is taking their new non-discrimination policy very seriously and these Sensitivity Seminars are mandatory. I attended one a few months ago and they'll let me count that, but you, Detective Jones, have to attend. Don't even try to get out of it, because they're holding a pretty firm line. Unless you're on your deathbed you just need to buck up and attend. Okay?"

He reluctantly nodded his agreement. "Okay, but I hate to take a whole week for that. But you're the boss and if you tell me I have to do it, then I guess I'd better." He gave the paper one more look and then placed it back in the tray. "Hey," he said hesitantly, "You want to grab a bite to eat."

"I'd like that – as long as I don't have to watch you eat coleslaw on pulled pork. That was just disgusting."

"You just haven't learned to appreciate my tongue action," he said wiggling his eyebrows at her.

"Detective Jones?"

"Yeah?"

"Shut up."

He laughed, pleased with their new camaraderie. She grabbed her purse, and he happily followed her as she led the way to her car.

❖ ❖ ❖

On Tuesday, John Brown camped out a few doors down from the Damerons' and watched the house. Sutton Dameron had not poked his head out all morning. John Brown knew he was home because his car was parked on the street. A few minutes before noon, he saw Mrs. Dameron come out of the house and get into her own car. John Brown pulled away from the curb.

She headed north and John Brown followed her as she drove out of the city, wondering where she was going. About ninety minutes later, she turned off the interstate and took an exit leading to the downtown area of the larger city, located just across the state line. He followed her closely until she'd parked, and then found his own parking place nearby. He watched in his rearview mirror as she got out of the car and hurried to a small shop located on the corner. "We Buy Your Unwanted Valuables" read the sign above the door. He got out of his vehicle and walked across the street, leaning up against a nearby building. Thirty minutes later she come out of the door and hurried down the street. He walked quickly toward her, bumping her shoulder as he passed.

"Watch where you're going," she snapped.

He turned and looked at her, letting an expression of surprised recognition cover his face. "Christina?" he asked, letting delighted surprise color his voice. "I'm so sorry I bumped into you! I obviously wasn't looking where I was going."

"Oh, it's you. What are you doing here? I haven't seen you since the charity event at your mother's home a few months ago."

"I'm just here on a job," he replied, giving her a charming smile. He glanced up at the sign above the door she had exited. "You buying or selling?"

She hesitated before answering, "Neither. Actually, I was trading some things I don't want any more for something that caught my eye."

"Oh? Anything interesting?"

"Just an old hunting knife – a gift for a friend."

"Sounds like a nice gift for the right kind of person."

"Yes. He lost the last one he had and I thought I'd get him a new one since he's planning on doing a little hunting in the next day or so." She glanced at her watch, and then said apologetically "I hate to cut things short, but I really need to be getting back home. I've got to pick my kids up from school and I still have a drive ahead of me. Give my regards to your mother."

"I probably won't see her for a while – busy schedules and all. But I'll let her know I ran into you – literally." John Brown gave her a small self-deprecating chuckle. "Again, I'm sorry about that – I need to pay better attention. See you soon." John Brown watched her hurry to her car and then walked slowly around the block to buy some time. When he got back to his vehicle, he verified her car was gone. *"This is getting to be very interesting now."*

On Tuesday as planned, Reightman met with Toby to go over the preparations for the next night. They met in the room at the back of Green Dragon since Toby needed to get away from the spa for a while and was feeling cooped up in his apartment. Reightman agreed, figuring that it wouldn't hurt a thing to talk over the details in Zhou Li's presence and the crafty old woman might have a few observations or suggestions to add.

With Zhou Li and Mitchell seated around the carved dragon table, Reightman and Toby reviewed everything they could think of from the Sunday episode with Dameron and then went over the plan for Wednesday night. "Anyone have anything to add?"

Zhou Li stood from here chair. "Please excuse me for a minute – I just thought of something and want to go gather a few things."

She returned a few minutes later and handed a small packet to Toby. "I want you to brew this and drink two cups before you meet with Sutton Dameron. No more than two cups, Toby – but no less."

"Okay, but what will it do?"

"The herbal mixture I have given you will help keep you alert. If Dameron encourages you to drink any beverage about which you are not one-hundred percent sure of the contents – try not to drink it. If you have no choice, this should effectively counteract any sedatives or incapacitating drugs for a while." Zhou waited until she had received Toby's acknowledgement of her instructions.

Toby weighed the small packet and his hands before replying. "Alright. I trust you, Madame Zhou."

"I will always try and honor your trust, Toby." She looked to Reightman. "That is all I have to offer, Detective."

"I'm sure your contribution will be very helpful and no one else thought about taking the same precautions." Reightman canvased the small group, "Does anyone have anything else?" When no one spoke up, she stood and picked up her purse. "Then I think that's all for now. I'll meet you at the spa at about seven o'clock tomorrow evening, Toby. Try and get some rest." She turned to Mitchell. "Stay vigilant, and take care of him." As he met her eyes and they exchanged the unspoken message, she added, "Anything you think you need to do, Mitchell – do it." When he nodded his understanding, she sighed. "Good night."

Toby and Mitchell said their farewells to Madam Zhou and went up to Toby's apartment.

Once inside, Toby placed the packet that Zhou had given him on the kitchen counter. "I don't want to take this."

"I know you don't, Toby. But you said you trusted her."

"I do trust her. I just hate the fact that I have to because that...slimy ass might try to drug me before slicing me up into a hundred pieces." He rolled his shoulders a few times. "I'm kind of tense. I think I'll go take a shower."

"You're going to wash away. I think this will be your third shower today, Toby."

"It'll be my fourth, but it's the only time I feel clean. I don't think I'll ever be clean again." The last was said with such disgust and self-loathing Mitchell couldn't meet his eyes.

Mitchell watched him walk back to the bedroom. He went to the fridge and took out a beer and then drank most of it. He sat the bottle on the counter and then picked it up and finished it off. Then he walked to the back of the apartment. He heard the shower start and took of his shoulder holster and removed his shirt. He laid it on the chair in the corner and finished undressing. After acknowledging to himself that what he was about to do would take all of his self-control to keep on task and prevent any misunderstandings, he walked into the bathroom and opened the shower door.

Toby turned in surprise when he stepped into the steamy stall. "Mitchell?"

Mitchell took the soap from Toby's hands. "Turn around," he said, "I'm going to wash your back."

Toby looked at Mitchell with a trace of suspicion, trying to figure out what he was up to. Giving up, he eventually turned around.

Mitchell lathered up the soap and began to wash his back. He worked the soapy lather across Toby's shoulder and around his sides and then knelt down and washed Toby's feet, picking each one up to get them clean. He worked his way up the calves and the thighs and then gently cleaned the rest. "Turn around," he instructed.

Toby hesitated, and then turned. Mitchell washed the chest and stomach, careful around the small purple bruise. "This looks better than it did yesterday. Now, wet your hair, I want to do that next." Toby put his head under the hot spray and let the water run over his head and down to his shoulder. Mitchell poured shampoo into his hand and then gently lathered Toby's head. "Rinse."

Toby put his head under the water and worked the lather out of his hair.

"We're almost done," Mitchell assured him. After giving Toby's body a few more swipes of the soap he positioned Toby under the falling water. "Last time under the water. Rinse off before the hot water's gone."

Toby stepped back under the spray, and when all evidence of soap was gone, Mitchell reached over and turned off the water. He reached over the door and pulled two towels from the hook. He gently dried Toby's skin, and then his own. He wrapped Toby in a bathrobe and wrapped a damp towel around his own waist. He then took Toby by the hand and led him the counter and combed his hair. He turned Toby toward the mirror. "Look Toby, you're all clean, not a spec of dirt anywhere, so don't tell me that you feel *dirty*." He looked Toby right in the eye and sternly said, "You're clean inside, too. What you're doing to help catch Geri's killer seems grimy to you, but you've convinced all of us – and yourself – that it's necessary. So, man up, Toby Bailey, and quit letting this eat you up inside."

"You're supposed to be the cop, not the friend," Toby whispered.

"I've decide I can be both. I don't really think there's a way to separate the two at this point, even though I thought I should try." Mitchell narrowed his eyes as he looked Toby over. "Oops. I think I missed a spot!" He leaned in and kissed him on the nose. "There – all gone."

"Mitchell, you're a dork and I don't know how I can stand having you around." Toby gave him a ghost of a smile, but it was the first thing resembling a smile Mitchell had seen from him in the past couple of days.

"You keep me around so you can keep cooking up elaborate schemes to get me nekkid." He nudged Toby's shoulder. "Loosen up. I'm curious about something, though. Do you ever wear clothes?"

"Yes, I wear clothes! Just not all the time, and almost never when no one's around. It saves on laundry."

"Oh, now I get it. You're just teaching me to save on laundry detergent and water? Or are you trying to find opportunities to feast your eyes on my manly beauty?"

Toby rolled his eyes and tied his bathrobe more snuggly. "Yeah – that must be it! All your manly beauty drives me wild with lust," he joked. "All that skin and those big puppy dog eyes. I must have amazing willpower."

"Yes, you do, Toby," Mitchell agreed seriously. "That's what's going to pull you through all of this."

Toby worried his lip for a minute and looked back in the mirror. "You think your hunky silver haired dream man will look this good in a bathrobe?"

"I don't know and I don't think I'll ever find out."

Tony raised his eyebrows at Mitchell's pitiful tone. "Why?"

"Because," Mitchell grinned at Toby's reflection in the mirror and then ruffled his damp hair. "Based on your most excellent example and your wise teaching and advice on how to cut down on laundry, I am going to severely limit the clothing I allow him to wear at home. In fact, bathrobes after hot showers will be totally banned."

This time Toby's smile turned into an outright laugh. Mitchell's work was done.

Wednesday morning, Mitchell fixed a quick breakfast and escorted Toby across the street to the spa. Toby had spent some time preparing himself for the day, and as a result, his mind was more at ease. Once in his office, he simply threw himself into the day, taking care of everything that needed to be done.

❖ ❖ ❖

At three forty-five in the afternoon, a well-groomed, well-kept woman entered the doors of Time Out and walked to the reception desk.

"I have an appointment in about fifteen minutes," the woman told SarahJune.

"Yes, I see you've booked an hour massage with Andre. If you'll have a seat, he'll be with you shortly." The woman thanked her and took a seat in the reception area, picking up a glossy magazine and flipping through the pages. A few minutes later, an exotic, light skinned man of mixed-heritage walked through the door from the back treatment area, and walked to the reception desk. After a brief discussion with SarahJune, he walked to the woman seated on one of the sofas.

"Ma'am, I'm Andre and I'll be your masseur today. Thanks for booking with me. If you'll come on back, we'll get you situated and comfortable."

The woman followed him back through the hallways and then asked, "Can you direct me to the ladies room please? I think I'd better make a quick stop there first."

Andre provided the needed information and the woman walked in the direction he'd indicated. After a few steps, she looked over her shoulder and saw him close the door to the treatment room. She turned and walked quickly to the breakroom. Once there, she unlocked the door to the stairs as she'd been instructed and went through. She hurried up the stairs and unlocked the door to the roof. After rushing back down, she exited the break area and almost ran to the ladies locker and shower room. When she had regained her breath from her excursion, she walked leisurely back to the treatment room. "I'm sorry for the delay," she apologized.

She undressed and positioned herself on the table, face down, and arranged the sheet over herself as Andre politely turned his back and pulled out some lotion from one of the cabinets and heated it in a small pottery bowl. "I'm ready," she said.

Andre walked to the table and placed his hands gently on her skin. The woman breathed out her tension and closed her eyes.

She'd done what she'd been asked to do – or rather, blackmailed into. She didn't like being in a position of forced obligation and was satisfied that she could wash her hands of the whole mess now. As the masseur's hands flowed down her back she found herself wondering if he'd be open to a more intimate arrangement. After a moment's consideration she decided that he was probably one of those morally degenerate queers. She could never understand how some men couldn't be satisfied with what she had to offer. But then again, she could also understand why they liked immersing themselves into a good healthy dose of masculine energy. Who didn't like a nice piece of meat?

She gave a small sigh at the thought.

"Is everything okay, ma'am?"

"Yes, Andre. Everything is just fine."

She enjoyed the next sixty minutes of the relaxing massage immensely, and when Andre indicated that – regretfully – their time was done, she sighed in contentment and sat up, letting the sheet fall from her generous breasts. Andre turned away, but not before catching a glimpse of a small flower tattoo on her pelvis. He didn't comment and didn't think anything more about it. The woman slipped on a robe and gathered her clothes. "That was wonderful, Andre! I think I'll take a quick shower before I leave. Thank you again." She laid a generous tip on the table and left the room. In the car on her way back home she made a short call. "It's done," she said, and hung up. Then she blocked the number. She hoped never to hear from that person again.

Reightman arrived at Time Out promptly at seven. She found Toby in a relaxed, focused mood. She looked toward Mitchell and raised an eyebrow. He held her eyes steadily but gave nothing away.

Shortly after seven, she met Jones out front and instructed him to keep an eye on the perimeter for the evening and to call her immediately if he spotted anything that was cause for concern. She went back inside and made another quick circuit. She looked over the larger treatment room carefully, and then, for some reason, she looked up to the ceiling.

The two hand bars hanging from the ceiling above the centrally placed table caught her attention as they shone silver under the lights. Her mind flashed back to the performance she'd attended with Zhou Li. She studied the bars as she walked underneath them and noted the scrape marks on the ceiling. "Oh my God," she whispered as an image of silky fabric dropping from above filled her mind. She rushed to find Toby and Mitchell. "Watch the ceiling if you can, Toby. I think…. he'll try and do…something with the bars above the table. Don't let Dameron near them. Be careful." As she started to turn, she remembered something else. "Did you drink the stuff Zhou Li gave you last night?"

"Yes," Toby answered. "I'm prepared."

She could tell from his voice that he *was* prepared. She smiled proudly at him. "Yes, you are. Good luck, Toby." And then, on instinct she impulsively pulled him close and gave him a hug, before going to his office and shutting the door.

Before making his way to the smaller treatment room next door, Mitchell, now more cop than friend, assured him, "I'll be listening, Toby. We'll be ready for any trouble.

At eight-fifteen, Sutton Dameron dropped his wife off at the corner and then pulled into the lot across the street. He watched as his wife ran quickly down the side street and disappeared from view.

John Brown watched Christina Dameron run down the dark back alley, carrying a small backpack. She was dressed in a tightfitting black body suit which tightly hugged her small, trim body. He thought it looked like something a dancer might wear, or maybe a circus performer. He followed behind her, staying in the dark shadows of the alleyway, hidden from sight. He watched her while she climbed the old ladder attached to the back of one of the building. "*I knew that ladder was going to be a problem!*" When she reached the top, he made a decision. "*If you hurt Toby Bailey, I'll make you pay. You won't get away.*" Not understanding why he thought it, but knowing it to be true, he added, "*Toby is meant for me.*" He leaned back into the shadows and waited.

As he stood hidden in the darkness, he wondered why he was so possessive of Toby Bailey. It wasn't like him to get personally involved like this. Maybe it all had to do with the fact that the young man was the first hit that had ever gone wrong for him.

Ever since he'd managed to crawl out of the hell of his dysfunctional family situation, he had avoided attachments of any kind – except those he paid good, hard cash for. These non-financial kinds of attachments just meant trouble. And he'd never messed up a job before. In his line of work, that could get you killed.

He thought there was something rotten about the whole thing, and that surprised him. It just wouldn't do for him to start questioning his client's motives. He'd learned that lesson the hard way and had it beaten into his thick skull a time or two. Yes, it would be best if he just minded his own business and let the events unfold as they may. At the thought of doing that, he felt something shiver down his spine. No, that wouldn't do at all. No one was going to take out Toby unless it was John Brown. After all, in some ways the hit was still active.

It would be a shame to have to shoot Toby. He'd miss seeing him around, even if it was from a distance. He enjoyed the sight of him jogging down the streets of downtown in his skimpy running shorts, and looked forward to watching him at night. He would have to do something about the cop that was hanging around though. He didn't think there was anything going on between the two of them, but wasn't about to take any chances. There'd be time enough to take care of that problem after tonight. Frist he had to make sure that no one else succeeded in taking Toby out.

It would be tricky and the timing would need to be absolutely perfect. All kinds of things could go wrong, and John Brown couldn't afford any other complications. After weighing the risks, he decided he'd just have to bide his time and look for the right opportunity. It was a complex problem to be solved and he liked that. He was good at solving problems. He guessed it was really two problems when you got right down to it; how to keep anything from happening to Toby in the next few hours, and then how to get close to Toby himself. *"Make that three problems,"* he corrected himself. *"Don't forget to take care of the young cop."* He had a few ideas about that already, and was sure that the first two situations would work themselves out – one of them possibly as early as tonight. Life sure was interesting these days.

"Hang in there, Toby. If anyone hurts you but me, I'll make sure they pay. I'm afraid that's the best I can do for you right now." He gave a quiet sigh and then smiled. It was a hard job he had ahead of him, but someone had to do it.

At twenty minutes after eight, Toby walked into the dark front reception area and took a seat on one of the chairs he'd so carefully selected when putting the spa together. He closed his eyes and listened to the wall fountain, calming and centering himself. He thought of the first time he'd met Geri and of all the times they'd made love – before things had gone so terribly wrong. He thought of Mitchell, standing beside him, body bare in the moonlight. Those were the thoughts he'd carry with him as he played this game with Sutton Dameron. When the knock sounded on the front door, he was ready.

Dameron entered the spa carrying a small bag. "I brought a few things to make our evening together more successful," he said in greeting as Toby closed the front door. Dameron didn't notice that Toby didn't lock it behind him.

"That's nice of you, Sutton," Toby told him with a smile. "Let's go on back."

Dameron followed Toby to the back treatment room. He entered the room and looked around. "Looks different."

"Different? Have you been here before?"

Dameron hesitated for a brief second and then replied, "Yes. I was here with your friend, Geri."

Toby smiled knowingly. "That figures! Geri was always meeting people here."

Dameron laid his bag on one of the counters and opened it. "I brought us some libations," he said as he pulled out a thermos of some sort. He removed the top and took a drink. "Damn! I forgot the cups and the ice. Do you have any here?"

"Sure. There should be ice and cups in the breakroom right down the hall. You can't miss it – the ice is in the freezer compartment of the fridge and the cups are in the cabinets."

"Excellent! I'll be right back. Why don't you get more comfortable?" Dameron smiled suggestively and then left the room.

Toby pulled off his shirt and slipped off his shoes. He tossed the shirt on the massage table in the middle of the room. He then slipped off his pants, adding them to the pile. He left on the pair of sheer briefs he'd selected just for the occasion. When Dameron returned, he stopped just inside the door, appreciating Toby's body. He brought him the drink, holding it out in one hand. "Here's a little something I whipped up just for you. I want tonight to be special – to apologize for the way I acted the other evening. You took me by surprise and, well, I don't do very well with surprises."

"That's okay. I understand." Toby took a very small sip of his drink. "Did you bring me what we agreed on?"

"Yes, I did," Dameron confirmed before he took a small swallow of his drink. "It's in the bag. I thought I would give it to you after we've had a little fun. Is that okay?"

"Sure, Sutton. I trust you."

Dameron started to put his glass down on the massage table and noticed the clothes Toby had left on top. "Let me move these out of the way. I wouldn't want them to get spoiled tonight. Here, hold this." He handed his glass to Toby and gathered up the clothes. As he carried them to the counter, Toby switched the glasses. He tensed when he heard something move across the ceiling.

"Do you want me to bring my shoes over there?"

"I don't think so. We can probably just move them out of the way." Dameron looked down at the loafers on the floor and nudged them out of the way before taking his drink from Toby's hand. "Let's toast to our new arrangement and special friendship. When I count to three, let's chug these babies down."

Toby smiled. "I'm ready whenever you are."

Dameron counted, and they both lifted their drinks and drank them down. Dameron took the cup from him and walked over and put it into the bag.

"Don't I get another drink?"

"Later, if I think you need it. Right now I have other plans." Dameron took off his shirt and folded it neatly and placed it in the bag. He slipped off his own shoes and then took off his socks and placed them inside the shoes and stowed them in the bag. He then unbuckled his pants and stepped out of his trousers. He wasn't wearing underwear. He folded the pants and put them into the bag. He rearranged the items slightly and Toby could see him searching for something with his hand. After a second or two, he apparently found what he was looking for. He made another slight adjustment and then turned back toward Toby.

Toby intentionally swayed at his approach and steadied himself by placing on hand on the table. He laughed softly. "Wow! I'm feeling buzzed already."

Dameron laughed along with him as he closed the space between them and circled his arms around Toby. "Good. Let me start taking care of you now." He navigated them toward the table and then leaned Toby back toward it. He leaned in and kissed Toby, thrusting his tongue into his mouth. Dameron stroked himself and then moved his hands to Toby. Toby concentrated on the other images he had tucked in his mind and felt himself respond.

"You appear…to be enjoying this better…than…than last time," Dameron commented appreciatively. Toby noticed he was having slight difficulty getting the words out.

Toby made himself moan softly. "I am. It…feels…so good."

Dameron smiled and went down on his knees. He licked Toby through his briefs a few times and then pulled them down around Toby's ankles. "Step out of…these," he said. "I think…think I'll keep them …keep them as a remembrance…of tonight."

Dameron was beginning to sound drugged. Toby obeyed the instructions, and even giggled when Dameron removed the sheer fabric from the floor and put it in the shoes. "Why…I mean…Sutton… why are you putting that…those in my shoes?"

"So they won't get meshed….messed up." Dameron moved back in front of Toby and took him in his mouth, shutting his eyes in hungry concentration as he engulfed the hard flesh. He worked diligently for a minute or two. "How ish…you …you feeling?"

Toby looked down at him and smiled a wide, silly smile. "I feel all….good and…floaty." He sighed and shook his head. "Those dinks……I mean drinks, were…real….strong.

"Ummmhmmm, they…was…..were strong." Dameron yawned involuntarily before taking Toby back into his mouth. Toby heard sounds again, this time from right above his head, but forced himself not to look up. A shadow fell across his face.

Dameron stood, grabbing Toby to support himself. "I need to….get….give….no," he yawned. "I mean I need to get something. Something…..I need. Don't…move."

Dameron headed for the bag, weaving and swaying on his feet. He reached inside and pulled something out of it. Toby couldn't see what he was doing, but felt a sudden tingle of unease which grew when something shifted above him. Dameron walked toward him with a hand behind his back. He stopped a few feet away and glanced up at a spot above Toby's head, and nodded. "Ready." The moment the word was out of his mouth a length of fabric dropped from above and twisted round Toby's neck. He saw a bright flash of silver as Dameron removed the large knife from behind his back.

Toby grabbed at the fabric, frantically trying to pull it from his neck. He twisted his body and saw the figure above him brace for leverage against the bars and the ceiling. The figure gave him some slack and he stumbled forward. Dameron moved toward him, unsteady on his feet. He knelt behind Toby and pulled his legs slightly backward, and Toby felt himself fall forward – held upright by the fabric. He clawed at his neck as he felt it tighten. "Help me," he croaked weakly, fighting for air. He struggled and twisted with as much force as he could muster, loosening the fabric for a split second. "Help!" he yelled before the fabric tightened again. The knife flashed and he spun away, but not before the flesh of his arm parted with sharp, slashing pain.

"Damn…………….you," Dameron cursed, finally realizing why he was so slow and unsteady. "You swished……..the…switched the…."

Toby torqued his body and finally found leverage. He scooted backward and as he did, he felt the fabric release at the unexpected lack of tension. "HELP!" he screamed before the fabric tightened around his throat again. The knife flickered in Dameron's hand and he tried to throw himself out of the way.

The door crashed open as Mitchell and Reightman rushed into the room. He heard them shout, but couldn't comprehend their words. He felt the fabric loosen and through a cloudy haze, he saw it flutter to the floor around him. Shots fired and then there was more shouting, but he couldn't understand the words.

Dameron screamed and fell to the ground. He crawled forward, frantically striving to reach Toby with the knife. Toby heard another shot and Dameron's leg jerked as blood began to quickly pool underneath it.

"Christina…!" Dameron wailed as Mitchell jerked up his arms and cuffed him.

Reightman ran forward and pulled Toby off the ground. "Toby….look at me. Look at me, damn you!" He felt her wrap something around his arm and she knelt down beside him. "Toby!' He understood she was shouting but didn't know why. He saw her arm draw back and felt her slap him.

Once. Then again. Then once more.

He shook his head and saw her arm draw back. "Stop!" he croaked from his bruised throat.

"Toby?" he heard her ask.

"Yes…Detective…….Melba."

He heard her laugh with relief and felt Mitchell's arms wrap around him. His eyes fluttered briefly. He knew he was safe, and then, he was out.

Christina dropped the length of parachute silk from her gloved hands when the door burst open. She heard the gunfire and the shouts as she pulled herself up into the ceiling and balanced herself across the metal tile braces to the service opening. She reached the small door and pulled herself out and raced up the few steps to the roof access. She flung open the door and stumbled out, breathing heavily. She took a few shaking steps toward the ladder and made her feet pull her forward. She crossed the first rooftop and then the next one. She stepped on the last few feet of asphalt between her and the ladder and managed to take a single step before a hard, brutal hand grabbed her by the arm and fling her to the ground. Dazed, she shook her head, trying to clear her head and to make sense of what was happening.

"Going somewhere, Christina?"

She looked up toward the voice and recognized the enraged face. "You! What are you doing? You have to help me!"

"No, I don't. You've been a bad girl, Christina and I'm the last person who'd help you tonight." John Brown pulled his gun from the back of his waistband. "You shouldn't have tried to hurt Toby. No one gets to do that but me. "

She reached her hand out in helpless supplication as he aimed the gun, and fired.

Christina Dameron fell back on the asphalt, already dead from the single bullet hole above her eyes.

Reightman left Toby in Mitchell's capable hands as soon as backup arrived to take Dameron into custody. She vaguely heard them read him his rights as she raced out of the room, heading for the stairs in the break room, futilely hoping she'd be in time to catch the other assailant. As she rounded the corner, she almost ran into Jones and the cop who was following close behind.

"We heard shots from the roof and couldn't find access to get up! It looks like the old ladder was ripped of the wall!" Jones shouted at her over his shoulder as he raced ahead of her up the stairs. The uniformed cop followed behind her as they climbed past the open access door.

"Dammit!" she swore when she saw it. "I should have double-checked that."

They stepped out onto the roof, searching frantically for the source of the gun fire. "There!' the cop pointed and they ran to the small form on the rooftop. Jones was there first and knelt down beside the body to check for a pulse.

"She's dead," Reightman said not waiting for his verification. "No one could survive that kind of shot to the head."

The cop walked up from behind her and looked down at the body. "Hey! That looks like…"

"Mrs. Sutton Dameron," Reightman said. "I think her name was Christina." She remembered the words Zhou had said over lunch with her and Sam one day not too long ago. "She was from Sarasota, Florida, and her family….they were circus people – big stars at one time. They taught trapeze flying….and the skill of maneuvering lengths of silk. Aerial silk is what they call it."

After shooting her a concerned and questioning glance, Detective Jones whipped out his phone and started talking to someone on the other end.

"Who shot her?"

"That's a good question, Officer," she looked at his name tag, "Wilson."

Reightman went to the edge of the roof and peered down at the ladder that had been pulled from the building. She knelt down and reached out, feeling the top part of the wall. She got back up and dusted off her hands. "The support brackets were shot away."

Jones approached her. "An ambulance and additional backup units are on the way. I've also called the Coroner and Tom Anderson."

"Thanks, Jones," Reightman said.

"Is Mr. Bailey alright?"

"Yes, I think he'll be fine. He was cut a couple of times and almost strangled, but I think… he'll be okay. Mitchell's with him."

"He's in good hands then. The EMTs will get him patched up, Reightman. It could have been worse."

"It could have been much worse. We'd better get back down there. Officer Wilson, please stay here with the body until additional personnel arrive."

"Yes, ma'am."

When they hit the bottom of the stairs, Jones said, "I'll go out front and wait for the others. I'll direct them to where they need to go."

"That'll be a big help. While you're handling that, I'm going to check on Toby." She walked into the back room and saw that Mitchell had Toby on his feet and partially dressed.

Mitchell was holding a rolled towel to the worst of the cuts. "This one's going to need stiches," he informed her as she approached.

"Just keep applying firm pressure until the EMTs arrive. They should be here soon." She looked into Toby's pale, but surprisingly calm, face. "I should have checked the roof access from the break room. I'm sorry."

"I checked it myself," he told her hoarsely, "between three-thirty and four o'clock this afternoon. I locked all the doors – the one up top and the one into the break room."

"Then that means someone unlocked them after that." She looked up at the hole in the ceiling where one of the large tiles had been removed. "Would any of the staff have gone up to the roof?"

Toby tried to remember who had been in the building. "The only people here were SarahJune and Andre. Andre had an appointment about that time and SarahJune hates going up to the roof. She doesn't like heights."

Reightman looked back up at the ceiling, trying to think of who else could have tampered with the doors. "I'll be right back. I want to grab the appointment book." She returned a minute later and showed him the page. "Am I reading this right? Andre had an appointment at four fifteen with a Ms. Marilyn Brown."

"Yeah, that looks right but I'll check with SarahJune tomorrow to be sure."

"Toby," she said reluctantly, "About tomorrow…I have some bad news. You're going to have to close for a day or two so that the crime techs can process this room, along with the stairwell and the roof."

"Why? We know it was Dameron who tried to kill me, and did kill Geri."

"Another person was killed tonight. The person who tried to strangle you was Dameron's wife and she was shot by someone on the roof."

He struggled to get the words out of his bruised throat. "So, you're telling me…there's a murderer still out there somewhere?"

"Yes."

Before he could reply the EMTs came through the door. "If everyone will step back we can start getting this gentleman patched up."

A short while later, Tom and Laurie arrived, followed by Doctors Evans and Bridges. "Fancy seeing you here," Tom greeted her. He took in her worried expression and tried to add a bit of levity. "Same accommodations as last time we checked into this joint to investigate a murder?"

Reightman smiled wanly, and then responded in kind. "Yep – the special suite – reserved just for you. Try not to wreck the place or you'll never get your deposit back"

"Same for us, Detective?"

"Oh, no – it's only the best for the Coroner's office. I've reserved the Penthouse for you, Doctors. The body is on the roof."

Toby came out of the back room followed by Mitchell. He went to the desk and picked up the phone. As he croaked into the handset to SarahJune, Mitchell updated her. "He only needed five stitches, Detective. They shot him with some painkillers though, so he's going to be kind of loopy for a while. I think I should take him back across the street as soon as he's finished calling the staff."

"That's fine, Mitchell. I can get your statements tomorrow."

"Thank you." Mitchell looked toward the reception desk and watched as Toby spoke on the phone. "Is it over, Detective?"

"No." Reightman looked out the front windows at the flashing lights that were once again illuminating Capital Street. "It isn't."

She stayed in her position by the window, watching as a wounded and drugged Sutton Dameron was led to the police car under the bright glare of camera lights. As he was placed into the back, and as she watched the car drive away, she realized it had been exactly four weeks since she first walked through the doors of the Time Out Spa. Exactly four weeks since the murder of Geri Guzman.

"And four weeks," she thought as she watched two young men cross the street and start up the stairwell, "since I first met Toby Bailey."

CHAPTER TEN

ON THURSDAY MORNING, accompanied his attorney, Sutton Dameron confessed to the murder of Geri Guzman and to the attempted murder of Toby Bailey. He brushed aside his lawyer's objections and told them all that he was more than willing to share how he'd taken care of Guzman, and how he'd almost taken care of Toby Bailey. He, in fact, told them all about how he and his talented and devious wife had arranged the murder so brilliantly.

Enraged at Guzman's blackmail and financially strapped to the point they couldn't continue to meet his demands, the Damerons made the decision to silence Guzman and end the extortion. Dameron maintained a semblance of lustful interest and, in fact, met with Guzman multiple times to scratch his itch, and to keep Guzman from suspecting that his blackmail scheme was at an end.

"Well, the thing is, I'm totally straight and happily married with two wonderful children," Dameron explained to those in the interrogation room. "But once in a while, I just have an itch for something different and Guzman was one hot piece of ass. But he really put the screws to us. All our money went to pay him off. Hell! I even had to give him Christina's big diamond earrings, and that was the last straw! She was really pissed when she found out I'd done that."

"So that's where the two earrings came from." Reightman nodded as she ticked them off her list. Geri Guzman had been wearing one of them when he was murdered, and Toby had discovered the other in the same lockbox that had held the ledgers and the photographs. She continued to listen in amazement as Jones asked the first questions

and the story began to unfold, filling in other unknown details of that night. With very little prodding, Dameron spilled it all, proud of his accomplishment and looking for verification of his cleverness and superiority.

"I met with Guzman a couple of times down at that damned fancy spa," Dameron told them. "One thing is for sure, those faggots sure know how to make a place look good. I scoped it out and one night Guzman even took me up to the roof for a little R & R – if you know what I mean. I shared the layout with Christina later and she even drew a little diagram for us to use to memorize the place. Christina figured she could get into the spa from the roof using an old ladder that was attached to the back of one of the buildings if I unlocked the door to the roof while I was there. I didn't even have to do that – Guzman took me up on the roof that night and we had a drink. You know, Christina is amazing. Her family were bigtime circus stars once, and she learned all kinds of things. She wasn't afraid of heights or anything,"

Reightman shot Jones a glance, and then stood and walked over to where Dameron was sitting. "Mr. Dameron, you and your wife were very clever. But Mr. Guzman was a strong man. How did you manage to handle him by yourself?"

Sutton Dameron thought it over and then gave her a confident smile. "You're right. Our biggest problem was how to handle Guzman without a lot of mess and without him doing some damage to us. As you pointed out, he was a solidly built guy – I should know – I had him naked on top of me more than a few times and I knew just how strong he really was. We finally decided the best thing to do was to drug him – get him drunk and give him something to make him almost comatose. I got some drugs from Lieberman. He had some stuff he used on guys occasionally, and he gave me everything I needed. I put it in Guzman's drinks the night we killed him. Once he was wasted and almost out cold, it was easy. I had a great big hunting knife – the folding kind – Christina picked up for some kid with the same name. We thought it was funny that it had the name 'Toby' on it. "That should confuse things," Christina said. Christina came up with the idea of restraining him with the big piece of fabric. She said it was very strong and she knew from experience even a little thing like her could handle Guzman if she could get it wrapped around him. She dropped it down over his neck. Guzman was so out of it that he just hung there, barely moving. I kicked his legs back and dragged him into position. I sliced him up a few times and put in a couple of good deep stabs. Man, it felt great to pay him back for what he did to us. I didn't even have to work very hard to keep him in place. Christina even played around some and showed me how she could swing him around, steering him with the fabric. It was kind of hot seeing her aim the blood spatter just like it was a water hose, and it was good to see her relax and have some fun. She'd been under a lot of stress with the campaign and it got worse when Guzman's demands got out of hand. I didn't want to spoil her fun, but I finally had to tell her to stop before she made too much of a mess. I didn't even get any blood on me, well not my clothes anyway, because I'd already taken them off, and moved them out of the way."

Dameron started giggling at how naughty he'd been and Reightman turned away in disgust, indicating Jones should take the next question. Jones raised his eyebrows to make certain she wanted him to proceed and when she gave him a curt nod, he picked up where she'd left off. "What happened next, Mr. Dameron?"

"Well, after I finished marking him up some more, I helped Christina pull Guzman – who I guess was just a dead body by then – back to the table in the center of the room and lifted him up. I tried to catch any drops of blood, but he'd stopped gushing well before that. He looked kind of creepy, so I arranged him more peacefully on the table. Even then he just kept staring. Christina rolled up the fabric when I took it from around his neck. It had a little blood on it so I wrapped it pretty tight. I think Christina got it out of the fabric later with some of that miracle cleaner that they sell on TV. She swears by that stuff and likes it because it's not harmful to the environment. I got some cleaner and wiped down a few places where I thought there might be a fingerprint, but I didn't do too much. I thought it would be suspicious, and besides, Guzman had explained to me that his faggot partner picked out the finishes in the room to make sure they wouldn't get smudgy from all the oils and lotions they used. I guess those are hard to clean up."

Jones shook his head, not believing what he was hearing. Dameron's lawyer hadn't made any objections so far, and both Reightman and the assistant DA were waiting, so he continued with the questioning. "That was smart thinking. What happened after that?"

"I knew that I had to figure out how to get out of the room without leaving a trail, so I wiped myself down, getting all the blood off my body, and took Guzman's clothes from where I'd folded them, Christina told me to make some cuts and slashes in them so they looked like Guzman had been wearing them when he was killed, so I did. Once I was cleaned up, I put on Guzman's athletic shoes and walked to the door. I had to stop and clean one sole off when I stepped in a small drop of his blood, but it wasn't too bad. I figured if there was any sort of footprint, it would have been made with Guzman's shoe and would confuse everyone. I'd already placed my own things into my bag so I picked it up with one hand and jumped across the big puddles by the door. I carried everything to the break room, and dumped it all into the washing machine. It already had some stuff in it so I just crammed the bloody clothes and the shoes right in and – for fun – I tossed in the knife. I thought it would a great touch for it to be found with the bloody clothes."

"And then?"

"It should be pretty obvious to you by now. I just got dressed in my own stuff while Christina put the ceiling tile back and went out through the ceiling. I bunched some paper towels around my hands and then locked the door at the top of the stairs. I shut the access panel and then came downstairs and locked that door. Then, I just walked out the front door – bold as you please. I couldn't lock it, and I didn't know how to set the alarm, so I just left."

"Didn't you worry about anyone seeing you, Mr. Dameron?"

He didn't even have to think about it. "No, why should I? I looked around once I got outside and there wasn't anyone around. I didn't think I'd ever be suspected of something like this. Everyone knows I'm an upright citizen and one of the city leaders. I do have to say one thing though. After I'm elected I'm going to make sure the city gets some better detectives on the payroll. You almost didn't figure this out."

"You're right Mr. Dameron, we almost didn't."

"I guess it's not all your fault, so maybe I'll be able to find a place for you somewhere in the department after the election. Maybe you can check all of the meters or give people tickets for jaywalking."

Sutton Dameron laughed at the idea, delighted with the situation and the looks on their faces. "But you know the real reason why you had such a hard time figuring this out?"

"No, I don't think we do. Why don't you tell us?"

"The real reason you had such a difficult time is simple. You didn't figure it out because we did a great job! Did Christina tell you how well I did?"

Jones started to answer and then turned away, trying to think how to break the news to him. Reightman cleared her throat and walked back to Dameron and stood by his chair. "No, she didn't Mr. Dameron. She was unable to tell us anything." Reightman looked down into his face, and when she was certain that she had his full attention, she told him. "Your wife was killed last night as she was attempting to flee from the roof."

Dameron's eyes clouded with confusion and he shook his head in outright denial. "No, that can't be right. Christina was too smart to get hurt. She wouldn't have had any trouble getting across the roof. I told you, she came from a family of circus performers. You must be mistaken."

"No, sir. I'm not mistaken. Your wife is dead."

"That's ridiculous! You're just telling me that to see if I break. I'm not stupid and I know how these things work. Where is she?" When Reightman didn't answer, he began pounding his hands on the table. "Christina! You need to get in here! They're trying to trick me and you need to straighten them out!" When those in the room failed to respond, and Christina didn't appear as demanded, Sutton Dameron glared at Reightman through narrowed eyes. "You're going to be very sorry for trying to trick me, Detective. Now, bring me Christina!" His agitation increased and his face contorted in anger. "Why won't any of you bring me my wife? I'll make sure everyone of you pays for this!"

To his credit, Dameron's attorney tried to calm him. "Sutton, settle down! You're just making the situation worse.

Dameron turned to him and yelled, "You're in on this too! Bring me Christina!"

Reightman took a step back to avoid the spittle that sprayed from his mouth as he continued to rant and rave. When he finally quieted down, and contented himself with glaring at them from his chair, Reightman spoke to him very calmly. "Mr. Dameron, I've already told you why we can't bring your wife here to this room. She was killed last night. She was murdered with a single bullet to the head by an unknown assailant. I'm sorry, but that's the truth, sir."

His eyes widened in shock and he looked into her face. It took a while for the words to penetrate, and once he truly understood his wife was dead and was no longer going to be able to take care of things for him, he collapsed and had to be carried from the room.

Later that day as Dameron sat across the table from Reightman and Jones, he was no longer boastful, but had withdrawn completely into himself. He gave only the most basic answers to the questions asked and it was obvious to everyone present he was broken man.

The questioning had gone on for time, and after confirming his confession from the morning, they had moved on to other links in the chain.

"Did you also kill Dr. Benjamin Lieberman?" Jessica Lautner asked from her place at the table.

"No, I had nothing to do with his death," Dameron replied, staring disinterestedly into the space in front of him.

"Did you know about the plan to put a hit out on Toby Bailey? A hit that resulted in the death of Detective Sam Jackson?" Jones asked sharply from where he sat next to Reightman.

"No."

"You expect us to believe you had nothing to do with those deaths, so I suppose you knew nothing about Helliman's death either. Or about his other activities?" Reightman asked him harshly, her disbelief of his innocence plain.

Sutton Dameron's eyes flickered briefly toward his attorney, before focusing again on some spot far, far away.

The lawyer cleared his throat. "My client had no involvement with former Officer Helliman, but," he paused and looked toward Jessica Lautner, "with some consideration from the DA's office....."

"What kind of consideration are you hoping for?" Lautner asked.

"Reduce the charges."

Reightman slapped her hand down on the table and stood from her chair. "You can't be serious!"

"I assure you, Detective," the attorney replied, "I am very serious."

Reightman turned toward Lautner and watched as the woman considered the situation. "Don't tell me you're actually thinking about making a deal like that."

Lautner held her eyes for a moment before shaking her head and turning her attention back to the attorney across the table. "We won't reduce the charges. However," she leaned back in her chair and looked toward Dameron, "if your client provides enough information – information helpful to the ongoing investigations into the other murders – I might see if I can take the death penalty off the table." As she saw the man consider her offer, Lautner added "Take it or leave it. That's my only offer. Otherwise, Mr. Dameron can take his chances, and as I'm sure you're aware, those chances don't look good."

The man across the table turned toward his client. "Sutton?"

Dameron refocused his eyes, and turned back to his attorney. He shrugged one shoulder. "He didn't help us when we needed it, so I don't see why I should help him." He looked at Lautner. "I accept your offer."

"This better damned well be worth it," Reightman muttered as she took her seat again.

Lautner leaned forward in her chair and picked up her pen. "Well, Mr. Dameron, start talking."

When Sutton Dameron had finished telling all he knew, Reightman looked at Jones and smiled.

Twenty-four hours later, and in the spirit of inter-agency cooperation, Federal agents seized all financial records – personal and business – of the Reverend Brother and Elder Ephraim Sawyer, the founder and CEO of the largest conservative evangelical church in the southeastern United States.

Reverend Sawyer was sitting in his palatial office located on the top floor of the business offices of the mega-church he'd founded many years ago, drinking twenty year old, premium scotch. He'd had a very trying day and deserved a drink or two. He was still finding it hard to believe that the Feds had busted in on him like he was some kind of common, low life criminal!

He swiveled his chair and gazed out the window, taking in the sprawling church campus as he held his glass in his long, thin fingers. He'd built this magnificent complex brick by brick from its humble beginnings in an abandoned shopping mall and he'd be damned before he'd see it crumble back to nothing. It was time to take care of the problem before things spiraled any further out of control.

He glanced at the gold watch on his wrist and tightened the lips of his hard, thin mouth as he waited for the visitor he was expecting. Thirteen minutes later, he heard the door to the office open and then close shut with a soft click.

"Hello, Dad," a voice from behind him said. ""I hear you had a bad day."

"Don't call me that! I am not your father," Sawyer said sharply from his throne-like chair, while continuing to look out the huge glass window to his wondrous creation below. "You haven't been responding to the many messages I've sent, and you're late. I don't like to be kept waiting." The Reverend spent a few more minutes admiring his view while pointedly ignoring his visitor. After he felt his visitor had been put off long enough, he finally swiveled his chair around to look at the man lounging casually in one of the plush guest chairs positioned in front of the wooden expanse of his desk.

"Aren't you going to offer me a drink?" the man asked.

"No, I'm not." Sawyer was tempted to turn back to the window, but thought better of it.

The man lounging in the chair took no notice of the cold, impersonal tone with which he'd been addressed. He'd had many years to become used to being addressed similarly by the Reverend Ephraim Sawyer. So many years to become used to being treated like he was less than dirt, unrecognized or given anything beyond the bare necessities unless he proved himself useful. So many years of being commanded to do the corrupt, sanctimonious bastard's bidding. The man mulled over the Reverend's refusal to provide him refreshment. "So much for the notions of Christian charity and Southern hospitality," he said a mocking voice. "Times just ain't what they used to be." When Sawyer didn't respond – other than to raise his glass in mocking salute before taking another swallow of the smoky, peat-infused liquor – the man asked, "So, how's Mom doing these days?"

"Your mother is very upset, as you might imagine. You might think about giving her a call to cheer her up, although that's probably too much to expect from you. You've never been concerned with anything or anyone unless there was a dollar or two attached. But that isn't why I wanted to see you. We're all in a hell of mess thanks to that fucking Sutton Dameron and his big damned mouth. I don't know what I ever saw in that pathetic excuse for a man." The Reverend raised his glass again, and took another drink. His fingers trembled slightly and it was clear that he was more disturbed by the turn of events than he wanted anyone to know – especially the man sitting across from him. He couldn't afford a show of weakness now. "If you had taken care of the situation earlier, like you were supposed to have done, none of this would have happened. Now we have a problem."

His guest thought over the Reverend's comment and then gave a dismissive shrug. "No, Dad, now you have a problem."

Sawyer placed his glass down his desk forcefully – enough to make the single ice cube inside click several times against the crystal. "We have a problem, you smartass little shit! You'll be implicated in much more than your mother or me if we don't get this under control. I may suffer grave financial reversals and the loss of all I've built, but I can recover. The stupid, misguided sheep in this world are always looking for someone to tell them how to think, and what to believe, and they'll pay lots of good hard cash for someone to do so. But you, son, you face the death penalty multiple times for your part in all of this. How many dirty little problems *have* you handled?"

The man in the chair shrugged again. "It doesn't really matter how many. They can only kill me once and they have to catch me first. But, I don't think there is much likelihood of being caught. After all, I've been very careful, just like you taught me to be. You beat that lesson into me time and time again. Besides, no one knows the full extent of my involvement except me. And you."

"And your mother."

"We both know better than that, Dad. She might have some idea of what's been going on, but we've both shielded her from the uglier side of this business so she wouldn't get her dainty, grasping hands dirty. She only knows what we've let her know over the years." The man in the chair smiled across the desk at the man he hated. "Like I said before, only two people know everything – me and you." The man stood up from his chair and smiled down at Sawyer. He reached across the desk and picked up the scotch and took an appreciative sip. "You always did have good scotch – it's too bad you didn't offer me one." He took another small sip to emphasize his point and enjoyed the look of outrage building in the old man's eyes. Now, I hate to cut this pleasant little get together short," he apologized as he wiped the glass down and set it back on the desk, "but I've got things to do and people to see, and one other problem to solve." He reached behind him and pulled the gun from the back of his waistband. Then, before the astonished Reverend Ephraim Sawyer could react, John Brown shot his stepfather right in the center of his head.

By Thursday afternoon, the news of Councilman Sutton Dameron's arrest and the death of his wife, Christina, was the featured news story in the state and was starting to be picked up by nation-wide news agencies.

Toby had already called Grams and given her the news before she could see a broadcast or read about it in the paper. He hadn't gone into much, if any, detail about his own involvement in the arrest or his near escape from death. When she asked about his weak and hoarse voice, he simply told her that he was suffering from a bad virus that was going around, and changed the subject.

He and Mitchell reported to police headquarters first thing that morning and provided their official statements about what had happened the previous night. Toby decided the best thing for him to do for the rest of the day was to take it easy, do a few things around the apartment, and maybe spend an hour or so in the sun. He knew that he hadn't had enough time to internalize the fact that Geri's killers had been found and he was waiting for the moment when his mind caught up to the facts. He worried when it happened, he wouldn't be able to handle the resulting breakdown.

A mid-morning thunderstorm changed his afternoon plans – at least the plans which involved sunbathing on the terrace – and he found himself indecisive about alternatives. Mitchell decided for him.

"Put on some shoes and grab your new gun. I think we should head over to the shooting range. You can use all the practice you can get."

"Hey! I did pretty well the first time, you said so yourself."

"Yes, you did – for the *first* time. But you need to be able to do better from here on out." There was a bullish tone to Mitchell's voice that Toby didn't understand.

"Why do I need to do better? Dameron's been caught and his wife's dead. I'm not sure I need to learn to shoot any better."

"Toby, if you are going to own a firearm you need to be the best you can be in order to use it effectively and safely. Those are part of the basic responsibilities that come with owning a weapon of any kind. You'll also need to plan time to practice so you keep your skills sharp."

Toby wasn't sure he cared for the Mitchell's lecturing mode. "Maybe I'll just sell the gun, now that this is all over. I've never wanted one in the first place."

Mitchell let out an exasperated breath and took a seat across from Toby at the table. "Toby, this isn't over."

Toby looked down at the table, refusing to meet Mitchell's eyes. "Sure it is," he said stubbornly, refusing to accept any other reality.

"No, Toby, it's not. As much as I wish it were – it's not over." Mitchell modulated his voice into a more reasonable tone. "Toby, Dameron and his wife are no longer a problem. But someone killed Christina Dameron on the roof last night."

"That may not have had anything to do with me."

"Maybe it didn't. Maybe it had absolutely nothing to do with you, and the person who shot and killed Dameron's wife was settling a personal score of some sort. But, Toby, are you willing to bet your life on it?"

Toby didn't respond and continued to look down at the table top, tracing the grain of the wood with his fingers. Mitchell considered other approaches – one which included forcibly dragging Toby from the apartment and shoving him into the car – when his phone rang.

"Office Mitchell," he answered. "Oh, hi, Detective Reightman."

Toby looked up from the table when he heard the name of the caller. He listened to Mitchell's side of the conversation, but wasn't able to make out much of what the conversation was about. He did, however, notice the hard set to Mitchell's jaw as the call progressed.

"Alright," Mitchell agreed, responding to something Detective Reightman said. "I'll tell him, Detective."

Mitchell ended the call, and sent a worried look his way. Toby stood from the table. "Tell me what?"

"That was Detective Reightman. She was calling to let me know ballistic testing confirmed the bullet that killed Christina Dameron matched the bullets fired at you – one of which killed Detective Jackson. She believes, based on the evidence, that same person fired the gun both times."

Toby's face blanched as his mind worked through what the information meant to him. Finally he turned his eyes to Mitchell. "The bullets that killed Detective Jackson were meant for me."

"Yes."

"This really isn't over, is it?"

"No, it isn't."

Toby turned and left the room.

"Where are you going, Toby?" Mitchell yelled after him, determined to finish their conversation.

Before Mitchell could follow him into the bedroom, Toby came back carrying a pair of athletic shoes and his gun case. "I went to get my stuff – just like you told me to do. I guess we'd better head to the shooting range."

"Toby, is it always going to take the possibility of death for you to listen to what I say and do what I ask?"

"Probably," Toby informed him agreeably. "Hurry up and get your stuff, Mitchell. I don't know why I'm always waiting on you to get ready to go somewhere."

Mitchell was always the first one ready to go anywhere, but he didn't respond to the baiting. He was just relieved that Toby had found some common sense, even if the reason was one neither of them wanted to contemplate.

On Friday morning, Sawyer's body was found. The debris from the shattered the window was discovered by of one of the church's administrative staff who arrived early to start her day. The confused woman looked up at the four story edifice, trying to discover where the scattered pieces of glass had originated. Spotting what looked like a badly damaged window on the top floor, she notified the maintenance team.

Sawyer's body was still seated in his huge, throne-like chair. The badly shaken worker promptly notified the Reverend's secretary, and she quickly followed him into the office to verify the shocking news. Shocked and horrified, she stumbled to the nearest phone and notified the police that one of the precious Lord's anointed prophets had been carried away from this earthly plane.

"The good Reverend looks the best I've ever seen him," Tom Anderson commented sardonically to Reightman as they stood a few feet from the body.

"I think he looks a bit pale." She studied the bullet hole which had been drilled into the center of the man's forehead. "Although, the manner of his death is disturbingly familiar."

"When I got the news, I was expecting suicide, Reightman. Having the Feds dig through his business must have been quite a shock to the old bastard." He stepped a few inches closer to the body and leaned in to take a better look. "I'd bet my hard earned money this wasn't suicide, but we'll have to wait on the coroner's ruling to be sure."

"I knew you were a man of unsurpassed wisdom." Dr. Evans told him, as she and Dr. Bridges made their way into the room. "Although, at first glance, I wouldn't bet against you this time." She began to pull on a pair of gloves and Dr. Bridges did the same. "It's a pity, too. I do like a good mystery once in a while and I rarely turn down a bet."

"I, for one, have had about all the mystery I can handle," Reightman commented, as she moved out of the way to allow the gurney to pass unhindered into the room.

"Is it okay for us to start?"

"Yes, Doctor Bridges, I'm done here," Tom confirmed. "I need to head downstairs to help Laurie and the rest of the team try and locate the bullet that blew out the back of this guy's head. I'm going to need that bullet to run ballistics, although based on the execution style, I'd say we're probably dealing with the same person that killed both Helliman and Christina Dameron. I just hope I don't have to get up on the *big* ladder to check the building walls, I hate heights and that ladder's kind of wobbly."

"Maybe you'll get lucky. The bullet must have been slowed as it went through his skull, the chair and the window. That had to slow the velocity and shorten the distance it could've traveled by quite a bit."

"It should have, but you never know. The places where I've ultimately located a spent slug would cause you to shudder in your sleep. I'll let you know what we do, or don't find, Detective."

"Hello, Anderson," Detective Jones said in greeting as he met the crime tech at the door. "Laurie said to tell you to get your lazy ass downstairs. She thought you should share in the fun of crawling around in the holly bushes in the courtyard."

"Thanks, Detective Jones. I was just on my way down. She's obviously past the deferential, respectful phase of our association. Having reached the one year mark of her employment, and receiving an exemplary performance review, has totally ruined our relationship." He grinned to show he didn't mean anything by his comment and went to join his team.

"Did any of the staff have anything helpful to share, Jones?

"No, nothing out of the ordinary. After the broken glass was spotted, the staff member informed maintenance about the problem, thinking maybe a bird had crashed into the window. The maintenance man discovered the body and told Sawyer's secretary, who called it in. The poor woman's really upset, and is adamant she didn't know of anyone who'd commit such a 'terrible sin against heaven'. Those are her words, by the way – not mine. Everyone else arrived after the body was discovered."

"That doesn't surprise me. If the killer's as smart as I think he is, he'd have made sure he was alone before he killed Sawyer." Reightman walked around the room once more, as the coroners supervised the movement of the body to the gurney. "I assume someone has notified Mrs. Sawyer?"

"Yes, the Reverend's secretary did, immediately after she called the police."

"And Mrs. Sawyer didn't feel the need to come down here? I find that interesting. She must've been concerned when her husband didn't return home last night."

"The secretary said Sawyer often stayed here overnight when he planned to work late. He had a small bedroom here in the building."

"I wonder if his overnight accommodations are as humble and low key as this office." Reightman's cynicism was plainly evident as she took in the immense, incredibly well-appointed room which had served as the man's office. "Let Mrs. Sawyer know we'll need to talk with her – tomorrow at the latest. I know she's grieving, but I want to verify her whereabouts at the time of the murder, and determine if she might have any helpful information."

"I'll set it up." Jones watched her progress around the room and joined her when she stopped in front of the wet bar. "It appears that the Reverend was a man of refined taste when it came to stocking his liquor cabinet. I bet this stuff cost more than I make in a year."

"Probably so, Jones." Reightman took one more glance around the room. "Let's go see if someone can help us locate Sawyer's nighttime accommodations. We might stumble on to something, if we're lucky. Grab a couple of pairs of gloves from the box by the door on the way."

Jones did as instructed, and followed her out of the door.

Jones and Reightman quickly commandeered a member of the church staff to lead them to Sawyer's bedroom. Once the door was unlocked and they entered the room. The small bedroom with attached bath actually held more resemblance to a very luxurious hotel suite than to the simpler accommodation they'd been led to expect.

Jones let out a surprised whistle. "These are pretty fancy digs!"

"Reverend Sawyer worked very hard, and the congregation felt he deserved the very best we could provide," the staff member sternly replied, making her disapproval of his comment clear.

"I'm sure he deserved everything provided," Reightman assured the woman. "We appreciate your help, but I think we'll be able to find the way back by ourselves. I don't want to keep you and I'm certain you have a lot of calls to make to notify all the church members of the Reverend's passing."

The woman gave Jones a final disapproving glance before she turned to join her fellow staff members in their collective grieving – and speculative gossip.

"You certainly managed to put her nose out of joint," Reightman told her partner, "and it only took a single sentence."

"Yeah," Jones replied gleefully, after trying and failing to contain his grin. "I have some pretty impressive communication skills."

The detectives pulled on the gloves and started their inspection. "Doing good works for the multitudes must pay a lot better than my job," Jones commented as he removed the expensively upholstered cushions from the antique reproduction sofa. "I should've made wiser career choices."

"Me too, Jones," Reightman agreed as she began searching through the drawers of the French Regency nightstands. "Compared to where I live, this place looks like a European palace. In fact, I bet it makes some of the smaller ones look pretty shabby in comparison."

He replaced the cushions on the sofa and started on the two co-ordinating armchairs. After he finished with them, he moved on to the desk which was the last remaining item in the room still to be searched. "You'd think the gigantic desk in Sawyer's main office would be enough for any mortal man," he said as he opened the center drawer and began removing contents.

"For a mere mortal, it would be." When he didn't respond, she looked up from her own search. "Find something?" she asked, moving across the room to join him.

"Maybe, maybe not," he said as he turned on the black phone he held in his hand.

Reightman looked over his shoulder as he scanned through the call history. After finding nothing of immediate interest, he opened the message app and scanned through the texts.

"I think 'maybe' is the right answer."

"I think you're correct, Reightman."

They both read the first words on the message screen.

I HAVE A PROBLEM

After scrolling through the entire series of exchanges, Jones turned off the phone. "Now we know who ordered Lieberman's execution and the attempt on Bailey."

"It sure looks that way. Now all we have to determine is who Sawyer hired to do the dirty work."

"Piece of cake, Reightman."

"I hope so, but I have a sneaking suspicion that identifying our hitman won't be as easy as just pressing the call button."

Jones decided to ignore her pessimism and focus on the positive. "At least your theory about how Lieberman died is proving out to be true."

"Time will tell, but we can rule out suicide after reading these messages. Dr. Evans is just going to love that." She took one last look around the room. "Let's get this down to Anderson and see if he can track down the recipient of Reverend's texts."

"If anyone can, Tom Anderson will."

Reightman took the phone from him and placed it in her jacket pocket. "Why don't you call Mrs. Sawyer and see if you can set up a time to meet. I'll meet you downstairs."

"You want me to send someone up to watch the door?"

"Yes, that's a good idea, Jones. Before we are done, we'll have half the force occupying space here."

"It'll be good for them. They might find they have a calling."

Reightman took the elevator to the first floor while Jones went to make his call. She found Laurie and a couple of other techs in the large courtyard watching Tom climb up a mid-sized ladder positioned to give him access to a garden statue. The large bronze was a depiction of Jesus Welcoming the Children.

"Looks like he found something." Anderson leaned forward, supporting himself by placing his gloved hand on Jesus's metal shoulder.

"Could be, and I hope so. I've had all the pricks I can handle today," Laurie reconsidered what she'd said. "I mean, I've had all the prickly rose and holly bushes I can handle today."

Reightman suppressed a smile. Tom extracted something from the head of the statue, and placed the item in a small evidence bag. He gingerly climbed down the ladder and walked over to where she was waiting.

"I brought you a present," he told her with a big smile as he wagged the bag in one hand. "I've been shopping for a while, since I didn't know what to get you. I figured any girl would love one slightly used slug from a preacher's head."

"You always bring me the nicest things, Tom. Where ever did you find it?"

"Ironically, in a place very reminiscent to where it first started the journey – right in the statue's head."

"Don't you find it slightly disturbing that the bullet was stopped in its path by a bronze Jesus head?"

"Nope," he grinned. "Come over here and I'll show you why it's ironic instead of disturbing." He led the way to the figural grouping near the center of the courtyard. "Look at the face of our wounded figure."

She did, and discovered that instead of depicting a compassionate and loving Christ, the statue's face was an exact match to the now deceased Reverend Ephraim Sawyer, and was forever frozen in a cruel, thin-lipped smile.

"This reinforces my belief in the Almighty," Tom told her.

"How so?"

"Well, the way I figure, the only way the bullet could have been guided here was by the hand of the Divine."

"That's almost poetic, Anderson." Reightman pulled the phone from her packet. "I found you a present too, but wasn't able to wrap it. I didn't have one of those nice gift bags you crime techs use."

"That's okay, I don't mind wrapping my own presents." As he took the phone into his hand he called out to his assistant, "Laurie, bring me another evidence bag."

"The best part of the present is inside, Tom. Go ahead and turn that baby on. Someone may have left you a love note. In fact, I know they did."

Tom – always a man to recognize a clue – immediately opened the message app. "This is one of the best presents anyone has ever given me, Reightman! I've always liked presents that take a little work to find the secret surprise." He turned off the phone and placed it in the bag Laurie handed him and sealed the top. "I'll see what I can find, but I have to admit I don't know if I'll be able to track anything down. The texts may have gone to a burner phone or a phone registered to an unidentifiable number. I'll get on it as soon as I get back to the office."

"Thanks, Tom. Will you be able to get to the bullet today as well?"

"Nope. I'm not going to do the ballistic testing." He handed the bag to Laurie. "My trusty side-kick is going to take care of that. She needs the practice."

Laurie rolled her eyes. "I don't need the practice, Boss Man. I'm already better at ballistics testing than you'll ever be. I have natural talent."

"In that case, I'll let you do all ballistic testing from now on."

"It'll sure beat dealing with the pricks I keep running into." Laurie replied as she walked away with her afternoon assignment.

"I like her, Tom – I mean, I really, *really* like her."

"She's a good kid," Tom said as he watched his assistant make her way back to the collection station they'd set up near the entrance to the courtyard. "In another couple of years she's going to be one of the best." He looked back toward Reightman. "Did you get me anymore presents?"

"No more presents," she answered regretfully. "But I did reserve a fancy suite for you upstairs – the same swanky place where I found the phone. Jones and I already went over everything, but I think you should give it your magic touch."

"That's what my wife says."

Reightman grinned at his quick comeback. "I bet you give her nice presents, too."

"You know it. I always have something ready for her to put into her firm, rosy palm."

"Alright, alright," she said, putting her hands up to surrender. "I can't take any more of this sexy talk – it makes me blush. Call me when you have some results."

"Will do, Detective. Will do."

Reightman met Jones on her way back into the building. "Did you reach Mrs. Sawyer?"

"Yes, I did. She sounded pretty torn up, but agreed to meet us tomorrow morning at eleven. She lives out by the lake, so if you want, I can pick you up and we can take one car."

"I'll take you up on the offer." She checked the time on her phone, discovering that it was later than she thought. "Let's head on back, Jones. I'll show you how to fill out all of the forms us poor folks in the Homicide Unit have to complete. You can watch while I get them started, and then *you* can finish them up."

"Why do I have to finish them up?"

"Because, the way I see it, you're my trusty side-kick and could use the practice."

Jones thought it over. "I can't even find anything to argue about in that statement. It wouldn't have done any good to argue if I had thought of something, would it?"

"Nope, not a bit," Reightman answered happily.

They headed to the parking lot, both perfectly content with the situation.

CHAPTER ELEVEN

THE CRIME TAPE was removed from the rooms of the Time Out Spa on Friday, and Toby and Mitchell made their way across the street a little before nine o'clock Saturday morning. Toby was in a surprisingly cheerful mood, and felt fairly optimistic about getting things back to normal – at the spa at least. His optimism lasted until he walked in and saw a very unhappy SarahJune sitting behind the reception desk.

"What's wrong? You look like something awful happened."

"It has, Toby. Something really awful *has* happened."

"What is it, SarahJune?"

"They've cancelled, Toby," she answered, beginning to panic.

"Who's cancelled?" Toby felt his cheerful mood beginning to dissipate.

"Everyone."

"Everyone has cancelled their appointments?"

"Yes, all but two."

"SarahJune, you're right. That that isn't good news, but we only had five appointments for today to start with. I'm not happy about the cancellations, but I don't think we should panic."

"You don't understand what I'm telling you! They've *all* canceled – all but two. Our clients have cancelled *every* appointment we had on the books for….for *forever*."

Toby found it hard to believe, but after looking through the appointment book he realized she was right. "What did they say?"

"A lot of them called last night and left messages, but I did talk to several more this morning. In a nutshell, they apologized – very politely, in most cases – but said that they couldn't continue to patronize a business where so many *horrible* and *scandalous* things have happened."

Toby focused on trying to remain calm and to keep the panic he was feeling from coloring his voice. "Did you try to convince them that all of that was over, SarahJune?"

"Yes, of course I did. Most of them were nice, even regretful, but they were all *very* firm that they would not be returning here – ever."

He continued to process her news, and tried to figure out how he could deal with the situation. "Is any of the staff here yet?"

"Brigette is the only one here right now. She had the first appointment and came in as usual to make sure everything was 'shipshape and orderly'. Andre's supposed to be in later. I think he's scheduled for an appointment at eleven, and usually comes in about twenty or thirty minutes before his appointments."

"Do they have anything at all today – after the cancellations?"

"No. I haven't said anything to them yet. I wasn't sure what you'd want to tell them."

"You did exactly the right thing, SarahJune," he assured her. "I'll go talk with Brigette, and then I'll call Andre."

"What are we going to do, Toby?"

"I don't know yet. But after I've talked to Brigette and Andre, I'll call some of my regulars and see if I can smooth things over and change their minds. Can you start making me a list of names and telephone numbers while I talk to Brigette?"

"Sure, Toby."

After he broke the news to Brigette and Andre, Toby took the list that SarahJune had prepared and went back to his office, trailed by a silent Mitchell. A few hours later, he knew things were bad. He hadn't been able to convince a single customer to give the spa another chance.

"I'm heartbroken for you, Toby," Adelaide Daniels said over the phone. "I've always appreciated how you made me feel pampered and special – even though I could stand to lose about thirty pounds. But…my husband won't allow me to continue coming to the spa."

"Would it help if I spoke with him, Adelaide? Maybe I could reassure him."

She hesitated before answering. "It won't help. I'm sorry."

After thanking her for her patronage, Toby hung up and went on to the next person on the list. The story was the same, although not everyone was as forthcoming about the situation as Mrs. Daniels had been. Finally defeated, he put the down the phone and laid his head on his desk.

"Is there anything I can do, Toby?"

He lifted his head and looked up at Mitchell who was sitting in one of the chairs in front of his desk. "I wish there was, but I don't think there is anything we can do to save this situation." With a heavy sigh, he sat back up behind the desk. "I need to figure out what to do now. In my worst nightmare, I never anticipated this."

"What are you going to tell everyone who works here?"

"The only thing I can, Mitchell. I have to tell them we're going to close." Toby turned to his computer and checked his bank balances and then opened the spreadsheet that he used to track and forecast the spa's operating expenses. He spent several minutes entering numbers and making adjustments and then finally shut the spreadsheet. "With the money I have on hand, and without wiping myself out totally, I can afford to give them each a small severance package. If I can convince SarahJune to help me manage the shutdown, I can probably keep her on for a couple more weeks and give her a nice check when we're finished. She's been with me since the very beginning. She was the first person I hired."

"Toby, when the spa had to close before, most of them were able to find some extra work to get them through. And, what about outcalls? Maybe they'll stay on until you can get things under control."

"I can't ask them to do that. Last time, everyone knew it was temporary and that we'd eventually be back to normal. This time, it's different. I don't see any way I can recover from this."

"You can't just give up!"

"I'm not giving up – I'm being forced to confront reality." Toby leaned back in the chair and closed his eyes. "Geri did all of those things to make sure I wouldn't have to worry about money or anything else having to do with the business. He thought he was protecting me, but the funny thing is, the things he did and what happened after are going to be the very reason I have to shut down."

"I don't think it's very funny."

"Me either, Mitchell. But it's the truth."

After a few minutes, Toby lifted his head and stretched to relieve the tension that was beginning to turn into a world-class headache. "I need to talk to Madame Zhou and see if she can help me get out of the lease. I still have about fourteen months of obligation. I can cover it, but it'd be nice if she could find a way to negotiate an early termination which would allow me to hold on to some extra cash. I'll need it until I find a job myself."

He spent a while longer contemplating his now uncertain future, then turned off the computer and stood from his chair. "Let's get out of here, Mitchell. There's no reason to sit here brooding about things. I'm going to talk with SarahJune and see if she'll agree to help me over the next few weeks. Then I think we should head back to the apartment. I can call Madame Zhou from there, and then I think I'll make myself a drink and drown my sorrows in the sun."

Mitchell followed him out of the office and waited while Toby locked his office and then turned off the lights in the treatment rooms and the breakroom. He spent the next several minutes looking out onto Capital Street while Toby told SarahJune about his decision to close the spa. Mitchell heard the soft sound of her crying and could hear in the distress in Toby's voice. Mitchell continued to watch the people on the street, going about their business like it was a normal day. *It is a normal day for most of them,* he thought as he heard Toby asking SarahJune if she would stay on and help in close the place down.

"Of course I'll help, Toby, I was the first one in the door and it's only right I should be the last one out of that same door. I'm just sorry it's come to this. I've loved working here and you're the best boss I've ever had."

Mitchell could see their hug in the hazy reflection of the window. SarahJune collected her purse and went out the door, wiping her eyes before she slipped on her sunglasses and stepped out into the sun. She walked down the street and Mitchell noticed that she didn't look back.

"I think that was the worst part of the day," Toby said as he walked to the front door. "Ready?"

They went out the glass door, and Toby locked up. "I feel a vodka and tonic in my immediate future, Mitchell. I know you won't drink one of those while you're on duty – which is all of the time these days – but could I interest you in a beer?"

"Sure, a beer sounds good about right now."

The two men walked to the corner and waited for the light to change before crossing the street. "I bet you'll be glad when this job is over, Mitchell. You can get your own life back to normal."

"Maybe, Toby. But, I think I might be bored without all of the excitement you seem to stir up."

They went up the stairwell, and the minute they stepped in the door, Toby began to shed his clothing. "Starting your nudist routine already? Don't you want to wait until you have talked to Madame Zhou?"

"There's no need to wait. Besides, she's already seen me nude."

"What? When did she ever see you nude?"

Toby's shorts hit the floor and he bent to pick them up. "She doesn't know I know, but she leases an apartment on the top floor of the building on the other side of her shop. Sometimes I see the curtains move when I'm out in the sun. I think she's taken a few peeks. I've never actually caught her, and after a while I didn't even try. If she's not bothered, then I'm not going to worry about it."

"If that's the case, I'm not going out on that terrace unless I'm fully covered!"

"Oh come on, Mitchell. It's no big deal. Besides, you could use some sun. You need some color."

"I don't tan very easy – so I think I'll just keep everything on anyway."

"I wouldn't let you get burned. I'll make sure you have on plenty of sunscreen."

Mitchell considered as Toby handed him a beer and then started mixing himself a drink. "I'll come out there with you, but I'll wear a pair of shorts."

"Suit yourself, but I think you are being silly. I'm going to call Madame Zhou. Would you bring me my sunglasses when you come out?"

"Sure. I'll be out in a minute."

Tony picked up his phone and called Green Dragon. After he had exchanged the obligatory greetings Zhou Li seemed to appreciate, he filled her in on the situation and told her what he'd decided to do about the spa.

"Considering what you have told me, Toby I think that is probably wise. I am proud of you for making this difficult decision."

"I think it is the best decision, but I'm having a hard time accepting the fact that the dream I've had since I was a teenager is dead."

Zhou was silent for a few seconds before she spoke again. "I have learned that when one dream vanishes another takes its place, if you remain open to the possibility. Try and remain as positive as you're able. You'll see I am right – I usually am."

"Thanks for the pep talk, Madame Zhou. When do you think you'll hear back from the management company regarding the lease?"

"I'll contact them on Monday and explain the situation. I will probably get an answer by the end of the week and I let will you know what they decide. In the meantime, try to get some rest. The last weeks have been trying."

"Yes they have been. I'll let you go now. I'm sure you have things to do."

"Yes, I'm leaving here shortly to attend a party that is being given by an old friend who lives out of town. It will be a nice get-away and I always enjoy a celebration. They have arranged for someone to pick me up and I am going to spend the night there and return tomorrow, after lunch. I'll talk to you soon, Toby."

"Well, that was certainly a waste of time," Reightman commented after she and Jones left their very unproductive meeting with Marilyn Sawyer. "She didn't understand half of what I was asking."

"Give her a break, Reightman. The combined shock of Federal agents descending on her husband's church, and his execution style murder has probably been quite a blow. We can follow-up again, after Sawyer's funeral. She did offer."

"You're right. I guess I was too hopefully optimistic about the whole thing." Her phone rang and Reightman pulled it out of her purse.

"Detective Reightman speaking," she answered. "Hello, Chief. Yes, I've got a minute….What?...No, Chief I don't think it's a good idea!– I think it is a very bad idea….Oh he did?" She glanced over at her partner. "I see. But……Yes, sir….I'll let him know. Goodbye."

She hung up the phone and stuffed it back into her bag. "That was Chief Kelly. He's decided it's time to reassign Mitchell." She watched his profile as he checked the rearview mirror and changed lanes. "He said he spoke to you about it and you thought it was a good idea." Jones didn't offer any immediate comment. "Mind telling me about that conversation?"

"I didn't tell him I thought it was a good idea…exactly. He asked me how I thought Mitchell was doing. I told him I thought he was doing okay, but could probably use a break. Kelly said he'd been thinking the same thing and had decided to pull Mitchell off and assign a rotation to Bailey. That way, no single person has to bear the burden of twenty-four hour coverage. That was the end of the conversation."

"Why didn't you mention it to me?

"To tell you the truth, it slipped my mind. With the Sawyer murder front and center, I just completely forgot about the conversation. What's the big deal anyway? It is probably time to make a change."

Reightman looked out her window, trying to decide why it *was* a big deal. "I think Mitchell's going to be upset, and I know Toby will be. They have grown very close over the last weeks. "

"Then it is definitely a good idea to reassign Mitchell. After this is all over, they can resume their friendship – or whatever they have going on."

Reightman didn't care for his tone. "What do you mean by that? You sound very disapproving."

"I don't disapprove – honestly. I'm concerned about Mitchell though. I don't want him get the idea that he's the only person who can keep Bailey safe. He'll put his own life on the back burner and who knows what he'll miss out on? I think he deserves better than that." He took the exit off the interstate. "Mitchell told me about the man he's interested in when we were working together. As long as he's tied to Toby Bailey, he'll never pursue another relationship and that would be a shame. Frankly, the change might do Bailey good as well. He can certainly remain friends with Mitchell, but maybe this change will prevent any inappropriate feelings from forming, especially feelings for the police officer assigned to protect him. He may very well start forming some kind of hero-based attachment and will be hurt if Mitchell fades away after this is done. One more dose of hurt won't do him a damn bit of good. He needs someone to help him heal – not provide him a roll in the hay."

"You may be right about some of it, but I still don't like it. I'd better call Mitchell and break the news." Reightman dug the phone again, and Jones listened as she spoke to the young officer.

Toby put down his phone and picked up his almost finished drink and went inside to make another. He was squeezing a wedge of lime when Mitchell entered the kitchen wearing a pair of flowered board shorts, accessorized by a beach towel displaying the local college mascot.

"I talked to Madame Zhou," Toby updated him as he put a few more cubes of ice into his glass. "She said she'd talk to the management company on Monday. She's going out of town to visit a friend and won't be back until noon tomorrow."

"Does she think they'll negotiate the lease termination?"

"She didn't say. She said we'd know by the end of the week." Toby put the ice bin back into the freezer and opened the fridge. He frowned when he got a good look at what Mitchell was wearing. "I like the shades – that mirrored look is very retro-cop. But those shorts are horrible."

Mitchell shrugged. "I like them."

Toby rolled his eyes, 'Of course you do! They cover you past your knees. You want that beer?"

"Sure," Mitchell exchanged the sunglasses he had fetched for the cold bottle, and followed Toby out onto the patio and adjusted the back of the lounger and sat down. "The only thing you need out here is some music."

"I can take care of that! I have a portable speaker that works with my phone. I just forget about it most of the time. I'll be back in a minute – I'll have to find it."

Mitchell looked over to the apartments to where Toby suspected Zhou Li lived. When he assured himself there was no suspicious curtain activity, he made himself comfortable and sipped his beer.

"How did it go," Jones asked as she ended the call.

She shrugged. "I didn't get a clear sense of what Mitchell thought, other than he's worried about Toby. He wants to make sure he's well protected."

"Toby Bailey will be very well protected – probably better protected than he is now. Not that Mitchell isn't dedicated, but with a rotation of officers they'll all be rested and more alert for possible threats. How much longer can this go on, anyway?"

"I don't know, Jones. I hope not too much longer. We're expending a lot of resource and not making much progress."

"Not much progress? Come on, Reightman! We stopped Sutton Dameron and his wife. That counts as progress."

"Yes, but we aren't any closer to finding the person who killed Lieberman, Helliman or Sawyer."

"Or Jackson," he softly reminded her.

Reightman turned her face back toward the window and kept her thoughts to herself for the remainder of the ride.

"Are we working tomorrow?" Jones asked when he dropped her off at her condo.

"I don't think so. We can all use the break. Thanks for driving today."

"No problem. It was worth it to see that huge house. Can you believe some people live like that?"

Reightman snorted. "No, it was quite a dump. I don't know how they manage. I'll see you Monday, Jones." He gave her a jaunty wave and drove away.

When Toby came back out, he looked Mitchell's way then set up the speaker and scrolled through the selection of music on his phone. "Jazz okay?"

"Sounds good to me."

Toby made his selection and turned back to Mitchell. "I have to say it's an improvement, but I thought you were worried about Madame Zhou seeing you without your trunks."

"You said she was going to be gone, so I decided I'd try some more of this naked stuff you're advocating all the time." Mitchell turned his head slightly to Toby, his eyes completely hidden behind the mirrored sunglasses. "I think you promised me some sunscreen."

"So I did!" Toby bent down and picked up the bottle of sunscreen by his lounger. "Should I make sure all of your all of your naughty bits are covered while I'm rubbing this in?" he asked with a very wicked grin.

"Thanks for the offer, but I can handle my own naughty bits."

Toby felt that was too good to let pass. "I bet you can, Mitchell! I bet you handle them *very* well indeed with those big, strong hands." Disappointed when Mitchell didn't reply, Toby walked over to Mitchell's lounger. "Sit up and I'll put this on your back. After that, you're on your own." Toby flipped the top up on the lotion. He bent down slightly and squeezed the liquid directly onto Mitchell's back.

Mitchell jumped. "Hey! That's cold!"

"Serves you right," Toby said as he worked the lotion into the skin, covering the back and shoulders. He worked down the lower back and then stopped. "I've reached the forbidden zone, so you can finish things up from here." He wiped his hands across Mitchell's back one more time and handed him the bottle. Mitchell stood and quickly covered his firm butt and the backs of his legs. When he finished and was about to reposition himself on the lounger, Toby reached over and took the bottle from his hands. "I think you missed a spot there, big boy. Hold still and I'll do it. I sure don't want you to get a burn. I'd never hear the end of that!"

Toby squeezed out more lotion into his hand and rubbed his palms together before placing his hands on Mitchell's ass. Mitchell shied away, but then stood completely immobile as Toby rubbed in the lotion, lingering for a moment on the small tattoo centered on the Mitchell's left cheek. "That should keep this cut of prime grade beef from burning," he said as he playfully slapped the now properly SPF covered ass and went back to his own spot in sun. He adjusted his own lounge and applied a little more lotion to his own chest and then closed his eyes, listening to the slow, smooth jazz.

Thirty minutes later, Mitchell lifted his head from his lounger. "I think it's time for me to turn over."

"Probably," Toby agreed. "I think that side of beef is done for the day."

Mitchell stood and moved the lounger to take advantage of the changed angle of the sun and then picked the lotion and began applying to his chest and stomach, working his way down the front of his hip and legs. He sat back down on the lounger. "Mitchell, I think you forgot something. Some *very* important somethings."

Mitchell looked at him through the mirrored shades. "Oh I did, did I?" With a flirtatious grin he poured a small amount of lotion into his hand and spread the lotion slowly over the missed areas, watching Toby through his glasses the whole time. Toby was suddenly taken back in time to several years ago, when on a sunny day by a pool, he'd first met Geri and had watched him apply lotion to his beautiful body. *"Mitchell is totally different from Geri,"* Toby thought as he mentally compared Mitchell's much fairer skin with its dusting of fine light hair to Geri's darkly tanned, satin smooth skin. *"He's every bit as handsome, just in a different way."* They lay companionably in the sun, listening to the music. After a few more minutes, Toby stood up and stretched. He applied lotion to his shoulders and back and to his own pretty nice ass. He caught Mitchell looking, so he took his time. Finally satisfied with his performance, he lowered the back of the lounger and then settled himself down.

They both enjoyed the sun and the silence until Mitchell cleared his throat and sat up in his lounger. "Toby? Do you every wonder what it would be like….I mean, do you ever wish we…..?"

"Yes, I have, and I do wish, sometimes." Toby felt the sun shining down and he allowed himself to just imagine what could be, before he continued. "But, I don't think the time is right for us to…you know, and I wouldn't want to ruin anything because it wasn't – for either of us."

Mitchell sighed. "I know. But sometimes – like now – I wish we could just…."

"Me too, Mitchell."

"Toby, there's something I need to tell you." Toby heard the lounge chair creak and something in Mitchell's voice made a small knot form in the middle of his chest. "Detective Reightman called while you were on the phone with Madame Zhou."

Toby didn't want to know what Mitchell was going to say. "Yes?" he made himself ask, turning his head to face him.

"She told me they've confirmed that the same person who killed the others killed Reverend Sawyer." He paused for a minute to allow that to sink in. "The other thing she told me was… I'm being reassigned. Someone will be relieving me tomorrow morning, on Chief Kelly's orders. I'll still be working with Detective Reightman, but…"

"But not here, with me."

"No, not here with you."

Toby looked away, hoping that his own sunglasses were hiding his eyes, which were brimming with unshed tears. Once he was sure his voice wouldn't betray him, he turned back to Mitchell. "Can we do one thing before you go?"

"Sure. What do you want to do, Toby?"

"Tonight, when we go to sleep, I want us to hold each other until morning. Just hold each other. You've kept me safe – even from myself – and helped me through the nights I woke up terrified and certain I was alone. Tonight, Mitchell, I'd like to us to keep each other safe."

Mitchell stood and knelt down beside him. Toby felt his hand on his shoulder, caressing his skin. "I'd like that very much." Mitchell lingered a minute more, and then walked through the French door and into the apartment.

Toby stayed on the terrace until the sun began to set. He never noticed when the curtains from the apartment across the way parted slightly, and then closed again. He had no way of knowing Zhou Li's ride had been delayed, and or that she'd witnessed the moment when Mitchell told him he was leaving. He never knew she'd watched as Mitchell knelt beside him and touched his skin. He never heard the soft, sure words she said as she wheeled her small suitcase to the door.

"…when one dream vanishes another takes its place…"

Once the sun was down, Toby went inside, showered, and fixed a simple dinner. They ate and joked and talked and tried not to think about tomorrow.

That night, Toby and Mitchell held each other until the sun rose again. Neither of them slept, but they did keep each other safe all night long.

CHAPTER TWELVE

SUNDAY MORNING, TOBY welcomed a new officer into his apartment and helped settle her into the guest bedroom. He then helped Mitchell carry his bags to the car. They had to make several trips, since Mitchell had a lot more to take home than he'd brought with him when he first took up temporary residence.

"Can you believe I managed to haul this much of my crap over here in the last few weeks?" Mitchell joked as they crammed the items into his car. "You'd think I'd decided to just move in permanently!"

Toby turned away, and refused to meet Mitchell's eyes. "Yeah. You'd think you'd decided to do just that."

"Toby, please don't be like this. There's no reason to be upset. We'll stay in touch."

"I know, but it won't be the same."

"No, it won't." Mitchell wanted to hug him, but held himself back. "Keep yourself safe, Toby. Don't forget to find time to practice at the shooting range."

"I won't forget."

"You'd better not! I'll have to come over here and whip your ass if you do." Mitchell shuffled his feet a few times. "I guess I'd better get out of your hair. See ya around." He held out his hand.

Toby hesitated and then took hold of his hand and shook. "See ya, Mitchell. Thanks for everything,"

Toby trudged up the stairs to his apartment. After he went in the door he locked it and then turned to the woman standing in the living room. "Officer Owens, can I fix you something to drink? Some coffee or tea?"

"Thank you for the offer, Mr. Bailey, but I'm fine. I brought my own with me. Just go on about your day as if I weren't here."

"Okay, but if you need something, feel free to help yourself."

"I'll be fine, Mr. Bailey."

Toby started down the hall to his bedroom to gather up a load of laundry and then turned back toward her. "Officer Owens, I don't suppose I could convince you to call me Toby, could I?"

"No, sir. I don't think it would be very professional for me to do that."

For the next couple of hours, Toby occupied himself with household chores. He fixed himself a sandwich and ate it, alone, at the table. He read a little during the afternoon, hoping to fall asleep. He didn't. Later, when the protection detail rotated, he tried to engage the new officer on duty, but didn't have any better luck than he'd experienced with Officer Owens. Depressed with the changes, he showered and crawled into bed. He picked his phone up from the nightstand and typed a short message before turning off the light.

His phone buzzed a few minutes later. He picked it up and read the return message from Mitchell.

I MISS U 2

He considered texting back, but finally laid down the phone. He tossed and turned for a while and reached over and pulled Mitchell's pillow to his chest. He inhaled deeply, trying to capture some trace of his scent. He finally closed his eyes, and slept.

The next few weeks passed slowly. Toby and SarahJune worked half days, making their way through the list of things needing to be done to close the Time Out Spa. Toby contacted a supply company and arranged a time for a used furnishings dealer to come and look things over and give him a bid.

At the end of the week Zhou Li called. "I heard from the management company, Toby. The building owner agreed to renegotiate better terms for the cancellation of the lease. They realize the situation which led to your decision to close was out of your control."

"What have they offered?" Toby asked.

"They have agreed to let you out of the lease at the one year mark, with no additional penalty. You'll be required to pay through the end of November. They also indicated that if your situation changed, they'd honor the original lease at the original terms."

"That's very generous of them, Madame Zhou, but I don't think the situation will change."

"You never know. Remember what I said to you about remaining positive."

"Yes, ma'am, I remember. Thank you for working this out for me. It's a big load off my mind."

"You're very welcome, Toby. I'll talk to you soon."

Toby wandered to the front reception desk to see how SarahJune was progressing with her paperwork.

"Toby, I got a call from someone wanting a massage in the next couple of weeks. He knew we were closing, but still wanted to schedule an appointment. I told him I'd have to check and call him back."

"Might as well – it'll buy us a few more lunches."

"Okay, I'll let him know. He said he wanted the ninety minute special."

"See if he can do next Saturday afternoon. Sunday would work as well. We'll be pretty much done by then. He can be my last customer."

"Toby, remember I'm not going to be here next weekend. I'm going to visit my sister. Will you be alright here by yourself?"

"I'm never by myself anymore," he said, nodding ruefully towards Officer Owens. "I'll be fine."

"Okay, I'll call him back and get it set up."

Reightman's next weeks dragged by as well. The team combed over evidence and worked through every possible lead, but nothing turned up. As she went over the evidence for the umpteenth time, she had a thought. Since she had the time, she could try the neighbors on Chutney Street one more time. She'd take the glasses with her, hoping that they might jog a memory or two.

"Tom, it's Reightman. I need you to do something for me. Do you still have the glasses found at the Lieberman scene?....What do you mean – you can't find them?....Yes, there have been a lot of instances of things being misplaced....I know and yes, you're right....just let me know if they turn up." She slammed the phone down, frustrated and disgusted.

At the end of the second week, things got worse. Chief Kelly broke the news he was going to cut back on the manpower assigned to the case. "There are not enough of us to go around," he gruffly informed her. "Other things are suffering from a lack of attention." He leaned back in his chair. "I've had several complaints about the reduced neighborhood patrols so I'm also cutting loose the team assigned to Mr. Bailey."

"But Chief, you can't do that! We haven't found the killer yet and he's still in danger."

"Reightman, we may never find the killer. You told me yourself that he appears to have vanished on the wind. We can't provide around the clock protection to one man if it means the rest of the population suffers."

"Chief, I think –"

"Reightman, I've made my decision," he interrupted sharply. "And before you can pull that old woman into it, I should tell you that the Mayor has also agreed, and so has Hollingfield."

Reightman felt a headache starting and rubbed her temples as she tried to take it all in. "So, you're pulling everyone off, except for Jones and Mitchell?

"I'm pulling everyone off, but Jones. I'm sending Mitchell over to Vice to get some street experience. We're down an officer since Lamont's arrest and the change will do Mitchell good."

Reightman tried to cover her disappointment and to push down the feeling of unease that crept over her. "When will the changes be effective?"

"The changes are effective immediately, Reightman. Bailey's detail will continue through tonight, but tomorrow they'll be back on regular duty." The Chief stood from his desk and made his way to the door. "I think that should cover things, Detective." As he opened the door, he turned back, obviously having thought of one more item he wanted to cover. "Reightman, about the Assistant Chief's position we talked about a few weeks ago…"

"Chief Kelly, truthfully, I haven't had much time to think it yet."

"That's why I'm mentioning it to you now. I've decided to look outside the current pool of departmental personal in order to bring in some new blood. I hope you're not too disappointed."

For some reason, Reightman was sure he was hoping that she was *very* disappointed. Maybe it was his small cold smile of amusement, or perhaps it was the anticipatory glint in his eyes which clued her in. *"He wants me to make a scene over this,"* she realized. *"He's hoping I'll cross the line and prove he was right about me after all."* She met his eyes and smiled as she went through open door. "I'm not disappointed. Not at all."

She didn't know how she felt, but a wave of helpless frustration washed over her when she realized that now, she might never find the person who had killed Lieberman, Helliman, and Christina Dameron. Worse, was the overwhelming sense of failure which rose up inside when she admitted that if she didn't find that person, the person who'd aimed for Toby Bailey and missed, she'd never find out who'd killed Sam.

A week later, SarahJune put way the files she had finished and walked back to Toby's office. "Toby, I finished the last of the files and I think I'll head on home. I have a long drive a head of me and I'd like to get started before it gets too much later."

"Thanks. Have a good visit with your sister. When are you planning on being back?"

"I'll be home late Tuesday and I'll be here on Wednesday. Hey, don't forget your appointment tomorrow."

"I have it in my phone and even set a reminder. Now, get out of here. Drive safe and have fun!"

Toby left shortly after she did, and walked down and visited with Moon until she closed. He drove to the grocery store and then re-stocked the cupboards. He downloaded a few books, and then took a long shower. He decided to go out to grab a bite to eat and was soon seated at a small table in his favorite Italian place, located a few blocks from his house.

"Hey, Toby!" He turned around searching for the voice and saw Mitchell seated at a nearby table, with an attractive man.

"Hi, Mitchell!" He got up and walked over to the table. "I wasn't expecting to see you here. "

"We decided to try this place. I heard it was pretty good." Mitchell cleared his throat a little awkwardly. "Toby, I like you to meet Bradley Clark. He's a … well, I think I might've mentioned him to you."

"Hello, Bradley, I'm Toby."

As the man stood to shake his hand, Toby appraised him quickly. *"Nice looking – maybe late thirties or early forties. He's a little shorter than Mitchell, and has kind of a stocky build. Not fat at all, just solid for his height. Looks like a nice amount of chest hair. Nice eyes and wait…silver hair at his temples and a neatly trimmed mustache and beard. This man – Bradley – is the silver daddy…..."*

They finished their handshake and Mitchell grinned, letting Toby know his suspicions about who Bradley was were correct. "Why don't you join us, Toby? We haven't even ordered yet."

Toby briefly considered it, but quickly discarded the idea. *"It's time for us all to move on,"* he told himself sadly. He smiled brightly toward the two men, obviously out on a date – maybe even their first. "I appreciate the offer, but I need to get on home. It's been a long week and I'm beat." Toby noticed the look of relief on Bradley's face as he made his excuses. "Bradley, it was nice to meet you, and I hope to see you again sometime. Mitchell…take care of yourself. I'll see you around."

Toby walked to the front of the restaurant and asked for his dinner to be packaged as a to-go order. Then he walked home, not paying attention to anything until he suddenly found himself at the foot of the stairwell that led up to his apartment. He looked up the stairs and realized he wasn't sure how he'd gotten there, or how long his walk had taken. Once inside, he stowed the food in the fridge – having decided that he wasn't hungry after all – and shed his clothes as he went into the bedroom. He looked at the bed, and then went to the linen cabinet and grabbed some fresh sheets. After the bed was stripped, he held on to a single pillowcase, stroking the fabric before he finally tossed it on top of the pile of used linens. He made the bed with fresh sheets. Toby read for a while, not paying any attention to the words. An hour or two later, he suddenly got up from the bed and rushed to the laundry hamper. He dug around until he found the item he wanted. He folded the pillowcase carefully and then placed it in the bottom of a dresser drawer, out of range of sight and smell, and out of the reach of his hand. But, he knew it was there.

Toby ran a few errands Saturday morning and picked up some packing boxes. After he was through with the afternoon's appointment, he'd start packing up his office. He started across the street, struggling with his load, and reached the door of the spa just as another man did.

"Here, let me help you with those so you can get the door," John Brown offered with a smile. "I'm supposed to be meeting someone here anyway."

"Thanks, I appreciate it." Toby handed the empty boxes to the man and dug out his keys. "I'm the person you're meeting." He unlocked the door and then opened it and ushered the man inside. He took the boxes from him and carried them behind the counter, and then went back and locked the front door.

"Are you the only one here today?" John Brown asked as he pushed up the dark-framed glasses which had slid down his nose.

"Yeah, just you and me today," Toby confirmed. "I think that SarahJune told you that we were closing, so we are not really staffed anymore."

"Yes, she did and said you'd only be here another week or so. I appreciate you fitting me in – I'm sure you must have other things to worry about."

"It wasn't any problem. I'm Toby by the way."

"It's good to meet you, Toby. I'm Bill Jones."

"Well, why don't we go on back to the treatment room and get you all set up?"

John Brown, aka Bill Jones, followed the young man to the back of the building, pausing as Toby stopped to flip on a few lights.

"It's warm back here," John Brown commented as they entered the smaller treatment room.

"I must have turned off the air conditioning system when I left last night. I forgot that I wasn't going to be in this morning. I'll turn it on, but it may take it a while to cool down. These old building aren't very efficient. I'll apologize in advance in case it's too uncomfortable."

"Shouldn't be a problem. I'm not going to be wearing clothes anyway."

"Most people like the room to be warm when they get a massage. The body temperature drops some as the blood flow gets going, so maybe it won't be too bad." Toby put a clean sheet on the table and smoothed down the corners and then placed another sheet on top and folded it back. "Alright, Bill, I'm going to go grab a couple of bottles of water for us. Go ahead and make yourself comfortable."

Toby left the room and John Brown undressed. He draped his clothes on the back of a chair and then sat down, waiting for Toby to return.

"Oh! I'm sorry!" Toby apologized as the nude man stood when he entered the room. "I thought you'd already be on the table or I would have knocked before entering."

"I wasn't sure what to do, except to get undressed. I've never had a massage in a place like this. Don't worry – this is just like being in the locker room at the gym. Plus, I'm not at all modest."

"Now that you mention it, I guess it is sort of like a locker room," Toby said as he carried the bottles of chilled water to the counter.

"Is one of those for me?"

"Sure – sorry. I must be kind of flustered for some reason." He started to walk across the room to give him one of the bottles, but Bill met him in the middle of the room.

"Thanks. I was getting thirsty."

Toby took a step back to give Bill more space, knowing that some men were really touchy being close to other men – especially when they were naked.

John Brown stayed where he was – totally unconcerned – and unscrewed the bottle cap and then took a long drink. Small drops of condensation fell from the bottle onto his chest. John Brown gently rubbed it in. "That's refreshing!" he teased and then shivered slightly. "I might be glad it's warm in here after all." He took another drink and then walked a step forward and handed the half empty bottle to

Toby. "Thanks." He maintained eye contact and asked shyly, "What am I supposed to do now?"

"Now you get up in the table. You're supposed to get under the top sheet."

"Won't it just get in the way?" John Brown asked doubtfully.

"No, I am trained to work around it to preserve the client's modesty."

"To late for that!" John Brown laughed and indicated his un-clothed state. "I vote we skip the sheet."

"I'm…ah…really supposed to do it that way."

"Who's going to tell? It's just you and me here today," John Brown said as he sat on the edge of the table. "What now?"

"Let me give you the run down." Toby walked him through the process, and answered a few questions.

"Thanks. Now I know what to expect," John Brown said with a grateful smile. "Should I lay back on the table now?"

"Yes, and while you make yourself comfortable, I'll put on some soothing music and grab some other stuff."

Toby put on the music and adjusted the volume, and then picked out a bottle of lotion. After looking back at the man on the table, he also picked up a bottle of oil, and a couple of long narrow towels. "I think we should try both lotion and oil. You can decide which one you like the best. Both are unscented and hypo-allergenic, so neither of them should cause you any problems." Toby pulled a small rolling table closer to him and sat the bottles down. He slung one towel around his neck and folded the other and placed it on over the man's groin. When Bill lifted his head slightly and looked back at the towel, Toby grinned sheepishly. "That's to protect *my* sense of modesty – not yours. Things are going to get up close and personal here in a minute."

"Thanks, Toby, but I'll be okay. I just plan to enjoy the experi-ence. I've been anticipating this for a while."

"Okay, but remember what I said. I'll also check with you about the pressure I'm using. Other than that, I'll try not to talk much un-less you want to start a conversation. Some people like it quiet."

John Brown nodded his agreement and Toby started the massage. After a few minutes, John Brown lifted his head. "Toby, could you take my glasses for me? It's still kind of warm and they keep slipping down my nose."

"Sure." Toby took the glasses and set them on the small rolling table. "And you're right – it's taking it a while to cool down. I'm already sweating and I haven't even really started working yet." Toby started on the arms and hands and picked up one of the man's hands to support it against his chest as he worked the delicate muscles and tendons.

Bill chuckled. "You *are* sweating. Your shirt is drenched already."

"Sorry," Toby said. "Let me grab a towel so it doesn't bother you."

"Doesn't bother me at all. But, you could take off your shirt. It's just us after all."

Toby looked down at his shirt and shrugged. "I wouldn't even consider it any other time, but if you really don't mind, I think I will." John Brown assured him that he wouldn't mind at all and Toby pulled off his shirt and toweled of his chest. "That's better already." He finished the initial portion of the session, occasionally exchanging some light banter with his client. 'Why don't you turn over and I'll start on your back."

Bill followed instructions and Toby repositioned the towel, and then opened one of the bottles from the table. "I'm going to try some oil now and you can tell me which you like better."

After a few minutes of working on the man's upper left side, he moved to the right. As he looked down, he noticed the tattoo on the back shoulder. It almost triggered a memory, but Toby couldn't quite capture it. He shook his head and focused on the man on the table. He slowly worked his way down the body and started working the man's glutes.

John Brown reached behind him and pulled off the towel. "I don't think that's needed and it seems to be getting in the way. Like I said, I'm not worried about you touching anything accidentally and it feels better without the towel."

Toby continued his work and Bill lay quietly on the table. Toby could feel the man begin to relax as he worked down the strong thighs.

John Brown let himself just experience the massage, enjoying the feel of Toby's hands and the slide of the oil. "*I didn't know if I would like this,*" he admitted to himself, "*But damn, it feels great. I could get used to this. I like his hands on me.*"

Toby moved to Bill's other thigh and bent the leg at the knee slightly and the moved the whole leg upward so that he could get to the large muscles. As he did, he heard Bill sigh on the table. "That feels great, Toby. If you could work just a little higher, it would be perfect."

"Here?" Toby asked moving his hands upward until they were just underneath the buttocks.

John Brown exhaled as Toby's hands massaged the flesh, enjoying every minute. "Yeah, that's the spot."

He didn't speak again for the next several minutes, but Toby knew he was enjoying the session from the small sighs of pleasure coming from the table. "Okay, I think you can turn over now and I'll finish up the front."

John Brown hesitated. "I…uh…I'm embarrassed to admit this, but I need a minute. I got so relaxed and your hands felt so good that I ….got excited, and it will take a minute for things to go back to normal. I'm sorry – I don't know why this happened."

Eventually, Toby realized what Bill was trying to tell him and shrugged it off. "Don't worry about it. It happens more often than you think." Toby handed him the towel and said, "Take your time and just drape this over yourself when you're ready. I'll get a drink of water."

Toby turned his back and opened his water. He heard the man turn over on the table and took another drink. He turned back around and the man seemed to be in control of himself, although Toby *did* notice the bulge of the towel on the man's groin was more pronounced than it was at the beginning of the session. Toby wasn't offended – he thought it was actually kind of endearing.

John Brown was surprised his body had responded so obviously to Toby's touch. He'd felt a growing attraction for some time, and had longed to be the man on the terrace with him on the summer evening he'd watched him and his friend in the moonlight. John Brown tried to reason through his physical reaction, and more confusing to him – his feelings. He didn't usually have feelings he needed to work through.

Toby walked back to the table and continued the massage. He worked the man's chest, using quite a bit of pressure on the firm pectoral muscles, and then worked his way down the muscles of the abdomen, moving his hands in slow circles as he progressed. He noticed Bill didn't have the typical six-pack everyone seemed to strive for, but his stomach *was* taunt and tight, and Toby could feel the muscles shift slightly under the skin. He moved to the hips and then down the thigh. As he worked up the inner thigh, he could see the towel beginning to rise again. He took his time finishing since the man seemed to be enjoying it, and then switched to the other leg. By the time he had completed the other, Bill was well on his way to being fully erect. *"I hope he's not embarrassed again, because it really does happen more than people think."* Toby moved his hand hands back up the man's body. *"He's really nice looking too, and he rocks those retro-glasses he was wearing."* Toby's hands stilled at the top of the shoulders. "We have about fifteen more minutes, Bill. Where would you like me to spend the time?"

John Brown knew exactly where he'd like Toby to spend the time, but knew better than to say. "Maybe on my upper back and shoulders?"

"That's where most people need extra attention," Toby told him. "Go ahead and roll over and I'll see what I can do."

When Bill turned over, Toby caught a glimpse of his impressive looking equipment. Noticing Toby's glance, John Brown took his time adjusting things before lying flat.

Toby looked away quickly and once Bill had repositioned himself on the table, he finished up by working the muscles of the shoulder and neck, noticing the tattoo again. *"Alias,"* he thought as he read the tattoo's lettering. *"Why is that familiar to me?"* He placed his hands on Bill's back. "That's it, I'm afraid. How do you feel?"

"I've never experienced anything like that," John Brown answered truthfully. "It was wonderful."

"Good, I'm glad you enjoyed it. I'm going to leave you here. Please take your time getting up – there's no rush. If you want, you can use the showers in the men's locker room down the hall before you leave. I'm going down there in a minute and rinse myself off, and I'll meet you out front when you're done."

"Thanks. I think I'll take you up on that."

Toby replaced the bottles on the table and then put the towels in the hamper in the corner. He quietly left the room.

John Brown stayed where he was for another couple of minutes, thinking about what he'd just experienced, and enjoying the hard, pulsing feel of his erection. Once it had subsided a bit, he slowly rolled over and put his legs over the edge of the table. He walked over to the counter and picked up a large, clean towel and secured it around his waist. He picked up his clothes and his shoes started for the door. He remembered the glasses on the table and went back for them, and then made the short trip down the hall. He walked into the men's changing room just as Toby was stepping out of the shower.

"Sorry I'm still in here, but the water felt good. I'll be out of your hair in a minute." He pulled a towel off a hook and wrapped it around his waist.

John Brown wished Toby hadn't been so quick with his towel, but the liked the current view of the man's damp skin just fine. "Please don't rush! I wouldn't mind the company."

"Okay. I don't have anything else to do after this, so I'm not in any real hurry. Why don't you tell me what you thought of your first real massage? Was there anything that would have made it better for you?"

John Brown ducked his head shyly as he unwrapped the towel from his waist and stepped into the shower. "It was great Toby." He turned on the water. "The only thing that would have made it better is something I'm not about to tell you – although you can probably guess after seeing my little…problem."

Toby laughed, but didn't comment.

John Brown smiled at the sound of his laughter and suddenly didn't want their time together to end. *"I wonder if there's a way to get him to spend more time with me."* He decided to take a chance. "So Toby, are you seeing anyone special?"

Toby was surprised by the unexpected question and it took him a moment to respond. "No, I'm not. I've had rough few months and right now there's no one special in my life – at least in the way I think you mean."

"Well, since that's the case…would you consider….going out with me?" This time John Brown was the one surprised by his own question. He didn't know what made him ask, but he could feel his heart beating in his chest as he waited in nervous anticipation for the answer.

Toby mulled over the offer. He thought about what his life had been like over the past months. He thought about Mitchell and seeing him with Bradley on what was probably one of their first dates. He admitted how appealing he found the man currently in the shower, and how nice and normal he seemed. He also admitted that he thought Bill was very attractive, in a shy, geeky science guy sort of way. It was a big bonus that this particular science guy obviously worked out and on top of everything else, was impressively hung. There was something which just drew him to this guy. "Yeah....I might."

"Really?" John Brown was stunned. He walked to the door of the shower stall and looked over, surprise written on his face. "I mean, you would?"

Toby grinned at the man's mixture of disbelief and eagerness. "Yes, I would, Bill. You name the time and the place."

John Brown figured there was no reason to wait. "Okay. How about...right now?"

"Now?"

"There's no time like the present! I think I'd better strike while the iron is hot and before you can change your mind." John Brown smiled engagingly over the stall door. "You did say you didn't have anything else to do tonight."

"You're right, I did say that." Bill's smile grew bigger, and that decided it for Toby. "Okay. What do you want to do?"

John Brown considered everything he'd learned from watching Toby these last few weeks and tailored his suggestion accordingly. "I don't know. My favorite thing to do is to grab a bottle or two of wine and some take-out food from somewhere, and find some place where we could talk and get to know one another. It'd be nice if we could find someplace near here, where we could just sit on a patio and watch the sun go down." John Brown ducked back under the water to rinse off some soap and then appeared back at the shower door. "I know that probably isn't exciting, but....what do you think?"

"I think it sounds....like a great idea. It's one of my favorite things to do. As a matter of fact, I know of a place very near here if you don't mind that it's a bit of a mess. I …uh…live right across the street and I have a great terrace on the third floor. The only thing is – there's no elevator. We have to walk up a couple flights of stairs."

"I don't mind stairs – if you're sure. I won't want to impose on you on our first date."

Toby liked the idea of having an actually first date. "It's not a problem – if that's what you really want to do."

"I can't think of anything I'd rather do." John Brown stepped out of the shower and dried his hair with the towel.

Toby watched him in the mirror as he removed the towel from his head and dried off. *"He certainly has no body issues,"* Toby thought. *"And there's not a damned reason why he should."*

John Brown walked naked to the mirror and combed his hair roughly into place with his fingers and then wiped off the few drops of water that still clung to his chest. He caught Toby's eyes in the mirror and smiled. "I'm afraid I didn't bring anything fancy to change into, Toby. You'll have to excuse me and take me as I am because I didn't plan on anything like this happening." John Brown found himself wanting to make a good impression, because he thought that was how dates were supposed to work.

Toby smiled back, trying to keep his eyes above waist level. "That's fine, Bill. I don't feel like getting dressed up anyway. Usually at home I wear as little as possible." His gaze flicked downward for an instant before snapping back to Bill eyes. "Besides, I've already seen you at your…uh…very best, back on the table."

John Brown had caught Toby's shifting eyes, and thought he might be flirting, so he decided to try it as well. He ducked his head again and grinned shyly. "About that, Toby?"

"Don't apologize again, it's kind of flattering."

"That's not what I was going to say. What I was going to say is, you weren't seeing me at my very best. There was still quite a bit of room for improvement."

Toby blushed when he realized what he was being told, and John Brown found it very appealing. He walked to the bench where he had laid his clothes, and watched as Toby walked to where his own clothes were waiting.

Toby dropped the towel and bent to reach for his underwear. He felt soft terry cloth touch his skin and stood slowly.

"You missed a place, Toby." John Brown gently dried the moist skin, caressing it and wanting to touch more. He moved the towel lower and stopped just above Toby's ass. "That's better," he whispered before realizing how he sounded. When Toby turned his head with his lips slightly parted, he cleared his throat and removed the towel from Toby's skin and went back to his clothes. "Now get dressed and let's go find a bottle of wine and some food." John Brown watched Toby dress as he pulled on his own clothes. *I wanted to just keep touching him. I feel happy for some reason, and I hope I'm making a good impression.* John Brown thought about Toby's lips as he buttoned his shirt. *I wonder if he'll let me kiss him tonight. I've never kissed a man before.* As he slipped on his plastic framed glasses, he decided that it was a very good thing that he hadn't killed Toby Bailey after all.

Their first date was very enjoyable and they talked and learned a little about each other over a bottle and a half of wine. They agreed to meet the following evening. When Toby asked what Bill wanted to do, John Brown responded, "Exactly this, Toby. I want to do *this* again if you don't mind. It's the best evening I can ever remember. I'll bring dinner and the wine. You provide the company."

At the end of the evening, John Brown walked slowly to his vehicle, enjoying the warm evening air. *He did let me kiss him, and I liked it, a lot.* He drove home, touching his lips and remembering the sensations he felt.

The next three weeks they were almost inseparable, and saw each other several times. Things progressed a little further, and they necked on the couch until they had to pull away from each other to catch their breath. John Brown buttoned his shirt and replaced his glasses as he stood up on shaky legs. "I better go." As much as he desperately wanted Toby naked, he decided not to rush things. He wanted to make these new feelings last, but if he didn't leave now, he knew he wouldn't be able to hold back. He picked up his blazer and put it on over his rumbled shirt. "I have a busy couple of days ahead so I won't be able see you until the weekend. Are you busy Friday night?"

"I'm disappointed that I'll have to wait, but I'd love to see you Friday."

"What would you like to do?" John Brown asked, while trying to analyze the word Toby used. *"Love."* He'd very little experience with that word in his life, and he wasn't sure what the associated feelings should feel like. Maybe it was time to try and find out about this love thing. He figured even a sociopath like him could learn if they wanted to badly enough.

"I don't know. What sounds good to you?"

"Well," John Brown hesitated, although he knew what he wanted, more than anything. "It's nothing fancy, but I have a small cabin about an hour from here. It's not much more than a single room, but there's a hot tub on the deck and the scenery's nice. The stars are amazing at night. It very secluded and I thought – if you don't have any other plans – we could drive up there Friday evening and come back on Sunday."

Toby wondered if it was too soon to be going away with a man he'd only met a few weeks ago, but pushed his doubts away. *"He just might be the one,"* he told himself. Besides, he thought it sounded like a nice change. "Sounds great. I could use a getaway. I'll get some food together and we can cook up there. Is there a stove?"

"Not a great one, but there is a nice grill."

"Perfect! I'll buy the food and you can cook it. I have no idea how to grill anything."

John Brown pulled him in for a kiss. "I'll take care of the cooking then."

"What should I bring? I mean, in the way of clothes and stuff."

"Bring a sweatshirt, because it can get chilly in the evening. Other than that, just a few casual things should do it."

They kissed once more and Toby walked Bill to the door. "I'm looking forward to it, Bill."

"Me too, Toby." John Brown said honestly, before he walked out the door.

CHAPTER THIRTEEN

REIGHTMAN WAS FED up with the lack of progress they were making on the case and as a result, was having a rough go of it at work. She was plagued by the feeling she was missing something important. Finally, she decided to let it go for a couple of days, and decided to visit her daughter and grandbabies. She arranged to take Thursday through Sunday off since there was nothing to hold her back from finally making the much postponed visit. Everything could wait until she got back. It wasn't like they were racing against the clock right now. She packed a small suitcase and a bag full of gifts and toys for her girls and then, on a whim, she called Toby.

"Hey, Detective Reightman," he answered. He sounded cheerful and more energized than she'd ever heard him.

"How are things going, Toby?"

"Actually, they're better than I could've ever imagined a few weeks ago. I've almost got everything shut down at the spa and I'm starting to think about what to do next. How about you?"

"I'm still trying to plug away, Toby. It's down to just me and my partner now, but I'm trying not to lose hope. I'm going to visit my daughter, though. I have been meaning to get to the upstate since...since the weekend Sam Jackson was killed." They were both silent for a moment, then Reightman forced some brightness into her voice. "I'm looking forward to seeing my granddaughters."

"How many do you have?"

"Two, and believe me, some days that's more than enough!"

"Somehow I get the feeling you don't really mean that. I bet you spoil them to death. When are you leaving?"

"Tomorrow afternoon. I'm going to stay until the last possible minute on Sunday."

"What a coincidence! I'm going out of town on Friday and will be coming back on Sunday too."

"Are you going to visit your Grams?"

"No, but I am planning a visit a few weeks from now. I need to spend several days helping her get the yard and the house ready for winter. She does a great job keeping things up, but she's getting older and I try to help as much as I can. This weekend I'm going away with someone I met a few weeks ago."

"Oh? Is this someone special?"

"Maybe, but I'm not sure yet. We do have a great time together and seem to like a lot of the same things. He has a cabin about an hour from here and invited me up to spend the weekend. It will be a change of pace, and I can use a change."

"Sounds nice. Sometimes a change is just what's needed. Oh, before I forget, have you heard from Mitchell? I don't see him much these days. They're keeping him busy over in Vice."

Melba caught his slight hesitation and wondered what caused it before he answered. "I talk to him occasionally, and he promised to meet me down at the gun range in a few days. We've both been busy and he's…he's seeing someone, too."

"Everyone seems to be seeing someone except me," Reightman laughed, after deciding that maybe there wasn't anything wrong after all. "Let's plan to catch up more when we both get back. Maybe we can take Madame Zhou to dinner. I miss her – I can't believe I just said that."

"That would be fun! Have a fun visit and enjoy your time with your family."

"You have a good time too, Toby. I'll talk to you soon."

Melba didn't realize until she was almost at her daughter's house that she hadn't asked the name of the man Toby was seeing. *"I'll find out when we go to dinner,"* she thought as she turned into the driveway of her daughter's small, neat home. When her grandchildren flew out the door to greet her, she forgot everything except the laughing, squealing girls she scoped up in her arms, and Abby's hug of welcome. At that moment, life for Melba Reightman was very good.

Unbeknownst to Toby, the new man he was seeing made a trip to his weekend cabin on Thursday evening to prepare for the weekend. He'd been reading up on this love thing and wanted everything to be perfect. The experts all said one of the things that showed someone you loved them, was when you made an extra effort to make things nice on special occasions. Since in his mind this qualified as a special occasion, he cleaned the place from floor to ceiling. He brought in a load of firewood, cleaned the hot tub and the grill, and put fresh sheets and blankets on the bed. As a final touch, he gathered an armful of foliage from the wooded acres around the cabin and placed then in an old glass jar in the middle of the rough wooden table. He stepped back to view his work, and was satisfied with all he'd accomplished. The last thing he did was check that he had a plastic tarp – just in case things went wrong. It would save a lot of mess in the end. Tired, but satisfied, John Brown went back to the city to get ready for the next day.

Toby likewise occupied himself by getting ready for the weekend. He shopped for food and wine, and picked up a good bottle of brandy, thinking it might be nice to enjoy in the hot tub while viewing the stars. Not knowing what provisions the place had, he filled a weekend bag with essentials. He put his portable wireless speaker in the bag and assembled a few clothes. When John Brown arrived to pick him up, he laughed hysterically at the assorted bags and boxes, but happily helped carry them down the stairs and load them into the back of his SUV.

They talked about their week and the ride went quickly. As they made the turnoff onto the country road, Toby realized just how secluded Bill's weekend hideaway was from the rest of the world. A few miles later, John Brown turned onto the rough gravel road.

"I think civilization stopped about twenty miles ago," Toby commented. When they pulled up to the small weekend retreat, he got his first view and gave a sigh of contentment. "But after seeing this, I think civilization is highly overrated."

"It's not much," his host apologized, "but it's a good place to get away to for a few days."

"It looks pretty fantastic to me." Toby took in the small clearing in front of the house and the mixed woods and foliage casting graceful shadows in the early evening sun. "How far away is the nearest neighbor?"

"At least a couple miles away. That's part of the reason I come here – it's nice and secluded and I can hear myself think." John Brown opened the front door and ushered Toby in. Toby set his arm load of provisions on the nearest surface and looked around the space.

The small cabin consisted of a single large room, about four hundred and fifty square feet of space. There was a large wood burning fireplace centered on the back wall flanked by two large windows which looked out onto the deck and then to the forest beyond. The kitchen was not really a kitchen at all, just a mid-sized refrigerator and – separated by a few feet of counter – a small and ancient three burner stove top and oven. Toward the back of the room, a large bed was positioned to catch the view from the windows. There was a roughhewn table and four chairs with a vase of foliage on top of the table. Toby noticed everything was very clean, as if someone had worked hard to make the room inviting. He suspected Bill had been very busy and was touched by the effort.

"What do you think?" John Brown asked nervously, as he watched Toby look around the room.

"I think it is wonderful! Let's finish unloading and when we have everything put away, you can show me around."

After they were done, John Brown opened a bottle of wine. He realized he'd forgotten to buy wine glasses, so he filled a couple of mason jars. He handed one to Toby. "I'd like to toast the first visitor I've ever brought to this place. I hope you enjoy your stay, Toby."

"And I'd like to say 'thank you' to the man I met just a short time ago, but feel I've known for much longer. Thank you, Bill, for inviting me for the weekend."

John Brown was pleased by the sincerity of Toby's words, and after they had taken the obligatory drink to complete the toast, John Brown showed him the cabin. "There's not really enough to call this a tour, but I'll show you around anyway. You can pretty much see everything there is to see in here without me showing you, but here," he opened a small door almost hidden in the wood encased door, "is the bathroom. It's small, but everything works and I've only had to chase out snakes a few times in the last three years."

"You forget that I practically grew up in the country. You can't scare me with the mention of snakes or any other kind of critter. "

John Brown laughed and led him out a door at the near the back of the room. "Here's my favorite part of the whole place."

The deck was huge and was filled with furniture made for outdoor living by local craftsmen. There were chairs with huge overstuffed cushions which Toby suspected had been placed there the day before, and the aforementioned grill and hot tub.

Toby imagined all of the good times they might have here. "This is amazing! Is the water in the hot tub warm?"

"It should be. Help me pull off the covering, and we'll find out."

The water was hot, having been heating since the day before. The grill, however, was not. "I'll just turn this on to warm up," John Brown said. "What did you bring us to eat?"

"I got easy stuff for tonight since I didn't know what time we'd get here. There's some rotisserie chicken and a couple of sides. I got steaks and a couple of chicken breasts as well, and a few breakfast and snack things for the next couple of days. You can choose. I'm just glad to be here."

"Then I'll turn off the grill and we'll take it easy tonight. Tomorrow, I'll teach you how to grill up the best steak you've ever eaten."

"That sounds good, but don't get your hopes up about my cooking ability. Right now I could use some more wine."

After both men refilled their glasses Toby took another look around the room. He liked the spare lines and the handmade furniture and thought it was a perfect weekend retreat. He was curious about one thing, though. "Should I assume we're both sleeping here?"

John Brown looked up from assembling their makeshift dinner to see Toby testing out the mattress. "Well, I thought maybe we'd be…"

Tony grinned at the worried expression on his face. "Bill, I'm happy to share the bed. It looks plenty big enough. You don't snore do you?"

"I, uh…I don't know."

"No one has ever mentioned if you snore or not?"

"No," John Brown replied, and decided to just tell him the whole truth. "You see, I've never slept with anyone for a whole night."

"But, you've …"

"If you're asking if I've ever had sex, the answer is, yes, many times. But, to tell you the truth, I've had sex with more women — many more – than with men."

Toby was surprised. Bill had been taking things slow, which he appreciated, but Toby had never expected part of the reason might be due to inexperience. "How many men *have* you had sex with, Bill?"

John Brown looked away for a moment. "Technically, two different men. And one more, which didn't work out too well. I cut things short with that one." He sighed, remembering his encounter with the fat doctor. He decided he'd better get it all out there. "With the other two, it was mostly fooling around and a little bit of oral, on their part – not mine. I've usually just been attracted to women."

Now Toby was confused. "Then why did you ask me out, and why have you been…courting…me?"

John Brown looked into Toby's blue eyes. "I've been attracted to you from the very beginning. I can't tell you why, but you make me feel….something when I am with you. If you're worried about that, all I can say is I'm open to about anything."

"Even the sexual aspects?"

John Brown thought about his question. "I'm not sure, but based on the reactions I get when we kiss, and the way I couldn't control myself when I had the massage, I'm almost positive there shouldn't be any problem."

Toby set down on the bed and stroked the quilt thoughtfully. "Come over here and sit down."

John Brown walked slowly over to the bed and sat down, worried about what Toby was going to say.

"First of all, give me those glasses." Once the eyewear was removed, Toby leaned in and pulled the man's head to his and brought them together for a kiss. As it grew in intensity, Toby placed his hand on Bill's thigh and worked it up to cup the cock and balls through his jeans. After a minute of heated mouth action, he pulled away. "There's a reaction – you're right about that! I have reason to know you've had that reaction before, so it's a good start. But here's the thing – I haven't been in a regular relationship with anyone in a long time. My romantic life has been somewhat curtailed, for many reasons."

John Brown knew that Toby had been through a lot over last few months, and he himself had even indirectly contributed to the trauma. After he thought about it, he could almost understand why Toby hadn't found companionship. In fact, he was happy that was the case. But, he was curious if Toby's lack of regular companionship had also put a damper on Toby's sex life. "You've told me a little about the things that happened, but did that keep you from having sex? Totally?"

"Pretty much. There were a couple of quick hook-ups, but they were all about getting off, and didn't even come close to what I'd consider to be anything more."

John Brown was trying to understand, but was having difficulty because he'd never really considered there could be anything more. He wondered what it would be like to have someone steady who cared about him and who he cared about in return. The idea intrigued him, in ways he didn't expect. "What would come close? I mean, what would it take for it to be more?"

Toby shrugged and thought about how to tell Bill what he wanted. He took his time before he spoke. "I think I want someone who will be a true partner. I've told you a little about me and Geri, and with him, I thought I'd found that. But Geri lied and did a lot of things, which in the end, I couldn't accept. He convinced himself that he was doing those things to help me – and maybe he really believed it. But they didn't help, and led to a lot of bad things happening. I want someone to share my life with who's my friend, and who's honest, and supporting, and knows right from wrong. I think it's the only type of relationship I could accept."

John Brown was perplexed, but decided not to think about it anymore. Instead, he asked the question foremost in his thoughts. "Do you think I could be that person?"

Toby looked him in the eye. "Do you, Bill?"

John Brown didn't know. He'd never had the opportunity before. He hesitated, but finally gave Toby the best answer he could. "Maybe. If you'd help me. No one has ever wanted me to be their…friend before."

Toby grinned. "Well, at least you're honest." Then more seriously, he added, "I like you a lot, Bill. I've enjoyed getting to know you, and if I haven't actually said it, I also think you're pretty darned hot." He could see he'd embarrassed Bill with his last comment, but needed to continue. "In spite of that, I'm worried you haven't had any experience with a real relationship and that makes me nervous."

John Brown might not have had any experience in this relationship business, but he had a lot of experience in making people nervous. Usually, he enjoyed it, at least when it was for a job. But he was dismayed that Toby was feeling uncomfortable with the situation, especially since the weekend was just getting started. He knew if he was going to have any hope of having a little fun, he needed to put Toby at ease. "You're right. I don't have that kind of experience. But, if you'll give me a chance, I'll try my best to give you what you're looking for." He looked over at the man beside him to see what effect his words had, and decided it wouldn't hurt to add a little more. "Just tell me what you need. I'm willing to try."

Toby was drawn to Bill's sincerity, and wondered if maybe, against all odds, this man was what he was looking for after all. Bill's earnest gaze from behind those geeky, sexy glasses said more than his words had. "I guess it can't hurt to give it a shot and see how it goes." Bill's eyes lit up and his lips curved into a slight smile. Toby had a few more things say and needed to get everything out in the open before he accepted Bill's assurances at face value. "There are a couple of more things." Bill's smile faded at his serious tone, and he gave Toby a somber nod. "I think we can figure out how to make this work. I hope so. But, Bill, just don't try to deceive me or lie to me. That is one thing I just can't handle. Tell me the truth, and I promise, I'll try to accept it." Bill's face clouded for a moment and Toby nudged him with his shoulder. "Hey, it's not like you're a nut case or a mass murderer! In comparison to those options, everything else is a piece of cake to work through." He gave him a goofy grin, trying to lighten the mood.

John Brown was suddenly very uncomfortable as he tried to interpret the silly, trusting expression on Toby's face. He knew he was supposed to react, so he nudged Toby back. "Yeah. A piece of cake." He forced a smile on his face, and then stood and went to the window, looking out to the green, lush woods.

"Are you okay, Bill?"

John Brown wasn't sure, but turned back to reassure him. "Yes. I'm just thinking about what you said." He looked back outside, and asked, "What about the sex part? What do you want?"

"Well, I like sex, a lot."

John Brown was relieved. Maybe this was going to be okay. "That's good!" He was encouraged by Toby's smile, and went back to the bed. "What do you like?"

"Well, I like a lot of things, but to cut to the chase, I like sex with a partner who both gives and takes in bed." Bill's looked at him quizzically, so Toby asked, "Do you understand what I mean?"

John Brown thought back to some of the things he'd seen and heard and thought he had a pretty good idea. But until now, he hadn't thought of much beyond kissing Toby and hoping Toby would eventually go down on him. "Yes, or at least, I think so. You're telling me you're versatile and you want a partner who is as well. Is that what you want between us?"

"Well, yeah! But don't get me wrong, If I thought you were just a one night stand or a casual fuck buddy who wanted to exchange blow jobs, or were looking to top or to bottom exclusively, I might be cool with it. Is that what you want us to be? Fuck buddies? I'd like to know before we progress too much further, so I know how I should set my expectations. I probably should have asked before I came up here, but I didn't."

John Brown was thinking furiously, trying to figure out how he *should* react and how he *wanted* to react. This was all so far outside his experience he didn't even know how to begin to answer. All he knew was he wanted a chance, and he'd hate to lose it just because he couldn't get his mind around the sex part. "I think I understand what you're asking, and I don't think I want to just be a casual roll in the hay. But the part about giving and taking? Well, I think I know the basic mechanics involved, but I don't know how I'd feel if I was....doing some of those things." He stood from the bed and stretched, trying to calm his mind. "Let's go outside. I can think better out there."

"I have a friend who thinks I think better outside too, but only when I'm not wearing clothes."

John Brown smiled at his memory of seeing Toby and his friend on the terrace, and fetched the bottle of wine. "We better take this with us. This might be a long conversation."

The two men carried their wine outside and took a seat in the deck chairs. For a long time they just set quietly. "Tell me what it's like, Toby. The good and bad parts about sex between men."

"I don't know if I can, because I don't think anything's bad. It's more a question of what someone does or doesn't like, and that can change depending on the circumstance, or who they're with. I personally think the only really bad thing is when someone is forced to do something they don't want to do, or when someone hurts another person just because they enjoy seeing someone else's pain."

John Brown didn't say a word, but he did think of the times he had caused other people pain. He decided he really hadn't enjoyed it – it was just a job. He figured he could adjust his behavior to fit Toby's thinking, at least regarding Toby himself, and maybe as it concerned any potential sex acts they engaged in. "Okay, I understand all of that, but tell me about the sex part. Like I said I have a basic idea, but tell me how it all works."

And Toby did.

After he finished, John Brown was astonished and spent a couple of minutes wrestling with his thoughts. Some of the things Toby described sounded pretty damn good, but a few – which didn't sound exactly bad – sounded uncertain to him. He closed his eyes to see if he could get a picture of himself doing the things Toby had described, and finally decided there was only one way to know for sure. He wondered if enjoying some of those things would mean he was gay. If it did, and he found it really bothered him, well, nobody needed to know about this little experiment. Only he and Toby would know, and Toby could be taken care of. After all, Toby was here alone with him, and there weren't any people for miles around. He could be killed very easily and no one would be the wiser. John Brown already had the big tarp pulled out to wrap him up with, and digging the grave wouldn't be hard to accomplish. It would be a shame to kill him, but it was a reasonable solution to the dilemma. Upon reaching this satisfactory conclusion, John Brown stood from his chair. "Let's go get some food and then we can try out the hot tub. We can talk about this more when we're in the hot water. I think it'll be relaxing for us both."

The two men had dinner and cleaned up and put away the leftovers. John Brown opened another bottle of wine and carried it out to the hot tub. He tested the water and went in and got a couple of towels. "Water's just right, Toby. Come on."

Toby followed him out the door and soon they had both stripped and were immersed in the hot, bubbling water. The stars were starting to come out, and the moon was bright. Toby laid his head back against the rim of the hot tub relaxed, enjoying the soothing warmth.

"So, I've been thinking about the things we talked about," John Brown said matter-of-factly after they'd been in the water for a while. "I really like you a lot, and might even have some feelings stronger than that, but I'm not sure. Like I told you, I've never experienced them before. But I don't know what I think about the physical part yet." He fortified himself with a swallow of wine and considered the stars for a minute. "I'm willing to try it all, as long as we take it slow and I can figure out what you like, and what I like. But, I need to be able to stop if we're getting to something I can't handle. I don't want to have to....I don't want things to turnout in a way that hurts you. If we discover we both can't get what we need, then I'll tell you and call it quits. That's the best I can do.

Toby was surprised at the usually shy man's straightforward pronouncement. Although it wasn't as heartfelt as he'd have liked, he understood that maybe Bill just couldn't bring himself to say it any other way. At least it was clear, and didn't leave any room for misunderstanding. *"He's probably been thinking about how to say this since before dinner,"* Toby decided. *"And, his position is more than fair. How can I expect him to know if he can do what he's never tried?"* Toby splashed a handful of water at him, and laughed at the surprised look on his face. "Way to get right to the root of things, Bill! So what do you want to do? Make a list and rank the things on it from the things you do think you'll like, down to the things you don't think you like?"

John Brown actually liked that idea, because maybe they could find some way to stop before he had to kill Toby. However, he got the feeling Toby wouldn't like that approach. He did want Toby to enjoy things, at least until he had to die. "I guess we can just fool around and see where things lead. As long as you take it slow, and stop if I get uncomfortable, I think we can figure this out without anyone getting hurt."

"I like that better than checking off a list and I think we have the fooling around part down pat."

John Brown lifted his body out of the water and sat on the edge of the tub. "Me too, and I know I like it. So, why don't you come over here by me? You're too far away."

Toby stood and walked toward him and when he got within a foot, Bill reached out and placed his hands on Toby's hips. He stood and leaned in for a kiss, and concentrated on the feel and taste of Toby's mouth and lips, since they were already familiar to him. Their skin was slick and steaming from the hot water and he could feel Toby's arousal. He stepped back and sat back down on the hot tub ledge then pulled Toby toward him and explored Toby's cock and balls. He marveled at how different, but alike, Toby's flesh was to his own. Very slowly and deliberately, he leaned down and took Toby into his mouth. He tasted the flesh and investigated the feel of it in his mouth and decided it wasn't bad at all. He felt Toby swell and extend further, and enjoyed the way the texture of the skin changed. He circled his tongue around the head and then took it deeper, and felt a sense of proud satisfaction when Toby gave a gasp and placed his hands on Bill's head. John Brown liked the idea his actions were causing those results. He reached between his own legs and checked things out, needing to see how his own body was responding. Everything was satisfactory and, in fact, the guy down there seemed to be very happy. John Brown tried a few more things he thought Toby would like, because, after all, John Brown had been on the recipient's end of this sort of activity many times. He pulled his mouth away, and looked up to see Toby's face. What he saw was encouraging, so he went back to work. After a while, Toby's hands tangled in his hair, and after a few minutes more, Toby told him to stop. He shook his head, having decided to see this through. If he couldn't accept and enjoy what came next, he might as well just kill Toby now and clean things up before heading home. Otherwise, the whole weekend was wasted.

"I'm getting really close." Toby's voice was now almost pleading, and his breath was heavy. "You need to stop."

John Brown tightened his hold on Toby's hip to keep him from moving away, and used his other hand to work the base of Toby's cock. Soon, he heard Toby's increasingly urgent and appreciative noises and felt the man's body tense. He worked his mouth and hand faster, until Toby was past the point where he could hold back. John Brown grabbed Toby's ass and felt the muscles clench and tighten. With a few more tense, throbbing thrusts, he spent himself and John Brown took it all, and waited until Toby's tremors had slowed before pulling away. He looked into Toby's eyes, which were glazed with pleasure. His pupils looked huge.

Toby gave him an incredibly sexy, lazy smile. "Wow."

Although John Brown hadn't minded any of it too much, and from the state of his own throbbing cock had liked some of it a lot, the best part was what he saw on Toby's face as the man pushed him down onto the edge of the tub and went down on his own knees in the hot water. The wanton smile on Toby's lips right at the moment they encircled him was like nothing John Brown had seen before, and he moaned involuntarily and felt his balls tighten. A few minutes later, Toby succeeded in his mission, and John Brown leaned back to catch his breath and gazed up at the bright stars, dazed by the experience. He'd been brought off by a willing and talented mouth before, but it had never felt like this, or affected him the way Toby did. As Toby's arms encircled him and brought their mouths together in a lingering kiss, John Brown experienced their mingled tastes for the first time, and decided no one was going to get hurt tonight, at least from engaging in this activity. He had a thing or two to learn so he could rock Toby's world the way his had just been rocked, and found himself anxiously anticipating the opportunity to get some more practice.

He stepped out of the water, and held out his hand. "Let's go on inside, Toby. It's starting to get chilly and we'll be more comfortable where it's warm."

John Brown started a fire in the fireplace and then turned off the rest of the lights. He gazed into the flickering flames, and felt the heat within himself rise to the surface as he anticipated the rest of the night. Toby kissed him gently, running his hands across his chest. Toby teased his nipples with hands and mouth and John Brown felt his world began to spin as he lost himself in the sensations. When he was aching with need, Toby went into the bathroom and came out with a few items in his hand.

Later that night, he lost himself deep inside the man beneath him. John Brown called out Toby's name as he spent himself. He then watched in spellbound wonder as Toby cried out to Bill, and found his own release. For a moment, John Brown felt himself fill with intense, jealous rage, until he remembered. Bill Jones and John Brown were one and the same.

Content, John Brown laid down beside his man, and fell asleep as Toby gently ran his fingers through his hair. He never knew or felt the moment when Toby kissed his tattooed shoulder, curious again about why the inked mark looked so familiar.

The next morning John Brown woke early, and over his first cup of coffee, thought about the last night and how Toby had guided him into his body. He'd loved it, but today it would be his turn to try. He knew Toby would never push the issue, and probably had no expectations, but John Brown wanted it over so he'd know what he had to do. He walked deep into the woods and dug a grave, making the ground ready in case he needed a place to put Toby's body. It was always good planning to have things ready in advance of a need. When he came back into the cabin, Toby was up, having showered and shaved, and was now building up the fire.

"If you'd put come clothes on you'd be much warmer," John Brown chided him gently, wishing they never had to put on a single item of clothing ever again.

"I'll be fine with the fire, and besides, I can think of better ways of keeping warm. Those involve getting you out of those dirty clothes. Where were you anyway?"

"I was in the woods, just... doing a few things," John Brown answered with a shrug. "I'll go clean up, and when I get back I think a walk in the woods would be nice. You need to put on some clothes for that."

In the shower, John Brown scrubbed the soil from his hands and from beneath his nails. He dried himself off and combed his hair. *"Today might be the day I have to say goodbye to Toby Bailey,"* he regretfully reminded himself as he walked to the bed. *"But first, I'm going to practice everything I learned last night. That way, the weekend won't be wasted. I'm going to try to give Toby as much pleasure as possible. At least if I have to kill him, I'll know he was happy with me."*

They made lunch and explored the woods. John Brown led them far from the site he'd prepared that morning, and practiced a few of the new skills he'd learned. He thought he was showing improvement, if Toby's sounds of intense pleasure were any indication. They walked back hand in hand and showered again, and started preparing things for dinner. After steaks on the grill and a few mason jars of brandy, they spent some time looking at the stars. Then John Brown led Toby back to the bed. "Show me, Toby. Do to me what I did to you last night."

So Toby did.

The next morning, John Brown worked in the cool country air, steadily shoveling dirt into the grave.

On the way back to the city, he thought about the weekend and the things he'd experienced for the first time, and the man with whom he'd experience them. He tried not to feel so sad that it was over.

"Cheer up, Bill. We'll have other weekends like this, although, this one will always be special to me."

John Brown turned to the man beside him and reached over and took his hand. "It's was a very special weekend for me, Toby – more than you'll ever know. I'm disappointed it's over, but you're right, we'll do it again. I'm just glad I didn't…"

"Didn't what?"

John Brown thought about the grave under the trees and what he'd been prepared to do. "I'm just glad I didn't hurt you, Toby."

"You were okay with everything?"

John Brown squeezed Toby's hand. "Yes, Toby. You would've known if I wasn't."

Toby had been amazed at Bill's insatiable curiosity and eagerness. He'd made it clear he wanted to try everything Toby could think of, and insisted he wouldn't let Toby leave until they had tried it all. He'd told Toby he wanted to be sure, and had even suggested a few things Toby had never done before. There were a few moments of hesitancy, but Bill certainly gave it his best shot – and in fact, had pretty much worn Toby out. All-in-all, Toby was surprised how compatible they were turning out to be, both in bed and out of it. Toby realized Bill was committed to proving he could be what Toby was searching for. He thought Bill might just be the one. Toby gave a hopeful smile as he squeezed the hand that was holding tightly on to his own. "Really? I wasn't sure you enjoyed some of it."

"Really. If there had been something I couldn't accept and didn't think I could grow to enjoy, and even desire, there was no way you could have missed it. I would have made sure of that."

Another week went by. Reightman enjoyed the visit with her daughter and granddaughters, and regretted she didn't see them any more than she did. She resolved to spend more highway time traveling the mere hour and a half to the upstate, so she could be more active and present in her family's life.

She'd met Will Cooper, the man Abby was dating, and she thought things might be getting serious between them. After watching him interact with Abby and the girls – who obviously adored him – Melba decided she liked the man quite a lot. Time would tell, but there might just be a wedding in her daughter's future.

As promised, she and Toby arranged to take Madame Zhou to dinner one evening, and she enjoyed the time spent with both of them.

After Toby and Reightman had seen Zhou Li safely inside Green Dragon, they stood on the sidewalk on Capital Street while Reightman brought him up to speed on the current state of the investigation, and told him she had pretty much resigned herself to the idea it was, for all intent and purpose, over.

Toby was disappointed, but understood. "Maybe it's for the best. I know it's hard to accept that you may never find the man who shot at me and killed Detective Jackson, but maybe that's just the way it is."

"I know. I just have a feeling there's a clue I'm missing." She leaned against the side of her car and looked across the street at the

Time Out Spa. "To tell you the truth, I'll probably always feel that way, but maybe I'm just going to have to accept it."

"If you think of something I can do, let me know. You know I'll help any way I can, Detective."

"I know, and I appreciate it." She considered possible next steps, and then shrugged. "I'm going to start consolidating all the information in the files, so at least I'll have everything organized if I should ever need to refer to it again. I suppose the file will sit, covered in dust, until it becomes one more unsolved mystery on the corner of an aging Detective's desk."

"I still have a file of pictures and a set of photocopied pages of the ledger book. I think you have the originals in custody, but I'll pull them together for you when I finish packing my office. Frankly, I'd rather have them out of my life. I know it sounds harsh, but I just want to move on."

"Thanks, Toby. I don't blame you at all for feeling that way, especially since you have a new person in your life. I keep forgetting to ask, but what's this mystery man's name? I feel silly referring to him as 'your special someone' or the 'the new man'."

Reightman noted the more than fond expression on Toby's face as he said the name; "Bill. Bill Jones. He's kind of a geeky – just like you'd expect with that name, but he's a hot geek, complete with retro glasses and a smokin' hot body."

"Kind of like a sexy university boy who studies engineering by day and let's his secret self out at night?"

Toby considered her description, amused to be having this conversation with her. "No, he's too old for that fantasy. He's about thirty-two I think, and he's more the shy, but personable, college professor type, who everyone has crushes on during class and imagines nude while he lectures about some boring topic."

"Oh! I had one of those professors back in the day! Everyone was always finding an excuse to drop by his office to get extra help with their assignments."

Toby grinned. "You better believe I'd be one of the students standing in line outside Bill's office door waiting for my private one-on-one! I'd be willing to pay extra for the private tutoring, and I know just how I'd pay that Bill!"

"Okay, that's enough of that, Toby! I get the idea. You're going to make this old lady blush. I'll have that image in my head forever, but it should help me remember his first name. All I'll have to do is imagine you paying the bill. The last name should be easy. My new partner's name is Jones as well, although he's a Vince, not a Bill. At my age, any little reminders are very helpful."

"Yeah, you *are* practically a geriatric, Detective Melba," Toby joked. "Before long, I'll be visiting you in a nursing home somewhere."

"As long as you promise to sneak me in all kinds of forbidden treats, I won't bust your ass for referring to me as Detective Melba."

"You know you like it!"

"Maybe I do, but you don't use it very often anymore. Maybe you should make more effort."

"I will." His mind went back to the things still to be packed in the office. "About those files – I'll get everything together and give you a call so I can officially hand them over and get them out of the way."

Reightman pushed herself off the car. "Thanks. Just let me know when you have them ready and I'll drop by to pick them up." As she opened her car door, she thought of something else she wanted to ask. "Toby, have you seen Mitchell lately?"

Toby's eyes flicked away and when he answered, Reightman thought she detected a trace of disappointment on his face before he forced some false cheer into his voice. "Yeah. We occasionally go to the shooting range. He's been real insistent I keep up my skills. But other than that, we don't see each other as much as I thought we would. He's spending a lot of time with the new man in *his* life and that's good. I'm happy for him."

"Thanks for the update. That's more than I knew, and I'm happy things are working out for him in that department. I'm glad we all went to dinner tonight and I think we should do this more often so we keep in touch. I've really missed seeing you and I miss Madame Zhou as well. I always enjoy her stories, and her very interesting observations about people and events. She always manages to work in some piece of advice, whether you want it or not."

"Yeah, I know what you mean. She's always offering a helpful hint or making a point about something or other. The thing is, she's usually right on the money. I really like her and I'm very thankful she agreed to help me out – that time you arrested me." He grinned to let her know he didn't mean anything by the comment. "She's a big part of why things have turned out as well as they have, and I'm very fortunate to have her in my life."

"We've both been fortunate in that regard, Toby. Now, I'd better get on home so I can drag myself out of bed and get into work tomorrow."

He'd noticed the weary disenchantment in Reightman's voice every time she mentioned work. "Are things bad, Detective Melba?"

Reightman shrugged. "It pays the bills, which is something. But, I'll admit I'm not as content or invested as I used to be. The last several weeks have opened my eyes to a lot of things, especially things having to do with human nature. I suspect what's bothering me now has always been there, but I didn't see what was right in front of my face." She gave a rueful laugh. "Just listen to me! Now I do sound like a bitter old woman in a nursing home."

"No, you don't, and I understand exactly what you mean. My eyes have been opened too. You know, I used to dream about having a place like the Time Out Spa. Soon, it won't be anything but a piece of my past. I thought I'd be devastated if I ever had to close it down, and I *am* sad it's come to that. But in a way, I'm relieved."

"Yes, I'm sure in some ways it is a relief." After a moment's more reflection, Reightman gave herself a mental shake. "Listen to us! We need to focus on making the future better instead of dwelling on the negative things which have happened."

"You're right! Thanks for giving me a dose of your ancient wisdom," he teased as she eased herself into the car.

Soon, he was on his way upstairs to his apartment and she was driving home to hers, both of them thinking of how much had happened over the past few months.

It was a day or two before Toby was finally able to focus on the last set of drawers in his office filing cabinet. He'd stepped in to help out the spa manager of one of the local high-end hotels who found herself with a facility of convention attendees and two staff members trying to recover from the flu that was going around town. She'd even approached him about coming to work for her full time. He'd declined, but had assured her he was happy to fill in anytime she needed some extra help.

Toby gave Bill the rundown on his day when they caught up by phone. Bill was out of town on a job, and they tried to touch base every day – sometimes more than once – and Toby was still amazed that this man had entered his life at exact moment he'd needed something good to happen. There were times when he admitted they'd moved very fast, and he was almost obsessed with the idea of their relationship. But he told himself he deserved a chance at happiness after the last several months, and put it out of his mind.

Tonight, Bill gave him some news he didn't care for, and Toby was working hard to get past his disappointment. "I can't believe it will be three more days before we get to spend time together," Toby told him, trying not to let his frustration show. "And, I can't believe you'll be totally unavailable even by phone."

"I know, Toby." John Brown's voice sounded as sad as Toby felt. "But sometimes jobs come up and there's just no way around it." John had accepted a little clean-up mission from an out-of-state client. He thought he could handle the client's problem sooner, but he'd built in the extra time, just in case he ran into unforeseen obstacles. He knew he couldn't indulge himself in maintaining daily contact with Toby while taking care of business. It just wouldn't feel right to let the job bleed into his personal life, especially since he knew how important it was to keep that part of his life off of Toby's radar. Besides, their time together was better spent on other things. "Why don't we plan to go up to the cabin next weekend, Toby? I'll make up for having to be away and out of touch for the next few days. I promise."

"And how, exactly, are you planning to make up for leaving me alone, all by my poor lonely, incredibly horny self?"

"I have a few ideas…."

"Yeah? Maybe you'd better share those with me right now. But first, let me get a little more comfortable."

John Brown thought that was an excellent idea and lay back on the hotel bed. He was as creative as he knew how to be and spent the next thirty minutes explaining in very vivid detail exactly what he was planning to do to – and with – Toby to make amends for his absence. He was getting good at this love stuff.

By the end of the next day, Toby finished packing his office, except for the bottom drawer of the filing cabinet – the drawer which contained copies of the ledger book and photos. He pulled them from the drawer, firmly resolved not to look through any of the materials. He held them in his hands for a minute, tempted to revisit them one more time, but told himself to just let go of the past and focus on the future. Feeling nothing but relief, he shoved them into a large envelope and sealed the top. He picked up his phone to let Detective Reightman know they were ready whenever she had the time to drop by and get them.

"Thanks for pulling these things together, Toby. You have to be relieved you'll never have to see them again."

"You better believe it! Just knowing they're on the way out of here makes me feel better. It doesn't change what happened in the past, and some of it I wouldn't want to change. But, I think....I think it's okay to focus on the future, and Bill."

"I can tell just by the way you say his name that he's very special."

"He is. He really surprised me – coming into my life just when I thought things were about as bad as they could be. And he's smart and nice and…well, you've already heard me go on about how sexy I think he is. There's something about him that just makes me tingly all over. Or maybe it's the glasses, and the tattoo, or maybe it's the unexpectedness of the combo. Whatever it is, he just does it for me."

"Yes, you've gone on and on about your sexy, geeky man but you never told me he has a tattoo. Is it some elaborate design on his chest or back?"

"No, it's just a little one, a name or something, on the back of his shoulder. But it gives him a little edge."

"So, you like the bad boy vibe, huh?"

Toby blushed and shook his head. "I don't think he's much of a bad boy, except maybe in the sack. I think he's more of a homebody with his cabin in the woods. We really have a great time up there, and it's like our own little world. I don't think there's anybody within a few miles of the place. I'm meeting him up there again this week-end." Toby looked off into the distance and then glanced back toward her. "Sometimes, I think I might be moving too fast, but when I'm with him, it doesn't seem to be moving fast enough."

Melba saw the longing on his face, and what might be the beginning of something much stronger. She wondered if he was moving too fast, and if he'd really completed his grieving for Geri Guzman. She was also concerned that if something were to happen to bring this relationship crashing down while he was miles away from people who cared about him and could support him through a difficult patch, he might not be equipped to handle it by himself. Someone might need to get to him fast – and she figured that someone might as well be her. "Toby, I want to say something, but, I'm not sure it's my place."

Toby pushed back the lock of hair that had fallen into his face and gave a very exasperated sigh. "After everything we've been through, I think you can say just about anything you want. I know you only have my best interest in mind, Detective Melba. Go ahead and say it. I promise I won't react, or over react, as the case may be – too badly."

She decided it was okay to interfere, just a little. She was probably spending too much time with Zhou Li. "Okay, if you say so. This might sound silly, but I kind of look at you as a younger brother. And, you're right; I only want the best for you. I'm happy you have a new person in your life. But, I am worried. I'm not going to butt in, unless you ask me to, but I'm uncomfortable knowing you're miles from here without anyone knowing how to get to you if something…"

He stopped her before she could go further. "I get it, Detective Melba." He gave her a hint of a pout, and folded his arms across his chest, reminding her of the boy in the picture she'd seen the first night she'd entered the Time Out Spa. For just a moment, he looked very young again. "How about this? If something goes wrong and I have some kind of crisis, you'll be the first person I call. I do, however-er, expect you to let me cry on your shoulder before you get to say I told you so. Deal?"

She chuckled in relief, glad he hadn't taken offense. "Yes, it's a deal, as long as you promise to return the favor for me if I ever need it. And one more thing – tell me how to get to this cabin in the woods in case I need to come rescue you."

Toby rolled his eyes. "You are like a big sister – bossy and everything! Okay, I'll draw you a map."

Later, as she was getting ready to leave, he took her by the hand. "Thanks, Detective Melba. I think you're being a tad over protective, but I guess I should be used to everyone thinking I need the extra help. Truthfully, I did need it a while back. Thank God that's over! Now, get out of here so I can finish closing this place down. I'll talk to you when I get back and hopefully, not before."

CHAPTER FOURTEEN

JOHN BROWN CROSSED the state line on his way to the cabin He'd stopped for lunch a couple of hours ago and enjoyed a delicious pulled pork sandwich, with all the fixings. He's savored the different flavor combinations while he read the local newspaper, paying special attention to the story about the shocking death of a well know State Representative. She'd been found dead in her home, from suicide, apparently. John Brown smiled as he folded up the paper and left it on the table for the next patron to read. He paid his bill, leaving a good-sized tip for his waitress and climbed back in his SUV.

About twelve miles from the cabin, he stopped at the grocery store and picked up a few things for the weekend, whistling as he shopped the aisles. He picked up a couple of steaks and a few bottles of decent wine and was soon pulling into the gravel drive of the cabin. He carried in the groceries and then went back to unload the rest of the things in his vehicle. He fixed a quick dinner and then poured a little brandy into a mason jar and went out onto the deck to enjoy the cool evening. He pulled out his phone and called Toby. "Hey, Toby," he greeted his man when he answered. "I have good news! I was able to finish up the job and stopped at the cabin instead of going on home. Do you think you can get away a day early and join me? I'll make it worth your while."

The silence on the phone lasted so long John Brown checked to see if he still had a connection. Sometimes service was spotty up here. "Toby, are you there?"

"Sorry, Bill," Toby's voice came over the phone. "I just dropped something. I'm here."

"So, do you think you can get away? I'm anxious to see you." John Brown was startled by the longing in his own voice.

"I'm anxious to see you too – really anxious, if you know what I mean. How about I drive up tomorrow and we can have the extra day together. I might be able to come up with some way for us to fill the time."

"I can think of some ways to fill the time, too, and maybe a few other things as well."

"That's enough of that, mister! I'll never be able to sleep tonight if you keep talking like that, and I need all the sleep I can get. I need to be rested up for what I have in mind."

John Brown smiled at the sultry tone in Toby's voice, and thought he might be getting the hang of things. "Okay, I'll let you go then – for now." He suddenly felt the urge to say something he'd never said to anyone since he was a child. It hadn't gone well then, so he thought it over carefully, wondering if the words he wanted to say were even true, or just a whim of the moment. A part of him wondered if his emotions were real or just part of the role he was playing when they were together. He knew he was fixated on Toby now and fiercely protective of their time together, and it didn't bother him a bit. After all, Toby was his. Given that, he decided the little words didn't matter all that much one way or the other. For now, he could imagine they were true, and for John Brown, that was good enough. "Toby," he said hesitantly, remembering the dismissive way his mother had reacted when he'd said similar words to her many years ago, "I think I ....uh....I...."

"Bill," Toby interrupted gently before he could stammer out the final words, "you don't have to say what I think you're trying to say right now. I don't want either of us to say it, until we're both sure, and really mean it." Toby listened to the silence on the other end, wondering if he'd said the right thing. "Bill, I..."

"You're right." John Brown knew he was correct and this wasn't the time, but he wanted to prove he was sincere about their relationship. He decided to add a few words for effect. "But, I think the time I'll really mean them will be coming very soon...at least for me."

John Brown smiled in satisfaction when Toby responded, "Me too, Bill."

When he hung up the phone he regretted he hadn't said the words after all. Part of the problem was he wasn't used to the way they felt coming out of his mouth. He wanted them to be perfect. Soon enough, Toby would expect him to make a declaration of some sort, and he wanted to be ready when the moment came. So, he practiced as he sat on the deck, by saying the words to the stars and the trees. "Toby, I think….I think I… might…love you." He tried again, putting more tender emotion into his voice, until the tiny drop of moisture in his eyes convinced him he had the words and the expected, accompanying emotion just right. "What do you think?" he asked his audience. The trees and the stars didn't answer, but, when the early autumn breeze moved across his face, he knew they approved. *"Good job, John Brown!"* he congratulated himself. *"I think he'll believe me if I say the words just like that."*

The next morning, Reightman walked to her desk and put her purse in the usual place, and went for a mug of tea. The breakroom was strangely deserted, and she wondered what could be going on to keep the usual addicts away from the coffee pot. Once she was back at her desk, she picked up the phone and called Nancy.

"A whole lot of people are out with the flu, and a few more are attending the week long seminar on sensitivity training," Nancy told her when she asked why the building seemed so empty.

"Oh! That's right. I forgot all about that."

"Well, all I can say is some of those guys could use all of the training in how to be sensitive that they can get!"

Reightman laughingly agreed, and hung up the phone. She spent some time listing everything she knew about the case, just to remind herself. She knew who had killed Geri Guzman. The same two people, Sutton and Christina Dameron, had tried to kill Toby and had either been captured or killed before they were successful. She knew who had given the orders to kill Lieberman, and that person was Reverend Sawyer. He'd also ordered the hit on Toby, which had failed, but had resulted instead in Sam Jackson's death. What she didn't know was to whom Sawyer had given the orders. She didn't know who the person was who'd fired the bullets that killed Sam, Christina Dameron, and Helliman. She had a hunch the same person staged Lieberman's suicide. Nothing else made sense. She was worried she'd missed some important clue which would tie everything together. She let her mind spin through a dozen possibilities, until she recognized she was sending herself down a useless path which would never bear fruit. She stood and stretched, easing her tense shoulders and neck. Then she single mindedly started putting all of the case files into chronological order, trying not to let herself think of it sitting forgotten in her desk drawer as she and the rest of the department moved on to other things.

She picked up the small notebook Toby had retrieved the night Sam was killed and flipped through the pages. When she came to the last page, she squinted to try and make out Sam's handwriting. *"Man with tattoo. Who is he? How is he involved in this?"* She wished she knew the answers to those questions.

Around noon, she walked to the coffee shop and grabbed a sandwich. Back at her desk, she settled down to finish the job she'd started that morning. She'd just put the last of the materials in their proper order when the phone across the desk from her began to ring. She let it go to voice mail. An hour later, she was tired and cranky, but was close to finishing the thankless job. The phone rang again. With a groan of frustration, she reached across the desk and picked up the handset. "Hello, this is Detective Reightman speaking."

"Hello. May I speak to Billy, please?" asked a woman on the other end of the phone.

"I'm sorry, ma'am. There isn't anyone here by that name."

The woman laughed in embarrassment at her mistake. "My apologies, I keep forgetting he doesn't use that name any more. He never did like to be called Billy – he much preferred Bill. But, I'm rambling. I'm trying to reach my son, Detective Jones."

"Oh! Sorry for the confusion, but I think he's out today, attending a conference. Have you tried his cell phone?"

The woman gave a frustrated sigh. "Yes, I have, and he's not answering. If you'd give him a message for me, I'd appreciate it. If you should hear from him, just tell him his mother called."

"He probably just has the phone turned off if he's in a training session."

"Oh! You know, I think he told me he was going out of town. I must have mixed up the dates. If he's in some kind of training, he won't be up at that place in the woods he calls his weekend cabin. The reception is spotty out there, and I can never get through."

"I'm pretty sure he's at the conference, but I'll give him the message if I hear from him. Is there anything else I can do for you?"

"No, that's all. Thanks for your help."

Reightman hung up the phone, and glanced at the nameplate on her partner's desk. She went back to finalizing the files, but something about the call bothered her. She picked up the phone again and called Nancy. "Hey, Nancy, I'm sorry to bother you again, but I have a question for you. Do you know what Jones's full name is?

"No, Melba, I don't think I do. But if you call human resources, they'll know for sure."

"Good idea, I'll try that."

Nancy gave her the number and Reightman picked up the phone again. When she hung up with the HR representative, she had the information she'd asked for, but wasn't sure why it seemed important. She sat back in her chair and looked at the name plate. She went back over the recent call in her mind, trying to figure out why her senses were on full alert. *"Is Bill there?....doesn't go by that name....at that place in the woods....Jones....Doesn't like to be called Billy....Is Bill there?...Jones....Bill...Jones. Bill Jones! Oh...my...God. Oh my God! Toby..."*

She pulled her cellphone out of her purse and dialed Toby, but after ringing a few times, she was shunted to his voice mail. She didn't leave a message, trying to convince herself it was all just some weird coincidence. She put the phone away and tried to focus on the next thing on her list, but she kept going back to the call and the terrible suspicion grew. Unable to let go of the idea, she quickly opened the file she'd just finished, and began pulling papers out and spreading them on the desks. She scanned the case notes, then rifled through the photos, looking for something which would prove her wrong. When she came to the final grouping of photographs, she could only stare down at the image in front of her, stunned. Against all odds, it unfortunately proved her hunch was right. She picked the image up and held it in her shaking hands, examining the photograph of a man's body, with no visible face, and a tattoo on the back of his shoulder.

"*Calm down, Melba!*" she ordered herself. "*Think! What do you know about the man Toby's been seeing?*" She went through their recent conversations, trying to recall the details. "*Good looking, sexy in a geeky sort of way – because of the glasses. And the tattoo.... of a name or....something... Goes by the name, Bill Jones. A homebody with a secluded cabin in the woods.*" She looked at the nameplate again. "*Jones' initials are VWJ, but if he goes by Bill instead of William, then the initials would be VBJ...and if he sometimes just goes by Bill, the would be ... BJ...bj.*"

Reightman felt her stomach churn as she dug through the scattered papers until she located the suicide note, which she'd never believed had been written by Lieberman. She scanned the note until she found what she was looking for, just two small letters down at the bottom of the note – "bj". Two letters at the bottom of a suicide note which had always bothered her, along with the pair of dust free glasses found at the scene, under the couch...glasses picked up and handled by Mitchell, until they were taken away from him by....Jones. Glasses with only two sets of fingerprint – fingerprints belonging to Mitchell and...Jones.

The pieces flew together in her mind and she picked up the phone and called Tom Anderson. "Tom, I have a question. Did any of the fingerprints on Helliman's truck belong to Detective Jones? Never mind that, could you check? It's urgent!" She waited and listened to the hold muzak, wanting to scream at the delay. When Tom came back on the line and gave her the answer she'd been dreading to hear, she started to panic. She hung up the call and yanked her purse from her desk.

"Detective Reightman, what's going on? You look like you're about to fly to pieces."

She jumped at the unexpected voice behind her. "Mitchell! I......."

"What's going on? And what are you doing with all of this stuff spread out everywhere?" When she didn't answer him, he looked over the materials scattered across the two desks and at the crumpled image she still held in one hand. "This has something to do with To-by, doesn't it? Tell me what's going on."

She hesitated, but one look into his hard, demanding eyes decided for her. She nodded her head and then, while trying to control her breathing, she told him.

When she had finished, he took the crumpled paper from her hand and stared down at image. His jaw tightened, and she knew the minute he made his decision.

"Let's go," he said simply.

"No, Mitchell! You can't go with me."

"Like hell I can't! You have a choice, Detective. I either go with you now, or I'll follow behind. The first choice will be easier on us both, but understand me – I am going to help Toby."

She thought about arguing, but knew it wouldn't do her a bit of good. They'd both made their choices concerning Toby, almost from the very beginning, and she couldn't think of a better person to have by her side.

They rushed to gather a few things they might need, and made one stop at the evidence room. Then they were on the road, headed for a cabin in the woods to try and save Toby from the man he knew as Bill Jones. The man with whom he was falling in love.

Melba tried Toby's phone, and again went to voicemail. This time she left a message, telling him to call her as soon as possible.

"Don't you think you should tell him what's going on?"

"No. I don't know how he'd react, and if Jones was around when he picked up the message, I…"

"You're probably right," Mitchell grimly agreed from the passenger seat. "Things could get really bad, really fast." After a few minutes of silence, Mitchell spoke up again. "What's the plan?"

Reightman glanced his way, feeling inadequate and unprepared for what was ahead. "I don't have one." It was very hard for her to admit, and she only had one excuse. "I wasn't thinking of anything other than the need to try to get to Toby as quickly as possible. That may have been a big mistake." She changed lanes, trying to get around a slow RV and then made a decision. "I need to call Chief Kelly, and tell him what's going on. At the very least, we're going to need back-up, and he's our best hope. He might be able to arrange something." She changed lanes again and then slowed as she pulled onto the shoulder. "You drive, Mitchell, while I call Kelly."

They quickly switched places, and Melba dug out her phone and dialed the Chief.

"You know better than to go tearing off to the middle of the woods, Reightman! I thought you at least had better sense than that!" he barked as soon as she updated him on the situation. "The best thing would be for you to get your butt back here so we can plan this out properly."

"I can't do that, sir! I wish I could, but we don't have the luxury of time. Toby might be safe until we get there, but I just can't take that chance. Jones is too dangerous."

"If Jones has pulled this off, you damned well better believe he's dangerous." Kelly grunted and Melba could only hope he was thinking over their options. "Let me see what I can do to call in some favors. The country sheriff up there hates my guts, but I'll try to get you some back-up." He ended the call before she could respond, and she held the phone in her hand wondering what to do next.

"What did he say, Detective?"

'He's going to try and get us some back up, Mitchell."

"You think he'll manage it?"

She didn't answer his question, and after seeing the expression on her face, he just kept driving. They were both silent for the next hour, wrapped up in their own thoughts and fears. "The next exit's ours, Mitchell. I'm going to try to reach the Sheriff."

John Brown dropped the gun he'd finished cleaning into the open bag on the floor and impatiently kicked it under the bed. He was jittery and nervous today, and was having trouble focusing on the separate parts of his life. He had a hunch that if he wasn't careful, all the separate facets would crash together, destroying the fragile, new identity he felt emerging from within. If that happened, he might as well give up now, because he was sure he'd break into a million pieces. It wasn't like him to wander down those sorts of paths, and he was uncharacteristically apprehensive about the weekend, even though he didn't know why. After all, he'd been looking forward to seeing

Toby for days, and he'd done everything he could think of to get things ready.

Earlier that morning, he swept the deck and cleaned the cabin, and the hot tub was filled and heating for the evening. He arranged the final payment details for his completed job, and was anticipating the bump it would give to his bank account. Soon he'd have enough stashed away to leave it all behind. He locked that part of his life away so he could focus on how to make the next few days special. He filled the old jar with foliage and placed it on the table. That helped some, since that caused him to remember their first weekend together. He made sure there were clean towels in the bathroom, and fresh sheets on the bed, and that help calm his mind some more. But despite his efforts, he worried throughout the day. Looking around the simple one room dwelling, he found himself dissatisfied with the place for the very first time. He found himself feeling inferior and unworthy, and wondered if this place, which some people would view as little better than a shack, would eventually lose its appeal for Toby. That led to other insecurities. He finally admitted there was nothing wrong with the cabin. Toby loved it. No, what he was truly worried about was the possibility of losing his own appeal. If that happened, he didn't know what he'd do, but he did know he'd never let Toby walk away from him. That would destroy him, and he'd do anything to keep that from happening.

He forced himself to cram those thoughts down deep into the recesses of his mind, where he kept all the other dark and frightening things. He rummaged through the kitchen, checking that he had everything they might need, and discovered he'd left a few things off the list. He picked up his keys and fled the cabin, knowing he had to get out of there to clear his mind. He drove into town to do the shopping for the provisions he'd forgotten the day before. He even picked up a load of firewood, anticipating the cooler evenings which would be perfect for a romantic fire in the cabin. After he returned, he sat on the deck looking at the woods around him, and refused to revisit the troubled thoughts which plagued him earlier in the day. Instead, he replayed the last several weeks he'd spent with Toby, and focused on how those weeks had changed him. He knew he wasn't just John Brown anymore, but also knew he wasn't only Bill Jones. The two had started to blend within him, and at times, it was impossible to let either one of them have total control. For a moment, he wished he could share this realization with Toby, and ask for help in reconciling his nature, but knew it was impossible. Toby would never understand the things he'd done and would be horrified by that part of his life. Worse, Toby wouldn't understand why he hadn't told him the rest, and why he'd hidden the fact he worked with Reightman. It had seemed so simple when he'd watched Toby on the terrace and then kept an eye on him during the following weeks. That had made him curious, which had led him to make the appointment at the spa. That day, he'd discovered more about himself than he had during his entire life. His world had changed the moment he'd recognized what he wanted and somewhere along the way, his want had changed to need. Maybe the best John Brown, aka Bill Jones, could hope for was a continuation of this half world, where he and Toby lost themselves in each other and the rest of the world didn't matter. Maybe, when he left this behind him, he could start over again with Toby. And, maybe not.

John Brown thought about the time they'd spent here, at this re-mote and secluded retreat. Here, there were none of the intrusions of the outside world, only two men curled together in the big bed as the fire provided flickering light. Here, there were Toby and himself – only two men taking their pleasure in each other, before they fell asleep in each other's arms.

John Brown put those thoughts away when he heard Toby's car coming up the graveled driveway. Holding only the last image firmly in his mind, he went to greet the man he'd been waiting for – the man he'd claimed as his own – the man he'd kill before he let him go.

Toby pulled his bag from the car and heard Bill's footsteps behind him. "I was able to leave earlier than I thought," Toby told him as he leaned in for a kiss. "I was going to call, but about halfway here, I realized I left my phone on the counter at home. I didn't want to turn around and go back for it and figured you'd just have to be surprised. I hope you don't mind."

"I'll show you just how much I don't mind when I get you inside!" John Brown took the bag from his hands. "What's in here, rocks?"

"Nope – no rocks, although to tell you the truth, I don't know what's inside. I just threw some things on top of what was already in there from a few days ago. I didn't even take the time to dump the stuff out to check. I'll see what it is when I unpack." Toby checked out Bill's ass as he started up to the cabin. "I was in a hurry to get here."

John Brown looked back over his shoulder and caught Toby looking. He gave him a slow grin. "Enjoying the view?"

"More than enjoying. I'm imagining all kinds of things."

"Really? Don't let your imagination get away from you – I have plans for you."

"Do those plans include you, sprawled out naked on the bed, waiting for me to have my wicked way with you?"

"Well, I was thinking of things slightly differently. In my mind, you were the one sprawled out on the bed."

Toby laughed and took the bag from Bill's hand as they entered the cabin. "Let's get to it, then." He dropped the duffle bag on the bed and greeted his lover with a proper hello.

John Brown felt the urgency in Toby's body, which fueled his own hungry aggression. He was excited by how the combination might translate into their weekend play. He felt his own body respond as he imagined what they'd do together, and the image in his mind grew clearer. He shivered with desire, and lost himself in the warmth of Toby's arms. Eventually, he pulled away and looked into the blue eyes. "I'm glad you're here." After another quick kiss, he stepped away, adjusting himself in his jeans as he did. "Are you hungry?" John Brown asked. "I haven't started anything yet, but it won't take long to fire up the grill."

Toby shook his head and eyed the tightly packed crotch. "Not really. I had an early lunch before I started the drive. What I'd really like is a glass of wine, and you and me together, on the bed. So, get out of those clothes. I want to see what I've been missing the last several days. From the way your jeans are fitting right now, you've been missing it too."

"I tell you what, why don't I get the wine while you start getting out of your clothes?"

"I think I can live with that change of plans," Toby agreed as he toed off his shoes. "Hey, can I borrow your phone later? I meant to check on Grams and intended to give her a call on the drive up. Since I left my phone, I couldn't, and I don't want her to worry. Ever since....ever since things got scary there for a while, she likes me to touch base every few days."

John Brown caught himself before answering. His regular phone was tucked away in the console of his SUV along with his department issued revolver, and he couldn't risk Toby using that one. However, he did have his other phone – the one he used for his jobs – here in the cabin. There was nothing on the phone to give him away, and if Toby happened to see any of the texts, they were easily explained. "Sure, Toby, but you might not have much luck with reception. You know how hard it is to get a good signal out here."

"Yeah, I know. If I can't get hold of her this evening, I'll drive to town in the morning and try from there." He unbuttoned his shirt and tossed it on the bed.

"Hey! You need to put that shirt somewhere else. That space is reserved."

Toby picked up the piece of clothing and grinned wickedly as he turned to take the glass of wine from Bill's hand. "I must have forgotten."

"I guess I need to remind you then." John Brown took the glass from Toby's hands and set it on the table. He unbuttoned his own shirt and slowly turned back to the man standing by the bed, sensing Toby's anticipation as he reached down and unbuttoned his jeans. He pulled Toby to him roughly, kneading the bare skin of Toby's back with his hands.

"Maybe you do…" Toby sighed in contentment and leaned into Bill's embrace. "Why don't you refresh my memory?"

John Brown removed his hands and slid his jeans down his hips while watching his partner's face. Then, he hurried to answer the need he saw in Toby's blue eyes.

Afterwards, the two men lay on the bed, satiated and lazy. Toby carefully unwrapped himself from Bill's arms and padded to the bathroom. After he had finished there, he retrieved his duffle bag from the floor and carried it to the table. He picked up his forgotten wine, and took a drink before starting to unpack his things from the duffle bag. *"I forgot that was in here,"* he thought when he discovered his gun case underneath his clothes. *"No wonder the bag was so heavy."* He refolded a couple of sweatshirts and tucked them in the small cabinet, and then carried a few things to the bathroom and put them away. He put the duffle bag back on the floor by his side of the bed and then went back for his wine. After taking another sip, he turned back to the bed.

The late afternoon sunlight coming through the windows illuminated Bill's body, highlighting his shoulders and back. There was something about the angle of the light, and the position of the man's body, which triggered some buried memory. Toby blinked his eyes, and walked closer to the bed, wine glass in hand. He ran his eyes over Bill's strong torso, and his eyes came to rest on the tattoo on the shoulder. For a moment, he lost himself in his thoughts, trying to figure out what was familiar. Just when he thought he had it, Bill gave a lazy stretch and rolled over.

At the sight of the man's body, all other thoughts went right out of Toby's head, except for the knowledge he was a very lucky man. Toby smiled at the sight of Bills heavy lidded eyes and messy hair. "Hey, sleepy head. Are you planning to stay in bed all evening?"

"That doesn't sound like too bad of an idea, at all." John Brown stretched again, this time less lazy and made more provocative by the way he arched his back and sighed. John Brown liked this game – it was one of his favorites. "Why don't you come and join me over here?"

Toby made an effort to avoid the very tempting distraction spread out before him. "I thought I'd try and call Grams, and get that out of the way. Can I use your phone?"

"Sure, I'll get it as soon as I remember where it is. I put it down somewhere – it's probably in my bag. But are you sure you don't want to come over here first? I'll make it worth your while…" He hands reached between his thighs and cupped his flesh. He loved the way Toby's eyes followed his movements so he worked himself some more until he hardened and strained upward. He kept his eyes on the man standing a few feet away from him. "See anything you like?" John Brown spread his legs a bit to give Toby a view of what was on offer. "Just take your pick."

Toby was mesmerized by the sight. He reached down between his legs with his free hand to help things along. "A few things, maybe. I think I might have to test drive the model again before I commit to buy, though."

Bill began to work both hands now, a little faster. "That can be arranged, but you'll need to start the engine before you put it in gear."

Toby set his glass down on the nightstand, and joined Bill on the bed. "I think I can do that." His hands roamed over the body spread out before him, working down their way downward, until they met Bill's hands, busy at work. He slicked his fingers with saliva, and let them delve into the creases and folds. They soon found the place they wanted to be, and he let them linger for a while, teasing and testing. He reached to the bedside table and grabbed a condom. He watched Bill's face as he sheathed himself, and the man held his eyes and shifted his legs to provide better access. When the man underneath him gave a moan of pleasure, Toby adjusted his position, until his body was where it needed to be. "If I remember, the key goes in…right here."

John Brown wrapped his strong legs around Toby's waist, and used his hands to guide him in. "That's the place, Toby." He exhaled at the sensations he felt, and when they shifted and became more intense, he gripped his legs tighter and lifted his hips to meet the first of Toby's thrusts. "Now, drive."

Reightman ended the call and turned to Mitchell. "I finally got hold of Sheriff Branson. She was surprised to hear from me, and wasn't too happy about the situation."

Mitchell looked over from the driver's seat and tried to decipher her expression. "Why was she surprised? I thought Chief Kelly was going to call and brief her."

"Mitchell, she told me she hasn't heard from him today."

Mitchell's eyes widened in shock. "That can't be right! Is there any chance she just missed his call?"

Reightman looked out the window at the passing countryside. "No, she said she's been in her office ever since she returned from lunch." She turned back to toward him and gave him the rundown on the current state of things. "She's going to send a couple of deputies out to meet us, but said it would be at least another hour before they can get here. Apparently, all her available men are on the other side of the county responding to a domestic disturbance."

"What do you want to do? Should I find a place to pull over and wait?"

Reightman shook her head, knowing they might not have much time. "Keep driving. Let's continue on until we're almost at the cabin. We can wait for them there. I just hope nothing happens before they get there."

"I'm worried too, but Jones doesn't know we're on to him, and doesn't have any reason to hurt Toby."

She wondered who he was trying to convince. She turned to gaze out the window and offered a silent prayer to whoever might be listening. "I hope you're right, Mitchell. But, Jones is unpredictable, and I don't have any way of knowing what might set him off."

Mitchell didn't respond, but Reightman noticed he picked up the speed.

CHAPTER FIFTEEN

"THAT WAS NICE," John Brown stroked Toby's back as they lay entwined together.

"Nice?" Toby asked as he raised himself up on an elbow. "You thought it was *nice*? After all the work I just did, I hope it was better than nice!"

"Well, maybe you're rusty. It's been awhile since we've done that." John Brown chucked at the expression on Toby's face and then pulled the man's head down for a quick kiss. "I wouldn't want you to get out of practice though, so I'll be up for another test drive before the weekend is over."

Toby glared at him in mock outrage, but his face cleared when Bill pulled him down for another kiss, longer and more lingering.

Then, Bill rolled his legs off the bed and stood up. "I think I'll go take a quick shower and then go check the hot tub. After that, I'll heat up the grill and we can start thinking about dinner."

"Sounds good. If the shower were bigger, I'd join you, but there's barely enough room for one."

"If the shower were bigger, we'd never get dinner started, and I, for one, worked up quite an appetite over the last couple of hours." He took one more lingering look at the man on the bed before he turned and headed to the bathroom.

Toby lay on the bed for another minute or two, enjoying the feel of the warm, tangled sheets and the memory of how they'd gotten that way. He heard Bill turn on the water in the shower, and made himself climb out of bed. He went to the kitchen and drank a glass of water, and pulled a couple of steaks out of the fridge. Then he decided to try and call Grams. *"I think I remember Bill saying his phone was in his bag."* He started searching for Bill's duffle bag and finally located it sticking out from underneath the other side of the bed. He knelt down to pull it out and saw it was opened. He reached in to see if he could locate the phone. His hand froze in mid reach as he spotted the gun on top. *"He probably brings it up here in case he has to chase away varmints."* Toby moved it aside and continued his search. As he dug through a couple of layers of clothing, he felt what he assumed was a wallet and lifted it out of the bag to put to one side. When he realized it wasn't a wallet, he lifted the leather flap, and was confronted with a badge. He examined it, noting the name on the ID and the seal emblazed on the metal. *"Bill's a cop?"* he asked himself as he sat back on his heels. *"A detective? This says his name is Vincent William Jones."*

His mind rushed back to an earlier conversation with Detective Reightman and he remembered her mentioning her partner had the same last name as Bill. He thought she'd also said her partner's first name was Vince. Was it possible they were the same person? If that was the case, why hadn't Bill mentioned it? He quickly replaced the badge when he heard the bathroom door open and nudged the bag under the bed. Just as he stood, Bill entered the room, toweling his wet hair with one hand and holding a phone in the other.

"Hey, I found the phone in the bathroom. I must have set it down in there earlier."

Toby stared at the man he thought he knew and took the phone from his outstretched hand. "Thanks. I won't be on it too long." He watched the man give his head a couple of more swipes with the towel and then glanced down at the phone he held in his hand. "I think I'll go out on the deck – the signal's probably better out there."

John Brown looked at him quizzically, as Toby slowly walked to the dresser and pulled out a pair of jeans and a sweatshirt. As Toby pulled on the jeans, John Brown noticed the bag sticking out from underneath the bed, and felt a chill travel down his spine. He studied Toby's face, but was unable read the rapidly changing emotions. "Is something wrong?" he asked. "Why are you getting dressed?"

Toby pulled the sweatshirt over his head and turned back to Bill. "No, nothing's wrong. I just felt chilled for some reason, and remembered it's probably getting cool outside." Toby tried to keep his voice level and to sound as normal as possible, while his mind was frantically trying to reconcile the man he knew with the cop he strongly suspected he was. He walked to the door and went out on the deck.

John Brown watched him with narrowed eyes until Toby closed the door and then he dropped his towel on the bed and bent down to his bag. He pulled it open and saw his badge sitting on top of the other items which had been disarranged. Overwhelmed by the realization Toby had discovered at least one of his secrets, a conflicted and suddenly infuriated John Brown threw the bag on the bed. *"I wish you hadn't dug through that bag, Toby! Because you did, it all has to end now."* John Brown strode to the cabinet and pulled out a pair of jeans and a button front shirt and quickly dressed himself. He pulled on a pair of socks and then his boots. He opened the bag and withdrew the gun he used when he was on a job, tucking it into the waistband behind his back. Then he went to the window, as stood watching as Toby spoke on the phone. For a minute or two, he tried to reason with himself, wondering if he was overreacting. After trying to think of any possible explanation he could give for what Toby had discovered, he reluctantly came to the conclusion that nothing he could say would make any difference. He saw Toby look back toward the cabin, with an expression John Brown had never seen on his face before. Toby was afraid.

Threatened by what this meant, his own mind divided, and everything he'd tried to be for Toby began to melt away until all that remained was a cold and calculating John Brown, the man who now had to eliminate a problem. *"Looks like you have another hard job ahead of you,"* he told himself, in resignation. He felt a pang of regret, but pushed it down and told himself it was nothing to worry about. *"After all, I've heard it's always messy when a love affair dies."*

Toby paced across the deck with the phone in his hand trying to find a signal to make his call. He finally found the right spot, and punched in the number he knew by heart. When the call was answered he cried with relief. "Detective Reightman," he said while trying to keep his voice steady. "I think there's something strange going on." He told her what he'd discovered and she carefully told him what she knew. By the time they hung up, he understood exactly how much trouble he was in. *"Oh, shit!"* The question now, was what he was going to do until help arrived? He turned the phone over in his hand while he tried to think. *"Don't panic!"* he told himself as he turned the phone over in his shaking hands. *"Pull yourself together, dammit! You need to try and act as normal as possible. They're just about twenty minutes away and you can manage until then."* He glanced down at the phone, and his hands stopped as he looked down at the case, noticing the long scratch running down the silvery back. *"This looks just like my phone – the one I lost, the night Geri was murdered."* He almost dropped it when he realized it very likely was his phone. He tightened his grip as he heard the back door to the cabin open.

"Were you able to make your call?"

Toby jumped at the sound of the voice, but somehow managed an embarrassed smile which he hoped was convincing. "You scared me, Bill! I didn't know you were behind me." He handed the man back his phone. "I was finally able to find a signal." He met the man's eyes. "Why don't you start the grill and I'll go hop in the shower? I guess I worked up an appetite, just like you did."

Even though his voice sounded fairly normal, John Brown could tell by the look in his eyes that Toby was frightened. That pleased the part of him which was the cold blooded killer. However, the small portion which remained of Bill Jones was remorseful. "Alright, I'll do that. Don't be too long."

"I'll try to hurry…Bill."

"How 'bout a kiss first?" John Brown asked, testing Toby's reaction.

Try as he might, Toby couldn't bring himself to meet his eyes so he turned away, averting his face. "I think I'd better brush my teeth first." Knowing how lame that sounded, he forced himself to look back and look at the man who he suspected would kill him without a thought. "I'll take care of that, right after I shower."

John Brown watched as the man he thought he might have loved – but now had to kill – walked back into the cabin. Bill Jones tried to think of any other alternative, but he couldn't take the chance Toby might mention anything to Reightman, because that would raise all kinds of uncomfortable questions. He'd have to explain to both Toby and Reightman why he hadn't just told them the truth, and he couldn't think of a plausible answer for that question. Toby had told him from the beginning he wouldn't stand for lies, not after what Guzman had done, and almost everything he had led Toby to believe was a lie. Even worse, if they somehow connected all the dots, he'd be in a world of trouble, and his carefully constructed persona would crumble. He walked to the grill and turned it on, deciding even though he was going to kill Toby, they might as well have dinner first. Otherwise, the evening would be ruined.

"It's the next turn to the left, Mitchell," Reightman instructed as she hung up the phone.

Mitchell slowed to make the turn and glanced her way. "Is he alright?"

"He's pretty shaken up right now. I hope he can hang on until we get there." She scrolled through her call list and punched the number she needed. "Sheriff Branson, this is Detective Reightman. Any idea how much longer your guys will be?...No, ma'am, but things have changed for the worse. We're about fifteen or twenty minutes from the location and we are going on to the cabin...Yes, I understand, but I can't wait any longer...No, ma'am...I will, and I'll be looking for that backup." She ended the call and turned to Mitchell. "Pull over at the next place you can find and we'll get suited up in the vests."

A few minutes later, they were out of the car and pulling on the protective vests. "Damn, I hate these things," Reightman complained as she tugged it into place.

"You'd hate taking a bullet more, Detective."

"You're right," she agreed as she checked her weapon. "But I can still bitch about how uncomfortable it is right up until the minute it takes the first hit."

"I hope it doesn't come to that." Mitchell finished fastening the side tabs and checked his own weapon. "Ready?"

"I guess I better be. I'm going to see if I can talk to Jones first. It might not do any good, but I have to try. You focus on trying to keep Toby safe."

"I'll do my best. I wish Toby had some protection of his own. He probably didn't bring his gun with him. There was no reason for him to do that."

"Probably not," she grimly agreed as she climbed into the driver's seat. "I'm not sure how much good it would do him anyway. He's only had it a few weeks and I bet he's just barely competent."

Mitchell settled into the passenger side and gave her a grim, lop-sided grin. "You'd lose that bet, Detective. The instructors say he's a natural talent. He's actually a very good marksman." The grin faded when he thought about his friend's situation. "If he doesn't have his gun with him, it's pretty much a moot point."

Reightman didn't respond, she just pulled out onto the two lane road and hit the gas.

Toby closed the door behind him and went to his side of the bed and picked up the bag he'd stowed on the floor. Then, glancing out the window to check on the location of the man on the deck, he went into the small bathroom and shut and locked the door. He turned on the shower and opened the bag. He removed his gun case and opened it and checked his pistol, just like he'd been taught. He pulled two large towels out of the bathroom cabinet and rolled the gun into one of them. He stripped off his clothes and stepped into the shower. As the hot water ran down his back, he tried to think of what he could do to keep Jones distracted. His head jerked to the door as he heard a small noise, like someone testing the knob.

"You about done in there, Toby? I need to know if I should put on the steaks."

"Yeah, Bill," he yelled back once he had the surge of fear under control. "I'll be out in just a couple of more minutes." He tilted his face up into the hot spray and thought through everything he knew. *"I should have recognized that damned tattoo,"* he berated himself. He turned off the water and quickly sluiced the moisture off his body before reaching for the towel. *"How could I have missed the connection? I looked at those photographs a million times!"* He dried off his body, pulled on his jeans and decided to leave off the sweatshirt. He wasn't cold anymore, and it wouldn't provide him any protection. A bare chest might distract Jones into thinking everything was normal, and every second might count before Reightman and Mitchell arrived. He hung his up his towel and quickly brushed his teeth, remembering the excuse he'd used to avoid contact. Then he stuffed the sweatshirt back in his bag, covering the now empty gun case. He picked up the two towels he'd rolled up and tucked them under one arm, and picked up the bag and unlocked and opened the bathroom door.

John Brown was waiting just outside when the door opened. "I thought you were going to wash away. It took you a long time in there."

"I know, but hot water felt good and it warmed me up. I'm not cold anymore."

John Brown stepped closer, forcing himself into Toby's space. "How about that kiss? Now you've brushed your teeth."

"Uh….sure. Just let me put these things down."

John Brown eyed the bag Toby held and the towels he had under his arm. "Here, let me take those for you."

Toby hesitated for a split second, then handed him the bag. "You can take this – just put it over by the side of the bed."

"You want me to take the towels too?

"No need. I thought I'd carry them out to the hot tub so we'd have them later. I'll take them out now and then I can come in and help you get things together for dinner."

Good idea, Toby. But I want that kiss first." John Brown waited as Toby made up his mind. He finally stepped a little closer and leaned in and gave him a kiss, but it didn't hold any of Toby's normal fire. *"Maybe we won't even make it through dinner,"* John Brown thought bleakly as Toby pulled away.

"I'll just take these out and I'll be right back," Toby told him before walking out the back door.

John Brown tossed the Toby's bag on the bed and went to the kitchen to season the steaks. He placed them on a plate and added salt and pepper, liking the way the shiny red, bloody meat looked against the dull finish of the pottery platter. He figured he might as well cook them, even if Toby didn't get to enjoy dinner. *"It's a shame,"* John Brown commiserated with himself, thinking about their last kiss, *"but, I guess I didn't really love him, after all. I wonder if he really cared about me."* He pulled out some lettuce and a couple of tomatoes to fix a simple salad. *"Still, I'm glad I didn't kill him the night I shot Jackson, and I'm glad I didn't kill him our first weekend together. If nothing else, we had some fun, and he taught me some things I'd never have tried on my own."* His knife sliced through the flesh of the ripe tomato and he wondered what else he should prepare. *"I probably should get the tarp back out since it'll be easier to carry him to the grave in the woods if he's wrapped up. I'm going to have to dig the hole out again, and I hope the dirt is not too packed. It took forever to get my hands clean last time. And, I guess I can throw a couple of pieces of thick toast on the grill to go with the salad and streaks."* He opened the cabinet to get out the bread, and heard the sound of tires on gravel. *"Someone's probably lost and needs directions,"* he decided, and rinsed off his hands.

John Brown went to the front window to check, and swore when he recognized the two people in the car. "Dammit!" He dug the phone out of his pocket and scanned the recent calls. His expression grew stormy when he recognized the last number dialed. "You've been busy, Toby!" He shoved the phone back in his pocket and pulled the gun from behind his back and then locked the front door.

"Well, at least we know he's home, Mitchell," Reightman commented cynically when she saw Jones briefly appear in the window. "I wonder if Toby's in there with him."

Mitchell turned to her with worried eyes. "I don't know where else he could be. His car's right there, so he must be inside. What do you want to do now?"

Reightman unbuckled her seatbelt. "I think I'll go on up to the door and see if he'll let me inside. Go on around the back and make sure he doesn't come out that way. We need to keep him here until our reinforcements arrive."

Mitchell unbuckled his own seatbelt and opened the car door. "How long before they'll show up, Detective?"

"I don't know, but I'm praying it won't be long. Just try to keep your cool, and if he starts shooting, try to keep out of the line of fire. "

She got out of the car and unholstered her gun. Mitchell followed suit. She watched as he started around the side of the house to make his way to the back of the cabin. When he was out of sight, she took a deep breath and marched up to the door, gun in hand. She gave two sharp raps on the door. "Come on, Jones, open up! I know you're in there." She tried the knob and found it was locked. "Jones," she called. "Why don't we have a little talk about things?"

John Brown hurried out to the deck and found Toby sitting on the edge of the hot tub with his head in his hands. "Toby?" he yelled. "You need to get in here. Now!"

Toby looked up at the angry shout, and immediately spotted the gun in the man's hands. He stood and dropped one of the towels. He quickly unrolled the other and took the gun he'd hidden inside into his hands, holding it steady with a double-handed grip. "I don't think so, Detective Jones, or whatever the fuck your real name is! I think I'll stay right here."

John Brown noticed the tremor in Toby's voice and he knew he was scared, but the gun in his hands never wavered. "What's that you have in your hand, Toby?"

"What the hell does it look like?"

John Brown aka Bill Jones was shocked by Toby's possession of a gun and even more so by the fact he even appeared to know how to hold it properly. He noted the angry, frantic tone in the man's voice, and decided that even if Toby wasn't a good shot, it was best to be careful. People were hurt by guns all the time. He took a couple of cautious steps toward him, and tried to reason with him. "You need to put it down, Toby. You'll hurt yourself if you're not careful."

Toby shook his head and bared his teeth. "I'm not about to put this gun down, and don't worry – I know how to use it. If you take one more step in my direction, I'll prove it.

Before he could reconcile himself with this new reality, John Brown heard movement from the side of the house. He wondered which one of the unwelcomed guests it was. "You have a couple of visitors, Toby. You should have told me you invited them."

"They were already on their way. Detective Reightman figured everything out before I did. I guess all of your secrets are out now."

John Brown shrugged. "Nothing good lasts forever, Toby. What tipped you off?"

"The badge in your bag. And the fact the phone you handed me to use was once my phone. The one I lost on the night Geri was murdered."

John Brown laughed at the irony, and remembered what Helliman had told him the night he put a bullet through his head. If he could create a little doubt, he might just get out of this with his skin intact. Good thing he had money sitting in the bank. "That phone could have belonged to anyone, Toby. What possible reason could you have for thinking it was yours?"

"The scratch on the back – in the exact place mine was scratched – is a pretty good hint. And it makes sense. Just like that damned tattoo on your shoulder. It showed up quite well in the pictures Geri left for me. I was just so wrapped up in you and how wonderful things seemed that I didn't put the pieces together. I should have known it was all too good to be true!"

John Brown was comforted to know Toby had been truly interested in him, at least if he understood what wrapped up meant. But he was confused by the rest of the statement. "What pictures?"

"Oh come off it, Jones! You were one of the staring attractions. You have to be familiar with the photographs since you've been working the murder cases, or at least, convincing everyone that's what you were doing."

John Brown's eyes widened, surprised by this new information. The day just kept getting better. "Reightman didn't share everything with me, Toby. I never saw all of the photos, and I never knew he took pictures of me." John Brown didn't want Toby to be unreasonably jealous of his little rub and tug with Guzman, so he tried to reassure him. "I was only with him once."

"You know what? It doesn't matter! I'm done believing anything you say. But I do have one question for you. Why, Jones?"

John Brown was disappointed by the predictability of the question. For some reason, that was always the first thing people asked him when they realized they were going to die. "That's not a very original question, Toby. I thought you'd do better than that. But, if you put down the gun, I'll think about giving you an answer."

"Put down your weapon, Jones!" Mitchell shouted as he rounded the corner.

John Brown narrowed his eyes at the interruption and fired once. Toby saw Mitchell hit the ground and roll.

Reightman also heard the shot. She stepped back and fired twice at the lock and pushed with her shoulder. Frustrated when it didn't budge, she stepped back and kicked the door open. She felt something tear in her knee – the same knee she'd injured the night Sam had been killed. Furious, she shoved the door open, and entered the cabin. The room was empty, but she could see out into the back of the property from the windows flanking the fireplace. "I guess he has his gun after all," she groaned when she saw Toby holding a weapon in his hand.

Reightman hobbled to the door, gasping at the sharp pain, and limped out onto the deck, taking aim. "Jones, drop the gun!"

A cold smile of pleasure formed on Jones' mouth. "Well hello, partner! I wondered what was taking you so long! I was starting to get worried. Congratulations – I see you finally figured things out."

Reightman took in the scene, noting Toby's resolute demeanor and the confused, manic look in Jones' eyes. She didn't see Mitchell, and wondered if Jones had already taken him out. She pushed down her fear, and took a step closer, biting her lip to keep from moaning at the pain in her knee. She did her best to keep her voice level as she responded. "It took me a while, but the pieces finally came together."

John Brown shook his head in sad resignation. "I worried about that, but I think this must just be fate, Reightman. Just when I find something wonderful, it falls apart. It's the story of my life. I don't know why this happened. I tried so hard to muddy the trail and confuse things, and I know I did a good job. I always do a good job."

She didn't understand what he was talking about, and didn't like the way he sounded. She could tell he was on the edge of some sort of breakdown. All she knew was she needed to keep him talking as long as possible. "Really, Jones? What was it you did so well? Tell me, so I understand where I messed up?"

"You didn't mess up, Reightman. There was no way for you to know your new partner was involved. If you'd had Sam around, you'd have figured things out much sooner. I do regret killing Sam Jackson. He…was a mistake."

She briefly closed her eyes in pain, both from her knee and the reminder of Jackson's death, but she couldn't allow the hurt to linger. "I regret that you killed Sam, too. He was a good man, and a smart cop. But, Jones, I know it was a mistake. This can end right now. Put down the gun, let Mitchell and me take you in, and we can get you some help."

She saw him think over her words, and an almost wistful, hopeful expression flashed through his eyes. But Jones shook his head. "You and I both know better than that. There isn't any help for me now. And I hate to tell you, but I think I winged young Officer Mitchell, so I don't think he'd be much help anymore. You know, I liked him, as long as he stayed away from Toby. That was part of the reason I made sure he was removed from the picture."

"What do you mean?"

"I didn't like it when they were together, so I convinced Kelly to reassign him. It just took a few hints that Toby was turning Mitchell into a little faggot, and Kelly was happy to pull him off. I didn't bother to let him know Mitchell was sucking cock long before Toby Bailey came along. After all, I promised you I wouldn't say anything about Mitchell's orientation. Kelly hates you now Reightman – ever since you backed him into a corner. He was the perfect man to help me, even if he didn't know what he was doing at the time." Jones laughed joyfully at his own cleverness, and then studied Reightman as she swayed and tried to keep her balance. "Reightman, you're looking a little wobbly over there. I'm worried about you. You know, I think you might have bit off more than you can chew, and you can't bring me in by yourself. You should have brought more backup." Jones suddenly moved his gun to his opposite hand and feinted to the right. He turned and fired a shot. Reightman felt the bullet strike her chest and she reeled from the impact, falling to the wooden deck and landing on the same injured knee. She saw Jones raise his gun again and take aim, but before he could fire, a shot rang out from the other side of the deck. Jones's gun hand jerked as the bullet hit, and he dropped the gun. But before it could hit the deck, Jones grabbed it in his other hand. He turned and fired two shots in the direction of his shooter.

Reightman heard Mitchell call out in sudden pain, and then, it was quiet.

"I guess I was wrong about Mitchell. He got off a pretty good shot," Jones said with true admiration, although he winced at the pain from his torn and bleeding hand. "It just wasn't good enough. I think I got him good that time, so he's probably done. If not, I'll finish him off later. Like I said," he shrugged, causing his now useless hand to swing at his side, "you should have brought back-up. You should pay attention to your partner, Reightman."

"Backup is on the way, Jones. This isn't going to end well for you unless you put the gun down and surrender."

Jones laughed again and slung the blood from his wounded hand onto the wooden deck. "It's not going to end well for me, anyway you look at it. But it's going to end badly for you, too."

He raised the gun again, but before he could fire, Toby called out to him. "Jones, you never did answer my question."

Bill Jones lowered his hand a few inches at the sound of the man's voice. He recognized it as the same voice he'd become accustomed to hearing when they were together, and doing such wonderful things to each other. It was the same voice which had urged him on, and sometimes begged him for release they strained together on the bed. Images of those moments ran through his mind and he shook his head, desperate to clear them away. Bill Jones couldn't respond, so John Brown answered for him. "Why did I do it, you mean? Why did I kill all of those people? It's very simple. It was just my job."

"No. That wasn't my question," Toby answered softly, hoping to keep Jones' attention away from Reightman. "What's with the tattoo? That's what I wanted to ask."

John Brown smiled grimly and nodded in approval. "That's a much better question, so I'll answer it for you." He closed his eyes briefly, deciding what to say. He probably owed the man something, so for once, he'd give him the truth. "I had it done when I was a young man," he said slowly, remembering why he'd selected the word inked on his shoulder "It was just an idea I had, of how I could explain my life."

"And does it? Does it explain your life?"

John Brown hesitated, unsure of the truth. He didn't know. He closed his eyes again, trying to determine what answer he could give to the man who'd asked it.

"Explain your life to me, Bill." Toby asked him, in a desolate voice, which told how hurt he was to have deceived once again, by someone he loved. "Explain it so I'll at least understand something."

Bill Jones opened his eyes and turned toward Toby, pleading with his eyes for him to understand, and hoping he could find the words to tell him the way things were for him then. "Alright, I'll try, Toby." His voice was almost a whisper as he remembered. "You see, when I was a kid, I didn't know where I belonged or who I was. I was just...lost. I didn't fit anywhere at all, no matter how hard I tried. My father was out of the picture from the time I was born, and I never learned what had happened to him. I tried to find him when I was older, thinking it was important. I never did, but he left me something. We share the same name – Vincent William Jones. Momma didn't like being reminded of him when she remarried, so instead of calling me Vincent, she called me Billy, or Bill when I got older. My stepfather never cared much for me, so I was raised by my mother's family, the Browns. They were a big family of white trash farmers, ignorant and bigoted, and mean. They had so many dirty, stinking kids running around the place – grandchildren and cousins and such – they couldn't keep up with us all, so they just called all of the boys "John", and all of the girls "Jane". I thought it was funny when I was a kid, but after a while, I understood they didn't give a damn what my name was. I could be John Brown, or Joe Smith, or Bill Jones – and it didn't matter. To them, I was just another belly that had to be filled. I tried to get their attention, and to show them I was something more than just another John Brown, but the only attention they were inclined to give was a hateful word or a slap in the mouth. Sometimes it was worse and took me a day or two to recover.

As soon as I was able and someone would hire me, I started working, just to get away from that place, and those mean, rough people. I wanted to be somebody, and to make something of myself. I guess I take after my momma that way. After a few false starts, I learned I could be anyone I needed to be in order to get a job, and then get the job done. I...changed myself...over and over again, to suit the situation and to make people like and trust me. I told myself all those people I had to become in order to survive didn't mean anything to me. They were the fake, the 'Alias', the part hiding the lonely, beaten boy in some safe place where he might find someone to care for him. That, Toby, is the story of my tattoo."

He saw a myriad of emotions cross Toby's face, but he didn't recognize most of them. John Brown had never allowed himself to have many emotions, except when he was with Toby. They got in the way of the job, and ended up causing their own problems. But the last, he did recognize. It was pity.

Before he could do more than wonder why anyone would feel pity for him, Toby's eyes hardened, and met his own. "What alias are you when you're with me?" Toby asked him.

A hundred images ran through Jones's mind and his good hand began to tremble in distress. At that moment, John Brown's mind splintered and fractured into a thousand pieces. "I don't know!" he shouted, terrified when he couldn't find an answer. A high keening noise began in the back of his throat and overwhelmed everything else. He shook his head frantically, until the noise died away. When he was able to meet Toby's pale blue eyes, what he saw in them made him feel worthless and inadequate. He tried to explain. "Sometimes, I just lose track of who I am when I'm with you. I've done things with you I never have imagined I would do – and I liked those things we did together, Toby. I like them because I was doing them to *you*, and with *you*. I close my eyes and *see* what *we* do together *in my mind*." Bill Jones/John Brown made a great effort to put it all into words. "Toby, I would have tried to be almost anyone you needed – or wanted me to be – for as long as we were together." He looked at the man with blue eyes and at the woman aiming her gun toward him, and knew it was useless. He turned back to Toby, resigned that the time had come. "It's too late now. I think it's just...too late for us, now." He put a hint of resolve in his voice, knowing how things were said when a great romance ended. "Toby, I think it's time for us to break up. Things have changed you see, and we've reached the end of the road." Bill Jones was crumbling, but John Brown knew he needed to finish the job. He steadied his arm and raised his gun, aiming straight at Toby's face and finding the path that would send the bullet between his eyes. Bill Jones struggled with John Brown, and managed to take control for a brief instant. "Toby! Did you love me?"

Toby answered immediately, voice shaking as he did, "Yes, I did love you. At least, I loved the man I thought you were."

As the words penetrated his mind, John Brown/Bill Jones/John Brown saw the gun waiver in Toby's hands. His heart broke as he realized what they were both going to lose today. He wished so many things were different, and his voice was like that of the lost, lonely child he once had been. "I have never loved anyone, Toby, and I didn't think anyone would ever really love me." Bill Jones/John Brown/Bill Jones smiled with heart-breaking sweetness, and regret. "But now, after hearing your words, I know someone did love me, for a while. I'm glad it was you and not anyone else. I'm so glad of that." Tears welled up in his eyes, and he blinked them away, remembering who he was and why he was here. He shook his head, trying to reconcile himself to doing the job he needed to finish. Bill Jones said the words he'd rehearsed once, on this very deck. "I think…I might love you, Toby." He waited and when there no response, Bill Jones drifted away, swirling down into despair. There was only one part of him left now and only one thing left to do. "I'm sorry," John Brown said with regret, "but I have to kill you now."

To John Brown's surprise, Toby began to laugh. No one had ever laughed at him before. "What are you laughing about Toby?" he asked, astonished by the reaction. "Why are you laughing when you are about to die? Don't you care?"

Toby tightened his grip on the gun and his laughter died away. "No, I really don't care! I'm sure you're going to shoot me, and I'll try to shoot you as well. But to answer your question, I laughed, because I finally realize just how fucked up this has been. You created this all in your mind, didn't you? You had to create this tragic, melodramatic scene, because you're incapable of feeling anything real at all. Now you're using it to justify what you're about to do."

John Brown/Bill Jones was wounded by the things he'd just heard. "How can you say that to me, after all we've shared? How can you doubt I care deeply for you?"

From the corner of his eye, Toby saw Reightman move closer and heard movement on the ground where Mitchell had fallen. He moved slowly backward until he felt the hot tub wall against the back of his legs. He held his arms steady, weapon in his hands.

John Brown sighted down the barrel of his gun. Reightman rushed a few steps toward him, her unsteady gait heavy on the wooden deck. He heard her approach and his finger tightened on the trigger of his gun. "I hear you, limping along back there. Back away, Reightman, or I'll pull the trigger now."

Reightman took a few steps back, hoping desperately someone from the Sheriff's office would arrive, but knowing they were out of time. "Alright! I'll stop, but please, put down the gun and let Toby go. You'd regret hurting him, just like I know you regret killing all of those others."

Bill Jones/John Brown shook his head at her foolishness." I don't regret killing any of them. They were each just a job, Reightman, and the last few deserved to die. I was well paid to end their lives – well, all except for one. I killed Christina Dameron for free, because she tried to hurt Toby." John Brown's eyes lost focus as something occurred to him. "I knew that ladder was going to cause problems, but I never did figure out who unlocked the door to the roof for her." He thought about it for another second, and then shrugged, dismissing it from his mind because it didn't matter any longer. John Brown turned back to Toby and looked into his eyes. He told him gently, soft and low, but steadfast in his resolve, "Toby, I'm going to shoot you now." He took aim at the spot between the eyes." It'll be fast, I promise. And –"

A shot rang out and Reightman saw the Jones stumble and fall to his knees. Blood soaked the back of his shirt where the bullet had exited, tearing flesh. He looked up at the man who'd shot him and struggled to raise his arm. "Toby, why did you do that?...I was going to kill you, and.....then myself.....so we would always be...together. You're supposed...supposed to be...with me...mine forever." Toby looked down at Jones as the man struggled to breathe. The hurt and dying man struggled to brace himself against the side of the hot tub. "I think...this is the end...and I'm glad. Please come with me...It'll be...quick..........I promise." He looked at Toby tenderly, with love shining in his eyes. He thought about the unfairness of life and the people and events that had led him to this place "I... wish I could hold you...one... more time." Using all that he had left inside him, he raised his gun to fire. Before he could pull the trigger, blood blossomed from the hole drilled through the center of his forehead.

Toby lowered his hands, still clutching his gun as Jones fell to the deck, and turned and ran to where Mitchell had fallen to the ground.

Forty-five minutes later, he watched as the ambulance took Mitchell away.

"He'll make it." Reightman tried to infuse her words with confidence as she struggled with her own pain. "He's hurt very badly, but he's young and strong." Reightman was laying on a gurney herself, with her knee packed and supported while waiting to be loaded into the other EMS vehicle. Her injuries were much less severe than Mitchell's, but she didn't know if her knee would ever be the same. She felt very old and very tired.

"We're ready ma'am," one of the trauma service personnel told her.

She looked up at Toby and reached for his hand. "Did you get it?"

He squeezed her fingers gently. "Yes."

She was smiling as they wheeled her to the waiting transport, knowing they had everything she needed to bring it all to an end.

Toby watched as the vehicle drove away, and he hoped her words about Mitchell were correct.

"Mr. Bailey, we're ready to go as well," the deputy from the county Sheriff's office informed him. Toby followed the man to the waiting car. He looked back once, as the car made its way down the long graveled drive, taking in one last sight of the small weekend cabin, illuminated in the night by the whirling lights of the remaining law enforcement vehicles.

Thirty minutes later, he followed the deputy into the county Sheriff's office.

"If we'd had more warning, this might have been prevented, Mr. Bailey." Sheriff Branson watched him carefully with her hard brown eyes.

"You were supposed to have been informed earlier. Police Chief Kelly told Detective Reightman he was going to call and alert you so that you'd be able to provide back-up."

"That's what she told me on the phone and I hauled ass to get my men freed up as soon as possible. But I can assure you I never received a call from Kelly, or anyone else in the department." She turned her stern weathered face away and contemplated the nighttime view out of her window. "I'll get to the bottom of this business with Chief Kelly. You can take that to the bank. If I even sus-pect that he let two of his people walk into this kind of confrontation without a safety net – well, let's just say things are going to get very ugly." Branson took a drink of her coffee and then turned back to him. "You're all very fortunate that it wasn't worse than it turned out to be. My deputies tell me that it looked like there was quite a bit of gunfire in a fairly contained space. Why don't you tell me what hap-pened from your perspective, and how you came to be in this situa-tion in the first place?"

Toby spent the next hour going over every detail, stopping only to provide more background or description when Branson wanted to clarify something.

Finally she stood up from her desk. "I think I have a pretty good understanding of what occurred. I'm going to leave you here for a few minutes while I make a couple of calls. I should be back before too long. If you want some coffee, the pot's right around the corner. Help yourself."

Toby didn't want any coffee. He was keyed up enough already. He stood and stretched for a few minutes as he waited for the Sheriff to return. About twenty minutes later she came back to her desk.

"You're free to go, Mr. Bailey. I've arranged for a couple of my deputies to bring you your vehicle, but it will take a while to do that. In the meantime, can I drop you somewhere? There's a small motel about ten minutes away that I hear isn't too bad."

"If it's not too much trouble, I'd prefer to go to the hospital where they've taken Mitchell and Detective Reightman."

Branson noticed the deep emotion in his voice when he men-tioned the badly wounded cop. "Then that's what we'll do. Come on then. It won't take us more than a few minutes to get there.

She soon pulled up in front of the entrance to the small county hospital. "Here's my card with all of my contact information in case you need it. Have Reightman give me a call when she's able. I think she and I have a couple of things to discuss."

"I'll be sure to give her the message." Toby looked worriedly to-ward the hospital entrance before turning back to shake her hand. "Thank you for everything, Sheriff Branson."

She noticed his worried look. "Mr. Bailey, this hospital may be small, but they know what they're doing. Officer Mitchell is in very good hands. My partner Cheryl – Dr. Cheryl Preston – is the doctor that'll be working to patch him up. She's one of the best trauma doctors in the state and you can be sure she'll do everything possible to see that he pulls through just fine."

Toby thanked her again and went through the glass double door. There he checked in and found a seat to wait along with the other worried people who were anxious for any news about those they cared for. After a few hours, a tired looking middle aged woman approached him, still wearing green surgical scrubs.

"I'm Dr. Preston," she introduced herself as she shook his hand. "You were asking about Officer Mitchell and Detective Reightman?"

"Yes, I'm Toby Bailey. I was with them when they were hurt."

"Well, Detective Reightman tore her knee all to hell, but she'll be fine. We have her doped up and are trying to relieve the swelling. She should be able to go home tomorrow."

"Toby sighed in relief. "Thank you. How about…Mitchell?"

"I'm afraid Officer Mitchell's situation is more complicated," Preston told him, the gravity of the situation clear in her eyes. "He's alive and in no immediate danger," she quickly assured him when she saw the panicked look on his face. "I have him stabilized and have arranged for him to be transported back to the city. He's going to need a level of care we can't give him here. The ambulance should be ready to transport him in another hour or so. I've informed the hospital there and they'll be ready for him. I've also informed his parents and they'll be waiting when he arrives."

"Has he said anything at all?"

"No, although he did open his eyes a couple of times before surgery. We have him pretty tanked up right now to help manage the pain and trauma. It's best for him to stay that way until he reaches his destination."

"Thank you for telling me, Dr. Preston."

"I would have wanted someone to tell me if I were in a similar situation. Now, I have to go check on some other patients. I'll let them know you're allowed to see Detective Reightman as soon as she's situated in a room. It shouldn't be more than another hour or two."

After she left, Toby took a seat again. He stared out the glass doors of the ER until he saw an ambulance pull up outside. He stood and walked to the doors, watching as a body was loaded into the back. When he saw Dr. Preston confer briefly with the team, he knew it was Mitchell. When the ambulance drove away, she turned toward him and gave him a single nod through the glass, and at that moment, Toby broke down and cried.

CHAPTER SIXTEEN

THE NEXT DAY Reightman was released from the hospital, with firm instructions from the doctor regarding care and follow-up. Toby drove her back home, and helped her into the condo, letting her lean on his arm rather than having to navigate with the crutches she'd been given. He helped her ease gently down onto the sagging coach before sharing the plan that he and Zhou Li had devised the night before.

"That's totally unnecessary, Toby. There is absolutely no need for anyone to go to that trouble."

"They've all offered and they all want to help. I know you think you'll be perfectly fine managing here by yourself, but there's no reason to try. After we see how you get along, we can adjust accordingly." His voice was tired and he turned away his anguished eyes. He was fighting to stay in control after the events at the cabin. "Just admit you need help, and let them get on with it. I'll be here as much as I can, but to tell you the truth, I'm not in any shape to do much more than just keep you company right now."

Melba knew what he was telling her, but also knew she had nothing to offer him. She wasn't in good shape herself, which meant she had to suck it up for both of them. She warred with the idea that anyone should have to take care of her, and discovered she was really more embarrassed that anyone should see her in her current state. Toby and Zhou Li she could deal with – she hadn't been given any choice and, she admitted, she was thankful for their concern and care. However, the thought of the rest of the characters from Capital Street descending on her was almost too much to bear.

Toby suspected what she was thinking, and decided it was time to bring out the big guns. "Detective Melba, if you don't accept this with the grace and gratitude their offer deserves, I'll have to call Madame Zhou and let her know you're being difficult. I don't think you want her expounding on the reasons why you should agree. It's a forgone conclusion that she'd prevail and you'd just wear yourself out anyway. You might as well just give in now."

"There is no need to make threats, Toby."

"That wasn't a threat."

She knew he was right. "Alright," she grumbled, "But only if it's just for a few days."

He was relieved she was finally seeing sense and decided to cut her a little slack. "We'll see how it goes and then we can decide."

Reightman knew how that would work out, but she was tired so she let the subject rest. "Who's the first person on cripple duty?"

Toby patiently explained the schedule her self-appointed caretakers had arranged, and she sat back against the sagging seat cushions and regarded him blankly. "Toby, why would these people do this for me?" She tried to find a way to explain what was obvious – at least to her. "They don't really know me. I'm a stranger, and they have no reason to go out of their way to do something like this."

He gave an exasperated sigh, and just wanted to shake her. She could be so dense sometimes. "Just accept the fact they're doing it because they're good people and they want to help. And because....well, you're not a stranger. You're part of the gang."

"What do you mean?"

"You're part of it now, Detective. You're a part of Capital Street. You've been involved with everything that has happened since Geri was killed, and they've gotten to know and like you. I guess you've become part of the family."

Somehow the idea wasn't as unwelcome and foreign to her as it would have been a few short months ago. "Really?"

"Really. Now, please stop talking and try to make yourself comfortable – or as comfortable as you can – on that sad thing you call a couch. I'm going to make some tea for you and then you're going to have a nap – if you can nap in here. All of this beige and brown is depressing, and I'm depressed enough already."

"The couch has blue and green in it," she said, defensively.

"Yeah, it does," he agreed from the kitchen as he filled the tea kettle. "But the shades of blue and green in that horrible plaid are the exact same shades found on moldy bread. It's not a good look – trust me, I got the gay decorating gene." After he made the tea and placed the mug in her hands, Toby covered her legs with a throw and then turned off the lamp. He sipped his own tea as he watched over her as she slept. *"Yes, Detective Melba,"* he thought with love, *"You're part of my family."*

Melba slowly recovered. She was thankful to everyone who had taken care of her and was dismayed to find she hadn't minded their presence nearly as much as she thought she might.

Herman the Red was the biggest surprise. The first day he showed up, he shyly presented her with a large purple crystal. "It'll help with the healing," he informed her gravely. "I know some people don't put much stock in things like this, but it'll help. Trust me and give it a chance. It just might work."

When she found out he was once a nurse, she relaxed and just let him do what he needed to do. He'd been a great help during the first days, helping her to the bathroom and into the shower with such professional care she was almost able to retain her dignity. She didn't know if the glittering rock had done any good, but it certainly hadn't hurt and she enjoyed the way the light played across its multi-faceted surfaces. Like the rest of the folks on Capital Street, Herman the Red was very different from what she'd assumed when she first met him. Remembering the advice Madame Zhou had given her the day after Guzman's murder, Melba tried to look beneath the surface and discover who these new friends really were. She was well rewarded for her efforts.

Lindsi was surprisingly good company, and Melba discovered that she wasn't nearly as doleful as she seemed when she was waiting on customers. She was Bernice's niece and – like every other teenager Melba had encountered – was just trying to figure out who she was and how she fit into the great big world. After a while, Melba even found the color-coordinated eyebrow piercing endearing, although she had firmly declined Lindsi's offer to hook her up so she could get one of her own.

Bernice kept her stocked with a selection of healthy and delicious food, and talked about the restaurant. One night as she shared stories about some of the more colorful customer's she'd had over the years. Melba thought back to her own first visit, and how amused she'd been when Sam discovered that Earth Fruits didn't serve meat. He'd gamely allowed Zhou Li to order for him and to his surprise, had enjoyed it so much that he'd cleaned his plate. That was also the day she had first heard Sutton Dameron address the public with his hateful rhetoric. She forced her mind away from that memory, and all of the unhappy events which had sprung from Dameron's pursuit of power.

Moon kept her entertained with her views – liberally sprinkled with a mind-boggling variety of descriptive adjectives – about fashion and the role it should play in everyone's life, and took it upon herself to rearrange the small closet while Melba napped. She suspected that she'd never see some of her old garments again, but decided it wasn't worth an argument – all things considered. She thought that maybe Moon had secrets and sorrows of her own, but didn't pry. Whatever Moon's story was, it was hers to tell in her own time.

Toby and Zhou Li were – just Toby and Zhou Li – constant and comforting, neither of them above bullying her when they felt she needed a push. Zhou Li would sit with her in the evenings and simply offer the comfort of another presence. Very occasionally, she would talk about her childhood, and Melba noticed she would often worry the joint of her missing finger as she reminisced.

On the surface, Toby was his normal self, but Melba saw the shadows in his eyes and knew he was thinking about his own part in the events of the last few months. He was having a difficult time working through things, but hadn't shared much of what he was feeling. He was headed for a breakdown and Melba knew that before long, someone was going to have to browbeat him into getting help so that he could come to terms with the fact he'd killed a man, even if it had been in self-defense. But the time for that wasn't here yet.

❖ ❖ ❖

Toby stopped by to visit Mitchell in the hospital late one afternoon. Mitchell had been in for several days, but was now doing well. When Toby entered the room, he felt uncomfortable for a moment when Bradley Clark rose from the chair and turned to greet him. Toby took a small step back when he saw the look in Bradley's eyes. He instinctively knew that if this man had his way, Toby wouldn't be seeing Mitchell very much in the future.

Before Bradley could speak, Mitchell's tired but happy voice came from the hospital bed. "Hey, Toby! It's about time you made it by."

Relieved at the distraction, Toby turned toward him with a smile. "Sorry it took so long, Mitchell, but to be fair, you weren't up to company until just a day or two ago."

"Yeah, I guess you're right. I'm ready to get out of here now though! The food is worse than your tuna casserole and that stuff you call spaghetti put together!"

"Hey! My cooking's not that bad."

"Toby…Oh, never mind! I guess I can admit it was filling, but that's about the best thing I can say about it. Anyway, that's enough about your awful cooking. Bring me up to speed on what's going on."

Toby spent the next few minutes filling in the details, and hearing about what Mitchell had planned for after his release. Bradley didn't say a word while they talked, and contented himself with shooting angry glares in Toby's direction. Toby pretended not to notice.

"They say I'll be able to go home at the end of the week, but I won't be going back to work for a while. I need to get my strength back first. But Bradley's going to help me."

Toby refused to look around and forced some enthusiasm into his voice. "That's great! I'm sure he'll spoil you rotten."

Toby noticed Mitchell was getting tired so he made his excuses, and promised to come back in a few days. He gave him careful hug and started for the door.

"Wait up, Toby, and I'll walk you out. I could stand to stretch my legs a bit anyway."

Toby suppressed an eye roll and waited for Bradley to join him. When he reached his side, they started down the hall to the elevators.

As they neared the shiny metal doors, Bradley cleared his throat. "I have something to say to you, Toby."

Toby continued walking as he addressed the comment. "I thought you might. It was pretty obvious that you weren't pleased to see me and I can tell by your tone that you're angry about something."

"You're damned right I'm angry! I don't know why Mitchell thought he had to be the one to pull your ass out of the fire, and I'll never understand it. You don't seem all that special to me. But that doesn't matter, and isn't really what I wanted to say to you anyway."

Toby stopped and turned to the man who was glaring at him, and knew he wasn't going to like this. "Okay. I guess I can see your point. I don't understand why Mitchell helped me either, but I'm grateful he did. He bought us a lot of time, and I know exactly what would have happened if anything else had gone wrong. You don't have to beat me up over it – I'm already doing that to myself and don't need any-one's help." When the glare was replaced by cold, hard anger, Toby sighed. "Please, just say what you have to say so I can be on my way."

"Alright, I will. I want you to stay away from Mitchell. I don't want you to make any effort to see him again."

Toby wasn't surprised, but he be damned if he'd give in just to please him. "How am I supposed to explain that?"

"Leave that to me. I'll do it in such a way he won't notice until a lot of time has slipped by, and then it will seem normal." Bradley held his eyes for a minute longer and then looked away. "You know, I al-most hate you."

"I am close to hating myself these days, so I can understand why you feel the way you do."

"No, I don't think you do understand. You see, I don't hate you for almost getting Mitchell killed. I hate you because there's some-thing about the relationship between the two of you which has inter-fered in my relationship with him."

"I won't apologize for being Mitchell's friend, Bradley, so you can just forget about that."

"If I thought you were just friends, I wouldn't feel the way I do."

Toby was surprised by the statement, and didn't understand where the conversation was headed. He just wanted to get out of here and back to the quiet of his apartment. "Bradley, Mitchell and I have never been anything more than friends."

Bradley Clark studied him with narrowed eyes and Toby knew the worst was about to come. "If that's the case, explain something to me."

Toby gave him a short, curt nod. "If I can, I will."

The man was silent for so long, Toby decided he wasn't going to finish the awkward conversation. Relieved at his escape, he turned to finish his walk down the long hall. Just as he took the first step, the man's voice stopped him in his tracks.

"Explain to me why the first night I ever spent with Mitchell – our first night as a couple – he pulled me to him in the middle of the night and said, "It's okay, Toby. I've got you. Go on back to sleep." If it had just happened once, I might be able to brush it off, but it's happened a couple more times since then. Explain to me why if you've never been more than friends, Mitchell calls your name when he's in my bed."

Toby was almost brought to his knees by the unexpected and telling question. After a moment of stunned silence, he forced himself to respond. "I can't explain it, Bradley, but I'm sorry it happened. I can't do anything about it, but I did tell you the truth. Mitchell and I are…just friends." When Bradley didn't respond, Toby offered all he could. "I promise you I'll stay away from Mitchell and not contact him myself. But, if he reaches out to me, I won't brush him off. I won't hurt him by pushing him away. I owe him too much for that. That's the best I can offer."

"You say you can't explain why Mitchell calls out you name, but somehow, I think you understand it." When Toby neither confirmed nor denied that it was the truth, Bradley gave him one last cold, pitying look before he cruelly added, "It's too bad for you that Mitchell didn't want what you were offering. I guess I was right and you're not so special after all. Keep your promise to me, Toby Bailey." Bradley Clark turned and walked away, headed back to Mitchell's side – Mitchell, who was there because he helped save Toby's life.

Toby added it to his pile of guilt and pressed the button to call the elevator which would carry him downstairs, away from the man who still called his name in the middle of the night. The man who'd caught him every time he'd fallen since Geri died.

He thought about how hard it would to lose another person he cared about, but maybe it was for the best. Mitchell had what he'd always wanted – too bad Bradley Clarke was such an ass. When the elevator doors opened, he decided he wasn't being fair. Bradley was just trying to protect Mitchell and had decided that Toby was bad news. Maybe he was right.

As he walked to the car, he decided that it was time for him to learn how to catch himself.

CHAPTER SEVENTEEN

AS THE DAYS went by, a handful of people dropped by to visit Melba; the most notable among them being Tom Anderson. During their conversation, she shared her misgivings about Chief Kelly and his lack of communication with Sheriff Branson the day Jones had been killed.

"That's interesting, Reightman, and not in a good way. What are you going to do about it?"

"I'm not sure what I can do about it, Tom. It'll be his word against mine. It would be easy for him to come up with some believable story featuring me as a hot headed detective running off into danger without proper preparation or warning."

"That might be exactly what he tries if you accuse him of anything," Tom agreed. "And, he would have a point. But are you just going to let it pass without comment?"

She shook her head, "No, Tom, I'm not. Before I'm done, he'll know I realize exactly what he pulled. Thank God things worked out as they did and no one other than Jones ended up dead."

"Have you heard how Mitchell is doing?"

"Yes, Toby was allowed to see him for a few minutes yesterday. Mitchell's recovering, although he's going to be out of commission for several weeks – maybe even a couple of months. He's supposed to be going home in the next few days."

"Is his family going to stay in town?"

"No. According to Toby, his new love interest is moving in to take care of him."

"Sounds like he has found himself a pretty good woman." When Tom noticed her cocked eyebrow, he amended, "Or a good man – or, whatever. You know what I mean."

Reightman smiled inwardly at his momentary discomfort, knowing Tom didn't have a prejudiced bone in his body, and his discomfort was caused by the assumption he'd made regarding Mitchell's romantic situation. Tom hated it when his assumptions proved to be wrong. She thought about giving him some grief, but decided she had better use for his time. She changed the subject. "I do have one small thing I thought I'd would ask you to help me with, Tom."

"Am I going to like it?"

"Probably. I know how you love a challenge. In fact, I'm worried you might find this one a bit of a letdown."

"When you say things like that, it clues me in that whatever you're asking might not be easy. I know your tricks, Reightman."

"I don't think it'll be as hard as it seems on the surface, because I have a hint or two I'm willing to give you – if you get stuck."

"Now I'm really worried. Okay, I'll bite. What's your little project?"

"Not so fast, Anderson! I have props to make it more exciting." Reightman reached into her purse and pulled out the evidence bag she'd retrieved from him as she rushed out of the building to drive to the cabin in the woods. She also pulled out a clear sandwich bag containing another item.

"I spy one thing I recognize and one thing which looks familiar." Tom picked up the unfamiliar bag and examined the contents. "This looks like Guzman's phone."

"It's not. Toby and I have a suspicion it is, in fact, the phone he himself lost the night of Guzman's murder. It's the same model, has the exact same case, and Toby says the scratch on the back is just like the one on his old phone. I know there are probably a million people with this exact combination and probably a few thousand of those have scratched cases, but given everything else, I don't think it's too far of a stretch to believe it is the same one. But that isn't really what's important about it."

"Okay, now I'm curious. What is important about it?"

"I was hoping you'd ask, Tom." Reightman picked up the black phone in the evidence bag – the phone which belonged to the recently departed Reverend Sawyer – and turned it on through the plastic. She then did the same with the phone in the silver case. "I've been practicing, so watch carefully. For my first trick –" she announced with a flourish as she turned the phone on, "I'll demonstrate and prove Jones was indeed the person hired by Sawyer to do his evil deeds." She typed a message on the black phone and then selected a contact and pressed send. The silver phone buzzed as the message was received.

Tom picked it up and read the text:

U R A STUD

"Thanks, my wife thinks so. Sorry to disappoint you though, but that little hat trick didn't astound and amaze me."

"You're such a difficult and demanding audience. It's a good thing I like you. What will astound and amaze you is there's a number on both these phones. The exact same number. I want you to track down and let me know who it belongs to."

"You did mention something about a hint…?"

"I have a hunch that the number belongs to someone who was very close to both Jones and Sawyer. Maybe even someone who was related to the both of them."

"You mean you think the number belongs to –?"

"Nope," Reightman interrupted with a smile. "I'm not going to say another word until you verify it yourself."

"Should I check it for prints while I'm at it?"

"You can, but I don't think there's any need. You'll find Toby's prints, my prints and Jones's prints on it, but I don't think you'll find anyone else's."

"You already know who it belongs to, don't you?"

"I have a strong suspicion. Based on something Jones revealed before he was shot, and a couple of other things I've pieced together, I think I do know. I also think I know who opened the door to the roof at the spa the night the Damerons tried to kill Toby."

"Same person?"

"Yes, and if we can tie them to both the phone, and to the assistance they provided the Damerons, then…"

"Then, you have an accessory to Guzman's murder, and an accessory to the attempted murder of Toby Bailey."

"See," Reightman smiled, "I knew you'd catch on, Tom. Also, if you could pull the prints you got off the door handles from the spa stairwell, we'd have pretty much everything we need to make the charges stick."

"Maybe so. It should make a good initial case anyway. Anything else you can dig up might be handy to have in your hip pocket."

"I'm one step ahead of you. I have Toby hunting for the final pieces to the puzzle right now."

"Reightman, you are soooo sexy right now – spinning your web from your secret lair. That cane by your side adds to the aura of evil."

"I hate this damned thing! But, it helps me get around while I carry out my nefarious plans."

"So tell me, oh evil mastermind, how'd you learn how to pull all these strings while sitting here all by your lonesome?"

"I can't tell all my secrets, but I will tell you I learned from the best. Most people would say that master manipulator is a harmless, old lady." She smiled at him, in a close approximation of what she called Zhou's dragon grin. "The people who've been lulled into thinking she was harmless have been proven to be very, very wrong."

The next thing she did was call the city's human resource department to discover who Jones had listed as his next of kin.

Toby dug through a couple of boxes before he found the item he needed to accomplish the task Detective Reightman had assigned him. Opening the spa appointment book, he flipped to the page listing the appointments booked on the day the Damerons tried to kill him. The page listed every client, and the corresponding spa technician who had provided the requested services. Locating the name he needed, he called Andre.

"Let me think a minute, and see what I can remember, Toby."

"Take your time, Andre."

"Well, I don't really remember much, and it was a while ago. But from what I recall, she seemed to be very nice and was apologetic about having to use the ladies room before we started her massage. I didn't think anything about it, because it happens all the time. The best I can remember is she appeared to be middle-aged, but it's hard to say how old she really was. She was very well kept and well groomed. She certainly didn't look like someone you'd suspect of having a tattoo, especially in the place she had it. I guess you just never know."

"Andre? Where on her body was the tattoo?"

"Well, it was right by her....lady parts. It was a flower of some sort. I just saw it for a minute when she kind of flashed me."

Toby thanked Andre for the information and ended the call. "Mission accomplished."

The next day Tom called with the news he'd verified the number on the phones. "Don't go alone," he warned her after he told her the name associated with the number.

"I won't, Tom. Thanks for doing this so quickly. I guess it wasn't much of a challenge for you after all."

"It was tricky enough, given that you're an amateur. However, I was so intrigued I put in a few extra hours. In fact, I stayed up all night and just finished a few minutes ago."

"I didn't intend for you to go to that length."

"I know, I guess I just want this all to be over. It's gone on way too long already, and has to be the damnedest chain of events I've ever seen."

"I agree. It has gone on for far too long. And too many people have paid the price of all the lies and deception perpetrated by some of this city's leading citizens and corrupt officials."

"Speaking of that, Reightman, I've been thinking about the conversation we had about Kelly, and I have a piece of advice, if you're open to hearing it."

"Sure. If you have any ideas on how to take care of Chief Ernest Kelly, I'd love to hear it. Any advice on that topic has to be better than what I've come up with."

"Sorry to disappoint you, Reightman, but I'm afraid my advice is just the opposite of that. The thing is, I'd like you to think about some things before you take him on."

As he'd expected, she started to interrupt, but he wasn't going to let that happen-at least, not yet. "Hear me out first before you shut me down. We all know Kelly holds a grudge forever, and you also know he has an ego the size of a large continent. Most of the time, he comes across as an old grizzly bear, grumpy and ready to smack everyone down, but folks think the bear's missing most of its teeth. But Reightman, you've seen enough to know that's all an act, and that the bear has plenty of very sharp teeth. He used to be hot stuff, from what I've heard – the best detective ever to grace the hallowed halls of this city. Right now, he's faced with a situation where at least three of his officers were directly involved in these murders, and he has a lot of egg on his face, both because of that and for the way this unfolded. He has to be embarrassed that he was wrong about everything, as you so adeptly proved. That adds to his discomfort. I'm sure he's had some explaining to do to the city brass, and word on the street is his own job might be in jeopardy. That may or may not be the case, but I know for a fact that he's persona non grata with the Mayor right now. The fact is, you outclassed him, and showed everyone he's not such hot stuff anymore." Anderson paused for a moment and then summed it all up. "Reightman, he's not ever going to forgive you for that and his resentment and anger is just going to grow."

So far, she knew he was right, but suspected there was more to come. "Go on."

"Well, people like Chief Kelly are old school, and however hard they try, they'll always be old school. They have old school ideas and fight by old school rules. All that being said, you have a couple of decisions to make. First, decide if your career as a Detective is really important to you. If it is, and if you're sure there's nothing more important than this job, do what you need to do. But be prepared for things to get much worse before they get better – if they get better. Prepare yourself for the hard reality they might just get very bad. If he thinks he needs to, Kelly will fight mean and dirty, and regardless of how he's currently viewed by the Mayor and a few others right now, he has powerful connections, and years' worth of favors he can use against you. And you can bet he'll go to the wall before he backs down."

If Kelly was out to get her, or thought he had to bring her down to salvage his misplaced pride, it would be a battle she might not win. "And my other option, Tom?"

"Get the hell out, Reightman. Get out while the gettins' good. Say whatever you need to say, but wait until your exit plan is in place. If you do that, and if you're lucky, he'll probably view it as a retreat and not a challenge. You don't want to challenge him, not if you want to get out of this intact."

"Tom, I can't just let the fact he almost got the three of us killed drop by the wayside!"

"I knew you'd say something like that. I agree that it would be a difficult thing to do. But next time, he might not just almost get you killed. Of course, you could just let him walk all over you in order to keep your job. Sometimes I wonder if that's what you want."

"What the hell do you mean by that, Anderson?"

"Melba, ever since Sam died, you've been hanging on by a thread. Oh, you've put on a good poker face, but face it; these days you can hardly drum up enough energy anymore to even throw a good bitch fit. As the case got cold, you just let it. You put up a good fight in the beginning and I thought you were going to pull through. I'd guess it would be difficult to get that fighting edge back, and frankly, I'm not sure you should even try, unless you want to sacrifice everything else in your life. And that would be a shame – a shame for you to not find the time to see your daughter and grandchildren because you were so consumed with trying to prove you were tougher than Kelly. It would be a shame for you to push away all of the people who you've come to know, and who've given up their own time to take care of a person they consider a friend." He gave her time to think about his last statement and then drove his point home. "Is it worth that, Melba? Are you ready to give up on your family and friends, just to make a point that doesn't matter to anyone else?"

He didn't offer more, and didn't need to. He'd given her more than enough to think about.

Two days later, Reightman, accompanied by two cars of uniformed officers and leaning on her cane, arrested Marilyn Sawyer.

Mrs. Sawyer, nee Brown, tried to bluff her way out of it. Reightman allowed her to talk, until she lost her patience and pulled out the black phone in the sealed evidence bag. She turned on the phone and dialed the appropriate number in the contact history. A phone buzzed in a nearby desk drawer. Reightman did the same thing with the other phone, and the buzz sounded again.

"Aren't you going to get that, Mrs. Sawyer?" Reightman asked the flustered woman. "It might be your son, Bill. But that can't be right. Bill Jones is dead, isn't he?"

"You have no proof that I'm involved in any of this!"

"Mrs. Sawyer, I have a chain of evidence reaching from the photos Gerald Guzman took of you, to the fingerprints you left when you unlocked the door for Christina Dameron the night she tried to kill Toby Bailey. The night she was killed by your son."

"My son was a fool!" Marilyn Sawyer spat as an officer placed the cuffs around her wrists.

"Maybe he was, Mrs. Sawyer. But the only mistake he really made was to fall in love with the man he was supposed to kill. For that mistake, he died."

Marilyn refused to say any more as she was led away to the waiting car.

The following afternoon, Reightman walked down the hall to Ernest Kelly's office.

"Hey, Melba," Nancy greeted her. "How's the leg?"

"It's getting better, slowly but surely. I think I have an appointment with Chief Kelly."

"You sure do, and you can go on in. He's expecting you."

"Thanks, Nancy."

Reightman knocked on the door – one knock – and entered.

No one ever knew what took place in the office, or what was said between the two of them, but when Reightman left the room, copies of the papers she'd filed that morning to trigger her retirement were on Kelly's desk. As for Kelly himself, he didn't take any calls, or open his office door for the rest of the day.

"In the end, I decided a battle just wasn't worth it," she told Tom when she stopped by his office on her way out to her car.

"I'm glad you saw it that way. I was afraid you wouldn't."

"Three months ago I wouldn't have, Tom. But, three months ago, I was a different person than I am today." She gave him a Cheshire grin as she thought about what was waiting for Kelly. "Besides, I don't have to do a thing. Sheriff Branson is going to be up his ass so far she'll be able to see light when he opens his mouth. I can just sit back and watch. He may very well face charges before she's done."

Tom returned her smile. "What are you going to do now?"

"I'm going to visit Abby and the kids, then start physical therapy so I can get rid of this damned cane. After that, I don't know, but I'm not worried. Something will come along."

CHAPTER EIGHTEEN

TOBY WAITED IN the reception room of the spa while Mr. Albertson finished up his walk through of the space and decided which furnishings he wanted to purchase. SarahJune was accompanying him, answering his questions and occasionally haggling over the relative value of a chair or set of treatment room fixtures. Toby was grateful she'd agreed to come in and handle that final part of the shutdown, because he just didn't care about any of it. He knew it was important to try and recoup as much as he could, but he also knew he was more than ready to close the doors and turn off the lights. Then he'd just crawl into bed and try to sleep.

He hadn't been doing much sleeping since the day he shot and killed Bill Jones. During the long nights, he replayed the events over and over in his mind until he'd nearly driven himself over the edge with the guilt and horror he felt. He didn't know how to get past it, or even if he could. He was exhausted, and overwhelmed by even the smallest thing. Maybe going home to Grams would help. He was leaving in the morning and planned to spend the next two weeks helping her get the house ready for winter. He guessed she'd need some help putting in the winter vegetables and there were always things to be done around the yard. He hoped she had so many things lined up that he could wear himself out, and then maybe he'd sleep for more than an hour at a time. He refused to think about the fact he hadn't told her what had happened. He didn't know how he could bring himself to tell her that he'd killed a man.

He looked up at the picture above the reception desk, debating whether he should keep it, or let it go with everything else. Grams had the original, still in its cardboard roll from when he'd returned it after having the extra-large copy made. He was still trying to make up his mind when he heard the front door open. He turned to look, and discovered it was Madame Zhou, coming to check on him as she'd been doing every day for the last week.

Belatedly remembering his manners, he stood to greet her. "Hello, Madame Zhou."

She didn't reply, which was very unusual, and he wondered if her hearing was starting to go.

"Hello, Madame Zhou," he tried again.

"I heard you the first time, Toby. Goodness, I am not deaf!" She walked to one of the plush green chairs and took a seat. She tilted her head and observed him for a minute, and then turned to the same framed photograph he'd been studying before she arrived. After a minute of contemplation she turned to him and scrutinized his face. "Yes," she informed him. "It is just as I thought."

Toby had no idea what she was talking about, and even for her, this was unusual behavior. "Madame Zhou, I'm sorry, but I don't understand."

"Well, of course you do not. One never does, at first." She waited politely for him to comment, and when he didn't, she gave a tiny shake of her head. "I find myself hesitant to say more, but I have decided I must." She waited for his response, and when none was forthcoming, she glared at him disapprovingly. "I can see you have reached the stage where it has become difficult to understand much of anything, except for the tangled emotions and regrets flowing inside. And that, Toby, is a very bad thing. It is to be expected I suppose, as there have been many layers building on top of each other since even before Geri Guzman was killed." Again she waited.

Finally, at a loss to figure out what she was waiting for, he said first thing which came to mind. "None of it should have happened."

"Perhaps. But, I regret to tell you, such is often the case in life. Many things should not happen. But they do. And when they do, we have choices to make. It's time for you to start thinking about what you will choose."

"But, Madame Zhou, I'm not ready to think about what I'm going to do now. I have a little money left and it will tide me over for a while."

"Toby, I am not talking about your choices of future employment. I'm talking about your choices of future life. Will you indulge this old woman while I share an observation with you?"

"Of course, Madame Zhou."

"Thank you. Now, my observation concerns your resemblance to that photograph hanging on the wall. I have always admired it, and if I recall, your mother took the picture." Toby affirmed she had, and Zhou turned to regard it again. "I have always admired her talent. It is difficult to create something so compelling without the use of color. The first time I saw that image, I noticed the remarkable resemblance you shared with the young boy in the chair. Of course, it was only to be expected, because he was you, once. Or perhaps, more correctly, you were he. Those things often become confused as we grow to adulthood. Even though this photograph is in black and white, and you are a startling combination of light and color, there was no way one could fail to recognize the person depicted, regardless of his age. You shared the same eyes, the same expression – your pout is quite famous here on Capital Street, as is the lock of hair which falls across your forehead, as it did even then when the photograph was taken. But underneath the small boy's pouting face, one can tell in a moment he will begin to laugh again and one knows that as soon as his expression changes, his arms will uncross and he will open up to possibilities. He will then be allowed off of the chair, and will soon be getting on with other things, exploring and learning from what is around him. You were much the same way when I first met you." She looked up at the photo again, and then turned back to face him. "That photograph captures but a moment, but offers the viewer the promise of much more. That boy teases us into guessing what happens next, and causes us to imagine what he will be experiencing the next time we are allowed a glimpse of his life. That, I think, is why it such a remarkable photograph. And that brings me to what I have hesitated to say, and now feel I must: You, Toby Bailey, no longer bear much resemblance to that child."

Zhou Li stood from her seat and walked over to him, and placed one tiny hand on his shoulder. "Toby, you need to make some choices, and make them soon. You can choose to remain in that hard-backed wooden chair with your hands crossed over your chest forever, or you can change, and free yourself. You may no longer be that child, and indeed, it is most probably time for you to move beyond what he represents. But don't stay in your wooden chair too long, or you will find your entire world is nothing but shades of gray. It can be powerful, and beautiful, in a photograph. However, it is seldom beautiful as a life."

"My life is nothing but gray."

Zhou Li heard the despair in his voice, but knew better than to let him wallow. "That too, is a choice, Toby. And even if it were true, there is no reason it has to stay that way."

"But I killed a man!"

"Yes, you did," she agreed. "You killed a man who was trying to kill you. You killed a man who had killed others. You killed a man who had seriously harmed your friend, Officer Mitchell, and who was also intending harm to Detective Reightman. Would you rather he had killed you, and them?"

"But...I loved him."

His heartbroken anguish was hard for her to bear, but inwardly she rejoiced at the words. "And isn't it remarkable you did, Toby? It is in itself a kind of redemption: You loved him, and he was, therefore, loved. That is the only redeeming thing I can find in Detective Jones's life. Don't let his life, and the end of it, poison yours. Find your way out of that chair."

Toby sat in the chair as she went out the door. He knew that she'd made several good points, but didn't know how to find his way out of the darkness he found himself in. As he started to descend into self-pity, he hurriedly stood from the chair and grabbed his keys from the counter. He hollered out to let SarahJune know he was leaving and then headed over to visit Moon.

When he entered the door to Passed Around, he looked around for her, but she was nowhere to be seen. The drapes separating the big front window from the rest of the shop were open and he could see the stripped mannequins in the window. One or two were missing their arms, and all of them were minus their wigs. There was a torn piece of netting on the floor. He reached down to pick it up and heard the door at the back of the shop open.

"I am so distressed to have left you waiting here alone without my presence," Moon announced as she came through the door with her arms full of boxes. When she saw who was in the shop, she gave a sigh of relief. "Thank goodness it was only you, Toby. It was terribly remiss of me to leave the shop vacant and unattended, but I felt the immediate need to take all of those fluffy and annoying prom dresses out of the window. They were almost all gone, and the display was no longer serving its cleverly intended purpose." She placed the boxes down on the counter and then glided toward him. "How are you doing, Toby? Have you recovered from your terrifying ordeal?"

"I'm fine Moon, but I don't think I'm recovered yet."

"I suppose that is not too shocking of a surprise. Horrible events take the toll on us all as life wings past. The best we poor, unworthy mortals can do is to hope that fortune favors us again with moments of peace and tranquility so that we are prepared for the next great and taxing test the mysterious universe presents us."

It took a minute for Toby to process her words and when he'd finally succeeded in untangling them, he discovered he didn't have much of a response. "I guess you're right."

"Of course I am. I have had a lot of experience with the capricious nature of the gods, and have more than once been a victim to their whims. Perhaps if you share what is troubling you, I might be of some small, insignificant assistance."

"Thanks, Moon, but I didn't come down here to cry on your shoulder. At least – not exactly. I just needed to get out of the spa for a few minutes. SarahJune is with the man who will be buying the fixtures and I was finding myself at a loss."

"It is such a shame you have to close, Toby. The Time Out Spa will always hold a special place in the glorious history of Capital Street. What are your plans for the future?"

"I really haven't decided yet. So much has happened that I just…I just need time to think."

"Hmmm." Moon tapped her long fingernail – painted a rich berry color today – against her matching lips. "Forgive me if this seems to be uncharacteristically intrusive of me, but during the long, dark nights when you were saturated with sadness and despair did you stop to consider that you might be allowing yourself to think too much?"

Once again, Toby had to decode her words. "I don't know. I just can't seem to help it. Everything bad that has happened has been my fault."

To his surprise, Moon broke out into throaty laughter. "Oh, Toby! That is hubris speaking. I know it is very tempting and pleasing to place all the blame on one's self – that is what misguided heroes do! If they weren't allowed to take all the blame when things went wrong, they wouldn't have to rage against the fates and set off on amazing perilous quests to make amends. Without the flawed and misguided desire to accept blame and atone for imagined wrongs, we'd be left with very few great works of literature – to say nothing of the beautiful and alluring tragic poetry which I so enjoy! However, although you have been exceedingly brave, I don't see you cast in the mold of the typical, predictable hero. You're much smarter than that and capable of finding another way to deal with misfortune. You have too much to offer to the world to force yourself to tilt futilely against the windmills of life. It doesn't do much good anyway."

"But Moon, you don't understand."

"You are wrong about that, my friend. I understand better than you think." Moon stroked his arm comfortingly for a moment and then made her way behind the counter to open boxes. She hummed under her breath as she worked. Just when Toby had decided to head back down to the spa, she looked up at him. He noticed her eyes were very sad. "I have had my own moments of hubris, Toby. I have accepted all the blame for too many things in my life. Sometimes I was right to do so, but many, many times I wasn't. That was a hard lesson for me to learn."

She held up the wig in her hand and gave it a little shake, and then dropped it on the counter. She reached in the box and pulled out another. "In case you haven't noticed, I tend to be somewhat dramatic." She looked up and winked and then went back to her task. "But the difference is I've created this fabulous person you know as Moon in order to confront my own reality – not hide from the things I don't want to accept. And there have been many things that have been hard for me to accept, Toby. I also know myself well enough to realize that I'm perfectly happy when there is a lot of drama. I could drown myself in drama if I allowed myself to do so. I could rejoice in the darkness of my thoughts and circumstances. But I made the choice not to. Instead, I created a new reality – one full of fashion, and glamor and fancy clothes. I learned that a new shade of lipstick could turn my day around." She fluffed out another wig and frowned. "I think this one has reached the end of its sorry life." She tossed it into the trash underneath the counter and pulled out another.

Toby stood silently as he watched her finish the first box and then she opened another. She pulled out yards of carefully folded black fabric and laid it on the counter. She considered it for a moment and then put it back into the box. "I had thought I might drape the window in black to mourn the passing of summer, but I've changed my mind." She picked the box up and began to carry it to the back door of the shop. "I've decided that instead, I'll embrace all of the colors of fall." She turned and gave him a wistful smile. "There's more than enough black to go around already. Don't you agree?"

Without waiting for his response, she turned and went through the door.

It wasn't until he was back at the spa that he realized the last few minutes of their conversation had been very unlike Moon. Her normal verbosity had been severely curtailed. She'd been letting him see a side of herself that she'd never offered before. He didn't understand what it meant, but he appreciated it, and knew it was significant.

He took a seat back on the sofa and looked up at the huge photo again. "*I think I'll keep it,*" he decided. "*There is still a lot to learn from that boy in the chair. Besides, I need to see if he ever gets up from there and goes on a new adventure. Maybe he'll teach me how to do the same.*"

The next morning Toby drove back to his childhood home and spent the next several days helping Grams. He worked without complaint or sass, which worried her, but not as much as his drawn face and hollow eyes. She knew something terrible had hurt her boy, but withheld her questions for the first few days.

Toby finished her list much sooner than he'd expected or hoped. He'd catch her worried glances from time to time, but did his best to ignore them. He wasn't yet ready for the discussion he knew he had to have with her. He was still exhausted and plagued by his internal demons. He still hadn't found the rest he wanted and needed and was on the verge of breaking down. He'd often find himself alone at the big kitchen table in the middle of the night, caught in a loop of anguish and guilt, unable to sleep but not wholly awake either. On one such night, at the beginning of the second week of his visit, Grams joined him at the table, wrapped up in her robe against the fall chill. She took a seat next to him, without saying a word.

After they'd sat together for a while, maybe as long as an hour, he knew it was time.

"Grams, I have something to tell you. Something that's going to be hard for you to hear."

She waited, silent in her chair, for him to find the words. When he eventually spoke, she thought her heart would break.

"Grams, I killed a man."

She listened for the next two hours as he told her everything that had happened after he found the photographs and records Geri had left for him. He told her about the things he'd done to catch Geri's killers and he told her about the other deaths; Helliman, Christina Dameron, and Sam Jackson. He told her how he'd met and fallen in love with Bill Jones, and how their relationship had evolved into everything he thought he wanted or needed. He didn't spare her much once he started, and she let him talk, uninterrupted, as tears ran down both their faces. He explained how he'd discovered Bill Jones' true identity, and how Melba Reightman had done the same, and come with Mitchell to rescue him from danger. Finally, he told her why and how he shot the man he'd loved between the eyes.

When he finished, he looked into her face, afraid of what he might see. The dam inside him broke when he found only sadness, acceptance, and love.

She opened her arms and wrapped him in comfort and compassion, stroking his head and crying with him. "My poor boy," she said as she brushed the hair from his eyes. "My poor, hurt boy."

Later, she sat by his bed as he slept, and she wept again, for Toby, for Geri, and for all the others who had been caught up in the lies and deception, and had lost their lives. And then, she prayed for forgiveness. Not for Toby – she knew the Good Lord had already done his part regarding Toby. After all, he'd brought him home to her. No, that night she prayed for forgiveness because all she cared about now was her boy was alive and that man was dead. Mostly she prayed, because if Bill Jones hadn't been dead, she would've done everything possible to kill him herself.

Toby slept straight through for ten hours. When he woke, Grams fixed him something to eat, and then he went for a run and did a few chores. After dinner, he helped clean the kitchen and then showered, letting the hot water wash over his skin. Suddenly exhausted, he went to sleep again. On that second night, he dreamed.

The cemetery was quiet and dark, except for the areas around each grave. Maybe the glow of the headstones was comforting, because Toby wasn't afraid. Instead, he felt welcomed and at peace, but he was chilled to the bone.

He walked through the rows of graves and found his Gramps, who said hello and told him to always be prepared, and his mother, who didn't speak, but laughed and snapped a photo of him. The minute the camera flashed, she held out the print in her hand, and Toby saw it wasn't her usual black and white, but was in full, vibrant color. The picture was of him. She held it out in offering, but he shook his head. "You keep it," he told her. "I'm not ready to appreciate it, yet."

She blew him a kiss and he caught it in one hand, letting it melt into his palm and warm him all over.

He walked a few more feet down the family row, and stopped at the site which was Geri's.

"Heya, Toby!"

"Hey, Geri. You're looking good." And he was. He bloomed with all of the beauty Toby remembered from their first summer together; bare chested, strong and tan, and his eyes glowed until they were the brightest thing around. There were no signs of the violence which had claimed his life.

Toby looked into his green, green eyes and when he blinked, they were both standing near the big pond at the park, and they each had a handful of small stones and pebbles.

Geri tossed one in and watched the ripples move across the pond. "I was hoping you'd stop by, Toby. I wanted to thank you."

"For what, Geri?" Toby skipped his own stone, and it skimmed the water until it disappeared out of sight.

"Why, for bringing me home, Toby. It meant a lot. Tell Grams thanks, for the chicken and cobbler she brought the day of my funeral." Geri tossed in two small stones and smiled at the sound they made when they hit the water. His teeth were very white.

Toby remembered the foil covered plate which Grams had carried to the cemetery that day. "You got that, did ya?" This time his pebble hung in the air a moment before it splashed down with a 'plonk'.

"Sure did. The birds brought it to me. I had to share, but still, it was about the best thing ever." Ripple, plonk, went the two stones as they left Geri's hand.

"I'll tell her, Geri."

"Toby...."

"Yeah, Geri?"

"Well, I...I wanted to say I'm sorry – for the way things worked out. I've been learning some things since I died, and I know I went about every-thing all wrong." He flung out his hand, and the single stone skipped four times before it disappeared.

Toby thought about all the days he'd spent with Geri, and shook his head. "Not everything went wrong... Some of it you got exactly right. It was just there at the end things got pretty rough." His pebble followed the path Geri's had taken, although it only skipped twice.

"Yeah, I know. But thanks for telling me I got some things right. It was all I wanted. I'm going to move on from here real soon, but I have a couple of things to tell you, if you've got another minute or two." Geri looked at the pebbles remaining in his hand, and motioned for Toby to throw one of his, instead.

Toby tossed in two, one for each of them. "Sure. I don't have much go-ing on right now. I'm sleeping and I don't think Grams will wake me up anytime soon. She's worried and wants me to rest. She says it'll help me heal."

"It will, Toby. Grams is usually right. Haven't you learned that yet?"

They both laughed at all the times Grams had proved how right she was, and in Geri's laughter, Toby heard an echo of the boys they had been. After a minute, Geri flashed his toothpaste smile, and then skipped another one of his stones. "The first thing I have to tell you is more of a message, really. The other day I met a new guy. Well, I guess I just saw him wan-dering around, all alone. He didn't have anyone here, waiting on him, so I thought I'd do the right thing and introduce myself. The strangest thing was, he knew me. After a couple of minutes, I recognized him, too."

"Who was it Geri?"

Geri hesitated before answering. "His name is Bill Jones." Toby felt his heart jump up in his chest, but realized it didn't hurt as much as he'd expected it to. After what seemed like a long time, Geri held out his hand to show Toby he only had one stone left, and then spoke again. "Anyway, he told me that if I should see you around, I should tell you two things. The first thing I'm supposed to let you know is that his tattoo is gone. Bill said he didn't need an alias anymore. He thinks he's finally figured out who he is." Toby nodded and Geri continued. "I didn't understand the other thing he told me to tell you. I know what the word means, but I don't know why he wanted to me to pass it along."

"What was the word, Geri?"

"Thanks." Geri shrugged his shoulders and tossed in his stone. "You have any idea why he wanted me to tell you 'thanks'? Seems kind of strange to me, given all that happened."

Toby threw in his last pebble and thought about it while he waited for the ripples to die. He decided he probably did know, but the only answer he gave was, "Maybe."

After he spoke, a small chime sounded in the distance. Geri looked over his shoulder and then back at Toby. "That's the warning bell, so I just have a second or two more. Listen up, 'cause I have two more things to say. The first is I did love you, Toby, and the second is, you'll find the real thing one day soon. In fact, I think you'll..."

The chime sounded again and Geri mouthed, "Sorry," as he faded away. The glow from the headstones slowly died away, and then there was another bright flash. He was no longer standing by the big pond, but was now seated in a high backed wooden chair. Everything around him was black and white, and his knew he was in his mother's picture. Toby saw her high above him, snapping away from different heights and angles. She let the camera hang from the strap around her neck, and held another print in her hands. She handed it to him, and this time, she spoke. "This is him, Toby, the one you'll love, and be loved by, for all of your life.... You want to see who it is?"

He thought about it, but decided he'd better not. Besides, he thought it might take a while before he was ready to know. "No thanks, Mom," he called up to her.

"Good choice, Toby Bailey!" She laughed again, and her voice sounded like a million ringing bells. "Now find a better mood to get into and get up out of that chair. There are wonderful things to do!"

In his dream, she blew him a kiss. As he reached out to catch it…

…he woke up, and felt better than he had in a long while. He rolled out of bed and stretched, and thought about his dream. After doing his morning business, he went to the kitchen and poured a cup of coffee. He could smell something baking in the oven. After thinking about it for a second, he hopped up on the counter and swung his feet.

"Toby H. Bailey, get down off that counter! There's a whole bunch of chairs in here so find one and sit yourself down in one of them."

He smiled and sipped his coffee, and then grinned down at his Grams. It wasn't the sunny grin from his childhood, but would do for now. "Not today. For today, anyway, I'm through sitting in chairs."

Grams, thought about swinging her dish towel toward the man sitting on her clean counter, but decided he really wasn't doing a bit of harm. "What are you going to do today, Toby?"

He swung his legs a little more, gently hitting the backs of the cabinet with his bare feet. "I think I might go to the park and walk around the pond. I might even skip a few stones." He hopped down and gave her a hug. "After that, I thought maybe I'd go visit Gramps and Mom. And Geri." Toby walked to the door, and turned back to the woman watching him from her place by the sink. "Hey, Grams?"

"Yes, Toby?"

He almost didn't ask. "You think you could…fry up some chicken? I thought maybe we could go together and maybe…have a little picnic while we visited."

She thought about it as she opened the oven door and pulled out the baking dish. "I guess I can do that, Toby. That's a nice idea, and we can take some of this cobbler."

She smiled as she heard his footsteps down the hall, and thought maybe he was beginning to heal.

CHAPTER NINETEEN

Two weeks before her retirement, Melba was invited to tea.

She entered Green Dragon and the small bells on the door chimed in welcome.

A moment later, Zhou Li called from the back. "Come on through, Detective."

Carefully navigating the space with the use of her cane, Reightman made her way to the doorway hung with wooden beads, and noticed the connecting door to the martial arts studio was open. There was a solitary figure kneeling on the floor, taking items out of various boxes and crates. Continuing to the door leading to the back of the shop, she parted the beads, causing them to sway and brush together with a tiny, rustling wooden clash. She entered the room with the carved dragon table and the four chairs. Seated in one of the chairs, as expected was Zhou Li. In another, not expected, sat Toby Bailey.

He rose as she entered and offered a welcoming smile. "Hello, Detective Melba. Fancy seeing you here."

Reightman noticed his pale blue eyes were shadowed in his drawn face, and underneath them were faint dark circles speaking to many hard, sleepless nights. *"He's finally grieving,"* she thought, both sad and relieved by what she saw.

Madame Zhou looked up from the teapot she was holding and offered her own smile, although it was different than usual. If Melba had to describe it, she'd say this smile blended both welcome, and secrets. "I'm pleased you have joined us, Detective. Please, take a seat while I pour, and then we will all have a little chat."

"It won't be "Detective" much longer," she replied, taking a seat across from the lady and stowing the cane on the floor beside her. "I'm retiring."

"Yes, I heard that was the case," Zhou studied her gravely before she filled three cups.

"Why are you retiring?" Toby asked from across the dragon table.

"I decided other things were more important, Toby."

"I hope it wasn't because of everything that happened."

Reightman shook her head to reassure him and banish his doubts. "No, or at least, it's not the whole reason. I'm retiring because of the things I've learned and realized over the last few months. That's significantly different than retiring because of all that has occurred, I think."

"I agree there is a difference, I think you have both learned, and suffered for some of that learning," Zhou commented as she passed them the cups. "And, so have I. That is part of the reason I asked you both to join me this afternoon. I would like to share what I myself have learned, and tell you what I'm planning to do. And then, I have a proposition I would like to discuss with the both of you. But first, let us sample this tea. It's a new blend."

Reightman noticed the jasmine fragrance she associated with Zhou Li's tea was much less noticeable in the warm liquid contained in the cup she held in her hand. The flowery scent was still there, but was more of an undernote than anything else. She raised the cup to her lips and took a sip. She took another drink, trying to determine what was in the new, complex blend. She thought she understood the first two flavors in a way she had never understood the jasmine tea, but there was an undercurrent of something which reminded her of…She raised the cup to her lips again, and sipped. The final flavor was almost bittersweet, but didn't say on the palate long.

"It's not bad," Zhou Li commented, after she had taken her own taste. "But, it is not quite right. Perhaps it needs time in the cup to age and mellow before it will be at its best. We will see."

"What's in it, Madam Zhou?"

"Oh, just a little of this and a little of that, Toby." She smiled peacefully, content to hoard her knowledge until it was time to reveal what she knew. "I don't think I'll tell you what is in it just yet. I am allowed my secrets." Zhou took another sip and then put her cup on the top of the table. "Now, let me share what I have learned, and what actions I am taking based on those learnings."

Before she could continue, there was a loud crash from the other room, followed by a few angry, mumbled words. Zhou Li tilted her head, bird like, and listened. "My great nephew Jon," she explained. "He is part of what I will share with you today." She lifted her cup and drank again, savoring the flavors for a moment. "It opens up a bit more after it cools from the heat of the brewing. Please, try it again and see if you can tell the difference.

Reightman tasted again, letting the tea slide across her tongue. The tea had changed, and the flavors seemed to blend together more. The bittersweet taste was softer now, more like something which had once been, instead of something still powerful and strong. Something else was beginning to emerge, but she couldn't identify what it was.

"I like it better now," Toby said as he put down his cup. "Before, there was something in it that was too strong for anything else to come through. And, I think I tasted something new, but I don't know what I think it is yet."

"Very good, Toby. You have a talent for this. But, I have always thought you showed incredible promise." Zhou folded her small hands on her lap and picked up the thread of conversation she'd started before the disturbance in the other room had interrupted her. "To continue with what I want to share, I have learned I am beginning to feel my age. I am perfectly fine," she assured them, "but I do find myself more easily tired these days. It takes me longer to recover from excitement or stress. I am also finding I am not capable of the same independence I have always enjoyed – especially in terms of transportation. It is becoming difficult for me to drive at certain times of the day. As you might imagine," she smiled ruefully, "these things are hard for me to admit, and harder to reconcile with how I have always viewed myself. But, I have," she said with a sigh. "And, I have decided I need help. That brings me to my great nephew, Jon."

Zhou took another sip of her tea, and the others followed suit. After the cups had been returned to the table, Zhou Li continued. "Jon, for reasons I will not share because they are his own, is also learning and admitting things, and is beginning to reconcile himself to what they mean. Between us, we have agreed he will be moving here, to help me with this shop, and with my transportation needs. He will also be opening the martial arts studio next door. He is very proficient in a number of the more respected forms of the martial arts, and I am confident he will make this venture a success. We shall get along well, he and I."

"Will he also be living with you, Madame Zhou?"

"No, Toby, not exactly. Jon will be taking an apartment directly below mine. We will both have our privacy and independence, but will be close to each other if needed. I think that arrangement will serve us both very well. I wouldn't want to interfere in his life, after all."

Reightman hid her smile with another drink of tea and noticed that Toby did the same. They both were familiar with the hesitancy Zhou Li showed when the opportunity to interfere arose. Their eyes met over the rims of the cups in perfect understanding.

"Before I tell you both about a proposal I have, I would like to ask you each a question. Please indulge me, because your answers are important to me."

They both nodded at Zhou's serious tone. She turned to Toby. "Toby, have you decided yet what you want to do with your life now the spa has closed?"

"Not yet, Madame Zhou. I have a better idea of what I don't want to do. I've decided not to find work in another spa, because I think I that part of my life is over, at least for now. I'll fill in if some place needs help, but only on a temporary basis. I think I want to do something which gets me out and about more, and gives me a creative outlet of some sort."

"By creative outlet, do you mean design or decoration of some sort?"

"No, I don't think so, Madame Zhou. Although I like those things, I don't think I could deal with people who think they know what they want, but don't realize it would be awful if it was actually done. I'm not sure what the right thing is yet, but I'm trying to keep an open mind."

"Very good, Toby. Thank you for answering." Zhou turned to Reightman. "Detective, have you decided what you will do after your retirement takes effect?"

"Other than visiting my family, no," Melba replied. "I'll have to find some new employment though – the retirement package for a retired detective isn't all that impressive. But I haven't decided yet what I'll do next."

Very good. Thank you for answering my question."

There were more sounds from the studio next door, and again, Zhou Li tilted her head to listen. "I think we need more tea," she said. After she'd finished pouring, she sat back in her chair and studied them both. Eventually she leaned slightly forward. "I have a proposal I would like to present to you both. Please indulge me and let me finish presenting my initial thoughts, and then I will answer your questions. Will you agree?"

"Of course, Madame Zhou," Toby agreed.

Reightman looked across the table and tried to find a clue in Zhou Li's eyes. Defeated in her effort by the old woman's inscrutable gaze, she shrugged her shoulders and replied, "I'll agree to hear you out."

"Excellent, then let me share what I am thinking." Zhou Li proceeded to lay out her thoughts, very precisely. When she'd finished, she sat back in her chair and waited.

After a moment, Toby looked at Reightman, and then back at Zhou with an incredulous expression on his face. "A Detective Agency, with all of us as partners?"

"Yes, but I prefer the term "Private Investigation Firm", Toby. A "Detective Agency" seems very film noir to me, and I never did care for that genre. And yes, we would all be partners, of a sort."

Reightman narrowed her eyes, trying to figure out what the old woman had up her sleeve. "How exactly would this partnership work?"

"That is a very good question, Detective. In the simplest terms, I would propose you and Toby run the agency, while I would provide any help or guidance needed. I would propose we all have an ownership in the venture. You and Toby would have a share equal to twenty-six percent of the business each, and I would hold the remaining forty-eight percent."

"Why would you have the bigger share, Madam Zhou?"

"Another excellent question, Toby. I am pleased you have asked. I would receive the larger share because I would provide the operating capital for at least the first year, and possibly for the second. This will allow you and Detective Reightman to build the business without financial worry, although I will expect you to maintain good financial practices and to watch expenses. I also bring to the table a large number of contacts and relationships which may well prove to be very helpful. The final reason is I propose we repurpose the spa facility into an agency, and I own the building."

"You own the building where the spa is located?"

"Yes, along with several other pieces of real estate around the city, and the state. I also have a few holdings outside of the state."

'Why didn't you tell me you owned the building, Madame Zhou?"

"There was no reason to, until now. I didn't want it to cloud our relationship, or for it to place added pressure on you as you worked through the things you needed to come to terms with over the last few months."

Reightman leaned back in her chair as Toby processed the information. "And what do you see us bringing to the table, Madame Zhou?"

"Detective, I think the skills you would be bringing into the venture are obvious. Toby's skills – while not so obvious – are equally important, and useful. He has good business skills, and he has a way with people. While you can teach him much in the area of investigation, he can teach you skills from the areas in which he excels. Over time, you will make each other stronger. I would expect you to each work to support and help each other, of course, but you have been doing so for the last few months – regardless of if you have done so intentionally."

Reightman cradled the delicate teacup in her hand and inhaled the scent. "It's almost too perfect," she said quietly. "I don't know what to think, to tell you the truth."

"I like the idea," Toby said, suspiciously, trying to understand what it was he liked. After a moment, he nodded to himself in understanding.

"Why, Toby?"

"Because, Detective Reightman, we've been doing this kind of work together already, and it worked. Madame Zhou is correct in her summary of the things we both bring to the table. I know we'd work well together, because we've done a fairly good job of that so far. I figure if we made it through the last few months, if we stick together, we stand a good chance of making it through just about anything."

Melba stared into her cup and thought about the past few months. *"Toby's right,"* she realized. *"We have been through a lot together, and we managed to come out the other side mostly intact. And in some ways, we may even be stronger than before."* She thought about the story of the phoenix and took another sip of the tea, trying once again to identify the elusive taste. She finally placed the cup down on the table, ready to see if both Zhou Li and Toby were serious about this idea. "I have a few conditions."

"I anticipated you might, Detective. Please tell us what they are." Zhou picked up her own cup and drank.

"The first condition concerns you, Toby. I want you to do the work to get licensed as a private investigator in this state, and a couple of adjacent states. It will mean a lot of work, but you need to do it if you want to be a real partner in this proposed venture."

"I can do that, Detective."

She saw the vulnerable eagerness in his eyes and responded gently, but firmly. "I have no doubt you *can*, but I want your promise that you *will*. This won't be a glamorous game, like in the movies, and we need to approach everything professionally." She remembered all he'd been through, and the worry she'd had for him and added, "You'll also agree to learn how to defend yourself so I don't have to worry about your ability to take care of yourself."

"Are you saying I need to learn how to fight?"

"Yes. I already know that you're not afraid of much and that you can keep your wits under pressure. You're also a damned fine shot, but I want you to be able to defend yourself with or without a gun – in any situation I can think of."

Toby's eyes clouded as he thought back to the evening he'd killed a man. "You sound like this is going to be dangerous."

She nodded. "It might be, sometimes, and I want to you to be prepared."

"Are you going to learn to defend yourself better as well, Detective," Toby challenged, shooting a knowing glance at her injured knee.

Melba thought his challenge was a fair one, given that she wasn't currently at her best. "I've been trained, and I've tried to keep myself in shape over the years. But, I'll admit I could use some additional instruction, and I'll need a lot of work to strengthen my leg and get back as much movement in my knee as possible. So, here's the deal: we'll both do what we need to do get into fighting shape and learn the skills we need to protect ourselves, and each other, without leaving any doubt in either of our minds."

Toby saw sense in her statement, and was glad she admitted she wasn't invincible either. "Alright. I can do that." When she looked at him steadily across the table, he amended his agreement. "I will do that." She smiled in approval and he grinned back in return. Then, he thought about all the responsibilities of the new business, and added new conditions of his own. "In return, you have to learn the business side of things so I don't get stuck doing all the paperwork and bookkeeping by myself. And I think we need at least one other permanent staff."

"What kind of staff, Toby?"

He turned to the address her question. "Madame Zhou, we need someone to be in the office when we're out finding lost cats and tracking down deadbeat dads, or whatever it is we'll end up doing to make this thing work. I know it's not going to be glamorous and I'll do whatever I need to make it a go. But, we need someone to make appointments, answer the phones and do the basic administrative work."

"I see your point. Do you have someone in mind?"

Toby thought about who his immediate choice would be and thought it would be perfect. "Yes, I do. I think SarahJune would be good at everything we need. Sure, it'll be totally different from working at the front desk in the spa, but we're all going to be learning as we go, and so can she."

Zhou Li inclined her head slightly and gave him an approving smile. "I'll agree to that, Toby, and I'll factor in the appropriate expense. I think she would be an excellent choice as well. I will even submit since the work she will be doing is more demanding, she should get a reasonable increase from her former salary. I am confident we can work out the details to everyone's satisfaction."

Melba decided she could live with his new conditions, although she hated paperwork. "I agree also, Toby. I'll even, grudgingly I admit, agree to learn the business side. It wouldn't be fair to you other-wise, and I might as well learn all I can."

"We are making excellent progress," Zhou Li said delightedly and clapped her tiny hands.

Melba didn't want to dampen anyone's enthusiasm, but needed to make something clear. "You haven't heard my final condition, Madame Zhou. My final condition is you will not interfere directly in any case unless we ask you to do so. You'll be involved in all of the general aspects of the business, of course, and I think you should always know the general nature of anything we're working on so you can advise us as needed, and provide your unique insight. But, when it comes to the actual workings of a case, you'll have to agree to stay out of the detail and let us do our jobs."

Reightman could see the surprise in Zhou's eyes, but her underlying expression wasn't shock, or disappointment or anger. Zhou Li approved of her words.

"Very good, Detective! I am proud of you for insisting on that, and I will admit that sometimes I meddle just for the joy of doing so. On this point however, I am happy to agree. I will always be willing to offer insight or advice if needed, but I agree to – as you say – stay out of the details."

Each of them looked around the table, gauging the reactions of the others. "Do we have an agreement? Zhou asked, satisfied by what she saw on their faces.

"I think we do, but I want to sleep on it. If I don't wake up screaming at the whole idea, I'll take it as a positive sign."

"I like it, "Toby said, "but, I agree we should sleep on it. Is that alright, Madame Zhou?"

"Yes, it is and I approve of the suggestion. A good night's sleep before making an important decision never hurts, and often helps."

Another crash came from the studio, this time accompanied by loud and audible cursing. Reightman heard the wooden beads crash together, announcing the entrance of an obviously agitated man. She gave him the once over as he entered the back room. He was about six feet tall, she decided, and his eyes – of some indefinable color – were flashing with irritation. As she watched, he flipped back his hair – worn in a long, thick braid – over his shoulder, and stopped short at the sight of the people seated in the room.

Zhou Li gave him a small nod of acknowledgement and looked up into his flushed and angry face. "Is something the matter, Jon?"

Her calm tone seemed to settle the man and he bowed in her direction. "I apologize for the interruption, Auntie Zhou. I didn't realize you had guests." Reightman saw him straighten the high-necked black tunic he wore and tug down the long sleeves as he tried to make himself more presentable.

Zhou Li allowed him a moment to get himself in order. "Please let me introduce you to my guests, Jon. This is Detective Reightman, currently the senior Homicide Detective for the City Police Department. Detective, this is my great-nephew Jon Chiang, whom I mentioned to you earlier."

Reightman shook his hand, noticing his firm grip and realizing his eyes were gray. *"How very unusual,"* she thought as she released his hand and reclaimed her seat. *"He doesn't bear much resemblance to Madame Zhou, and I'd hazard a guess he's not fully of Chinese descent."*

Zhou turned to Toby. "Jon, please allow me to make known to you, Mr. Toby Bailey. Mr. Bailey owned and operated one of the city's premier new spas, located across the street."

Reightman watched as the two men shook hands and then broke away quickly, as if their hands had generated some kind of electrical charge. There was a startled expression in both pairs of eyes, as if they'd recognized someone unexpected.

After the social forms had been observed to her satisfaction, Zhou Li continued. "As I believe I mentioned to you, Jon, Mr. Bailey has closed his business due to a series of unfortunate events far outside his control. Detective Reightman is also in the process of leaving her current employment. I have been working to convince them to join me in a new business venture."

"And they haven't agreed yet? You must be losing your touch, Auntie Zhou."

Zhou Li bridled at his tone. "Jon Chiang, I'll remind you, pleasant impressions are made through good manners."

Jon had the grace to be embarrassed by his flippant and sarcastic comment. "You are right to remind me, Auntie. My apologies to you, and to your guests."

"Thank you, Jon. I'll let it pass this time." Although her tone was firm, Melba could see the faintest hint of a twinkle coming from the eyes behind the thick-lensed glasses. "Now, I believe you must have rushed in here for a reason, if the sounds coming from the studio were any indication. Is there something I can help with?"

"I ask for forgiveness for all of the noise, Auntie. I have been trying to manage some of the larger crates by myself, and I find them to awkward to handle alone. I was wondering if you might know someone who could help me for a few minutes. They are somewhat heavy, but it is more the size which makes them impossible for me to handle without additional help." Reightman could tell the admission was difficult for the man. He looked very strong and capable, and it almost certainly hurt his pride to ask for help, especially in front of strangers.

"I can help," Toby offered.

Jon Chiang met his eyes and then looked away, uncomfortable for some reason. "I appreciate your offer, Mr. Bailey, but I couldn't take you away from Auntie Zhou. It would be unforgivable."

"Madame Zhou, is there anything else we need to discuss right now?" Toby didn't look toward Zhou as he asked his question. His eyes were firmly on Jon Chiang, who was searching the room for anything to settle his own gaze on – as long as it was not Toby Bailey.

"I believe we are finished for now, Toby. After you and Detective Reightman have had time to think over our discussion, we will get back together to answer any additional questions and handle any concerns which may have arisen. We can then formalize our agreement. Is that acceptable to you both?"

"That's sounds fine to me, Madame Zhou," Reightman answered, as she watched the silent interaction between the two men.

"Thank you, Madame Zhou. If I might be excused, I will be happy to help Mr. Chiang with the crates."

"That would be much appreciated, Toby. Will his help be sufficient, Jon?"

Jon snapped his eyes to Toby's face and then turned back to his Aunt. "Mr. Bailey's help would be much appreciated, Auntie, and will be sufficient to get the crates moved." Jon Chiang's voice as he answered her sounded slightly dazed, as if he was wondering what was happening. He turned to Toby, and bowed slightly. "If you would follow me, Mr. Bailey," he said softly, "I'll lead you to the crates."

As Toby exited the room, Melba heard him begin his now familiar spiel, "About that Mr. Bailey stuff, I'd prefer you to call me Toby." She was unable to hear Jon Chiang's response, but she knew from experience that Toby would eventually get his way, regardless of any possible objections. Melba mulled over what she'd observed in the last few minutes, then picked up her cane, and stood. "Since we've finished, I think I'd better go for now, Madame Zhou. I find myself tiring much faster than I did before my injury."

"I understand. It will take a while longer to be back at your full strength. Your body is using a lot of energy to heal itself. Let me walk you out to the front, Detective. I want to pull a few things from stock so I can work on this tea blend further. I am not quite satisfied with it, yet."

"What are exactly are you attempting to capture with the tea, Madame Zhou?" Melba asked her, intrigued with the possibilities.

Zhou looked up with her dark eyes and considered Melba for a minute before answering. "If you wouldn't mind, please tell me what *you* sensed in the tea, and then I will answer."

"Well, I can't describe the ingredients, but I think I can describe what I tasted." She hesitated, thinking about what she might say. "This may sound foolish."

"Nothing about tea is foolish, Detective. Please share what you sensed."

"Alright, I'll give it a shot." Melba closed her eyes and tried to remember the taste of the tea. She described what she'd tasted, thinking back to the day Moon had asked her how she felt wearing a particular set of clothing. She opened her eyes and looked at the old woman, who was gazing back at her with surprised eyes.

"I am astonished, Detective! The first three are exactly what I was hoping to invoke. The fourth, which you describe as healing, is almost, but not quite what I am trying for."

"What *are* you trying for, Madame Zhou?"

"I think I will keep working on the blend some more, before I share my goal. I wouldn't want to spoil it by giving myself away. I hope you will indulge me, Detective."

"Of course I will, Madame Zhou," Melba answered, knowing she really didn't have much choice in the matter. Zhou would only share her secrets when she was ready, and not one second before then. She bent down awkwardly to give the woman a brief hug. "I'll call you in the morning to give you my decision."

"Thank you. I will await your answer with anticipation. Please get some rest, Detective."

After she'd shown her guest through the door, Zhou Li gathered a few herbs from the shelves, and turned to walk back toward the beaded curtain. She paused in the doorway of the studio, and watched the two men standing inside the bare, unfinished room. They'd finished moving the crates, and were now talking quietly together, with grave and serious expressions. Their eyes were troubled, she noticed, and their postures were closed and guarded, as if each was prepared to defend himself from an unexpected attack. However, as she watched, they leaned closely together, sharing private thoughts with each other. She smiled as she noticed their eyes never left each other's face, even though the expression on each was carefully neutral.

She parted the wooden beads, and took a seat in her chair by the dragon table. She sipped her tea, sampling the flavors as she thought about Melba Reightman's descriptions. "Hope" was correct, as was "promise". The bittersweet taste of "loss" which faded slightly with time – after the heat of despair had cooled – was also correct. She was very pleased with the perceptions of her protégé. She took another drink, striving to capture the final element. "Healing" wasn't *quite* what she was striving for, but maybe it had to come first, to balance the flavors appropriately before the final quality could emerge. She sipped again, searching once more for that final thing she was hoping to find in the taste of the tea. It wasn't there yet, she eventually decided. But, before she was done with the blend, it would be.

Later that night, Toby called Reightman at home.

"So, I was wondering…"

"What were you wondering, Toby?"

"Well, I was wondering, since you aren't going to be a Detective anymore, and we're going to be partners and everything… what do I call you?"

Reightman lifted her mug of tea to her mouth and took a sip. Then she made a suggestion.

"Really?"

"Really. Now, it's late, so I'll say good night now, Toby."

There was a moment of comfortable silence before he replied, "Good night, Melba."

As she put down her phone and raised the mug again, the smell of jasmine rose around her, and she smiled.

Acknowledgements

I hope that you enjoyed this second book in the Reightman & Bailey Series as much as I enjoyed writing it.

I've continued to learn about the world of book publishing and as HARD JOB comes to the end, I'm reminded again that books might get written in isolation, but they don't make it out of the computer and into a reader's hands without the writer getting a lot of help and encouragement. Once again I need to thank two close friends: Dr. Rhea Ann Merck, and Julia Prater.

Rhea helped immensely as I delved into the damaged mind of John Brown and as his character unfolded, I relied on her to point me in the right direction to help us all understand what made him the man he was. I took a lot of liberties with the information she so generously provided, but nonetheless, he wouldn't have appeared on these pages without her help and guidance.

Julia agreed to take up her purple ink pen again to search for and destroy my typos and incorrect word usage. I always quake in fear when I open the notebook she returns to me, but thankfully this time around, there wasn't as much purple on the page. She always has excellent observations and points out inconsistencies that need to be resolved with humor and grace and is ready to offer me a glass of wine when needed.

I'm so thankful they are some of the first readers of the words I put on the page and can't find the words to show my true appreciation and gratitude. I'd also like to thank other good friends and supporters who bought my first book and who listened to me talk about this one while it was underway. Their support guides me back to the keyboard day after day for another round of writing.

I have to give a special shout out to Kathy LaLima of LaLima Design for another outstanding cover. She listens to my concepts and then politely tells me where the problems are, then sets about solving them. I couldn't ask for a better collaborator to help me bring these characters to life.

The world of writing is a fascinating one. I was fortunate that I came from a family who enjoyed reading and taught me to do the same. A good book doesn't always solve the problems in front of me, but it does allow me a moment of escape and reflection. While I always enjoyed a good story, I never realized what it took to get a book into someone else's hands. As I struggled through the process and seemingly endless steps, I was fortunate to have the best support of all – that of my husband and partner, CPK. He continues to help me solve my technology problems, reads the multiple drafts and kicks me in the pants when I need it. I am so very, very lucky.

About the Author

JEFFERY CRAIG is the writing pseudonym of the author and is used for fictional works. Jeffery resides in the southeastern United States and shares his life with his husband and partner, and a menagerie of much loved pets. For several years he worked an executive providing technology and consulting services to help clients meet their business needs. He's an avid supporter of the arts and co-owns a local art gallery/gift store that provides an outlet for area artists and craftspeople to showcase and sell their work.

When he isn't writing, he might be found working on a painting or enjoying the covered porch of his historic southern home with a good book in hand. He can be contacted via his webpage (www.jefferycraigbooks.com) or on social media.

Coming Soon!
Skin Puppet
Reightman & Bailey Book Three

Toby's head hit the hard wooden floor as he went down — hard. He rolled and pulled himself to his knees, groaning at the effort. He knew he had to get on his feet fast or he'd be finished. He shook his head, trying to clear his dazed mind, and in the process scattered bright ruby-red droplets around him. The sight of the blood distracted him for a minute, bringing back a host of images and bad memories from the last time there'd been blood on the floor. He touched his split lip gingerly and then struggled to his feet and turned to face his attacker.

The man in front of him was standing a few feet away, eyeing him with emotionless gray eyes. He was about the same height as Toby, but probably had twenty or so pounds on him – all of it muscle. The gray eyes narrowed and the man shifted his blunt wooden stick from hand to hand. Before Toby was anywhere near ready, he attacked again. Toby dodged out of the way, trying to get into a position he could defend. *"Damn! This guy is fast!"* he thought as the thick wooden stick came at him from the side. *"I don't think I can hold out much longer."*

He quickly glanced to the side where his friend and partner, Melba Reightman, was trying to get up from the floor. She looked like she was in pretty bad shape herself. He didn't have the time or the energy to spare her much thought, and he had to keep his attention on the stick. She'd have to look out after herself.

They'd been ambushed the minute they'd walked in. Neither of them had been prepared for the fury of the surprise attack and had barely managed to fling themselves out of the way. They'd regrouped and for a minute or two, it looked like they had the upper hand. That had seemed perfectly reasonable. After all, there were two of them and only one bad guy. Boy, were they wrong about that!

He dodged again, trying to avoid another hit and flinched as a fist came at his head from the other side. He lunged out of the way, desperately trying to catch his breath while thinking about his next possible move.

He'd been fighting a losing battle for the last few minutes, and he knew it. He'd had tried to protect his head and face and at the same time, keep his focus on the man in front of him. The stick came flying again and narrowly missed his temple. To avoid the flying foot that followed, Toby dropped to the ground and rolled. The man was on him in a flash and Toby knew he had to get up and put more distance between them. "I could use some help here!" he yelled, hoping Melba was ready to step in. At this point, he wasn't ashamed to admit he needed help.

To his relief, she was ready. She launched herself into the fray with fists flying. He heard her give a blood-curdling yell as she attacked the man from behind. The attacker turned like lightning and with two jabs had her back on the floor. Quicker than he believed possible, the man was in his face again and Toby knew his fate was sealed. *"Think, Toby! What are you supposed to do in situations like this?"* He knew he needed to focus, but was having difficulty just staying out of the man's reach. *"Think!"* he commanded himself again. There had to be something he could do. He took a quick look around the room, hoping to spot something he could use to defend himself. There were a couple of possible weapons but he had to figure out how to get to them. Before he could come up with a plan, the stick struck him hard across the left shoulder. Toby barely kept from crying out in surprised pain. He knew he only had one option left. *"When it's time for a last stand and you're almost out of gas, focus and then give it everything you've got. And remember – fight dirty."* He took one more breath, then narrowed his eyes and went on the offensive. He barreled his way into the man's space and dropped to the ground. He kicked out with one leg and made contact. The man stumbled for a minute and taking advantage of the unexpected opening, Toby levered himself up and punched him in the back of the knee. The man grunted in surprise and dropped to one knee.

Toby felt a surge of elation. "Take that, asshole!" he shouted. He punched his fist into the back of the other knee and moved to the side as the man went down. "*I think I've got him now!*" He felt a thrill of excitement and thought maybe he'd survive after all. He started to stand while the attacker was still on the floor, but lost his balance when he stepped in a few drops of blood. The man jerked up and swept a foot in front of him, catching the back of Toby's ankle. He stumbled and tried to regain his footing. He started to panic and looked away for a moment trying to see where Melba was. He never saw the fist that laid him out cold. The last thing he remembered before he passed out was thinking he forgot to protect his head. Again. Jon Chiang was going to be so pissed-off about this.

Chapter One

HE BLINKED IN the light and tried to lift his head.

"Can't you just stay down?!" The exasperated voice of his instructor rang in his ear. Everything hurt. With a groan, he laid his head back down and closed his eyes. He wasn't ready for the inevitable lecture just yet.

"Is he going to be okay?" Leave it to Melba to ask the obvious question.

Toby opened one eye and caught a glimpse of his partner. She didn't look too good herself. Her curly hair was tangled and matted with sweat and her white gi needed to make a trip to the washing machine in the very near future. He grimaced and decided that his probably wasn't in any better shape. To make matters worse, she was on her feet and he was on the floor. Plus, he was bleeding and as far as he could tell, she wasn't. Sometimes, life just wasn't fair. He shut the eye quickly when she moved a little closer. He didn't have the energy for any of her fussing. Monday mornings were bad enough without that. Besides, it would be more fun to listen to what they said when they thought he was out of it.

"He'll be fine. It'd take more than a little whack on the head to do him any real damage."

"Yeah, he's pretty hard headed."

"You're telling me? His skull cracked the stick on one end. I didn't even think that could happen in a sparring lesson, and this is the second time he's done it. I need to charge more for this."

Reightman gave him a snort. "Since this is the second time, you probably should add it to the bill. But then again, since the lessons are courtesy of your great-aunt, you'd have to take it up with her."

"It'd take a braver man than me to broach the subject with her. She'd just tell me I needed to be more careful and remind me to take better care of my toys."

Toby heard the sound of rustling cloth as someone knelt down beside him. He felt a rough palm on his forehead and knew it belonged to Jon. He suppressed a shiver as the strong hand felt the front of his skull and worked its way over the top of his head to the back. "There's no blood from anywhere other than the split lip, and other than a little goose egg, there's no swelling. I don't think he has a concussion."

"Then why hasn't he woken up? Do you think we should call someone to make sure?" Toby almost grinned at the sisterly concern in her voice, but managed to keep his expression under control. If she found out he was faking, he'd be in for a world of hurt.

"Let's see if he comes to in the next few minutes. If not, we'll call the EMS. Why don't you check with Auntie and see if she can make up a cold compress. It might help – if the ice can penetrate his thick skull."

"Okay. I'll be right back. I'll get one for his lip too. It's still bleeding."

Toby heard Melba head toward the door that connected Green Dragon, the herb and tea shop, to the martial arts studio, He recognized the sound of the door opening and closing. After a minute, Jon removed his hand. "You can open your eyes. I know you're awake and listening to everything we've said for the last few minutes."

"Have not."

"Yes, you have. Now open your eyes so I can check out your pupils."

Toby reluctantly opened his eyes and looked up at the man leaning over him. Jon's gray eyes were calm, although there was a tight set to his smooth jaw.

He gently opened Toby's lid wider and peered into one pale blue eye. Toby could feel the man's gentle breath across his check as the man leaned closer. He did the same to Toby's other eye and then sat back on his haunches. "You'll live to fight another day." He gave him a considering glance and then held out a hand. "Let's see if you can sit up."

Toby held out one hand and let Jon pull him up into a sitting position, groaning at the stiffness in his neck and back. It wasn't even noon and he felt like he'd been put through the wringer. He touched his lip and discovered that it was still bleeding and was also puffy. He felt his left shoulder and could tell he was going to have a nice bruise. "I…I hate fightin' againth da' stick!" He couldn't quite form the words since his swollen lip was getting in the way and it hurt to talk. "How come you geth to be de one to whack usth around all de time?"

"I get to whack you around because I'm trying to teach you to defend yourself against anything I can think of. It's not too farfetched to imagine someone might come at you with a shovel or a broom, or even a broken tree branch."

"Yeth, but dey wouldn'th be twained de way you arh."

"You never know how well someone is trained or how skilled they are until the fight is on. Then it's too late. It's better to be prepared." Jon stood and reached out his hand again.

Toby grasped it and used the leverage to pull himself to his feet. He was a little unsteady and he felt a headache coming on. "You weally goth me goo dat time."

"That's because you forgot to protect your head."

Toby mumbled something under his breath but stopped when he caught sight of Jon's arched eyebrow. "You we wight. I justh can'th seem to geth the hang of this stuff."

"I wouldn't say that. We just started training a few months ago. You do pretty well with the physical aspect, but you don't think things through and get over confident. The only time to be confident is when your opponent is totally vanquished and you are absolutely certain that he won't get up again. If I've told you that once, I've told you a million times!" Jon gave a resigned sigh and then added, "But you've made better progress than I expected. You're fast and have good coordination. You just forget to focus."

"I hardry ever geth a hith in!"

"Toby, you have very unrealistic expectations. I've been practicing the martial arts since I was a little boy so I have about thirty years of experience you don't have. Realistically, you should be pleased you ever get a hit in." Jon gave him a small smirk. "And today you did very well. The punch to the back of the knee was a surprise. I wasn't expecting you to try something like that this early in training, and it worked. It would have given you time to get in another shot – or better yet – get away if this had been a real fight."

"Yeth, I know. But somehow wunning away doesn't theem like de besth thing to do."

Jon's gray eyes shadowed for a minute and he looked away, gazing off into space as if watching something only he could see. "Toby, there are times when running away is the not only the best option, but the only option. Especially when the odds are against you and there's no way you can win. You need to recognize when that's the case. You'd better start learning that lesson now."

Before Toby could respond, the door opened and Melba hurried through, followed closely by Madame Zhou. Reightman was carrying what Toby assumed was an ice pack and a couple of towels. Her hair was still a mess and Toby would have made a smart-ass comment if he hadn't noticed the concern in her eyes. And if his lip and head didn't hurt so much.

Madame Zhou was completely unruffled by the situation and this wasn't the first time she'd been called on for help. The tiny old woman was wearing her gardening cloths and looked about as disreputable as Melba. The tattered green tunic had seen better days, as had the large, brimmed straw hat. She must have been puttering around out on her terrace, getting her pots and planters ready for spring. He grimaced when he noticed she held a steaming cup of something in her hands. He was getting used to her brews and potions, but wondered why they always had to taste so bad. He knew better than to ask.

He glanced over at Jon, and saw that he was standing up straight and quickly tidying his appearance. His great-aunt Zhou had that effect on him. Toby had noticed early on that whenever Jon Chiang was in her presence he was much more formal and polite than normal. He even gave her a tiny, but respectful bow.

"Let me see that bump."

Toby started to object, but Reightman's tone caused him to reconsider. When she used that voice it was better just to go along with what she said. He obediently bent his neck so she could check out the small knot on the top of his head. Since she stood only about five foot four in contrast to his own height of nearly six feet, he had to bend down a considerable distance.

She quickly finished her none-to-gentle inspection, and brushed few damp strands of hair off his forehead. She handed him the ice pack." Put that on the sore spot and keep it there until I tell you to take it off." She handed him a smaller pack. "And hold this one on your lip."

He knew he'd better just do as she said, although he felt like a fool holding one ice pack to his head and another to his mouth while they all examined him. He probably looked like some sort of 'see no evil – speak no evil' monkey.

Madame Zhou stepped forward and thrust out the mug. "Toby, drink this down. It will help with the headache I am sure you are experiencing." Her tone was much milder than Reightman's, but once again he knew better than to argue. He took a swallow, grimacing at the bitter taste. He started to lower the mug, but caught the glint in Zhou's eyes. Resigned to his fate and determined to get it over with, he tilted the mug and finished off the nasty brew. He dribbled a little out the side of his mouth because his swollen lip got in the way.

"Tanks, Madame Thou. I'm thure ith will help." It never hurt to be polite, even if he sounded like an idiot.

"You're welcome, Toby. Now, if things are under control here, I need to finish my gardening. I assume we will still meet for lunch."

Toby inwardly groaned. The last thing he wanted was food, but her comment had not really been a question. "I guessth tho, but I'm noth weally vewy hungwy."

"Give the tea time to work. By the time you have finished with your much needed shower and are presentable, I think you will find your appetite will have returned. Although, you might have to ask Bernice to prepare one of her delicious smoothies for your lunch, given the current state of your lip." Madame Zhou held out her tiny hand for the mug, and when Toby gladly relinquished it, she checked to make sure he'd finished every drop. She gave him an approving nod and turned and went back through the door to her shop.

Toby repositioned the ice pack and rolled his left shoulder to try and ease the stiffness. "I tink I'll head upstairs and sower."

"Not yet, you won't. The shower can wait for a few more minutes. First we're going to talk about what went wrong this morning and I want you both to give me a couple of ideas of how you might've handled things differently."

This time it was Melba who groaned. However, she'd also learned not to argue with their instructor. He had ways of making it unpleasant if they didn't give him the respect he felt was his due during class. And this technically was a class. "We weren't expecting an attack when we walked in and weren't paying attention to our surroundings. That was our biggest mistake."

Jon nodded and turned to Toby. "And?"

"And, I losth my focus and wath unable to concentwate on whath I needed to do to defend usth."

"And?"

Toby sighed. "And I didn' keeth my eye on you de entie time. I wasth wowwied abou' Melba."

Jon pursued his lips as he considered the answer. "I commend you for your concern. It is not a bad thing to be aware of your partner's situation. However, you need to assume that they can either take care of themselves or the situation is worse than you anticipated. If you don't protect yourself, you'll be unable to help them." He raised his eyebrow and waited, while pointedly looking at the ice pack.

"And, I fogoth to pwotect my head." Toby hoped they were done with this part of the Q & A.

"Yes, you did forget to protect your head. Again." Satisfied that he'd made his point, Jon turned to Reightman. "What will you do next time you are in a similar situation?"

"I'll take a good look around to make sure I know what I'm walking into," she answered. "I should have known better – I do know better. I had that drummed into my head as a rookie cop. I just wasn't expecting to be attacked when I entered the studio my regular lesson. That was sneaky, Jon Chiang!"

"Yes, it was," he agreed. "I've been planning it for a couple of days. I wanted to see how you'd both react so I'd know how you were progressing with this little training program." He turned to Toby and arched his brow again. "What else could you have done?"

Toby thought it over before responding. Now that the heat of the moment was over, he thought he had a good idea of how things could have been handled better. "Once we wealized whath wasth happening we kind of…sepawated and I guess we wost focused on pwotecting ourselthes. Instead, we should have given ith evewything we had and done our besth to beath you to a pulp. When we focused on ouwselves, we losth our edge and the advanthage we would have had."

Jon considered the answer and gave a tight nod. "That may have made a difference with a normal attacker. I'll see what I can do to create another few surprises so you can test out that hypothesis. We'll see if you're correct in your thinking." He gave them an evil grin. "I'll enjoy planning that scenario."

Melba glanced at Toby and glared when she saw he'd removed the ice pack. "I said to keep that on until I told you to take it off!" When he hurriedly replaced it, she rolled her eyes before turning back to Jon. "We should have also determined if there as anything we could have used as a weapon."

"Such as?"

She took a minute to look around the room. There wasn't much in the spare, clean space but there were a couple of possibilities. "Well, there is one chair in the corner and another set of fighting sticks hanging over there on the wall. There is also some of that resin powder in the box by the door."

"How would dat have hepped?" Toby asked, curious to hear the answer.

"Well, if one of us had picked it up and thrown it in his face, it would have distracted him and would have probably burned if any got in his eyes."

"Yes, it would have," Jon agreed. "There is still another choice of weapons you haven't mentioned."

They both looked around the room, but neither of the spotted anything else. "What?" Toby asked.

Jon simply grinned and shook his head. "I'm not going to tell you. You'll need to figure it out for yourselves." He ignored their disgusted looks and added, "We'll meet here again in the morning."

"Awe we going to wowk on sticth fighting some more?"

"No, Toby. No stick fighting tomorrow. We're going to work on meditation."

"Meditwathon?"

"Yes. I realized this morning that I've neglected an important part of the process. As my first teacher told me any times, it is as important to train the internal as it is to train the external."

"You'we gwoing to teach us to meditwait?"

"No. Tomorrow you will have another instructor." He refused to tell whom that would be and, instead, turned away and headed toward the back door of the studio. "Now it's time to shower and make ourselves presentable for lunch. We just have a short while before we need to meet Auntie, and she would disapprove if any of us were late."

Since they all knew Madame Zhou felt that punctuality was one of the ultimate forms of courtesy, they agreed. Melba headed to the back changing rooms and Toby went out the front door and headed to the stairwell that lead up to his third floor apartment. As he undressed and tossed the filthy and blood spotted gi on the floor he had a thought. He looked at the clothes where they lay, and decided he had an idea of what possible weapon Jon had been thinking of. He just had to find the right opportunity to test his theory. He turned on the shower and when the water was hot, he stepped into the stall and under the spray. If he picked exactly the right moment, this could be fun. After he finished and had dried off, he stepped up to the mirror and took a good look. He touched his swollen lip. The bleeding had stopped but it was still swollen and probably would be for a while. He might have to wait until he healed a little before he enacted the scenario he had planned. Jon Chiang would never know what hit him.

www.ingramcontent.com/pod-product-compliance
Lightning Source LLC
Chambersburg PA
CBHW030659120726
47905CB00001B/291